THE PRICE OF PASSAGE

"You wish to strike a bargain, but I warn you the price may be high. Tell me your terms"—he smiled coldly—"and I'll give you mine."

He finally seemed to have had an effect on her. The color in her cheeks rose; her steady gaze faltered. "I wish to reach another port." She hesitated only a moment. "Take me, and I will be yours."

Brent McClain arched his brow still higher and kept silent for a moment. "Perhaps I should get you something to eat."

"Then you accept my offer?" she asked.

"Not yet," he drawled. "But whether I do or not, I don't care to have you swooning upon me again. I want a few more minutes to decide whether or not you will be worth the passage."

For a moment she lost her elusive calm; she stared at him as if she meant to slit his throat. But the color drained from her face, and the murderous gleam left her eyes. She stared at him and smiled. "I assure you, Captain, I'll be worth the passage."

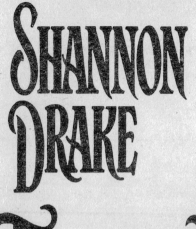

SHANNON DRAKE

TOMORROW THE GLORY

PINNACLE BOOKS
WINDSOR PUBLISHING CORP.

PINNACLE BOOKS are published by

Windsor Publishing Corp.
475 Park Avenue South
New York, NY 10016

First Trade Edition Printing: April, 1985
First Paperback Edition Printing: March, 1994

Printed in the United States of America

*To my husband Dennis Frank Pozzessere,
with love and thanks for Gettysburg, Appomattox,
Fort Sumter, and all the rest.*

Prologue

The night was dark, the weather cold and damp, yet on no other December eighteenth had the holiday spirit ever so charged Charleston. Church bells tolled, cannons thundered, guns burst out in revelry.

The cheers of the crowds could still be heard upon the Battery. Madness had come to the people.

South Carolina had just declared herself out of the Union.

There were a few men who did not celebrate the final coming of secession, although most had realized it was inevitable after the election of the Illinois farmboy, Lincoln. As long ago as May, South Carolina's governor had sent letters to the leaders of sister cotton states regarding secession.

Yes, most men of intellect had seen this day as inevitable. But there were a few men, loyal to the South, who did not join in with the drunken crowds and dream of glory. A few men knew that conflict would come, that brother would face brother, and that the land they cherished would be bathed in blood before any declaration of independence could stand as fact . . .

One of these men stood on the wall of the Battery, his

rugged face turned seaward, his powerful work-roughened hands stuffed into the pockets of his frock coat. He was a southerner, and yet he mourned tonight. He was well traveled and well versed in politics and he knew damned well that Abe Lincoln wasn't going to bow a courtly goodbye to any state. . . .

It was early yet, of course. Today South Carolina stood alone. But Mississippi and Florida were ready to spread their wings of independence. Texas, Georgia, Arkansas—many would follow the lead of the Palmetto State and secede from the Union.

Already Brent McClain had been approached by prominent leaders in the South. More states would certainly vote for secession; a southern coalition would be formed. And just in case the damned Yankees felt like causing trouble, the South would need to form an army. And a navy. And when the navy was formed, the South would call upon her loyal sons to give of themselves and of their ships.

With his steel-gray eyes focused broodingly on the water, Brent thought wryly that his reputation as a sea captain who could face any tempest at sea and maneuver safely among the most treacherous shoals would now cast him into the thick of things. Well-informed men knew already that the North would try to block southern harbors; when that happened, men of cunning and courage would be needed to run the blockades.

Brent felt a sharp stab of pain as a shiver riddled through him. No one could prevent what was unfolding; time and destiny were upon them all. Yet he had a fear that everything that was unique and beautiful about a certain breed of men and women was about to come to an end. He pictured South Seas, majestic beneath magnolias and Florida moss, and with just that vision of his family's St. Augustine plantation in his mind, he felt a warmth seep into him. He eschewed a number of the so-called gentlemanly pursuits, but he had loved the

8

drawing room where his mother had once played the spinet; he had a penchant for fine brandy after the hunt, for sleek Georgian columns that stood graceful sentinel.

He had built South Seas with his father and brother. He had tended the fields along with the freed blacks and Indians. The plantation had cost them blood and sweat and tears, and he'd die before . . .

He sighed. When the fight came, he'd be ready. But he couldn't believe that the Yankees were all damned cowards. Or that it would all be over in a few months. He had sailed into too many northern ports to live with such a delusion.

It was cold on the Battery. Why he continued to stare seaward, facing the brisk breeze of winter, he didn't know. He should seek shelter within his comfortable master cabin aboard the *Jenni-Lyn*. A good tot of brandy and he could forget the portent of things to come.

Something, some slight movement, attracted his attention northward along the Battery.

A woman stood there, a silhouette framed by the harbor light and the glow of the moon. She was too far away for him to have actually heard her; the movement alone must have caught his eye.

She stood perfectly still now, her attention focused on Fort Moultrie, a Union outpost.

First curiosity, then irritation, compelled him to move toward her. The hour was approaching midnight; no respectable woman would be alone on the harbor at this time. Yet as he closed the distance between them in a long-legged stride, he discovered to his surprise that she could be no common harlot; her clothing was far too rich. Beneath a mantle of deep black velvet she wore a silk receiving dress in shimmering silver pearl. The bell of her skirt informed him that her crinoline was of the latest fashion, as was the waterfall effect of her honey-blond hair.

She was a lady of consequence, and yet she was alone in

the darkness when even some good men were so filled with bourbon that they were potential rapists and thieves.

He came to an abrupt halt within feet of where she stood, and she remained still, shivering against the cold.

Brent uttered a curse of exasperation beneath his breath; he was not taken in by the lures of the female sex; he had known too many women, both ladies and harlots, not to realize that most members of the "gentler sex" were capable of conducting themselves like spitting alley cats. The finest drawing room tactics in the world couldn't always hide the claws of some of the female sex. In fact, he thought a bit dryly, he preferred the company of a good honest whore over that of the southern belles who were determined with wide-eyed innocence to drag him into their bedrooms.

But he had been raised in the gallant South. And he couldn't leave a woman standing alone on the Battery when the streets were full of overzealous revelers. She might deserve whatever came her way, but . . . hell, he had to find out what she was doing. It would plague his conscience if something happened to her.

"Madam," he began, only to stop short when she whirled to him, emitting a startled cry of alarm, obviously shocked to have her silent vigil broken. It was apparent she had thought herself alone.

And as she turned, he discovered that she was incredibly beautiful. Stunning blue eyes as dark and turbulent as the night sea met his, eyes that hypnotized, framed by lashes of darkest midnight velvet. Her nose was small and straight, set between high cheekbones in the slender face of an aristocrat. Her mouth, ruby red from the cold, was compressed in a grim line, yet it gave hint of defined fullness and passion.

She was one cat he'd be glad to meet in the night, no matter how sharp her claws.

"Madam," he began again as a strong breeze whipped in from the sea. The wind caught the balloon of crinoline and

10

skirts, and before he could say anything else he found himself reaching out to fold her swaying form into his arms before she could plummet to the icy waters below the wall.

She was very light, and very, very cold in his arms. As he held her he heard a sound that was part whimper, part sigh. Her face turned parchment white, and her slight body went limp.

"Jesus," he murmured, his tone harsh with both concern and irritation. He should have left her alone. Now he had a swooning woman on his hands, and he hadn't the faintest notion where she belonged.

He stood in uncharacteristic indecision for several seconds, wondering what to do with his fallen beauty. He was not a native of Charleston; he had nothing to offer but the hospitality of his ship, and with his crew aboard, it was hardly the hospitality one would want to offer a well-bred lady.

If she was a well-bred lady. Despite all outward appearances, no southern lady should have been alone on the Battery in the midst of the city's celebrations. He shrugged. The majority of his crew were probably still celebrating. And just as he had no delusions about Yankees, he had no great delusions about women. He'd spent many an amusing night in the bedroom of a "chaste" widow.

She grew colder in his arms. With another exclamation of irritation he turned smartly on his heels and briskly carried the woman to the berth of the *Jenni-Lyn*.

Thankfully, most of his men were still reveling within the taverns and whorehouses of Charleston. He met only Charlie McPherson as he boarded the *Jenni-Lyn*, and one look from the captain's storm-gray eyes silenced any mocking comments that might have come from McPherson's tongue. Charlie stood aside as Brent strode the deck toward the master cabin, curiously eyeing the lovely burden his captain carried, but asking only if Brent would be requiring anything.

"Brandy, Charlie," Brent replied. "And smelling salts."

"We don't carry no smelling salts!" Charlie declared indignantly.

"Then brandy," Brent replied impatiently. "And fast."

"Aye-aye, Captain McClain! Aye-aye!"

Grumbling something about women, Charlie moved to carry out his errand. Brent kicked open his cabin door and carefully laid the woman on his bunk.

She was still deathly pale, deathly cold. He reached for a heavy wool blanket and attempted to cover her, then gave up in disgust as the hoop of her crinoline sent the blanket flying back at him. Cursing softly in annoyance, he slipped his hands beneath the cumbersome silk folds of her gown until he found the hooks of the crinoline, released them, and eased the monstrosity of fashion from its wearer.

His annoyance abated somewhat as he touched her. He felt the curve of her hips, and the trim roundness of her buttocks. Her belly was smoothly flat, and as he drew the crinoline from her, his hands grazed over flanks that were long and lean and wickedly shapely. Heat rose in his loins from the intimacy he had begun with irritation, and it created a greater anger within him. He didn't know who the hell she was, and he'd be damned if he'd be trapped into marriage by accusations of having compromised someone's daughter. He'd seen the innocent little trick played one too many times.

She moaned slightly as he maneuvered her frame, but still she remained pale, the thick curls of her lashes never leaving her cheeks. Brent wrapped her in the blanket, cradling her onto his lap and against the warmth that exuded from his own frame. Charlie appeared with the brandy; Brent gruffly requested that he pour a glass.

"Where'd ye find her, Captain?" McPherson inquired curiously, studying the girl and apparently gaining interest as he discovered her startling beauty.

"On the Battery," Brent replied briefly. "That will be all, Charlie. I can handle things from here."

12

Charlie scratched his grizzled face, loath to give up the excitement of the captain boarding his ship with the beautiful mystery creature. And stone cold out, as it were! Charlie could barely suppress a chuckle, he was so dying to rib his captain. Last he'd seen, Captain Brent McClain would need to knock the ladies out to make them leave him alone, not to secure their company. McClain liked women well enough; and his steel-gray stare seemed to devastate them. But whether he chose his conquests from the streets or the plantations, he assessed them with his bold gaze first, playing his bedroom games only with those who knew the rules. He was reputed to be a daredevil rogue, and though he lacked the polish of a number of his contemporaries, women seemed drawn to the very rough edges that set him apart. His hands were callused and his muscles hard from the work he chose to do; his features were ruggedly hewn with determination and his manner was never that of indulgent flattery. It was damn surprising that he was ministering to a woman with the vapors; normally if a girl thought to flutter her lashes and faint, Brent would step back with contempt for her airs and let others do the "rescuing."

But though Captain McClain could drink and roar and whore with the best of them, he was, in general, a discreet man, a gentleman, born and bred in the South. He was a second son who had won his own fortune with the sweat of his brow and the strain of healthy muscles, but still he had been raised to uphold a certain code of honor. He did not seduce innocents.

In short, Charlie found it hard to believe Brent had accosted a young lady for immoral purposes.

But then what the damned hell else was he doing with her in his cabin? No man in his rational senses could look upon the face and form of that girl and not think a few immoral thoughts . . .

"Charlie!" Brent growled.

13

"Aye-aye, Captain," Charlie mumbled, backing toward the cabin door. "But I'd get rid of her corset, if'n I were you, Cap. I seen a lady pass out in a play at Richmond, and they blamed it on those damn bone traps. Yep, Cap," Charlie repeated, meeting McClain's frosty eyes and moving backward more hastily. "That sure is what I'd do."

Charlie closed the door behind him. Brent eyed the woman and with an irate growl, took a long swig of the brandy.

Then he touched the fiery liquid to her lips, tilted her head and the bottle, and allowed the brandy to trickle into her mouth. She choked and sputtered and coughed, whimpered slightly with a limp wave of a hand, and slowly opened her indigo eyes.

There was pain in them, Brent thought at first, pain so sweeping that it darkened the color to something deeper than the sea, more tempestuous than a storm that thundered and lashed the oceans, but that look of pain was gone so quickly that he thought his own eyes had played a trick.

Still, she didn't appear at all horrified to find herself in his cabin. She glanced at him, straightened, and allowed an astute gaze to ascertain her surroundings. Her eyes returned to his.

"Where is this place, please, sir?"

"You are aboard a ship, madam, the *Jenni-Lyn.*"

"And you cared for me?" she queried, her cheeks at last darkening with the hint of a blush. Apparently she did realize she was minus her crinoline.

"Yes," he said bluntly.

She continued to look at him, digesting his information with a calm interest. Again he felt his anger grow. "I found you on the Battery," he said harshly. "You fainted; I brought you here."

"It is your ship, then?"

He offered her a grim smile. "Yes, ma'am. It is my ship."

She stood, then, and he saw that she was tall for a woman.

14

He noted again how very beautiful she was. Without the distortion of her crinoline he found her figure very lithe and graceful, and now that she had awakened, he noticed that her skin was exceptionally fine, like silk. With her pallor gone, a fresh color brightened her cheeks, a natural pale rose that beautifully complemented her honeyed hair, the inky smudges of her lashes, and the bluer than blue of her arresting eyes.

She moved about the small cabin with a restless grace. "I apologize, Captain. I have never before fainted in my life. I'm afraid I neglected to eat with the excitement of the day."

"I see," Brent replied, crossing his arms over his chest as he observed his mysterious guest. "Too busy celebrating?"

Her lashes lowered over her eyes. "No, sir, I do not celebrate this day."

"Are you a Unionist?" he demanded.

"No, sir," she murmured. Her eyes lit on her discarded crinoline, yet its removal seemed to mean nothing to her. She appeared to totally accept her situation with calm interest. "I am a native South Carolinian, Captain." Her lashes had remained lowered; suddenly they rose; the smile she offered him was dazzling. Her lips were so beautifully shaped, her teeth small and white and perfect.

Who in their right mind had allowed this beauty to roam the streets alone?

"And you, Captain?"

He was wise to her charming questioning, her abrupt attempt to bring the focus of the conversation from herself to him. That was all right, he thought, his eyes narrowing. He'd play her game for a while.

"And I?" he inquired. Standing, he clasped his hands behind his back and circled his guest until he reached the wooden planking of the cabin door. From there he continued to observe her.

"Did *you* celebrate today?" she pressed, offering him another of her dazzling and coquettish smiles.

"Did I celebrate?" he repeated somewhat bitterly, as if the question were a new one he must phrase to himself.

"Sir!" She sounded impatient. "If we should come to war, where will your loyalties lie?"

"With my state," he answered quietly.

"Which state?" she queried huskily.

He cast an amused frown in the direction of her blue, blue eyes.

"Florida, madam. I am a Floridian."

"Florida," she repeated, smiling very slowly. She lowered her lashes again, and idly glanced at the charts that covered his desk, touching the edge of one with a slender finger. She returned her glance to him. "I had always thought the state nothing but swamps and Indians—and backwoods. Is that true, sir?"

Brent allowed himself a hearty laugh. "No, madam, some of the loveliest plantations you would ever wish to see grace our landscape. The soil is rich and fertile, the weather warm, the sun brilliant. The ocean is ever blue, ever beautiful."

Once again her lashes lowered. She had the capacity to act the perfect southern belle, and yet she was like no other woman he had ever met, great lady or harlot. She played prettily only when required to receive an answer she desired; yet one could almost see the sharp workings of her mind. Each of her questions was planned; she sought something.

It appeared that she, his guest, was putting him through a strange test. He was being judged.

Suddenly anger surged through him. He wanted to shake her. Didn't she know the folly she had almost brought upon herself? Just watching her was arousing him, the soft, natural undulation of her hips as she sailed about his cabin. He could feel his blood grow hot . . . pulse and surge . . .

"Enough, madam," he said curtly. "I haven't time to

16

amuse you or to satisfy your curiosity. I want to know who the hell you are so that I might return you to father or husband."

Her lashes lowered. "There is neither," she said softly.

"Then pray, madam, what would you have me do with you?"

"Do you sail soon?"

"With the morning tide."

Her direct gaze met his. "I'd like to sail with you."

Very slowly, and with calculated assessment, Brent allowed his eyes to roam his visitor from head to toe, lingering upon the lush swell of breast and hips. "You do not look the whore," he said roughly.

She flinched slightly; her lashes swept down over her eyes, but then she was facing him again, the indigo of her eyes so sultry he was certain he had imagined the flinch. "I am not a whore, Captain." Her voice was husky; it sent a new wave of heat rushing to his loins. "I merely wish to reach another port. And"—she allowed her tone to fall lower, her eyes to rake suggestively over him—"I find you quite . . . appealing."

Her reply thoroughly startled him, but he arched a brow high with skepticism. Despite her words and manner, something about her didn't ring quite true. She was stunningly beautiful. Her clothing was of the finest quality. Her speech was gently modulated.

He sat at his chart desk and rudely leaned back to clunk his boots atop it while he struck a match to light a slim cigar, assessing her all the while with a frank scrutiny that should have made her blush. "Lady, I wonder if you know what you ask. If fortune has struck against you, I don't believe I am the man you seek. I am not the marrying kind."

"I have no wish to lure you into marriage!" she said with an irritated exclamation. Seeing the mocking smile that curved his lip and raised his brow at her display of temper,

17

she swiftly lowered her lashes again, and spoke with soft seduction. "I wish only to strike a bargain." Her laughter rang out suddenly like a sweet melody. "Really, Captain." She glanced toward her crinoline. "I do believe I've already been compromised. And a southern gentleman—"

"Don't count on my being a gentleman," Brent warned her, inhaling on the cigar.

But even as he spoke, he felt the pulsing need and desire strengthen. Sharp gray eyes, the hue of granite, swept over her again. When he looked at her he wanted to touch her; to see the parting of her rose lips in anticipation of his, to see the incredible blue of her eyes misted with passion . . . but he would not be used, not by any man or woman.

"Lady, what is this?" he inquired shortly. "If you have hopes to irritate a lover, bring him jealously to my steps for a duel to delight your nature, I will not participate. I would not waste life for the vanity of a foolish woman seeking attention. I fear, madam, that soon enough plenty of the gallants of our region will lie dead."

She inhaled slightly. "I have told you, sir, no gallant will rush to my defense."

Sweet Jesus. He wondered what power she held over him. If she taunted him much longer he would cease to care; he would find himself ripping off the remainder of her clothing and taking her on the floor. . . .

What was she? The finest of courtesans? How else could she offer herself with such aplomb? Perhaps a widow, long without a husband? Whatever, she was no innocent maid, and if she wanted to hop into bed with him, he sure as hell didn't have any objection as long as she expected no ties.

"You wish to strike a bargain, but I warn you the price may be high. Tell me your terms"—he smiled coldly—"and I'll give you mine."

He finally seemed to have had an effect on her. The color in her cheeks rose; her steady gaze faltered. "I wish to reach another port." She hesitated only a moment. "Take me, and I will be yours."

Brent McClain arched his brow still higher and kept silent for a moment. "Perhaps I should get you something to eat."

"Then you accept my offer?" she breathed.

"Not yet," he drawled. "But whether I do or not, I don't care to have you swooning on me again. I want a few more minutes to decide whether or not you'll be worth the passage."

For a moment she lost her elusive calm; she stared at him as if she meant to slit his throat. But the color drained from her face, and the murderous gleam left her eyes. She stared at him and smiled. "I assure you, Captain, I'll be worth the passage."

He opened the door he had leaned against and harshly barked for Charlie. When a curious McPherson appeared, Brent asked for some food and said he wished to remain undisturbed. It annoyed him to see McPherson grin like a monkey for the lady, about to trip over his own fool feet for her. She had granted him one brilliant smile, and he was entranced.

While they waited, he turned to her sharply. "I am Captain Brent McClain," he said coldly. "What is your name? If I am to whisper in passion, I want to know whom to address."

Again she blushed, but still she held her ground.

"Kendall," she said clearly. "Kendall Moore."

He nodded distractedly, moving near the open door. "Charlie, damn your hide, what's taking so long?"

Charlie, appearing with commendable speed, glanced at him reproachfully. In a matter of minutes he had managed to create a handsome tray of cold fowl, bread and creamery butter, and wine.

"That's fine, Charlie, thank you," Brent said firmly, shutting Charlie out of the cabin.

Brent sat at his desk and watched her. She said nothing

19

as she seated herself across from him, eating ravenously but with an elegant delicacy. She made no apology for her appetite. He knew that she covertly watched him as she imbibed freely of the wine. It appeared that she craved the relaxation it might bring . . .

Kendall wasn't really craving the wine; she drank out of nervousness. She was frightened by the man she faced; he was built like Goliath, and moved with a deadly, pantherlike agility. His face was not so handsome as it was extraordinarily arresting. It showed strength, character. The angular planes were rugged; the jawline was firm and square. His eyes were level, straight and direct. He was a man who would demand much. A dangerous man if crossed, she was certain. If used . . . and she planned to use him. His eyes seemed to sear into her soul; they made her shiver. Dear God, she had chosen the wrong man. He didn't squander his energy on gallantries. But she had to get out of Charleston, so she had to carry it off.

Covertly she gazed at him again. He was tall and broad of shoulder, narrow and trim at the waist. From his form-hugging trousers and knee-high boots she knew that his legs were long and as sturdy as tree trunks, finely muscled and shaped. The fingers, too, that tapped on his desk appeared powerful, like his hands—long, broad across the knuckles.

The shivering assailed her again. How would such a man touch a woman? she wondered. And then she bit into a piece of meat so that he wouldn't see her tremble. All she had known of men thus far had been misery.

She sipped her wine again, almost gulping it. She had made a mistake. He radiated masculine power and virility. It was natural, something he breathed and walked. Such a man would also be ruthless. She could feel it by the sear of his eyes as he probed her. How will I keep him at bay? she wondered desperately. If I fail, and if he discovers that I am a liar, he will be relentless. God help me. I must have been mad; I will never succeed. But I must! I must!

Where she had come up with her plan, she didn't know. It had only come to mind when she had seen him. And then she had brashly opened her mouth. Now she had begun something that she had to finish. And whatever came, it would be worth it, because she would disappear before the radical events in Charleston today forever made her a prisoner in a land that was foreign to her.

I am mad. . . .

She had eaten all that there was to eat. Willing her fingers to steadiness, she poured herself more wine and brought her cool gaze level with his.

Why was he so angry? she wondered. "Are you quite finished . . . Kendall?" he inquired in a mocking drawl.

She nodded.

"Then will you stand, please?" His voice was pleasant. Too pleasant.

He raked his gaze over her again, letting her see how he mentally stripped her with a practiced eye. She was no debutante, he decided. She was young and beautifully fresh, but past the age when a southern girl was presented to society and married. Was this a game she played often? Did she often seek out lovers? Her eyes professed a mysterious innocence; they also seemed to promise the enigma and the wisdom of all seductive femininity . . . With a cruelty he couldn't suppress, he demanded disdainfully, "What makes you think, madam, that I should find you worth the passage?"

It was not the ashen color he had seen earlier, but her high-framed cheeks went white. He wasn't particularly proud of his triumph, and yet it was justice. He had known that she had observed him closely, as he had her, since her eyes had opened; she had judged his physical attributes, he thought wryly, and she had obviously decided he passed inspection.

21

Kendall suddenly knew deep and devastatingly how slaves felt when they stood on the block at auction. And for the first time, she lost sight of her plan. A black fury seemed to overwhelm her; she was speaking before she thought. "Because I had figured you as a gambler—you backwoods bastard!" she hissed. And she spun on her heel, groping blindly for the cabin door.

"Oh, no, madam!" he suddenly roared, and then, with lithe steps he was upon her, jerking her into his arms. "You have teased me long enough with your bold proposition, with the promise in your eyes. I will have you tonight, Kendall Moore. Your bargain is sealed."

Her head fell back; her eyes, as deep and storm-tossed and mysterious as the ocean, met his.

"We reach a new port first!" she insisted icily. "That's the deal I offer!"

His lips tightened grimly within the strong line of his jaw. The steel of his eyes ripped through her with the brutality of a knife. "Your deal? Well, madam, I'll have a sampling of what I'm being offered before I agree to terms!"

His lips fell on her bruisingly. He plundered her mouth, forcing it to his, his tongue delving between her teeth in an invasion that swept away any chance of denial. His fingers tangled into her hair, his hand spanned the small of her back, forcing her to him. But then . . . his intent changed. He had wanted to savage her with the fever that had gripped him. Now he found that he did not. He drew his lips from hers, then touched them with a light and teasing brush, mingling his breath with the sweetness of hers. She smelled of mint and roses . . .

He stood back from her, pulling his shirt from his trousers and undoing the pearl buttons. He raised a brow at her as he removed the silver cuff links at his wrists. He paused. Waiting. Determined.

"Now, Kendall," he told her hoarsely. Relentlessly. "If you want passage, *I will have you now."*

She was shivering, shaking from his assault. She could not resist his strength; neither could she drag herself from the effect his *gentleness* had had on her senses. He had touched something within her, something that made her want him, as dangerous and demanding as he was . . .

But he would know! He would discover that she was a fraud, and he would throw her off his ship.

"Now!" he demanded again, gray eyes sharp and nakedly displaying a desire that could no longer be taunted.

She watched as his shirt fell to the floor. She stared at the broad expanse of his chest, at the rippling muscles of his shoulders, at the tawny hair that tapered to a line at the waistband of his breeches.

"I . . ." She lifted her chin. He might not be a typical southern gentleman, but surely he would keep his word. "Your promise," she said, trying to still the quiver in her voice. "Your promise that you will deliver me to another port."

His lips were set in a grim line. She had to have his promise before her shaking became so uncontrollable that she panicked and fled. She couldn't do this! She didn't know the game! But she *had* to play it. Now.

Kendall smiled sensually, reaching gracefully for the hooks of her gown. She allowed the silver dress to fall in a rush of silk to the floor, forcing herself to remain tall and proud as her breasts were bared above the corset. "I promise you I'll be worth the passage," she murmured, slowly, seductively untying the drawstrings of her corset and allowing that, too, to fall to the floor.

Brent tossed back his tawny head and laughed. "Madam, you are worth it already. It will be no difficult task to transport you from one berth to another."

Kendall pouted, allowing her fingertip to hover over her

23

lips. Then she clenched her fist over her heart, between her breasts. "Your word, Captain," she murmured prettily, lashes fluttering as she prayed that she would make the right moves in this game that was totally new to her. "Your word . . ."

As Brent stared at her, minus stays and corset, he discovered with a pleasure that brought his breath to a rasp that her perfection was real. Firm, high breasts, cream-colored, rose-tipped, met his view. Beneath them lay the visible line of her ribs, narrowing to a waist his hands could circle. With pulse beginning to pound, he reached for the cord of her pantalettes, pulled it loose, and watched their path as they fell to her feet.

Her belly was concave; her legs long and sleek. The deep shadows of her hips lent fascination to the honey brush of feminine hair, an intoxicating contrast to the cream silk of her flesh.

He stepped back again as she stood, devouring her with his eyes as his senses came to a lava boil. Sitting in the chair that had been hers for her meal, he began to pull off his boots. Still their eyes held; but who hypnotized whom he wasn't sure.

"Your word, Captain," she insisted. Dear God! She couldn't stay here like this much longer.

He smiled rakishly and shrugged. "My word, Kendall. As I said, giving you passage will be no hardship."

She had to bite down on her lip. She was worth passage only because passage was so cheap. And she was standing naked before this arrogant but arrestingly handsome stranger who appeared even more awesome as he shed his clothing.

With boots cast aside he stood again, walking to her slowly. His cheek nuzzled against hers as he sought her lips, this time taking them deeply. His hands found her shoulders, caressed the feel of silk, then glided slowly over her spine, appreciating the fine indentation. He felt the soft touch of her fingertips coming up to press against his chest. . . .

Her lips parted, and he drank of the taste of mint, plunging ever deeper into her mouth as his passion grew. Her response was hesitant, but it was sweetly there.

Then suddenly the fingertips that had pressed so teasingly against his chest were shoving, and she jerked her mouth away. In astonishment he saw that her eyes had gone wild; she glanced at him and spun toward the cabin door.

"Jesus Christ!" Brent swore, catching her in a step and securing her wrist. "Are you mad? You can't go running out of here stark naked!" He swept her slender form into his arms. "And you're not running out on me at this point, madam!"

He dropped her on the bunk with a lack of decorum born of anger. She stared at him again, the liquid blue of her eyes registering a return to sanity. He dropped his trousers.

One didn't grow up on a plantation without knowing a fair amount about life. Still, Kendall wasn't entirely prepared for Brent McClain. He was, as she had imagined, magnificent. Waist and hips were whipcord lean; shoulders and chest were rippled in firm musculature, bronze and satiny from exposure at sea.

But her eyes fell to his hips and the strong columns of his thighs and the desire that was hard and strong between them.

He is magnificent, she thought again, but with that thought came a terrible panic. She didn't know what she was doing. How could she cope with such elemental command? Would she scream? Would she fail? Yet, in the black hell of her life, what mattered what happened here tonight? What humiliation or shame could matter, be worse than what life had tossed her thus far. Any price would be well paid.

His palms came down on either side of her head as he hovered over her, balancing himself above her. She started to quiver in earnest, but he suddenly smiled, and the smile was very gentle.

"Lady," he murmured, "do we or do we not have a bargain?"

Her choice. Even now, it was her choice. She moistened her lips with her tongue at the passion and kindness in his eyes. Her voice was a whisper, but it didn't falter. "We do have a bargain," she murmured.

"Then, madam," he whispered in a husky caress, "do not tremble so. I will love you very tenderly."

She felt his weight and searing warmth as he lowered himself over her; the potency of his need brushed her thighs like a brand.

But he had promised her tenderness, and that he gave her generously. He gently held her head as he trailed light kisses over her face . . . her chin, her cheeks, her eyes, her temple, and finally his mouth came down on hers, sensuously parting her lips with his tongue, reaching deep, slowly probing . . .

His hand cupped her breast, fondling it, his thumb grazing the rose of her nipple, until his mouth moved over it. And then as his lips teased the sensitive spot where his hand had taunted, she felt that appendage move downward, sliding firmly over her belly and hips to her thighs, sinking between them. Kendall gasped aloud and dug her fingers into his hair, feeling as if his touch had turned her to liquid fire, robbed her of all cohesiveness . . .

His mouth roamed up to the hollow of her throat, over her collarbone, to her other breast, suckling the nipple until it was hardened and taut, until her breathing was as labored as his. Still he roamed her flesh with the moist warmth of his lips and tongue, pulling back now and then to watch the manifestations of passion on her body and letting the sight of her fire his own need. She was made to be loved, he thought. She responded to him with a natural beauty that was drugging.

To look at her was *drugging* . . . with the honey and fire fan of her hair spilled over the white of his pillow, her sea-blue eyes wide and misted, her lips parted and moist, her perfect form spread before him. He didn't need to touch her to fill to bursting with desire. But he couldn't stop touching her. He couldn't stop tasting the sweetness of her flesh.

He ran the tip of his tongue down the cleft of her ribs and felt fever grip his loins at the sound of her whimpered moan. Thus driven he caressed her breast as he brought the hot demand of his lips lower and lower, holding her as she jumped as if to protest but writhed and arched uncontrollably. He murmured things against her flesh, teasing her, and then he demanded all of her with probing fingers, following his touch with his kiss, still watching the effects and thinking that every inch of her was incredibly beautiful, incredibly, sensuously, responsive . . .

She tightened slightly when he shifted to move between her legs, but he gently placed a hand on her thigh along with the firm wedge of his knee. Softly, sweetly, she opened to him. "Easy," he murmured, "I know you want me. You are warm and damp and inviting . . ."

She did *want* him, dear Lord, she *wanted* him, she thought incredulously. Had she known when she saw him that it could be like this? The liquid fire was racing through her, making her moist and aching and burning because he touched her . . . and touched . . .

Now, she thought, with what remained of her reason . . . *now!*

But in his own fever, he tortured them both. She had become pliant beneath him, a writhing creature of exquisite, erotic beauty. He started kissing her again, moving her about so that he could explore every inch of giving flesh, easily parting her to him then, touching and touching and touching with passionate teeth and tongue and fingers until he heard her call his name. How sweet it sounded from her lips, how exotically sensual . . .

"Touch me," he commanded her huskily.

27

She did, with trembling fingers. He was pulsing with life, and it was wonderful and frightening and she needed him so to still the need he had created in her . . .

Neither of them was aware of the soft padding of feet on deck. The sound of their whispers, of their heartbeats, had deafened them to all else.

Suddenly the cabin door burst open.

"It's that damned Rebel McClain, all right!" someone shouted.

Brent started to turn, ready to fight the intruder. The muzzle of a gun was pressed hard against his cheek, and he gritted his teeth, holding still.

The voice continued, husky, grating. "Kendall, you ingenuous little vixen, you did find yourself just the right brand of southern bastard! You did damned well for yourself, eh, Kendall?"

Seconds . . . it all happened in just seconds. The door slamming open, the shouted words. Atop Kendall, Brent's eyes met with hers in just those few seconds. Filled with his startled belief in her malicious betrayal, filled with loathing and steel-gray fury and condemnation and rage . . .

Then he didn't give a damn. His fury was so great. He started to turn, swiftly, like a panther, to leap from her, to wrest the gun from the intruder or die in the attempt. Yet he moved too late. No matter what his speed and grace and ability, his attacker had come prepared, while he had let down all his guard in the arms of . . .

Kendall. Kendall Moore. With her wealth of honey-blond hair. With her mystery and intrigue and beauty and absolute gift of seduction.

He never even saw his attacker—or attackers. More than one, he was certain. He wasn't shot, but he felt the tremendous pain, the explosion in his head, as the butt of the gun cracked down upon it.

As the world went black before him, he could think only

one thing. Indeed, he had been a fool. Completely duped. She had set a trap for him; she had set him up to be taken. Naked and unarmed, he had been such a damned easy target. Someone had wanted him out of the way. A Yankee officer, a past associate, someone who knew that he would be a threat now that the war was imminent. She had been the tool, the perfect, seductive siren. She had taken him down, led these men right to him. Traitorous little witch! How she must have been hoping that her companions would come in time. They'd called her an ingenuous little vixen, perhaps just plying her trade in a different manner . . .

What had they done with his crew? Sweet Jesu, and what could he do? The world was all but faded out completely, and he was nearly gone from it. Consciousness faded to a void with just one last thought in his head.

If he lived, he would find the men who had done this.

And he would find her. She would regret what she had done to him, so help him, God. She would pay. Dearly.

No more thoughts plagued Brent when the intruder spoke sharply again; Brent McClain was out cold. The man was tall, dark-haired, with a dark mustache and trimmed beard, striking, handsome himself. Except for his eyes. They were a cold blue, harsh, almost like a void themselves within the cruel lines of his face. "You bitch!" he told Kendall softly. "Maybe I will just kill you."

He grabbed the shoulders of the unconscious McClain and jerked his naked body to the floor. Then he wrenched Kendall up by the arm and brought his open palm across her face so hard that she cracked her head against the bulkhead of the cabin.

But not a word, or cry, or moan escaped her.

She lifted her bruised face to his. "I despise you, John," she said coldly. "And one day I will escape you."

He wrenched her from the bed and struck her again, this time sending her sprawling to the floor.

But before the man could strike her again, another stepped forward, touching his shoulder.

"John, I helped you find Kendall, but I can't stand by while you beat her senseless. Let's get out of here."

"Not until I cast this rebel bastard overboard, Travis!" John stated, his lips forming into a sneer as he kicked Brent's body with a booted toe.

Travis Deland stepped past his childhood friend with a shiver and offered a blanket to Kendall. She murmured a thank-you and then rose painfully to her feet. But her chin rose high as she faced John, and she stood with the blanket around her. "If you kill this man, John, I'll find a way to bring you to trial for murder. And I'll see you hang."

"John," Travis said quietly, "it *would* be murder."

"The bastard's a Rebel!" John bellowed.

"We're not at war," Travis protested.

"We will be!" John exploded. "And this bastard will be at the head of the fleet if the southern traitors muster up a navy." His eyes fell on Kendall with a lethal glaze. "Besides which, Miss Southern Belle, when I finish with you, you'll be as good as dead. Might as well hang for two murders as one."

"John—"

"Oh, I won't kill her. She's still in one piece. If she'd spent another few minutes with him, I might have had to stab them both. As it is—"

Kendall suddenly spun on Travis, her eyes wide and pleading. "Travis! How could you have been a part of this! How can you make me go back with him?"

Travis felt as if a heavy hand were squeezing his heart. He glanced at John, at the murder in the man's eyes. And he glanced at Kendall, at the misery and fear concealed behind a blue wall of pride. And suddenly it was so sad he could hardly bear it. He wanted to tell Kendall that there had been a time when John Moore had been a kind man, a good man.

A time when John had laughed, a time when he could have loved her with the tenderness and caring that she deserved . . .

And he wanted to rail against God. He wanted to know what kind of justice it was for a man like John to be so riddled with disease that the unbearable consequences to his manhood had poisoned his mind. Made him into this beast.

Poor Kendall. All she had ever known from the man she had been sold to for a "precious" piece of land was brutality. He couldn't blame her for trying to run away. But Travis had known John all his life; he kept praying things would get better. But they didn't. And he'd never seen John strike her before. He'd never realized just how bad it was. They had found her with another man and she was John's wife . . .

He looked at Kendall and shook his head sadly. "He's your husband, Kendall. You . . . you have to go with him."

John picked up Kendall's clothing and threw the various garments of silk and lace at her. "Get dressed. Quickly. Before I change my mind and stab you and your southern lover in the heart."

Shaking, Kendall walked into the corner and began to dress, glancing surreptitiously at the southern captain to assure herself that the blow to his head hadn't been fatal.

Forgive me for involving you! she prayed silently. Forgive me, for I will never forget you. You are the only beauty I've ever experienced, and it will all be so much harder now.

She flinched as she heard John stoop over and then grunt under the solid, muscular weight of the man as he hefted the Rebel captain over his shoulder.

"Don't let her move, Travis. I'll be right back."

John left the cabin. Kendall hurled herself across the space into Travis's arms, panic rising to her eyes. "Travis! Stop him! Maybe I deserve whatever happens, but that man doesn't."

"Hush, Kendall," Travis soothed her. "As soon as he gets

back, go with him meekly. It will . . . it will go better for you if you do, and I can circle back and check on the Reb. John has another five men on deck. He took the crew by surprise."

The cabin door burst open. John returned. He jerked Kendall's arm viciously, his eyes narrowing as she held back a cry. "Come with me, Mrs. Moore." He laughed bitterly. "My wife. The great southern belle. The great southern—whore!"

Kendall lowered her head and squeezed her eyes tightly closed. Dear God, how I hate this man, she thought. But she was worried about Brent McClain, so she readily followed her husband's cruel lead.

"Brent McClain," John said mockingly. "She knows how to choose, eh, Travis? Maybe she's just done the Union a hell of a favor."

"Sure, John," Travis muttered.

Travis hung back as John Moore led his wife off the ship. Frantically, he searched the deck. He began to breathe more easily. A few crew members were strewn about, but they were all breathing. But where was McClain? Overboard. Oh, hell—overboard!

Travis rushed to the port side. He could see the man, naked in the freezing water, struggling with the rope tied about his wrists. Doffing only his boots, Travis quickly jumped into the water, almost losing consciousness himself at the shock of contact with the freezing water. He reached the captain and dragged him to the dock.

"Vixen," the Rebel muttered. "Damned beautiful vixen. Seduced me into a trap. I'll find her."

Brent McClain opened his eyes briefly. He stared at the stranger who had pulled him from the water. "Thank you."

Don't thank me, Travis thought. I was a part of this, and it's all so sad and ugly. And don't blame Kendall. You don't understand. Travis smiled ruefully. "Just remember one day that all damned Yankees aren't all bad," he said out loud.

"Shades of gray," the Rebel captain muttered.

Travis heard a commotion coming from the ship. The crewmen were rousing; they would find their captain on the dock. And Travis was freezing to death himself. He stood, glanced at the Rebel one last time, and broke into a run down the Battery.

Shades of gray . . . he thought, pondering the strange words.

Yes, it was coming to shades of gray. Life would never be a simple matter of black and white.

One

November 1861

The water was beautiful. In some spots it was aqua, shimmering beneath the sun with a gemlike dazzle. And as it stretched out across the Straits, it became a blue as deep and mysterious as night. Challenging. Compelling. Up close, it was crystal clear. Tiny, brilliant little fish could be seen within its translucent depths. If Kendall narrowed her eyes and allowed them to mist, the fish appeared as colorful and magical as a rainbow, as a distant burst of mystical promise.

She sighed and opened her eyes fully. There was no promise in the water, or in the hypnotizing beauty of the reef fishes. The heat might be shimmering about her with a fury in the middle of winter miles and miles south of the Mason-Dixon Line, but she was still on Union soil. She stood within the boundaries of the third state to secede from the Union, but although the state belonged to the Confederacy, Fort Taylor and therefore the whole island of Key West were a part of the Union.

Although the citizens of tiny Key West could do little to combat the Union troops, Kendall knew that the majority of them considered themselves Confederates. It was comforting to know, even though she was never allowed beyond the boundaries of Fort Taylor by herself. She could still dream. One day a soldier would let down his guard and she would escape, and kindly Confederates, knowing she hailed from South Carolina and longed to escape the Union hold, would help her. She would tell them how she had been forced into marriage.

Tears blurred her eyes, and she impatiently wiped them away with the back of her hand. After all this time, it was ridiculous to cry. And after the outrageous stunt she had tried last Christmas season and failed, she was probably lucky she was still able to walk.

She turned back to the sea, her eyes misting again and creating a crystal rainbow dazzle of the water. Life might have been more pleasant—no, never pleasant, but perhaps bearable—if John hadn't always hated her so. Why had John Moore wanted her so badly when he had so thoroughly despised her from the beginning?

Travis kept telling her that John loved her. That he prayed nightly that his illness would ease and that he longed to love her as a husband should. But Kendall didn't believe that. John kept her just as he kept his Union blue uniform, his swords, and his rifles. She was a symbol to him; John Moore is a man, her presence told the world, a man, a man . . .

If he had ever been kind, ever, she would have tried to understand. She would have willingly proclaimed anything he desired with a voice that challenged dispute.

Maybe she had created the loathing herself, she thought dryly. But who would have ever guessed . . . ?

She closed her eyes again, remembering the day at Cresthaven those three long years ago when she had first set eyes on John Moore.

Cresthaven . . .

Rightfully, it should have been hers. Her father had built the plantation from the ground up. And when she and then Lolly had been toddlers, William Tarton had carried them

36

about the estate on his huge shoulders from sunup to sundown. She could still recall his words.

"Sons!" he would laugh. "I don't need them! Kendall, my little beauty, you have a mind like a whip! Cresthaven will someday be yours, and you will put the men to shame, for I will see that you know its workings from cotton to cooking. And you will marry a man you choose, my precious daughter. A man who can love a woman with strength. You will marry because you love a man with wisdom, wit, and tenderness and power, never because it is arranged that you should take an advantageous place in society."

Tears suddenly streaked down Kendall's face. Damn you, Father! she cried out inwardly. You allowed me twelve years of that dream, and then you died, and although you gave me your knowledge and love of the land, you never gave it to Mother!

Kendall winced. How she had loved her father. And despite it all, she loved her mother, too. Elizabeth Tarton had been raised to be an ornament. She could play the spinet and hold beautiful parties, but she could barely count money.

And despite Kendall's pleas, Elizabeth had married George Clayton and allowed him to run the plantation.

George Clayton had run it, all right. Run it right down to the ground.

And so John Moore had entered her life. He was stationed at Fort Moultrie, an ardent military man. He and some friends had come to the outskirts of Charleston for the horseraces, and there he had met George Clayton. George brought him home. And John Moore saw Kendall.

The Moores were monstrously rich. Without mentioning the fact to Kendall, her stepfather offered her to the Yankee for an outrageous sum.

Kendall felt herself shaking. A fine sweat broke out over her forehead. She could remember the scene that followed all too clearly. The argument in the drawing room . . .

37

"No!" she had screamed, shocked and horrified. "I will not marry *any* Yankee. You are a fool, George. Anyone can see what lies ahead! The country is going to split."

George tightened his lips grimly. "Don't you shout at me, Miss Uppity-Pants. You've had airs about you ever since I first put eyes on you, but they don't mean a thing to me, missy. I'm your pa—"

"You aren't my pa! You married my mother, but you'll never, never be my pa! And you'll never order me to marry just because you squandered my father's property on your whoring and gambling!"

"Why, you uppity little bitch!" George took a step toward her, loosening his belt. "I'll beat you black and blue, missy!"

It wasn't an idle threat. He had beaten both her and Lolly many times. But Kendall didn't flinch. She had grown hard and strong, and though George was a big man, he was wasted with laziness and drink. "Touch me, you filthy swine," she told him coldly, "and I'll rip your heart out."

At the cold, calm assurance in her voice, and the narrowing of her icy eyes, George hesitated. He turned from her to light one of his fancy Havana cigars. "All right, girl, maybe you've gotten too old for me to take a belt to. I'll let your husband break some humility into you."

"I will not marry your Yankee friend. I'm not marrying anyone at your say-so, George. And when I do marry, I won't marry a man who needs to take a belt to a woman."

George turned back to her, sneering gleefully. "Oh, you'll marry him, all right. 'Cause if you don't—"

"I won't marry him! He's rude and obnoxious and has no manners whatever. He stares at a woman as if he already had her undressed. And he's a Yankee, and *I'll never marry to please you!*"

That was when Kendall looked across the room to see their guest, John Moore, standing in the doorway. Blue eyes venomously cold, harsh features tightly drawn. She was sorry that a guest had overheard her cruel words, but she couldn't back down.

"I apologize, Mr. Moore, that you had to witness this exhibition of poor hospitality. But I will not marry you."

Surely, she thought, they would both back down.

But John Moore merely glanced at her stepfather with grim anger tensing his posture and features, and then turned away. George laughed shrilly. "Kendall, you've just sealed yourself into a life of misery. 'Cause you will marry him, girl. Either that, or I'll give your precious little sister Lolly to Matt Worton. And he won't care if she says yes at a wedding ceremony or not, he's real fond of young virgins, 'specially blue-eyed, wheat-haired blondes like that little girl."

"She's only fourteen!" Kendall lashed out in desperate fury. "You wouldn't dare do such a thing. Mother would kill you!"

George tapped his cigar ashes onto the polished floorboards. "Now, you know your mother is too ill to believe anything you say about ol' George, honey. Your mother needs a man to cling to. And I'd see that Matt got ahold of Lolly without Elizabeth ever knowin' what happened."

Kendall felt the blood draining from her features. Lolly was so much more like their mother than their father. So gentle and ethereal. George would bully her. And Matt Worton beat and chained his female slaves and used bullwhips. Two of his wives were already dead, although nobody could ever prove his treatment had killed them.

"You marry that Yankee, Miss Priss, and I'll sign an agreement that nothing will happen to precious Miss Lolly. I'll see that only you can approve a choice of husband for her. And I'll see that she never wanders too far away from protection. You know what I mean now, don't ya, Kendall?"

Kendall had known from the moment she saw John Moore's eyes on her that he despised her.

But she was shocked on her wedding night. He slapped

her across the room as soon as the door closed on them. And he ordered her to undress. Shaking, but with defiance and loathing in her eyes, she obeyed him, her fingers trembling so that it seemed to take forever to rid herself of her mother's cumbersome wedding gown.

But then he had merely stared at her, devouring her with his eyes. And then the moody blue had filled with hate and misery and clouded despair. John Moore had slammed his fist into the wall and stalked out of the room, slamming the door behind him.

The scene had been repeated a dozen times during their marriage.

It was Travis who told her that John had caught some kind of a disease fighting the Indians in Florida during the Second Seminole War. He had almost died in 1856, but he had pulled through. Only Travis—and now Kendall—knew that the misfortune had left John only half a man. Kendall tried hard to understand the devils that plagued him and made him cruel and venomous, but understanding came hard when he directed the hate at her.

She had withstood it all with silent dignity for the first year. When he was angry, he struck her, but he was always careful not to leave marks. She could withstand any physical pain, keeping her chin high, her pride about her like a wall that no lash could breach. What she couldn't bear was the isolation. Many of John's New York friends were pleasant, and the city itself was bustling and fascinating. Both of them maintained the facade of a normal marriage.

But a year and a half into Kendall's mockery of marriage, Lolly had fallen in love. The letters Kendall received were full of enthusiasm and devotion, and despite the fact that her baby sister was only fifteen, Kendall had given Lolly her consent to marry. The young man so in love in return was the son of one of Charleston's most respected and affluent planters, and Kendall had always liked him well. Gene McIntosh was all the gallant things that the South stood for; he was intelligent and kind and well read, and he would cherish Lolly and keep her safe forever.

And so, with Lolly safe, Kendall felt a new freedom. She listened avidly to the news that came to New York, and after John Brown was hanged for leading an abolitionist uprising, she felt certain that there would be a civil war. And she wasn't going to be in the North when South Carolina seceded from the Union.

Travis had helped her convince John that she should visit her mother despite the rising tide of tension. But she had already tried to escape once in the streets of New York; she should have known John would follow her with his navy friends.

"Oh, God!" she moaned, burying her face in her hands. What folly! She had almost cost a man his life! How could she have known she had stumbled upon a southern captain whom northern navy men already feared and hated? Not that it mattered. In the compromising position in which she had been found, it was only Travis's restraint that had kept John from trying to kill them both. And Travis had assured her that the man lived . . .

The man. Brent McClain.

She shivered, thinking of him. How many times since that fateful night had her thoughts unwillingly turned to him? How many times had she trembled, filled with heat and cold and then liquid, shattering heat again? She had often wakened to find herself trembling and covered with a sheen of sweat.

No matter how she tried, she couldn't forget him. The husky drawl of his voice. The deep gray of his eyes, hard as steel when they narrowed with anger, smoky and almost silver when they misted with the heat of passion . . .

He was arrogant! she reminded herself. Arrogant and self-assured and mocking and . . . splendid in a raw and primitive and wholly masculine way. She would never erase the picture

41

of his naked body, so strikingly muscled, yet so trim, the broad shoulders narrowing to stomach muscles so tight that they were like bands of iron. He could move with the agility of a wildcat despite his height and cleanly sinewed size. He was, in fact, a bit like a beautiful wild beast, full of keen health and virility and restrained power.

"Oh, God . . ." she whispered again. And then she inhaled and exhaled slowly, wincing. Another thing she would never forget was the look in Brent's eyes when the barrel of John's gun crashed against his skull.

Never had she seen a look so cold and threatening. Never had she felt so riddled with fear, not even when she had turned to find the eyes of her husband on her . . .

It was good for the South that Brent McClain had lived. She heard his name whispered among the Union barracks with awe. He could slip past any Union blockade; he ran supplies from the islands into Florida, Georgia, and Louisiana, and he managed to sail right beneath the Union soldiers' noses without ever being apprehended.

Confederate President Jeff Davis had given Brent McClain a naval commission, Kendall knew from the southern papers she read voraciously when Travis could smuggle them to her. And McClain had twice been commended for bravery.

Dear God, Kendall prayed silently, don't let him be caught! And she added, "Please, don't let him be caught—and don't ever let him be brought here . . ."

She shivered again despite the heat of the day. Never in a thousand years could she forget the steel-gray daggers in his eyes when he had looked at her that last time. Were she surrounded by a hundred Union soldiers, she would quake in fear. He would, she was certain, find a way to kill her . . . unless John got to him first. He had been furious to discover that McClain lived. He and Travis had argued so violently that the rift between them would never really heal.

But still Travis had asked for the transfer to Fort Taylor

with John. He had come to protect her, the best he could, anyway, she thought. Travis—such an honorable man! Even for a Yankee. No, Kendall thought, biting her lip. She didn't mean that. There were a lot of honorable Yankees. Men were men, she had learned. The color of the coats they wore did not determine the degree of their honor.

Half of her misery was that she was what she was. South Carolina was her home. The cotton fields were her pasture. The soft crooning of the slaves as they worked was the music she knew best. She was loyal in the core of her heart to her homeland, and she would not evade the danger of being a Rebel in a Union stronghold. Everywhere she looked—now toward the guard tower—loomed a uniform of Union blue.

"Kendall!"

Hearing her name called, Kendall spun around on the fort's catwalk. She did so with a smile, for she knew it was Travis hailing her, not her husband. One benefit to being here was that John was seldom about; he was constantly sailing along both coasts, from Pensacola to Jacksonville, where most of the sea skirmishes took place. Florida, whose past and present governors were ardent secessionists and totally loyal to the Confederacy, was sadly being stripped by the very cause it so wholeheartedly supported. Most of its troops were called to fight in Virginia and Mississippi where the key battles of the war were taking place, leaving miles and miles of vulnerable coastline open to attack.

"Hello, Travis," she called softly.

Travis smiled at her in return as he joined her on the walk where they looked out over the ocean. Guilt plagued him every time he came near Kendall, yet he often sought her company. He was more than a little bit in love with her. She was beautiful, but his feelings went deeper than that. The southern slur of her voice was soft, yet laced with pride and strength. No matter what befell her, she stood tall, facing the

43

world defiantly with matchless dignity and poise. She was, under any circumstance, a lady.

And if he had not helped John find her, she might have escaped him . . . Travis dug his nails into his palms. She was John's wife, legally tied to him. That was why he had helped find her. And because he feared John might have tried to kill her, and she might not have cared enough to fight.

"Want to go sailing?" he asked her.

He saw the blue in her eyes alight, matching the splendor of the sun-touched water. "Might I, Travis?"

"Yes," Travis said happily. "I've been assigned to a small scouting excursion. Captain Brannen said it would be a routine trip. There's no real danger this close to the fort. Since John's been gone almost four months now, the captain thinks you need an outing."

Kendall smiled again. Captain Brannen was a good man. He didn't know the root of her misery, but sensed it. And as John's superior officer, he was often in the position to do little things to ease her life.

"Oh, Travis! Thank you!" Kendall exclaimed. "When do we leave?"

"Now."

"Just let me fetch a shawl."

She was already running down the catwalk to the steps, flinging her words behind her. Travis sighed as he watched her go. She really was so very beautiful. She had quickly learned in the heat of the island to do as other women did—discard the voluminous petticoats and restricting corsets that were so fashionable on the mainland. The gown she wore was a light-colored cotton, and it clung to a body that was not overly voluptuous, but feminine and shapely and graceful. The cut of the gown was modest, but not even modesty could hide the swell of her firm young breasts, or their rise above a naturally slender waistline. A wide, floppy straw hat protected her complexion from the merciless rays of the sun,

44

but even the hat added to her beauty, giving a shadowy mystery to the stunning blue of her eyes, which seemed to change color like the varying shades of reef-strewn waters.

"I'll wait for you at the gate!" Travis called after her.

She waved in response, then raced in to the small room she shared with John when he was at the fort, and luxuriated in when he was not. She snatched her white shawl from the foot of the bed and raced—with little decorum—to meet Travis at the gate to the dock. She had discovered one passion since she arrived at Fort Taylor: sailing. She loved the ocean, and the wind in her hair. She loved the sway of the decks beneath her, and the salt spray that bathed her and seemed to refresh her, giving her spirit new life.

"What are we sailing on?" she demanded breathlessly.

"The *Michelle,*" Travis said with a grin. "We're a small party. There's myself and Seamen Jones, Lewis, and Arthur. How's that sound?"

"Delightful!" Kendall laughed. She liked all three men. Tactful and considerate. None would make comments about "smashing the bejesus out of the backwoods Rebs" in her presence; nor would they whisper that she was one of "them slave-whipping traitors to God's own Union." The barracks at Fort Taylor were filled with a mixture of men; the majority were decent folk caught in a sad war. But there were a few swaggering asses, convinced—despite the Union humiliation at Bull Run—that they would "womp the snot-nosed Rebs in a lick and a split and hang 'em all high like the goddamned Injuns."

Travis gripped Kendall's arm and led her along the dock to the small *Michelle.* The schooner was equipped with no guns. More pleasure craft than navy vessel, the *Michelle* functioned solely as a scouting vessel.

"I'll let you take the helm," Travis told her with a wink as he slipped his hands about her waist to lift her aboard.

"Why, bless you, Travis!" Kendall laughed delightedly.

She greeted the three other men with a smile and took a seat near the helm as they cast off lines and maneuvered the boat out of the harbor. She faced the wind as the men hoisted sail, dreaming that she could sail forever and ever on aqua seas.

The breeze was brisk, not heavy. Kendall stared up at the billowing canvas, glanced at Travis where he sat at the wheel, and then closed her eyes. One day she would escape John. And Florida had opened new frontiers to her. There were places, she knew, islands and inlets, where people could disappear. Pirates had used these islands as hideouts for centuries. She wouldn't need much. She had been raised in luxury, but she had learned to work hard, too, and she could survive quite well. She would find a way to trade for a living, and she would buy a boat, smaller than the *Michelle,* one that she could manage alone. And then she *could* sail forever and ever on aqua seas. . . .

"Look, Kendall!" Travis's voice broke into her beautiful daydream. He had opened his shirt for comfort, and was leaning back casually against wooden planking as he pointed across the water. Kendall followed the direction of his arm to see a pair of playful dolphins leaping high and diving deep, keeping pace with the *Michelle.*

Kendall smiled, but something in her eyes must have told Travis that he had brought her from a pleasant dream to harsh reality. His smile faded, and he glanced quickly aft, where the three crewmen were scouting the inlets of the tiny islands north of Key West for other small craft.

"Kendall," he said. He stopped, grimaced, and then began again. "Kendall, I've never had a chance to tell you, but I'm sorry about . . . about last December. I . . . I grew up with John, you know. He was my best friend all my life—"

"It's all right, Travis," Kendall interrupted tonelessly. "You did what you felt you had to do."

"No, it's not all right." Travis hesitated again, noting that she had half closed her eyes, shielding them against him with the thick fringe of her lashes. "Kendall, I . . . Oh, hell! I just kept thinking that John was going to be all right one day. But he isn't. John's like a wounded animal, Kendall. When you shoot a wildcat, you might as well kill it. Otherwise, it will suffer for the rest of its life, dying a bit at a time. John should have died. The pain isn't in his body; it's in his mind. His spirit is poisoned and twisted."

Kendall at last opened her eyes and stared into Travis's warm brown gaze, dark now with the heartache he bore for two people. Poor Travis!

"Travis," she said quietly. "I admire your loyalty to John. He was your friend, and you loved him. And you've been a good friend to me. You've made my life bearable. You've . . . you've kept John from killing me, and you've kept me from wanting to die."

Travis cleared his throat, and glanced quickly aft to assure himself that the seamen were still talking among themselves and keeping their lookout.

"Kendall, I don't think you understand. I believe John has gone over the brink. His own men think him mad. I . . . I want to help you escape from him."

Kendall straightened and gazed at him eagerly. "Oh, Travis! Bless you! I'll go anywhere, do anything! Charleston, maybe! I'd be careful. I'd go to Lolly's, and I wouldn't travel anywhere near town. No, maybe not Charleston. My stepfather would give me back to John if he caught me. Unless I could get a divorce! Oh, yes, Travis! That's it. I could plead to a South Carolina court! They wouldn't make me go back, not when my husband is a Yankee!"

"Kendall, Kendall!" Travis warned. "Even during a war, maybe especially during a war, a divorce isn't easy to get. And your stepfather is so afraid for his money that he'd ship you back to John. Don't . . . don't count on a divorce, Kendall. We have to plan for you to disappear entirely."

"Commander! Commander Deland!"

Travis's speech was halted by a sharp cry from Seaman Jones. Travis frowned and pulled Kendall's hands to the wheel. "Excuse me, Kendall," he said, as confusion and worry filtered into his gaunt features.

Kendall held the wheel, and watched with knitted brows as Travis nimbly scurried aft. She pulled the brim of her straw hat lower to shield her eyes against the glare of the sun. Seaman Jones, a boy of about eighteen, was pointing excitedly behind them. Squinting, Kendall felt her heart beat harder as she saw that they were being followed by three long, slender vessels, all with only one mast and one sail. Dugouts, she thought instantly, each about fifteen feet long. Dugouts with sails, bearing down upon them swiftly . . .

"Jesus Christ, preserve us!" She uttered the prayer tensely as Travis scrambled back to push her from the helm.

Tremors of ice-cold fear fanned up and down Kendall's spine. "What is it?" she demanded, her voice shaky as Travis turned to face her, his expression one of amazement—and a panic he couldn't quite hide.

"Indians," he told her briefly. He turned around again. "Jones! Hoist the jib! We have to pick up knots!"

"Indians!" Kendall repeated incredulously, the cold fear that had touched her developing into raw panic. "What Indians? Why?"

Travis shook his head impatiently. "I . . . I don't know why. Seminoles, or maybe Mikasukis. There's been some isolated violence since the last war. They hate the Union." Travis twisted around to see that the dugouts were gaining on them. "Of all the days for me to bring you along. Goddamn the U.S. government! They cheated and lied all those years and pushed the Seminole into the swamp, and now they're attacking my boat. *On the Keys no less!*"

"It's not your fault I'm here," Kendall said swiftly, but she couldn't keep the sick terror from her voice. Horror tales about the Indians in Florida had reached her when she was a girl. They had burned out Florida plantations, killed the white planters, butchered women and little children . . .

"Load your pieces!" Travis yelled out. "Take the wheel again, Kendall."

Kendall grabbed the wheel with sweaty palms. She glanced back and saw the dugouts surrounding them. The three seamen were hurriedly loading their weapons, ripping their powder packets open with their teeth. The men would be able to get off only one shot apiece. Then they'd have to battle with bayonets.

Travis was loading his own rifle. "Travis!" Kendall pleaded shakily. "Give me a knife! Give me something!"

He glanced at her uncertainly, then at the dugout coming up on their port side. A scantily clad brave, his knife between his teeth, was about to leap from the dugout to the *Michelle*. Travis hastily snatched the knife strapped to his calf and handed it to Kendall. Then he aimed his rifle.

Kendall flinched at the first report. One brave went crashing into the water in midleap; another leapt onto the deck with the grace of a cat, squatting low to spring into an attack. Kendall sprang to her feet, holding her knife in a death grip and stumbling toward the stern of the *Michelle*. The second dugout had come up along the starboard side; three browned and well-muscled braves, clad only in loincloths, were making agile jumps from their vessels to the deck. crying out in bloodcurdling war whoops as they did so. Kendall watched in horror as Seaman Jones caught a knife in his neck and plunged into the foaming sea. And then, clear above the burst of powder and shouts of men in hand-to-hand combat, came a harsh voice, speaking flawless English.

"Surrender, Yankees! Your lives will be spared!"

Travis, as stunned as Kendall, made the mistake of freezing in astonishment. The Indian who had spoken butted

49

Travis's rifle from his grasp and sent it flying over the side into the sea.

Leaning against the mainmast and holding on to it as a support, Kendall watched sickly as Travis straightened to face the warrior brave. "Who are you?" Travis demanded.

"Red Fox," the Indian said, turning toward the stern where the two remaining seamen had gone ghastly pale as four Indians surrounded them. Red Fox jerked his head, and his braves grabbed the struggling men to hurl them overboard.

"Just a minute!" Travis cried out. "You said our lives would be spared."

His voice broke off as Red Fox turned to stare at him once more, his dark eyes hard and seemingly amused. "You are a brave man, my friend. And I do spare your lives. A dugout is yours. And now, brave man, you, too, will jump overboard and swim to a dugout. And hope that no hungry shark is in between."

Travis stood tall. Kendall saw that he shook a bit before the tall brave with his sleek, well-muscled brown body, but he did not back down. "I will go after the woman."

"The woman stays," Red Fox said determinedly. "You go. Or else you die."

"I cannot—" Travis began, but that was as far as he got. Red Fox laughed aloud, picked Travis up as if he were feather-light, and tossed him into the sea. Kendall heard a long, high-pitched scream—and realized it was her own.

Red Fox was approaching her.

In panic she let go of the mast and brandished her knife menacingly. Several Indians scrambled over the decks, as silent as cats in the night. Kendall darted her eyes from left to right, ready to plunge her weapon with desperate intent in either direction. But low laughter rang out again—that of Red Fox. He said something sharply in his own language, and the other Indians backed off, one of them taking the wheel of the *Michelle*.

50

Red Fox kept coming—alone. Kendall stared at the Indian as he approached her, fear making the blood rush furiously through her system. His black hair fell shining and straight to his shoulders, his face was an arresting sculpture made of granite. Only the sneer on his lip, and the cunning sparkle in his wide, dark eyes betrayed the presence of emotion. She knew now what it was to be a mouse cornered by a cat.

"Woman, give me the knife," he demanded.

"Never!" Kendall vowed. Fear, more than courage, made her do so.

Red Fox placed his hands on his lean hips and laughed loud and heartily. "Fire lady!" he said, admiration touching the rough edges of his voice. "I would much like to deal with you, but"—he shrugged, his amusement evident—"the Night Hawk has claimed you for himself. I bow to his wishes."

Kendall had no idea what he was talking about. She had never encountered an Indian before in her life. And it didn't matter which heathen thought she was some prize, because she was going to fight until . . .

Until what? The only avenue of escape seemed to be the water . . .

Red Fox took another step toward her, and she lashed out desperately with the knife. He hopped back a step and began to circle her. She turned with him, lunging, drawing back. Warily they eyed each other. Then Kendall leapt at him with a vengeance, gratified to hear him curse softly as she drew a line of blood on his chest with her knife. But his arm snaked out before she could retreat. He caught her wrist in an iron vise and snapped the knife from her hand. She screamed out in pain and fury, and wrenched her wrist fiercely, managing to escape from his hold.

The water probably offered only death. She couldn't swim, and she was hampered by the length of her skirt. They were at least a mile from land.

Nevertheless, she lunged for the port side and threw herself overboard with a fury. Into the crystal depths she sank and sank, her lungs becoming heavy, the pressure of her held breath pounding against them. But then her limbs sprang into life; instinctively she gave a ferocious kick and propelled her body toward the surface.

Even as her head broke the water and she sucked in a huge gulp of air, she felt a talonlike grip on her shoulder.

She turned and saw it was Red Fox, his handsome features irritated.

Kendall tried to strike him. He placed his hand on her head and dunked her, holding her under the water so long that she struggled fiercely, her only thought to breathe again. Suddenly he jerked her back to the surface by the hair.

This time she didn't have the strength to fight him. Black spots before her eyes threatened to become an all-encompassing curtain. She was barely coherent when he began to swim with her in tow. She was drawn back to consciousness by the pain in her scalp as he pulled her by the hair.

Two of the braves caught her limp form as Red Fox let go of her and heaved himself aboard with his powerful arms.

The two braves dragged her aboard and dropped her on the deck, and for moments she just lay there, her eyes closed as the heat of the sun bore down on her drenched body, drying the sea salt on her skin. At last her mind began to function again.

The Indians were speaking among themselves quietly. The *Michelle* was moving now, picking up speed.

Kendall's eyes flew open, and she prepared to leap to her feet and spring into the sea once more. But even as her muscles tensed, a large, bare brown foot balanced threateningly on her abdomen. She stared furiously into Red Fox's dark eyes.

"Get your filthy foot off me."

Red Fox grunted and reached down to grip her arm and

jerk her none too gently around so that she lay on her stomach. She tried to struggle, but it was useless. He tied her wrists together with little effort, using a leather band from about his neck. And then he tied a piece of rigging rope to that, like a leash, so that she couldn't go far.

Left with no other recourse, Kendall began to curse at him viciously, rolling to kick and thrash with the remainder of her failing strength.

Red Fox grunted as she landed a sharp kick on his shin. He jerked on the rope so that her arms were pulled back roughly. The pain was searing.

"Woman!" he told her fiercely. "You are more trouble than the soldiers in blue. Cease! Or I will forget that you are for my brother the Night Hawk and I will extract his vengeance for him."

Beaten for the moment, Kendall closed her eyes and lay still. She felt the soft pad of footsteps as he walked away from her, and then the light jerk of the rope, a firm reminder that she was still tied to him.

Dripping and miserable as she lay in sodden dishevelment on the hard planks of the deck, Kendall tried not to think of her situation. She had to rest, to regain some strength.

But the *Michelle* was sailing ever northward. And she couldn't stop herself from thinking . . . from feeling terror wash over her again and again . . . Who in God's name was the Night Hawk? And why would he seek vengeance on her?

Two

The sun did not stay out long enough to dry Kendall's clothing. With the approaching darkness, the hot winter day became a cool night. Cramped and miserably cold, Kendall wondered dismally just where the Indians were taking her.

Northward was all she could really tell. They had passed a number of islands, but that seemed to mean little, because it was ridiculous that Indians had come as far southwest as Key West to stage a surprise attack . . .

Her captors did not molest her in any way. They had talked among themselves in their native tongue as the long afternoon had waned. Except for the abundance of naked bronze flesh they displayed, and their long, jet-black hair, they might have been any sailors out for a pleasant sail. And for all the attention they gave her, she might have been just a sheet of canvas or a coil of rope. She had been grateful for that fact.

But it was strange what a human being could bear, and what one could not. She had managed to keep her pride and not fall weeping to her knees when she had first faced Red Fox with a dagger, certain that she would shortly die. Now . . . now she was not so sure she could maintain her pride much longer. She was so cold. So damp. And the leather about her wrists was drying tightly; it was slow and constant torture against her flesh. She hadn't eaten for hours, and salt seemed to have become a permanent taste in her mouth.

Constant, nagging pain could drive one crazy, she thought. Drive one to plead for release, like a sobbing child. Kendall swallowed, almost emitting a cry at the terrible dryness that wracked her throat. There was water aboard the *Michelle,* Kendall knew. In the small cabin there were dozens of jugs filled with crystal-clear drinking water.

Red Fox had seemed almost civilized. Not quite the complete savage that had always been her vision of an Indian. The complete savage would have killed all the men aboard the *Michelle,* raped her, cut her throat and tossed her carcass to the sharks.

She was being saved for the vengeance of the Night Hawk, she reminded herself, and a quiver like a tide swept through her. But if she was being saved, then she could ask for water and a blanket so that she would not catch pneumonia and die, thereby denying Night Hawk his vengeance.

Kendall opened her mouth to call Red Fox, but just as she did so, a light flared suddenly in the darkness. In eerie shadow she saw the face of an Indian in another vessel about twenty feet away. One of the dugouts had drawn up next to the *Michelle.* A spatter of their Indian language rang out in the night, and then the warriors aboard the *Michelle* began hurriedly lowering the sails. She heard the huge plop as they heaved the anchor overboard, and then, without a sound, Red Fox seized her and, despite a vicious verbal protest on her part, tossed her over his shoulder. A cry escaped her as he carried her over the port side with a jarring leap into the sea. The water rushed over her trailing arms and hair and the shock, when she was already shivering with dampness, made the temperate water seem as cold as the arctic seas.

Red Fox hauled her ashore and set her down beside the warmth of a fire that blazed on a spit of white sand. His dark eyes registered a certain concern as they stared down at her. "You are cold?" he demanded.

Kendall could only nod.

He dropped the rope when he left her. Kendall assumed he did so because he thought it unnecessary to keep her on a leash any longer; there was nowhere for her to go. All she could see was sand—and beyond that the dangerous black sea.

Kendall stared into the flame of the fire, then narrowed her eyes again to search out the shoreline. Four of the braves were pulling the dugouts high onto the sand. They talked as they worked, but their conversations were low and subdued. Two other braves spoke quietly to Red Fox; then they joined the others at the dugouts. They took from the dugouts colorful shirts and woven blankets as well as a number of leather satchels. Kendall watched as Red Fox slipped a long-sleeved shirt over his head, then clutched a satchel and a blanket and returned to her.

He tossed the satchel down to her. "Clothing," he told her briefly.

She kept staring at him and he lowered himself to face her closely, a sneer touching the fullness of his lip. "Do you tremble, tremble, white woman? Do you fear a glimpse of your pallid flesh will make my warriors like stallions at stud to a mare in heat?"

Kendall wanted to laugh and to cry. This Indian knew nothing about her life; she had endured humiliation so long that there was little he could do to her in that quarter.

She smiled. "If I tremble, Red Fox, it is with cold. And I do not rush to accept your gift of dry clothing because my hands are tied!"

She was glad to see that Red Fox was at first taken aback. But then the Indian chuckled, and that strange glint of admiration returned to his eyes. He slipped his knife from his belt and walked behind her. She felt the jagged rasp of the knife as he slit the leather.

"Your hands are no longer tied, white woman. You may go to the trees and change and take care of your needs. Do not try to run. There is nowhere to go. This island is small with no fresh water. It is fringed by reefs where the sharks prowl hungry in the night."

Kendall rose painfully, rubbing her chafed wrists. She grabbed the leather satchel she had been given, and smiled bitterly at her captor once again. "I'm not going to run, Red Fox. I wouldn't dream of quitting myself of your benign hospitality." She started walking off past the amber glow of the fire and then suddenly spun back. "I have a name, Red Fox, and I do not like being called 'white woman.' My name is Mrs. Moore. You may so address me if you wish me to respond."

Red Fox crossed his arms over his chest. "I know your name, Kendall Moore. Now go, change quickly. I am growing weary and will not wait long to give you food and water for the night."

Kendall turned again and kept walking into the darkness, now more puzzled than frightened. How could this Indian possibly know her name? It was as if the *Michelle* had been attacked with the sole purpose of taking her hostage.

There *was* more than sand on the tiny island. She came at last to a straggly mangrove stump and ducked behind it. Her confusion increased further as she opened the leather satchel. She had expected to find Indian clothing inside, a dress like the colorful shirts the men had donned.

There was a dress in the satchel, yes. But it was not Indian. It was a cotton day dress, not unlike the damp one she began to remove in jerky, thoughtless motions as her head spun in bewilderment. *What* was happening?

Kendall began to hurry, determined to return quickly to the warmth of the fire—and to Red Fox. She was becoming more and more convinced that the Indians intended her no harm—not at this time, anyway. She was for the Night Hawk. And apparently the Night Hawk wielded at least as much power as Red Fox—and he had ordered that she was not to be molested. That thought could give her courage for the moment.

So thinking, Kendall fastened the last of the buttons on her dry dress, gathered up the soaked one, and stalked back to the camp.

Blankets were strewn about the fire. Some of the men were eating, chewing strips of meat they held in their hands. Three of the warriors were already curled into their blankets.

Red Fox sat cross-legged exactly where she had left him. The only surprise was the coffeepot that sat on a chunk of coral in the center of the fire.

Kendall emitted a little cry of joy and boldly sat cross-legged before Red Fox. "Coffee! How nice. However, I would like some water first."

Red Fox was willing to extend only so much hospitality to his captive. He tossed her a tin cup and a flask. She opened the flask and poured herself a generous amount of water, drank it thirstily in what seemed a single gulp, and then re-peated the procedure. She suddenly felt the heat of his hand on her arm. "Not so fast. You will cramp your belly."

The dark eyes were enigmatic. Kendall nodded, and slowly sipped the rest of the water, bluntly staring at him. He grunted with impatience when she finished the last of the water, and poured her coffee with obvious annoyance. When she had accepted the tin once more, he waved a piece of the dried meat beneath her nose. She accepted that, too, biting into it hungrily while she continued to survey him. "Thank you," she murmured with sweet sarcasm after she swallowed her first bite of the meat, which was not at all bad tasting. "You're ever so kind. Southern hospitality—southern Indian style, that is."

Red Fox grunted again. "Eat, white woman." ·

"Mrs. Moore."

The only reply was another grunt.

"Are you a chief, Red Fox?"

"Yes."

"Of what?"

His dark eyes now narrowed suspiciously. "I am a chief of my tribe."

"Yes, yes, I gathered that," Kendall said impatiently. "I mean, are you a Seminole?"

"No, and yes. I am a son of the great Osceola. Who was *Creek*—and Seminole. But my mother is Mikasuki. And you are too talkative. Eat your food, white woman. I want to sleep."

Kendall glanced about her. She had sensed a quiet, and she noticed now that all the warriors had curled into their blankets. She exhaled a little breath, surprised by these strange bronze men with their dark eyes and fathomless expressions. They truly ignored her and left her care entirely to their chief.

"We are not beasts, white woman. Nor are we savages. No more than any man when his land is attacked."

Kendall flushed as her eyes returned to those of Red Fox. Then she asked softly but bluntly, "Then why did you attack us? Why did you kidnap me?"

"The Night Hawk wishes to see you," Red Fox replied.

"But that is insane!" Kendall exclaimed. "I have never seen a Florida Indian before in my life! I have never harmed an Indian!"

Red Fox stood and picked up her blanket and tossed it over her. "Be quiet and go to sleep. And don't think to stab us in the night. We awake at the smallest rustle of the breeze, and if you disturb me, I will tie you for the rest of the journey."

Kendall tossed the blanket from her head and sipped her

coffee slowly, aware that the irate Indian stood over her. "I hardly think little old me could stab seven braves in the night," she replied dryly. She did not look at Red Fox, but somehow sensed delightedly, that he stared at her with confusion and discomfort. At last he emitted another of his very impatient grunts, and picked up his own blanket. He did not move far away, and when he lay down—his back to her in challenge—she continued to sip her coffee. But at last she, too, felt the weariness that gripped the Indian. Her words had been true. It would be suicide to steal a knife and try to stab seven healthy, husky braves in the night. And there was only the eternity of the black night sea and the brief span of sand and stumps to escape to.

Sighing tiredly and fighting tears of despair, Kendall stretched out, trying to find comfort on the hard-packed sand. She could never sleep on such hardness.

But she did. Her eyes closed even as her weary body gave out, and she didn't feel discomfort at all as she laid her cheek on the rough blanket. She sank into a sweet oblivion almost instantly.

Dawn broke with pink-streaked sunlight. Kendall felt the growing heat on her eyelids, and as she blinked awake, she became aware of pleasant aromas and the still strange sound of Indian voices.

Shielding her eyes as she sat up warily, she looked around her. The fire still burned. And once again, it heated a battered tin coffeepot. But a cast-iron skillet also sat over the heat, and the smell of fresh fish cooking brought a growl of hunger to her stomach. One brave tended the skillet while another was busy with a knife, carving more neat fillets to place on the fire.

"You slept well, white woman."

Kendall turned with a start. Red Fox stood behind her. She hadn't heard a sound, and the fact that he could come upon her so silently was disconcerting. She scowled up at him.

"Not badly," she agreed, adding a sarcastic, "considering the circumstances, brown man."

She was pleased to see the Indian's features tighten—for him, a stark expression of anger. She smiled sweetly, and deepened her rich Charleston accent until her voice was as syrupy as maple sugar. "I do declare! More coffee! May I impose upon you, brown man? I do just adore my mornin' coffee."

Red Fox at last emitted a sharp growl of irritation. "All right, Kendall Moore. I will call you by your name." He lifted his finger toward the fire. "Jimmy Emathla will see that you have food. Go to him."

Kendall smiled and did as she was told. Jimmy Emathla was apparently the brave cooking, and so she approached him. He wasn't half bad, she thought, once he smiled. Like Red Fox, he was all muscle and athletic grace, but he didn't appear forbidding this morning. She knew that the other warriors, pouring coffee and preparing tin plates of fish, eyed her and whispered about her, but they offered her no menace now that she seemed reconciled to her situation.

Kendall wondered what they would think if they knew that, so far, she was actually finding her situation more palatable than it often was among her own people.

Seeing Red Fox standing on the shore where the waves broke in ripples of foam, Kendall gripped her plate and cup and hurried after him. He turned with a scowl as she approached, as if his captive were a bad penny that kept reappearing to plague him. Kendall actually laughed.

"If you would just release me, Red Fox, I would not annoy you so," she told him with both humor and a pleading sincerity.

He stared at her, neither smiling nor scowling. "You will not be released, Kendall Moore."

61

The quiet conviction in his voice frightened her far more thoroughly than any threat could have done. Swiftly determining that he would not see how badly his words had shaken her, she raised her cup to him. "This is really delicious. It surprises me. I didn't know that Seminoles were morning coffee drinkers."

"The coffee is good," Red Fox agreed stoically. "It is Colombian." He twirled the word on his tongue, as if he had a natural curiosity about the place with such a name. He shrugged, and his next sentence chilled her further. "We have much coffee. It is a gift from the Night Hawk."

He turned, calling to his men and leaving her standing on the shore with the waves breaking and the coffee churning in her stomach.

"Eat, Kendall Moore," Red Fox called back to her. "We leave now. We have far to go this day."

Kendall sank to the sand with her back to him and ate the fish. It was good; not the tiniest bone remained in the fillet. These Seminoles, she decided, knew how to wield their knives.

The camp was broken in a matter of minutes. Two braves departed in the dugouts, while Red Fox rather rudely escorted Kendall back aboard the *Michelle* with the rest of his warriors. He made no attempt to tie her today; perhaps he had decided she was not the suicidal type, and a plunge overboard now, away from anything familiar, would surely be suicidal.

Her worst torture of the day was provided by her own mind. Left alone as the Indians sailed, she asked herself questions over and over. Where were they taking her? Why? Who was the Night Hawk? How could she possibly have offended a Seminole Indian when she had never even seen one before?

By late afternoon they were traveling through an area where small mangrove-fringed islands dotted the sea, becoming more and more numerous. She feared somewhat for the safety of the *Michelle,* yet it appeared that her Indian navigators did know these waters well. The hull struck none of the reefs that seemed so prevalent in the water.

Where were they? Kendall wondered. Close to the Florida mainland? Yes, surely, for soon they were entering a river, and to both port and starboard all she could see was mile after mile of thick long grass and swamp and mud.

Panic seized her heart. Dear God, she should have chosen the ocean. Now there was nothing, nowhere to go. From the muddy banks of the river she saw a log move, and then as it neared, she saw that it was not a log at all. It appeared to be an immense and grotesque monster from another age. The creature made a plopping sound as it moved into the water, but then its body became sleek and quick with movement; only the eyes and tip of the snout visible above the surface.

"Alligator."

Kendall jumped and swallowed quickly at the sound of the voice whispering in her ear.

Red Fox appeared quite pleased to have frightened her. "He is hungry. It is dusk, and he seeks his dinner. An egret. Gulp. One bite. Wild boar. Two bites. A man . . . or a woman. Four or five bites. Maybe six."

Kendall searched out the Indian's eyes. They were dark and fathomless in the waning light, yet she was sure she still offered him amusement. She turned to stare at the bank of the river once more. "How very interesting," she murmured.

She felt the Indian's whisper close to her ear. "Interesting, Kendall Moore? Are you not frightened?"

She turned to stare at him again, her spine stiffened, her shoulders squared. "No."

"Do not be stupid. You should be frightened."

"Do you intend to feed me to the alligators?"

"I intend to do nothing—except give you to the Night Hawk. I tell you only that the land does not welcome the white man. There is mud that will suck you under. Alligators that will eat you. Snakes that can give you a poison with such strength that you die where you stand."

Despite herself, Kendall shivered. Red Fox spun around to face the stern, about to leave her. Impulsively Kendall clutched at his arm, drawing him back around to face her. "Please! What have I done to this Night Hawk?" she demanded. "I swear to you I have harmed no Indians! I've never been on the Florida mainland."

Red Fox stared at her a long time. Kendall stood tense as she waited, certain her plea had touched whatever heart lurked beneath the strength of his bronzed chest. But at last he shook his arm free. "The Night Hawk is not a murderer of women. I tell you these things because you are brave and possibly stupid. Do not try to escape. Whatever the Night Hawk decides your punishment, it will not be as cruel as the fangs of the moccasin."

Kendall clamped her hand over her mouth to keep from crying out as Red Fox strode to the helm. Dear God! He was telling her her choices. The vengeance of the Night Hawk, or the fangs of a snake. Or the jaw of an alligator. Or quicksand.

"What could I have done?" she whispered pathetically. From the port side a bird whooped out a sharp and lonely call, sending a wave of cold terror through her. Night was falling fast, and darkness was bringing horrid shadows to the swamp. A mosquito buzzed about her face, and she slapped at it furiously. Something crashed into the water from the bank, but the dusk was so murky that she could not see the creature. Another alligator? "Sweet Jesus!" she whispered in a soft plea. Then she spun about on the deck and passed two of the braves to hurry down the few steps to the small cabin. She heard Red Fox's pleased laughter follow her, but she didn't give a damn.

Tears filled her eyes when she was alone. Somewhere far away, there was beauty. A beauty she had survived this far to return to someday. A manor with tall Georgian columns reaching clean and white to the sky where meals were served on a long oak table polished with beeswax until it gleamed. Where men read in the library and smoked small cheroots as they consumed their brandy. Where beautiful women chatted and gossiped, where the cotton fields grew as far as the eye could see and the manner of living was as gracious as the soft clouds of a summer's day . . .

Cresthaven.

And men were fighting for that way of life now, far away, and not so far away. She had been imprisoned within a Union barracks, and now she was being dragged into a swamp . . .

The Confederacy, she thought with a dry bitterness that almost brought hysterical laughter to her lips. She was at last within the Confederacy. This dismal swamp was part of Florida, part of the Confederate States of America . . . Men were dying for saw grass and quicksand and alligators. Men were fighting . . .

John! Oh, dear God. This was all John Moore's fault. She knew her husband to be a cruel man—and he hated Indians. Perhaps on one of his trips he had run into Indians, and perhaps he had done something to this Night Hawk. What? Slain his family? John considered all Indians savages; he would shoot a Seminole child as easily as he would a wolf.

Kendall clasped her hands together, unaware that her fingernails dug so deeply into her flesh that they drew blood.

The fangs of a snake were beginning to seem preferable to the treatment she would receive at the hands of the Night Hawk.

Kendall remained in the cabin until she heard shouting on deck. From the movements of the braves, she knew that the anchor was being cast. She moved to the companionway, but tripped on the hem of her dress. Struggling to her feet, she started when the area was suddenly illuminated. Glancing up, she saw that Red Fox held a lantern for her. "Come," he said. "We can go ashore only in the dugouts."

With no other choice available, Kendall followed him. The other braves awaited them in the dugouts. "Take this." Red Fox gave Kendall the lantern, then grabbed the rail and jack-knifed over the side. His body splashed water high, but Kendall saw that he stood in the river, which was very shallow. She felt the blood drain from her face as she remembered the alligators they had passed, but Red Fox showed no fear. "Come," he told her impatiently.

He wanted her to walk in the swamp river in the darkness. She started to back away, shaking her head.

"Come!" Red Fox persisted. He held out his arms. "Hold the lantern high. I will carry you."

She bit her lip, but then hurried to the rail. If she aggravated him now, he might change his mind, and she might find herself dumped into the swamp.

She held the lantern high as he lifted her from the boat, and into the hold of his strong arms. Kendall held the lantern with her left hand; her right arm instinctively curled around his shoulder and neck so that she would not fall.

His body was warm, his flesh smooth and brown and slightly oiled. Studying at close range his strongly chiseled features, Kendall blushed, aware of her intimacy with the strange Indian. His eyes fell on hers, barely inches away. Nervously, Kendall began to talk. "Your English is excellent."

He grunted. Red Fox offered information, it seemed, only when it was in his interest to do so.

"Where did you learn to speak the language so well?"

His eyes fell on her again, and the dark, brooding depths within them warned her she wouldn't like the answer.

"I spoke the white man's language as a boy. I was but a small child when the white men tricked my father with a white flag of truce. I was eight years old when Osceola died in the walls of their prison. Osceola warned us all that it was well to understand the English words spoken, for always a trap lay behind them."

Kendall fell silent as Red Fox walked through the waist-deep water. Osceola had died at Fort Moultrie. She hadn't been born until two years after the chief's death, but the story of Osceola had become popular among Charleston's children. It seemed strange to her now that Osceola should have died in the same city where the first shots had been fired in the Civil War that now raged.

Another of the infernal night birds shrieked, and she tightened her hold around Red Fox's neck. She saw the snicker on his lips and snapped at him in anger. "I do not know the swamp, Red Fox. But as the Indian has learned it, so can the white man—or woman."

He twisted his head and smiled at her, ignoring her comment. "It is thanks to the Night Hawk that my English improves with the years."

Their eyes locked in combat as Red Fox at last reached a dugout. Kendall realized that he parried each of her thinly veiled threats with one of his own.

He set her down hard on her rear in the dugout, and then climbed in himself, waving a go-ahead to the braves who waited. They began to pull through the shallow, grass-flanked water with long poles.

"We are not far," Red Fox said.

They weren't far indeed; the trip in the dugout was too brief for Kendall's liking. Before she had time to worry further, she saw a glow of light through the trees. They rounded a bend in the river, and at last approached the Seminole camp.

Her first impression was of strange buildings that seemed to blend into the trees. Many such buildings filled the clearing, built on posts several feet off the ground and roofed with thatch. Some were cabins with split-log walls, while others were open to the night air. Campfires dotted the clearing in the wilderness, and women and children in bright cotton dress busied themselves about those fires. Then suddenly a joyous cry went out, and scores of brown-skinned Indians came rushing to the river.

Kendall shrank into the dugout with trepidation. These were the Seminoles. The women scampering to reach the dugouts were young and old and in between. Some had coarse features, some were beautiful, their faces chiseled with nobility like that of Red Fox. A few of the young children were naked; others were dressed like their parents in clothing that ranged from cool loincloths on the younger men, to western shirts and trousers, and every possible combination in between. The colorful shirts the braves had donned in the cool of the night just past were prevalent; the women's dresses and skirts were much the same. The village would be fascinating, Kendall thought vaguely, if she weren't so very, very terrified.

The cries and shouts became louder and louder. The braves at last stood in their dugouts, and their families and friends rushed through the shallow water to embrace them as they pulled their vessels to the banks of the river. Kendall's eyes darted from the homecoming scene to Red Fox, and she saw that he searched the shoreline. A broad grin broke out across his face, and he stood, rocking the dugout precariously. "Apolka! Apolka!"

Kendall followed his gaze. A young woman, slender and lovely in bright calico, gave a happy shriek and raced toward him. As she came closer, Kendall realized that, in an exotic way, the Indian girl was truly beautiful. Huge brown eyes with luxuriant lashes dominated her delicate face; she was as lithe and agile as a doe.

"Red Fox!"

He jumped from the dugout so quickly that it almost tipped. Kendall gritted her teeth as her fingers gripped the rough planking tensely in a desperate effort to steady herself.

When she was at last convinced that she would not teeter into the swamp, Kendall looked up to see Red Fox embrace the woman enthusiastically. But if she had hoped to be ignored for any length of time, Kendall was sadly disappointed, for the girl laughed, disentangled herself, and turned curious eyes to her, speaking hurriedly to Red Fox. He answered her in his native tongue, and then both stared at Kendall. She lifted her chin and returned their scrutiny.

Red Fox smiled. "It appears that you will wait, Kendall Moore. We expected the Night Hawk to be here by now. But these are troubled times. No matter; he will come. For now, you will go with Apolka."

Kendall hesitated, eyeing the girl who continued to stare at her with open curiosity.

"Kendall Moore, go!" His voice was a sharp growl, but still Kendall hesitated. There were so many Indians in the camp. How many? she wondered. It seemed that they were everywhere . . . and more and more of them were flocking near to stare at her. The very young with their round, cherubic faces, the old who were worn and leathered from their harsh existence beneath the merciless sun. The men, and the women . . .

"You will go!" Red Fox commanded again.

Apolka touched his shoulder and said something softly. Red Fox shrugged impatiently, but stepped back, his brawny arms crossed over his chest.

The girl stepped forward. Her slender, work-roughened, and darkly tanned hand reached out, palm upward as if she offered friendship. Kendall stared into the doe-brown eyes, and saw that they were soft, not pitying, but sympathetic. She paused just a second longer, and then accepted the small-boned hand that offered surprising strength.

Kendall winced as her feet sank into the mud of the riverbank. Then, knowing that she would walk through the curious crowd of Indians, she forced herself to maintain an expression as stoic as Red Fox's, and to walk tall with pride.

They grabbed at her as she walked into the clearing. Pulling at her clothes, touching her hair. She didn't flinch, but held on desperately to her dignity and poise. She heard the constant cackle of high-pitched, mocking laughter as the women and children jeered her, but she fought the panicked longing to bring her hands to her ears in a desperate attempt to still the taunting sound.

At least they did not hurt her!

Although she couldn't understand their words, Kendall was certain that Apolka scolded the other women. When they at long last reached a sturdy cabin built on a platform, Apolka pushed her toward a rickety ladder, then turned and said something to the gathering of tormenters who still followed. Sullenly, they began to move away.

A small lamp burned on a squat table in the one-room structure. Kendall glanced hurriedly about, noting that the two windows were unobstructed, but very high. A pile of colorful blankets lay in the corner of the room, and next to the lamp was a rough pottery pitcher. Water, she hoped.

Besides that, the room was bare.

"Kendall."

The soft pronunciation of her name sounded very strange on the young Indian woman's lips, but Kendall turned to her, sensing that Apolka had elected to offer her the only kindness she might receive. Apolka made motions that Kendall quickly realized referred to eating. She nodded eagerly. She was starving.

Apolka turned gracefully on her heel and left, closing the planked door behind her. Kendall heard a sharp thud—and realized that although Apolka had decided to be kind to her, she was taking no chances. The door apparently had a slip-log bolt. And it would always be bolted.

Kendall nervously walked about the room, vaguely noting

that the floor and the blankets left her were surprisingly and pleasantly clean. The pitcher did contain water, and when she greedily reached for it—then paused, forcing herself to drink slowly and carefully—she was gratified to find the contents clear and deliciously fresh.

Apolka returned before she had set the pitcher down. Apolka handed her a wooden bowl filled with an awful-looking gruel. But Kendall was too hungry to accept the protest of her mind, and she whispered a soft thank-you as she took the bowl.

"Koonti," Apolka said.

The word meant nothing to Kendall, but she gave the girl a wavering smile. Apolka said something else, then shook her head with exasperation, aware that Kendall didn't understand her. Then she pressed her hands together and placed her head on them, mimicking sleep. Not knowing what else to do, Kendall nodded. Apolka seemed satisfied. She left Kendall again, closing the door firmly, and sliding the bolt.

Kendall exhaled a long and shaky sigh, and sank to the floor with her bowl of gruel. She tasted the mixture and shuddered. It felt grainy and coarse in her mouth. She set the bowl aside, and wondered if they had dragged her all this way just to poison her.

And with that thought, her mind began to spin again. She had to escape. She couldn't escape. If she did escape, she could be lost in the swamp forever. No, not forever. Until she encountered a snake or an alligator or a pit of quicksand . . .

"Dear God!" she whimpered, folding her arms about herself and rocking on her haunches as terror seemed to rush about her in a conscious sapping sweep. "No, no, no, no," she repeated over and over. There would be a way. She would find a way.

Pull yourself together, Kendall, she told herself silently. You can endure; you will find a way. You have survived all the blows that have come your way so far. What can they do to you? No one can take your pride or your spirit. You survived John; you survived life in a Union barracks while war raged . . .

At last she stopped rocking. There *would* be a way. She was unharmed and strong and healthy. She would watch everything around her. She would learn, and she would escape.

She picked up the bowl of gruel again and forced herself to eat. She couldn't allow her strength to wane.

When she finished the gruel, she drank another few sips of water, then snuffed out the lamp and fashioned a pillow from one of the blankets. She lay down and drew the other about her. She was going to sleep, just as she was going to eat, so that she would remain alert and calm and healthy.

But tonight she couldn't sleep. She stared up at one of the windows, transfixed by the pale moon that glimmered in the otherwise total darkness.

Who was the Night Hawk? A brave like Red Fox? She was protected from harm now because of him. But what happened if he put in his appearance before she could escape?

She groaned and twisted on the floor, closing her eyes tightly. The Night Hawk did not murder women, Red Fox had told her. And yet he sought revenge. What *did* he intend? Rape? Mutilation? He would not need to kill her to chop off her fingers one by one and feed them to the alligators.

A low moan escaped her. Stop, she chided herself. Stop. Over and over she repeated the word, as if she were counting sheep.

At long last she drifted into a restless sleep plagued with nightmares in which the strong figure of a man came to her in the darkness while night hawks shrieked, and she shuddered because there was no escape . . .

Three

"Damn!" Kendall groaned, wincing as she scraped the largest blister on her palm against the rock with which she strenuously beat the clothes she had been given to wash. Of course, as a southern lady she really shouldn't be using such a word, but she had never felt less like a southern lady. She sat back on her haunches and studied her hands. Her nails were cracked and broken, and her flesh appeared raw.

In a spurt of fury she tossed the shirt she was laundering out into the river and watched with satisfaction as the slow-moving current took the colorful garment out of sight. Then she sighed, for the act of defiance had done her little good. A large stack of clothing lay beside her, and if she tossed it all away, the Seminoles might decide to wreak a little violence upon her, although such actions were apparently taboo. But she sat back, determined to rest. She had been with the Indians a full week now, and she was learning.

She had feared at first that they would keep her constantly bolted inside the high cabin, but that had not happened.

Life was busy in the swamp. Braves, she learned quickly, left the camp with the morning's light. They spent their days hunting the hammocks for deer and fowl and scouting to keep the territory safe. Old men whittled and did minor repairs, relating stories of their past days of glory to one an-

73

other as they worked. Children tended chickens and pigs, and women cooked and sewed and laundered, performing the most strenuous and tedious tasks.

No woman was ever allowed to sit idly in a cabin. From her first morning onward, Kendall had been taken from her prison at dawn and set to some task. The first Indian word she had learned was the once mysterious *koonti,* mentioned the night of her arrival. It was a root that constituted a staple of the Indian's diet. It was ground and made into bread and gruel, like the gruel she had finally managed to consume in her hunger and determination that first night. And grinding *koonti* all day was backbreaking labor.

Kendall glanced at her hands again and sighed. It was hard to imagine that she had once been a dazzling southern belle, stunning in silks and velvet and crinolines so numerous she had lost count. Hard to imagine that only a week ago she had been treated like a prized pet by the Union soldiers. Too late she realized that when John had been gone, her life had actually been pleasant and easy. She had been in Union barracks, yes, but the news that came to her always told of thrilling southern victories.

Kendall glanced down the river to where two dugouts were dragged up on the bank. "Tomorrow!" she whispered.

As she had promised herself, she remained always alert. She had meekly accepted all the tasks given her, and she had watched every movement in the camp with meticulous care and cunning. She believed that the Indians had come to trust her; they were probably certain that she would never try to escape into the swamp. It would be suicide . . .

But it might not be.

The darkness had terrified her so that first night. By daylight, she could be reasonable and weigh her chances. As long as she armed herself with plenty of food and water—and succeeded in her plan to steal a dugout—she should be all right. She would follow the river, and never leave the dugout. The alligators were dangerous, but if she remained in the safety of the dugout, she needn't worry about them or the gripping muds or the snakes. The moccasins might lurk beneath the surface of the river, but she would not stick her hand out searching for them.

And she could steal the dugout easily, she was certain. The Seminole had grown so sure of her compliance with their rules that they left her alone on the riverbank each afternoon with the laundry. Each day was the same. Mornings she ground *koonti* root; afternoons she washed clothes. And for the last five days, she had come to the river with Apolka to bathe before dusk settled. She had felt terribly vulnerable as she stood naked in the water, which could be filled with God only knew what frightening creatures, and also within close range of several dozen healthy young braves—but she had slowly come to realize that the Seminole were a very moral society. Marriages, even when polygamous, were sacred, and the young women were strictly guarded. Apolka was Red Fox's wife, or woman—Kendall wasn't sure which—and none of the men would entertain the idea of molesting their chief's property. Kendall's time in the river with the gentle Apolka, bathing and learning how to swim, proved to be her salvation many a day when she was certain that the humid heat would drive her to a burst of rebellious temper. That sort of outburst she had to avoid, for her escape depended totally on her docility. And when the other women weren't exasperated with her lack of expertise as she fumbled at her tasks, they were kind enough. Apolka had accepted her; the others grudgingly went along with that acceptance. In the short span of a week, it seemed that she had become adopted, somewhat like a curious pet, into the tribe.

She took her meals with Apolka and her two children, and spent a portion of each evening in the chickee that belonged to Red Fox and his family, and then she was returned to her bolted cabin. And each night she pleaded with Red Fox that he release her, and each night he refused. But she was no longer at all frightened of Red Fox. She believed that he granted her a certain admiration, and if she weren't a gift to be packaged and handed over to the absent Night Hawk, he might have decided she was worthy of release. After the initial awkwardness passed, she grew used to the chickee that was home to Red Fox and Apolka and their two small children. Kendall had discovered a maternal instinct within herself when she played with the little Seminole boys. Their large, dark eyes stared at her with such solemn curiosity, and they were more than willing to crawl up on her lap while Apolka busied herself at the communal cooking fire.

Red Fox had quickly decided that Kendall would never cook. He had told her after her one experiment with *koonti* gruel that the food she prepared tasted worse than swamp muck.

Kendall compressed her lips as she again set herself to the task of the laundry with vigor. "One more night, you arrogant savage!"

She bit her lip as she worked, admitting silently that Red Fox wasn't a savage at all. He was blunt and brusque, but he had never truly harmed her, no matter what the provocation. And he was tenderly devoted to Apolka and the two toddling boys she had borne him. He was a far better husband and father than many a "civilized" white man she had seen.

Kendall paused in her work again, slowly making another secret admission. She didn't mind being with the Seminoles. She longed to be home, but home to her would always be Charleston and Cresthaven and cotton fields, and that was not the home she had been taken from. The truth of it was that it was far more pleasant to be with the Indians than it was to be with John Moore. Were it not for Red Fox's certainty that the vengeful Night Hawk would eventually make an appearance, she would have been more than pleased to remain—and to pray that the Rebs would whomp the Yankees in no time flat and she could make her way back to Charleston and reclaim the land that was rightfully hers . . .

Kendall gave herself a furious shake. She had to make reality better than dreams. Although population on the Keys was thin except for Key West, there were settlers here and there. She had to escape and find someone. If she could do that, she could go somewhere. Maybe not Charleston, but perhaps Atlanta. Or even Richmond. With the war growing more fevered daily, she could find something to do that would help the cause of the Confederacy. She could surely find work in a hospital.

With that determined thought in mind, Kendall gathered up the wet laundry and headed back toward the camp. One more night. She would be prepared to go when she meekly set off for the river tomorrow afternoon.

Kendall stopped short before the clearing, certain she had lost her mind. There were visitors to the Seminole camp. About twenty of them. Men. Men who laughed and joked in soft, familiar drawls. Men dressed in butternut and gray . . .

Confederates! It was a squadron of Confederate soldiers. "Oh, my Lord!" Kendall whispered in stunned joy. She didn't need to escape through the swamp at all! These gallant soldiers of the South would take her to a safe harbor.

She clasped the wet laundry to her chest and hurried joyously through the trees toward the clearing. But she stopped short again on the trail. Red Fox and a white man, tall and broad-shouldered, stood between her and the clearing. What did that matter? she asked herself impatiently. She would issue her plea to the man with the tawny gold hair whose back was to her now.

"Sir!" she cried out, dropping the laundry and racing ecstatically toward him. "Oh, sir! Please, you must help me. These Indians have taken me prisoner, and they intend to give me to a savage named Night Hawk and—"

Her voice broke off and she halted in a dead freeze, her heart thundering in her chest, as the man turned toward her.

She knew him. She knew him far too well. He had haunted her sleep for almost a year, with erotic dreams, with chilling nightmares . . .

Gray eyes bore into hers, eyes that darkened and hardened to steel as they fell upon her. Kendall stood transfixed in horror as she watched the man's strong features grow tense, his lips compress into a grim white line. His jaw went rigid with hard anger, and she could see the ripple of curling muscles beneath his butternut shirt.

"You . . ." she whispered with incredulous dismay. Dear God, she had hoped to never see him again. In her worst dreams, he had appeared as a prisoner in a Yankee barracks. Dear God, dear God, dear God . . .

She remembered him all too well. The voice that could quietly command, the fingers with their brush of steel . . . and his tenderness . . .

Tenderness. Hah! He would kill her! The tense explosiveness within him didn't fade a hair as he doffed his cap and bowed low with gallant ease. "Yes, Mrs. Moore. Captain Brent McClain, madam, Confederate State Navy. Better known in these parts as the Night Hawk."

She wanted to scream; the sound caught in her throat. Terror greater than any she had ever known rose to smother her breath and wind her stomach into knots. No, never had she been so frightened. Not facing John, not facing Red Fox when he had attacked the *Michelle* . . .

McClain. Brent McClain. Oh, God. She had never forgotten the look in his eyes that night. The look that was still in his eyes, seeming to pierce through her and impale her on a burning stake of raw fury.

His compressed lips curved into a sneering, determined smile that left his eyes as heatedly furious. He took a step toward her, and Kendall at last managed to scream out her raw panic. She spun around to flee with a speed born of sheer terror.

Her flying run took her back past the laundry rock, and toward the beached dugouts. But, fast as she moved, she heard relentless footfalls following close behind. Her heartbeat took up a thunder that sounded as explosive to her ears as gunshot. He was coming after her, of course; he was pursuing her, and his strength and stamina were far greater than hers.

"No!" she gasped as she ran, not daring to look back. The odds were ridiculously against her. She was like a hunted fox; she had to run until she fell.

Moss and branches slapped against her face as she reached the river's edge and the dugouts. But as she leaned low, grunting as she attempted to move the vessel from its mudbank into the water, she quickly realized the futility of such an action. The bow of the dugout was firmly grounded; she hadn't the strength to push it into the river.

Glancing quickly over her shoulder, Kendall saw that the steel-eyed Rebel captain was almost upon her, slowing his gait as he smiled with ruthless satisfaction. In panic she heaved the dugout again as he approached her like a Florida panther. She was prey, being calmly stalked, while the beast luxuriated in the ritual moments that preceded the kill . . .

The dugout refused to budge. Looking back Kendall saw that McClain, his handsome features tense despite the sardonic smile that curled his hard mouth, was less than twenty feet away. She could almost feel the heat and tension bombarding her from his still distant body, the coil of sinewed muscle ready to strike.

"No!" she cried again. Spinning about, she gathered her skirts into her hands, leapt over the dugout, and stared about in desperation for a place to hide. In back of her was the river; to her right loomed the Indian camp. Ahead of her was a thicket of moss-encrusted trees that rose in a tangle so dense they might have been spiderwebs. Desperately Kendall tore along the riverbank.

"Come back here, you fool woman!"

Kendall didn't sense the warning in his irritated command; she only knew that he was after her, and that he looked like he would enjoy throttling her, slowly.

Her breath came in ragged sobs as she ran, and she muttered incoherent prayers as the muck of the bank sucked at her shoes. The riverbank was changing; the ground had no firmness here. Tall grass suddenly loomed before her, and she couldn't tell where the land ended and the river began. Mangroves dotted the area, their myriad roots reaching out like grotesque tentacles.

"Kendall, *stop!*"

A desperate sob escaped her as her foot caught on a grass-hidden root. The impact cost her her balance, and suddenly she was wavering, careening toward the mucky ground. The saw grass cut the bare flesh of her arms and face like an army of miniature razors.

"Oh, God!" she gasped, reaching for the trunk of a mangrove. She touched something that felt more like leather than bark, and in horror she looked up quickly, recoiling and screaming as she saw that she had been about to grasp a colorful snake.

She pitched into the muck and saw grass, her terror increasing as she wondered with frenzied horror what other creatures lurked nearby, ready to strike.

"No! No, no, no . . ." Heedless of the sharp saw grass, she clutched at it and stumbled to her feet. Ahead was another mangrove—a patch of sure footing, she was certain.

"Kendall!"

She glanced hurriedly over her shoulder. Brent McClain, eyes now as dark and stormy as a thundercloud, was gaining on her. He hadn't changed, she thought stupidly as she sobbed again and staggered through the grass and muck. He hadn't changed at all since that December night.

Oh, God! Why hadn't she guessed that he was the Night Hawk? She had known he was a Floridian; she had known he harried the Union navy all along the coasts, both east and west . . .

He was the only man who had reason to want to harm her. He believed she had deliberately lured him into an ambush that December night. Why hadn't she remembered the vengeance in those steel eyes as they had hardened above her, and the promise of retaliation in the granite features that hadn't eased even as blackness had overwhelmed him?

"Stop, you fool!" he shouted.

She reached for a hold on the mangrove, checking hastily to see that she didn't grab another snake. Finding an insecure footing on a gnarled root, Kendall turned back again.

He was standing in the muck, hands on his hips as he stared at her coldly. His butternut frock coat was open, as was his shirt. She could see his pulse beating against the strong cords of his neck, and beneath it the hint of the tawny curls that grew in profusion on his well-muscled chest. His legs were spread apart in a challenging stance, their sinewed strength straining against his form-fitting breeches. His fingers were tense over his hips—wire tense. And his mouth was so tightly compressed that she could barely see his lips against the twist of his jaw.

Kendall closed her eyes for a dizzying moment.

"Don't be a fool," he warned her, his biting, mocking tone deathly quiet. "There's nowhere to go."

Kendall opened her eyes and stared at the danger in his explosive form and features. She twisted to look beyond the mangrove. The river had all but disappeared. All that loomed before her was grass, as high as her waist.

"Stay where you are," he drawled with soft menace. "I'll come for you."

Kendall heard him take a footstep; the muck seemed to groan as it released its hold on his boot. She glanced his way wildly, then sobbed, choosing the danger of the saw grass over that of his deadly steel eyes.

But she had barely taken a step before she discovered with horror that she could go no farther. The muck refused to release its hold on her. Madly, desperately, she struggled to free her foot and calf, but she sank deeper. It was as if the ground had truly embraced her. It was holding her tightly, drawing her down. Even as she struggled, its grasp on her became more secure. She clutched at the grass nearby, but succeeded only in cutting her hands. The suction grasping her increased in pressure, and in abject horror she realized that it was sucking her surely downward; the black, oozing muck was up to her waist now, and with each movement it rose higher . . . and higher . . .

"I told you not to be a fool!" The soft drawl came to her from the magrove tree.

Brent McClain had propped one booted foot against a root and casually leaned one elbow against a thick branch. A flicker of amusement glinted in the gray of his eyes, and his teeth flashed white against the dark tan of his features as he offered her a charming smile. But the hardness was still fully about him; she could sense the sparks of angry tension emanating from him like heavy, threatening ripples of heat lightning, charging the distance between them.

For several horrible moments Kendall was certain that he intended to lean back with that satisfied smile cruelly curling his lips as she sank and sank until the mud swallowed her completely, choking off her air, crushing her lungs like dry tinder.

"Do you know, madam—excuse me—Mrs. Moore, you do look a fright. I wonder if I would have been taken in so easily last December had I seen you covered with mud rather than garbed in that lovely receiving gown. Silver. Yes, that

82

was the color. I remember it so well . . . Of course, I remember removing it, too. What a perfect seductress you were! And what a clever trap you set. A bit dangerous, though. Had I been your husband, I could not have let things go so far—not even if I believed I could rid the Confederacy of General McClellan himself."

Kendall was alarmed by his bitterness and his certainty that he had been the target of an ambush. She momentarily forgot that the muck was encroaching higher and higher on her body. No, it wasn't encroaching higher and higher; she was sinking lower and lower, closer to death. And he still believed she had seduced him with the sole intent to set him up for an assassination . . .

He was going to let her die. And he wouldn't have to raise a finger. He could watch with relaxed enjoyment as nature doled out what he must surely consider fitting justice.

Suddenly anger flooded through her in a white-hot flash. How could he be so damned arrogant and judgmental? He had been an arrogant son of a bitch that long-ago night, too.

"You are an unmitigated ass, Captain McClain!" she lashed out, then quickly paused in horror. He was her only hope for life at the moment. She softened her tone quickly, noting the caustic arch of his brow as her voice softened to that of a well-bred Charleston girl. "I didn't trick you, Captain I was desperate to get away—"

"From your own husband?" The query was scornful.

Kendall took a deep breath and tried not to quiver. The muck was up to her breast now, and her smallest movement seemed to make it rise even faster.

"Captain McClain," she pleaded in her softest drawl. "I swear to you that I'm innocent. I—"

"Spare me, please!" he drawled, a hard ring of steel beneath his mocking gallantry. "Lawd, honey, I'd expect any woman with a whit of intelligence to plead innocent while she was mired in a pool of quicksand. And, Mrs. Moore, I never did take you for a fool!"

"Well, you can't possibly have taken me for a Yankee!" Kendall burst out.

"Oh, no, Mrs. Moore. You're too well versed in the ways of the southern belles for me to have made such a mistake. However, you *are* married to one of the most notorious Yankees in the South . . ."

His voice trailed away as he doffed his coat and rolled up the sleeves of his shirt. Kendall caught her breath as he squatted down to balance on the balls of his feet, wondering if he intended to pull her out or push her head beneath the surface of the muck.

"What are you going to do?" she whispered sickly.

He smiled again, but Kendall didn't like the tight twist of his rugged jaw, or the glitter that touched his narrowed gray eyes.

"Am I going to let you go down?" he queried softly. "Not on your life, Mrs. Moore. I've a score to settle with you. I won't allow a pit of quicksand to rob me of my vengeance!"

He suddenly flattened himself out over the roots, digging the toes of his boots into the earth. He stretched out his arms to her, his broad powerful hands forming a vise over her upper arms. Instinctively Kendall wrapped her fingers around his arms, grateful for her reprieve, but shivering nevertheless as she touched him. She could feel the strain and bulge of his biceps, the frightening, hot power within them. She caught his eyes, close, so close to hers, and she bit her lip to keep from crying out. He was so calm, controlled, and yet she sensed a violence in him so volatile that his very control made her tremble anew.

"Pull!" he commanded tensely.

She pulled. His fingers bit into her soft flesh with such intensity that the pain was excruciating, but still the muck refused to release her. His face tightened further with the strain; he clenched his teeth and ordered again, "Pull!"

Kendall tossed back her head and cried with pain as the earth's suction constricted tightly about her. The tug-of-war on her body was almost more than she could bear. She was about to beg to be left to die when suddenly—so suddenly that she felt she flew into the arms of the hostile Reb—the quicksand released its hold and catapulted her from the earth. Together they rolled over the mangrove roots and into the field of cutting grass.

For moments they both lay panting beneath the burning sun. Kendall closed her eyes, not noticing the bruises and scratches she had received in her gratitude at being free of the clutching, smothering black ooze.

But she was covered with the stuff. From her breast to her now bare feet, she was blanketed in it. Spatters of the black muck smudged her face and tangled into her hair; it was even clogged in her eyelashes.

She stopped thinking about her condition and bolted upright as she heard Brent McClain move, rising in a swift and agile cat-curl to his feet. He strode the few feet toward her, and Kendall warily attempted to back away on her haunches, but it was futile. Mindless of the mud clinging to her, he bent down and grasped her arm, rising again with a grunt as he crudely tossed her over his shoulder. Hard bone and muscle butted into her abdomen and she gasped at the indignity in panicked protest, pounding furiously against his back with clenched fists.

"Let me go! Let me be!" she wailed. "This is kidnapping. There are laws!"

He stopped short, delivering a stinging open-palmed blow to her backside. "Mrs. Moore, there isn't a law in the world that can help you now. I heartily suggest you shut that sweet southern mouth of yours, unless you want to pray nice and soft."

He started walking again with strides so swift and purposeful that her dangling head smacked roughly against his back. Kendall braced herself, clenching her teeth and closing her eyes to keep from bursting into a humiliating storm of tears.

"I don't deserve this!" she hissed defiantly.

"This? Darlin', you haven't seen half of what you deserve yet!"

"I'm telling you that you're an ignorant ass!" Kendall wailed, her fight returning with his soft words of ruthless menace. Frantically she struggled against him, writhing, kicking, pounding, scratching. Suddenly both of his hands spanned her waist and he set her down. She stared at him wildly, then realized they had reached the clearing.

An audience awaited them. Like a center-stage attraction, they were ringed by the Seminoles—and by the Confederates.

Kendall knew she would receive no help from the Indians. But what about Brent McClain's crew of Confederate Navy men? Surely they wouldn't allow even their sacred captain to attack a young white woman of breeding. She spun about, searching out white faces. "Help me!" she cried. "Dear God, help me! This man has gone insane!"

Her voice trailed away as she realized she stared into stony faces and unblinking eyes. Of course! she thought sickly. These men had been with McClain last December in Charleston! Some of them had been attacked aboard his ship, left to lie where they fell.

McClain's hand suddenly descended on her shoulder. Again she was cornered, and like a frantic, caged animal, she lashed out, clawing wildly as she hurled herself at him. She managed to rake her nails across his face, scratching so fiercely that she drew a line of blood from his eye to his chin along the rugged plane of his bronzed cheekbone.

"Dammit, you little vixen!" he swore, his jaw then clamping with serious intent as his gray eyes narrowed to slits. Kendall paused at the sound of his harsh voice, and instead of attacking, decided retreat would be the better part of valor. She spun about to flee, but screamed instead as his fingers wound into her hair and jerked her back. She did not know, as Brent McClain did, that a man would have to handle such a situation quickly and deftly or lose face with the Seminole braves; she knew only that she had pushed him to a truly dangerous point, and she was so terrified that she would gladly have returned to the quicksand.

He sank down on one knee, and she screamed as he pulled her hair viciously once more, drawing her down to him. Kendall flailed her arms wildly, but to no avail. He released his hold on her hair and grimly and silently secured her wrists; then, before she quite realized how, she found herself crudely tossed over his knee. She struggled, but her fight was useless against the power of his hold. He jerked up her skirt, tossing it so that it fell over her head, momentarily blinding her. And then she screamed out in humiliation and raw pain as his palm truly lit into her, the blows hard and determined and shattering, with only the thin material of her pantaloons to protect the bare rounded flesh beneath . . .

How long did it go on? Nine purposeful swats? Or ten? She had lost count at five, so mortified and furious was she. But that wasn't to be the end. Just as smoothly and swiftly as he had begun, he ceased, rising so suddenly that she pitched to the ground in a sprawled heap, tangled in her own clothing, her hair a sodden and muddied plaster about her face. She couldn't see the loathed face of the Rebel captain who towered above her like some pagan lord; she only heard his contemptuous voice as he called to several of the Seminole women. He spoke in English, but apparently they understood him as they rushed toward her.

"Clean her up, will you? She's filthy."

Kendall saw his booted feet spin smartly and stride away.

Four

Brent McClain looked ruefully at his reddened palm as he strode to the chickee of his friend, Red Fox. He hadn't meant to strike with such force, but, damn her cunning little hide, she was like a wildcat, and she had left him no choice. He had been so stunned to see her, and when he had heard her soft, cultured voice with its melodious southern drawl and turned to see her wealth of shining golden hair, her delicate, aristocratic features and wide, guileless eyes, something within him had snapped. An explosion of fury like a bursting shell had raked through him, and he had shuddered with the intensity of his rage.

Perhaps it had been because she was still so beautiful. In the swamp she stood out like a perfect red rose. In seconds he had taken in again the perfection of her lithe form, the fullness of breasts and hips, the slender tuck of her waist, the leanness of flanks that were not concealed by the thin cotton of her dress.

And the innocence! The guileless plea in her voice when she had thought she could wrap a "gallant" Confederate officer around her sweet little finger! She deserved the spanking. He had never intended to take his revenge in that manner, but she definitely deserved the punishment he had meted out.

Besides, he thought grimly, his eyes darkening with remembrance, he had done nothing to her compared with what she had wrought upon him. As long as he lived, he would never forget that night. Thrown overboard to die in the winter cold water of Charleston harbor. Struggling desperately to hold his breath when to inhale would be to fill his lungs with seawater. Sinking, fighting, struggling to free his wrists, which had been bound together. Had it not been for the Yankee officer who had dived into the sea and pulled him to the docks . . .

Brent shuddered suddenly in the heat with the memory of the terrible cold. He ground his teeth together. How he had longed for revenge! A chance to stare into Kendall Moore's bluer than blue eyes again and harshly decry their bold beauty and innocence . . and treachery.

He had made inquiries. And he had discovered who she was. He had sworn that he would find her—and her husband, John Moore.

Moore . . . Brent *had* believed he would find Moore one day. The man roamed the Florida coast with near reckless insanity. With more than normal Yankee loyalty and devotion to Abe Lincoln's war.

But he hadn't believed he would ever again get his hands on the blue-eyed seductress who had lured him into the trap. No matter what his personal dreams of vengeance, he was a captain in the Confederate States' weak navy. It would be folly to attack the Union fort on Key West. He couldn't lead his men to certain suicide or capture and incarceration in one of the prisons that were reputed to kill more men than they held.

But now Red Fox, with a tiny band of braves, had accomplished a feat he would never have dreamed of executing. Brent was still somewhat amazed by the turn of events. He had not told Red Fox exactly what had happened in Charleston. But Red Fox knew him well, and when Brent had come to the swamp to ask the Seminole chiefs help in keeping supplies running to the small Confederate outposts in the lower portion of the state, Red Fox had quietly demanded to know what troubled his white brother. Brent told him only that he had a score to settle with a certain Yankee—and a bigger score to settle with the Yankee's woman. Brent's dreams of vengeance had been vague at that time, something he would deal with when the war was over. He had never imagined that Red Fox would be so determined to please his "brother" with the gift of revenge.

The chief was laughing now as Brent climbed the ladder to his chickee. Brent grinned in return as he hoisted his frame up on the platform. He hadn't seen such an expression on Red Fox's face since they were youths and Red Fox presented him with a hunting knife that had been Osceola's and which Brent had coveted as only a small boy could covet such a treasure.

"My friend," Red Fox said, "you have not yet won the war with that one. The battle, yes; the war, no. I have come to know her well, and she is a fighter. She is like the Seminole. We can be bested by strength, but never beaten."

Brent sat crossed-legged before Red Fox and smiled at Apolka as she handed him a steaming mug of coffee. He waited until Apolka had left them to give his full attention to his friend and speak. "I am amazed, Red Fox, that you have managed to present her to me. Now that I have got her, I'm not really sure what to do with her."

Red Fox lifted a skeptical brow. He found it difficult to believe that a strong white warrior like his brother Brent didn't know what to do with a difficult woman—especially when the woman was young and pleasingly curved and stunningly beautiful, even to the astute Seminole eye.

Brent laughed, but his voice was grim when he spoke. "Don't worry, Red Fox, I intend to finish a few things we started, but what then? In a way I'd like to wring her neck and beat her black and blue, but—"

Red Fox snorted out a taunting interruption. "But you cannot do that to a woman, my friend. All your breeding and culture are against it. Tell me, what would happen if you turned her over to your generals?"

Brent took a sip of his hot chicory coffee and shrugged. "Not much, Red Fox. Female spies have been caught on both sides of the Mason-Dixon Line. Seems the Yanks can be as gallant as the Rebs. Worst that has happened to any woman has been a short stint in a prison, although I guess that can be pretty rough. Wounded men die like flies in prison camps, in both the North and the South."

"It is better to die in the field," Red Fox said softly. Brent was silent for a moment. They could both remember how Osceola had sickened and died at Fort Moultrie. The proud chief—dying in prison. Red Fox hadn't even been able to join his father's family at the time; he was not the son of a legitimate wife, and therefore the government had ignored him. Brent had begged his father to intervene, but Justin McClain had been able to do nothing. The anti-Indian sentiment had been too high at the time. And Justin had tried hard. He had never forgotten that Osceola had spared his son, and cared for him like a member of his own family until he had been returned to the plantation house at South Seas.

Brent would never forget Osceola himself. The chief's strong, handsome features were forever imbedded in his memory. He could see Osceola now just as he had all those years ago, riding up to where Brent stood staring at the desolation that had once been a settlement of planters south of Micanopy. The planter he had visited lay dead, and the elaborate manor house that had been the planter's home had been burned to the ground.

Brent had been only five years old on that day in 1835; he hadn't known that the United States government had broken every treaty it had ever made with the Indians in the Florida Territory. He didn't know that the whites didn't intend to honor any treaties; they wanted the Indians removed to the reservations in the distant west. He didn't know that the Indian agents and the men from the Bureau of Indian Affairs lied and cheated, and that many settlers moving into the territory regarded Indians as fair game for the hunt.

He knew only that a man with grave, intelligent dark eyes approached him on a pinto pony. A dark man wearing a band that held a single feather about his brow. An Indian. Brent drew his pocket knife and stood ready to do battle.

Osceola paused before him, and for a long moment they stared at each other, the frightened child, and the chief already old in wisdom though young in years. Osceola at last spoke.

"Put the knife down, boy. You have stood with the courage of a warrior. But Osceola does not make war with children."

Brent had ridden in front of Osceola on the pinto pony to the Seminoles' central Florida camp. Osceola had seen that messages were sent to Brent's parents, but Brent had lived with the Indians for many months before Justin McClain came to claim his son.

That had been over twenty-five years ago. The Wars of Indian Removal had gone on; Osceola had died. The Seminoles and Mikasukis who had fought relocation to western reservations had been pushed ever southward until now, here in the Everglades, they made a stand. They had never surrendered, and they had never been conquered. They had learned to eke out a living in the forbidding swamp. They knew it as the white man never would.

"How does your war go?" Red Fox queried, drawing Brent from his reminiscences.

Brent finished his coffee in a gulp and stood, pacing the platform as he searched for an answer to the question.

"It goes like any war, Red Fox. Men die. Many of the

great battles are taking place in Virginia. Thousands die, mown down like corn in a field. There was a battle at Manassas, at a little creek called Bull Run. Young men from both sides dropped like flies. They called it a southern victory. The Union troops broke and ran back to Washington. But it taught everyone that the war wouldn't be quickly ended. Right now the southern armies are doing well. Our generals think and see more clearly. Why not? The majority of them were West Pointers, men trained at the U.S. Military Academy. They were in the Union Army until their states seceded. And now, it seems that their battle strategy is superior. But I am afraid, Red Fox. The North has many men. They die, they are replaced. They are like a tide that cannot be held back."

Red Fox watched his old friend's face as Brent at last stopped pacing and stared out upon the peace of the coming dusk. The Everglades could be very beautiful as twilight approached. The sun set, a great flaming ball of orange and crimson, and the moss-covered trees and high grasses swayed beneath a breeze that cooled the humid heat of day. Egrets and cranes formed graceful dark silhouettes against the golden backdrop of the sky.

"You do not like this war," Red Fox said. "Why do you fight it?"

Brent shrugged. "St. Augustine is far north of this swamp, Red Fox, but they are both Florida, and my home is here, as is yours. Florida is a Confederate state, but it is raped to serve the Confederacy. Its troops fight and die in faraway places. The land is left scarcely protected while the Union soldiers and sailors raid the coastline. *I* fight as you have always done, Red Fox. To preserve what is mine." He fell silent, and then shrugged again, meeting Red Fox's eyes. "And maybe I do fight to preserve a way of life. I don't really know. Sometimes I fight only to bring medicine to those who are old and sick. To bring food to the children.

And sometimes I carry arms so that men may continue to butcher one another. I don't always know what I feel, Red Fox. I know only that a man must follow what he is, choose his side, and fight and give his total loyalty where he is committed."

Red Fox was silent as he digested the words. Then he eyed Brent squarely once more. "The slavery of blacks is wrong. We have harbored runaways here whose backs appear like butchered meat."

Brent did not look away from Red Fox. "I do not own any slaves, Red Fox. But my father does. Those he owns he cares for gently. They are well fed and clothed, and even taught to read and write."

"Justin McClain is a good man. Not many of your planters are like him."

Brent shrugged. "Not many men own slaves, Red Fox. More than half the soldiers in the Confederacy never owned anything but a few feet of dirt. Slaves are expensive. Rich men own them. Rich men fight, of course, for honor. But some rich men pay others to fight for them, and most of an army is composed of poor men. But the Indians have practiced forms of slavery."

"Yes, but like you, I do not believe that a man can be owned. He is not a beast to be whipped and shackled and sold."

"Yet you support me," Brent said quietly.

"I fight the blue uniform, blood brother. I fight the cavalry and infantry that my people have always fought. The Seminoles have learned to hate the blue Federal uniform. When the war is over, we shall see whether I wage battle with the white man again or not." Red Fox watched his friend, but Brent said nothing. They both prayed that the Seminole would be left to live peaceably in the Everglades when the whites at last stopped fighting one another. "But explain to me, please, what is this you call a navy? You sail in your own ship with your own men. How is this a navy?"

Brent laughed dryly, and the sound was bitter. "When the Confederacy formed, it had an instant army. Men left the Union Army for the Confederate Army. The Confederacy even had some naval officers. But it had no ships. And so it called upon its citizens." Brent shrugged. "It is best the way it is. My schooner is seaworthy, better than what I might be given. I can take to the ocean with speed, and I can slip into narrow rivers at will. We have just begun this war, yet food and clothing supplies already begin to tighten all through the South."

Red Fox began to speak, but he broke off as Apolka's head appeared at the top of the ladder. She climbed gracefully with one hand, carrying in the other a tray laden with food for her husband and his guest, the handsome white warrior to whom the Indians had given the name Night Hawk—a name that was spreading among the Confederate ports where Brent daringly ran Union blockades.

"My wife brings us our evening meal," Red Fox said. "We will speak of pleasant things."

Brent returned to his position in front of Red Fox and crossed his ankles to sink to a sitting position. He smiled at Apolka, and thanked her for the dish she handed him. Venison stew, Brent noted with appreciation, inhaling the rich, appetizing aroma. The warriors had been out hunting to provide for him and his men.

"As always, Red Fox, I thank you for your hospitality."

"She is a fine cook, my Apolka, is she not?"

"The finest," Brent agreed, smiling at the chief's wife. He could not really carry on a conversation with Apolka, for although whites often grouped the Florida Indians together under the term "Seminole," the Seminole and Mikasuki languages were different. Both tribes hailed from the Georgia Creek, but from different factions. Brent was well versed in

96

the Muskogee tongue, but the Mikasukis spoke a dialect of the Hitichi language, and Apolka was a Mikasuki. The customs of the Indians were very similar, however, and intermarriage among the few hundred Indians left in the vast Florida wilderness was not at all unusual. Apolka's command of the Muskogee language grew constantly, however, and despite the slight language barrier between her and Brent, they were fond of each other—warm friends through the language of the heart.

Women ate apart from men in the tribal society, and so after Apolka gave them their food, she started to descend the ladder once more, but then paused. She whispered in Red Fox's ear, and the Seminole chief gave a hearty laugh and his dark eyes twinkled with brilliant humor as he looked at Brent.

"Apolka tells me that Kendall Moore has been bathed and fed and secured within the cabin."

"Thank you," Brent said quietly. He lowered his eyes to his food and began to eat, not really tasting the savory food. What was the revenge he really wanted? he wondered.

He had come incredibly close to death at her hands a year ago, but he flirted with death now each time he sailed.

The woman had wounded his pride. His ship had been the victim of her stealthy attack.

But something more than a desire for revenge had kept him determined to find the woman. Something that had made it a torture to watch her today as the quicksand sucked her into the earth.

He still wanted her. And not just for vengeance. He wanted her because he could seldom remove her completely from his mind. He could remember the silken touch of her flesh, the warmth of her slender body, the look in her eyes when he had made love to her.

Fraud! he reminded himself. Her part in the fiasco had *been* to keep him occupied. Oh, she had done that. He had lost himself in her, in the need to touch and feel and know her . . .

But, he thought grimly, she had also responded to him. No one could act out such a trembling physical reaction. He had felt her heartbeat, the swell of her breast to the caress of his palms, the quivering hunger of her lips. The arch of her sweetly curved body to his . . . Or was even that sweet piece of heady seduction practiced and learned?

Maybe that was it, he thought with a sigh. Part vengeance, yes. By God, she had seduced him, and she was going to finish out what she had so boldly started. A man didn't go through what he had endured and forget what had happened. But beyond the desire for vengeance he felt a deep longing. A need to know what it was about her that still clouded his memory. If he could at last have her, he might be exorcised of the spirit that haunted him. A blue-eyed spirit with golden hair.

Brent glanced up to see that Red Fox hadn't yet touched his food; he stared at Brent. "I've a suggestion to make, Night Hawk."

"Oh?" Brent queried, a tawny brow rising curiously.

"Leave her in my care."

"Kendall?"

Red Fox nodded. "What would you do with her? Send her back to the Yankee you despise?"

Brent paused, surprised at the pain that seemed to constrict his gut. "It sounds as if she has seduced the red man as well as the white man."

Red Fox shrugged. "I admit that I like this woman. She is a fighter; she is proud. She does not know the meaning of defeat. I do not know what she has done to you, but she is a valuable prize. Were she not yours, brother, I would keep her."

"Might as well keep a pit of 'gators," Brent said dryly.

Red Fox laughed. "True, Brent McClain. But taming any

creature is a task that must be done with care. No man wants to ride into battle on a steed that has been broken in spirit. Neither does he crave a cowed and sullen woman in his bed. This one, this Yankee's woman, she will not be broken. Her spirit is strong. She has the heart of a great warrior. If gently tamed, she could give to a man what few receive beneath the sun."

"Umm, a knife in the back," Brent muttered.

Red Fox lifted a brow, but said no more. Brent chewed his last piece of meat and set his plate down. "She is your captive, Red Fox."

"No, she is mine no longer. I have given her to you, and therefore she is yours. I offer only to keep her for you when you must sail again."

Brent mulled the words over. He stood. He had waited long enough, searching his own soul. Talking about Kendall Moore was affecting him more than he cared to admit. Flashes of heat seemed to tear him, bringing a growing ache to his groin. It was time to discover what he did want, why the memory of her gnawed at him still.

"Thank you again, my friend," he told Red Fox. "I will decide what to do with her in the morning."

Red Fox laughed, a chuckle that was low and insinuating. "Sleep pleasantly, Night Hawk. You will not be disturbed."

Brent crawled down the ladder. As he approached the high cabin with the bolted door, his strides were long and determined. Tension knotted his muscles and he clenched his jaw tightly.

Kendall had paced the confines of her small cabin in an agitation so severe she was close to a hysterical frenzy.

In the clearing she had been so soundly defeated. When they had taken her to the river she hadn't cared; she had felt like an invalid, a person so long ill that every movement was

99

an effort. Like a child she had needed assistance and guidance. She hadn't had the strength to protest the vigorous washing of her hair and body, nor would it have made sense to do so. Had she escaped the industrious Seminole women, what could she have done? Run? She could have escaped . . . right into another quagmire.

She hadn't been docile so much as numb. Even when they had returned her to the cabin she had been numb. But she had been hungry, and once she had eaten the tasty venison, her strength had returned to her, and her body had rallied.

But rallying had done her little good. She had never been spanked in her life, and although she had endured worse treatment, somehow being tossed over a man's knee like a child was more humiliating than being struck in anger. She had never experienced anything like the smoldering rage she felt toward the man who had so abused her. She wanted to scratch his eyes out. But she was trapped, and she knew it. There was no way to escape, nowhere to go. All she could do was pace and worry, working herself into a fevered pitch, awaiting a man who believed she had seduced him into a setup for murder.

Arrogant son of a bitch! she thought, viciously kicking the pine wall of her prison. How dare he assume his death would be worth such an elaborate scheme.

A shudder jolted her slender frame even as she walked. He was going to kill her. He had been knocked unconscious and tossed into cold winter waters. He was definitely going to kill her.

But he could have killed her already. Or merely stood by and watched as the muck did the deed for him. No, his wrath was too great for that. That was what he had said. He intended to finish things between them. Was his threat a statement of his intention to rape her? Rather foolish from a man who had already received more from her than any other. A hot flush rose from deep inside her to darken her cheeks, coloring them crimson. She wanted to gouge him to ribbons, but she could remember with disgustingly excellent precision how it had felt to be touched by him, how splendidly male he had appeared in bronze and muscled nudity, how the brush of his hot and pulsing masculinity had both frightened and excited her. He had taken such care with her, touching her with such sensual expertise that she had longed for fulfillment of the hunger created with wild abandon.

But he hadn't hated her then. And she hadn't despised him.

A wave of cold air like a wall of snow swept over her body. He wouldn't take care with her now. He would think of her as rancid garbage to be quickly tossed away.

He was capable of being cruel. Of being ruthless. Perhaps he wanted only to rip her nails from her fingers one by one, carve her features into a pulp, chop off her ears . . .

Kendall paused in midstride and suddenly gripped her hands into fists and banged furiously against the pine. Damn him! Damn him a thousand times over! He was already creating the torture of revenge; he was leaving her to shake and quiver with dread and to worry herself sick!

The bloody hell with him! Surely he couldn't behave barbarically, so just what could he do to her? Beat her, humiliate her?

Laughter that bordered on the hysterical hovered upon her lips. Nothing could be worse than what she had already endured. And she had always survived. No matter what John Moore had said or done to her, she had raised her chin and stared him coldly down, and she had survived.

But this man wasn't John Moore. He was young and virile and powerful, and the searing menace in his steel eyes warned that he was not a man who gave quarter when he discovered that he had been used. And he wanted to finish what she had begun.

The tension that wound itself up in her abdomen knotted

so acutely that the room swam like gray mist before her, and she had to reach out and hold the wall to keep from falling. No, he would not be an impassioned and tender lover when he came to her this time. His sole intent would be to extract a savage revenge.

"I have to talk to him! I have to reason with him. I have to convince him that I never intended him harm," she said aloud.

It would be a difficult task. But she wasn't going to keep pacing in an agony of anticipation. She was going to sit, and wait patiently. And she was going to remember that she could not be broken, that she was a survivor, and that although she could be abused, nothing could be done to her heart and soul and will that she did not allow.

Kendall sank to the floor, gritting her teeth as her still raw posterior came in contact with hard wood. Tears rose to her eyes with the bite of pain and humiliation.

I never intended you harm, Brent McClain, but from this day on, you'd best not turn your back on me!

Crossing her legs carefully beneath her, Kendall stared at the door. Without thought she arranged her plain cotton skirt around her, as if she were bedecked in the most elegant of ball gowns and about to graciously welcome visitors to Cresthaven.

This isn't over, Captain McClain. You judged me without benefit of trial; you found me guilty. I will not shiver and plead at your feet. I will rationally try to explain.

He was never going to believe her . . .

She forced herself to compose her features. She calmly folded her hands on her lap.

Still, when she heard the sound of booted feet on the ladder to the cabin, she couldn't control the erratic pounding of her heart or her short and ragged gulps for breath.

The cabin door did not bang inward. It drifted open slowly and smoothly. Brent McClain placed his boot on the landing and entered, staring at the woman who coolly awaited him. Irritation freshly flamed his temper. She looked as if she should be sitting before a silver tea cart, and assuredly, her first words would be, "One lump, or two, Captain?"

He kept his eyes on her as he moved into the cabin. For several seconds he merely stared at her, then, with unhurried determination, he firmly closed the door in his wake. "Well, Mrs. Moore, your appearance is quite improved."

"If you didn't care for my appearance, Captain McClain, it was your own fault."

"Was it?" A tawny brow rose. "I don't recall pushing you into the mud."

Kendall's determination to remain calm wavered as her temper rose. "I was running from you. If you hadn't terrified me half to death—"

"Terrified you? I hadn't said a frightening word, Mrs. Moore. It was, in fact, a pleasant surprise to find you here," he drawled softly.

"Surprise?" she queried politely. "Hardly a surprise, Captain. Red Fox and his crew obviously attacked under your orders."

Brent chuckled, but the sound held little humor. It was as dry as a tinderbox and seemed almost as explosive in the tension that crackled in the humid air. "You are quite mistaken, Mrs. Moore. I would never presume to order Red Fox to do anything."

"You might have easily fooled me, Captain."

"Ah, but you did easily fool me, Mrs. Moore, didn't you?" The quiet question was low and polite, so polite that it sent shivers racing along Kendall's spine. He strode across the room and gazed out one of the narrow windows, his hands planted on his hips. "Are you married to John Moore in appearance only, Kendall?"

Her mouth suddenly felt very dry. She couldn't answer.

He spun from the window, and his question was now a deathly thunder. "Well, Kendall?"

Don't let him intimidate you! she warned herself. Hold on . . . hold on to your dignity. "I am legally his wife," she replied coolly. "But truly, Captain McClain, you don't understand—"

"Oh, Mrs. Moore, I'm just dying to understand," he murmured sarcastically. "Pray, do expound upon the situation for me."

Sitting had been a mistake, Kendall decided. He slowly sauntered behind her. She felt him as if he were a fire, scorching her back. Each of his quiet footfalls sent shivers down her spine, each spasm of shivers further undermined the control she had determined she must maintain. She did not want him to see her fear, yet the temptation to spin to face him was great. She couldn't! She couldn't allow herself to betray the effect he was having on her. Yet she had to swallow before she could speak; it was like trying not to run when a deadly water moccasin snake slithered up one's back.

"I'm waiting, Mrs. Moore."

The whisper touched her ear like a heated sizzle. Still she didn't move.

"It's very simple, Captain. I was born outside of Charleston. I knew when South Carolina seceded that war was inevitable. I didn't want to be taken back to the North when—"

"Your husband just happened to be right behind you?" The scornful query was now closer to the rear of the cabin. "And he just happened to intervene at the . . . moment of truth, shall we call it?"

Kendall stiffened her spine. "Yes."

"But you told me, madam, that you had no husband."

"I—I lied."

"That I do believe!"

Kendall cried out as his fingers raked into her hair, jerking her head back, twisting her neck into a painful arch. The muscle-hewn columns of his long legs were spread in a firm stance behind her; his thighs brushed her shoulders as he held her relentlessly. He towered over her, his eyes boring into her with a ruthless steel-gray fury. She did not try to twist from his grasp; she raised her chin of her own accord and returned the fury of his eyes with a volatile blue sizzle.

"You egotistical ass! No one was after you!" Her words ended in a shriek as he knotted his fingers more tightly into her hair with a vicious tug, then threw her from him.

"Then tell me, Mrs. Moore, how it happened that I was thrown overboard to die with less chance than a drowning rat! You think quicksand is bad, Mrs. Moore. Try being bound and naked in winter waters."

Kendall fell forward with the force of his push. She picked herself up and stood, whirling to face him. She *had* been a fool to keep her back to such a snake no matter what the circumstances. And his touch stripped her of calm. She *had* to hold her temper! Somehow, she had to reason with him—and keep both her fear and fury in check.

She stood straight and stared at him, painfully aware that his wrath was like a tangible force in the air between them, but determined to best him. "Sir," she said coolly, "you were pulled out of the water—by a Yankee, I might add. You are quite alive. Whether you choose to believe me or not is immaterial. The situation is long past, and I would think you would already have taken whatever petty revenge you desire. I have been abducted by savages, dragged into a swamp, frightened to near heart failure by quicksand, and . . . and beaten in a most humiliating fashion. If anyone is owed justice, Captain McClain, it is I. Now I am asking you, sir, as a Confederate, a captain in the service of the South, to desist with this boyish foolishness and make arrangements to have me taken to a southern port as soon as possible!"

He stared at her incredulously for several seconds, and

then laughed, tossing back his tawny head with the force of it. "Boyish foolishness, is it?"

His tone was light. Kendall relaxed slightly. "Captain, I just know that an officer of the Confederate States Navy must in all justice show kindness to a wretched lady of that realm."

"Mrs. Moore, you are so right." He took a casual step toward her, hands on his hips as he assessed her with a smile that brought a smoky hue to gray eyes that half closed in somnolence. "We of the CSN do try to show gallantry to the wretched ladies of our realm. I have found, however, that true ladies are harder to find than silk stockings in Jacksonville."

His tone was seductively rich and pleasant. Even here in the backwoods he smelled pleasantly of the sea. As he spoke he continued his slow saunter until he stood directly before her. Kendall stared up at him, mesmerized and lulled by the husky quality of his voice. He had suddenly changed so drastically. Of course! She had reminded him of the honor of the South. And he *could* be a gentleman when he chose. Broadshouldered and sleek in the gold-trimmed uniform of a Confederate captain, rugged features made handsome with the rakish and slightly crooked grin . . .

Kendall was taken completely by surprise when his powerful fingers bit into her shoulders and he shook her so that her hair spilled behind her to her buttocks and her eyes were forced to meet his. "The way I see it, madam, you acted toward me as nothing better than a conniving, tawdry little slut—"

His words were cut off by a sharp, stinging slap as Kendall wrenched a shoulder free and raised her hand in a vicious fury against him, striking so quickly that he hadn't a chance to avoid the frenzied blow. "Scurvy low-blood! Backwoods bastard!" she hissed, cursing to quell the terror that rose in her as she watched his jaw clamp tightly and his eyes narrow

106

to steel slits that had lost their lazy nonchalance. The mark of her hand was imprinted in clear red against the bronze of his hard, chiseled features, but the line about his lips was growing taut and white as he returned her stare. His hand whipped out suddenly, clamping around her wrist like a coiled snake that had been waiting to strike. Kendall wrenched at it furiously, pure panic outweighing her determination to remain coldly calm.

"Let me go!"

She grasped at the hand restraining her with her free fingers, clawing at the flesh. She kicked out at him insanely, managing to draw grunts of pain as she caught his shins with a number of her wild strikes.

But just as he had captured her wrist, he reached for a flying foot—and where she had been standing one second, she seemed to be flying the next, jerked cleanly off her feet. The flying sensation was only to last the briefest second—to be replaced with a hard and jarring thud as she hit the floor, stunned, on her backside.

Before she could rally her bruised body, she was gasping out a curse of protest as his weight landed on her, legs straddling her waist in a clasp from which there was no escape. She stared into the hard and merciless steel of his eyes, and primal fear more than courage drove her to fight again, lashing out at him with flailing fists, writhing, trying desperately to elude the iron clamp of his legs. He cursed softly at her wild strength, but still subdued her, drawing her wrists high over her head and securing them with a single hand in a humiliatingly brief span of time. Panting and praying that she wouldn't burst into tears of hopelessness, Kendall again met his eyes, close . . . so close to hers. "Madam, you were intent upon offering me something last December, but you never did give it to me. Well, darlin', you are in a different port now. With the gentleman you decided to use well."

She lay quiet, but he could still sense the fight within her,

her breasts heaving provocatively, her hips pressed taut against his upper thighs. Just as she had that night long ago, she elicited a raw desire in him that overwhelmed all thought and clouded his mind. She was beautiful. Even as she stared at him, loathing giving the crystal blue of her eyes a gemstone quality, he could think of nothing but the way her lips had given in to his in hesitant but thirsting pleasure, the way her body had come alive under his hands, her full firm breasts thrusting to his chest . . .

She had almost killed him, he reminded himself. Brought him to that stage of total beguilement and animal passion only to witness his complete, unguarded downfall. "Truly, Mrs. Moore, I don't see why you are so resistant tonight. The last time we met, you were more than willing to welcome my embrace. What? Are there no Yankees nearby this evening to grasp you from the hands of fate?"

She went rigid beneath him, her stunning eyes still staring challengingly into his. A brittle laugh escaped her. "Captain McClain, you may believe this or not, but I find the Yankees almost as loathsome as I do you. So you just do whatever you want. I can't beat you. I won't even fight you."

Kendall continued to stare at him, praying she had shamed him into searching his conscience. He paused above her, watching her with an enigmatic glare that told her nothing. Not a flicker of expression touched the strong square jaw, or the grim line of his full and mobile mouth. One brow was slightly arched, as if in mocking query. "You *won't* fight me?" he asked softly.

Kendall felt heat flush her face again. The memories of that night in Charleston came back to her vividly as they engaged in their duel of wills; she felt the strength of his thighs and the power of his hands as they held her an intimate prisoner. She felt the heat of him as she had that night, the aura that was dominatingly male. A pulse ticked within the corded column of his neck, and in it she could see the tension and fever of his emotion. Through the thin cloth of her dress and the strong material of his breeches she had even become aware of the rising beat and growth of his male sex.

Kendall swallowed; they were both aware as they stared at one another.

He smiled slowly, a subtle movement that twisted his lips but had no impact on the hard steel in his eyes. He released her wrists suddenly and placed one palm beside her head, trapping her hair within his fingers. His left palm he placed on her breast, cupping it, and grazing his thumb over the nipple. The material of her dress provided him little obstacle. He felt the seductive fullness and warmth, the erotic hardening to his touch. And the rampaging pulse of her heart. She did not strike out at him, but remained still, her eyes mirroring a subtle change . . . she was defiant still, but frightened . . . ?

Of him, he wondered, or of herself?

Suddenly he wanted to stroke her cheek. To whisper to her softly words that told of the web of intoxication she spun, of the allure and fascination of her sleek and fluid beauty.

He bit down on his lip savagely, drawing blood. She was the woman who had cunningly used him. And she was practicing a calculated seduction on his soul once again. He leaned closer to her, his mouth not an inch from hers. "Do what I wish, Kendall?"

"I can't stop you," she whispered.

"A repeat of Charleston?" he murmured.

She didn't seem to be able to make her mouth work. Her lips barely formed words. "I can't stop you," she repeated.

His lips suddenly fell upon hers with a bruising intensity. She tasted his blood as his tongue plundered her mouth, savagely demanding entrance. Kendall whimpered a protest at the intrusion, yet her heart was beating madly; she could barely breathe and the smothering sensation left her faint. She tried to twist to fight him, but his palm held her hair firmly to the floor. She gripped his back, digging her fingers desperately into his hard, rippling muscles. For the barest second his assault eased; then it began again. But the cruelty was gone. The motion of his lips became persuasive, caressing that which was bruised and in need of tender care. Kendall fell prey to the abrupt change of his touch, shivering as she succumbed, and finding, in spite of herself, that she still felt a hunger for him.

His head at last rose from hers. His features were strained, his voice was harsh when he spoke. "All that began in Charleston ends here."

There was a fight in him; somehow Kendall sensed it. She also knew he meant what he said. If she opened her mouth and pleaded honestly, warned him of one truth he would shortly discover, he would be gentle . . .

She wanted to tell him, but she couldn't. The words refused to form on her quivering lips.

All she could do was lie there as he rose and methodically began to strip, watch him as he stood high above her, bronze shoulders glistening in a narrow streak of twilight from the rear window, gray eyes as dark and stormy as the night sea.

Transfixed, she watched as he took a step toward her, fluidly lowering himself to her side, his sleek, muscled body as finely honed as a panther's. He drew her against him and undid the buttons of her dress. A hoarse grunt of impatience escaped him, and the fabric came away, ripped open in a clean stroke.

"Brent . . ." His name at last formed on her lips, but she could say no more. She closed her eyes as his hands touched her waist, stroking her flesh with irrevocable purpose as he stripped away the pantalettes, her only remaining garment.

His body covered hers. Heated power. She tensed as his knee abruptly forced apart her thighs, but even then, she couldn't find her voice. He hovered above her, his eyes seeking hers. She returned his stare, but still she could say nothing.

She closed her eyes as his mouth touched hers again. The movement was a gentle caress. His tongue rimmed her lips. His lips trailed down her chin, the moisture and warmth of his mouth grazed her ear, his teeth gently captured the lobe. Again his kiss wandered erotically. It touched her throat, found the shadow above her collarbone, and returned to her lips.

Time, reason, life itself . . . all seemed to fade and shift and change. It might have been Charleston again. His was a touch she remembered all too clearly, all too sweetly. He had threatened, he had warned of vengeance, he had waged his private wars with himself, and she had kept silent, and still, none of it mattered. If he had sought to hurt her, he had failed. For he seduced. His kiss upon her lips seemed to rob her of both breath and protest. The sweep of his tongue seemed to bring with it a sweet, volatile storm of searing heat, touching her there, filling the length of her . . .

He kissed her still as his hand cupped around her breast. Kissed her as he stroked and touched . . . drugging her. Then suddenly it seemed that his long bronze fingers were entwined with her, holding them free from him on either side of her, and she realized that she had dug her nails into his shoulders, torn her fingers into his hair . . .

Not fighting . . . him. Just the storm of sensation.

Yet so much more was to follow . . .

She heard the slightest sound. A soft cry, a whimper. It came from her own lips. She remained gently but firmly imprisoned as he continued his . . . revenge. The searing caress of his mouth covered her flesh, the rough tip of his tongue slid over the hardened peak of her nipples, circling the underglobe of her breasts with liquid fire. She trembled, writhed, fought to escape the honeyed sensations that cascaded into her being with his touch, strained to free her hands, to twist, to move.

Ah, revenge! He would have no mercy. His fingers remained tightly laced with her own. The wicked assault of his kiss became ever more intimate. The length and strength of his body parted her. The hot molten seduction of his touch and caress covered the bare innocence of her flesh, bathing her abdomen, creating sizzling sparks of fire upon her thighs, finding then the very heart of heat and desire within her. Not even the shocked cry that escaped her, the wild convulsions that seized her, could sway him from his purpose, his desire . . .

His revenge.

She wanted to die. She thought that she had died, would die. The night had exploded into stars, into blackness, into stars again. She tugged furiously upon her fingers again, desperate to free herself . . . or to touch some unknown magic that seemed to glitter just beyond her comprehension. She cried out, cried out his name . . .

And he was there, over her again, his lips now upon her own once again, fevered, tasting of the force of his passion. Her hands were free, she realized dimly. And just as dimly she felt the shift in him, the sudden tension. She felt him, the heated tip of his sex against the portals of her own, like a hot steel blade. Dear God . . . she had been so seduced, she had not thought . . .

The magic was cleanly ripped away by the staggering sensation of pain. Tears swam in her eyes; she tried not to scream, but a sob tore raggedly from her even as she instinctively writhed to escape the invasion of his sex.

She wouldn't escape. Just as instinctively, she knew that. They had come too far. Damage done.

Revenge . . . not quite taken.

"Kendall, damn, Kendall, you little fool, you should have told me you . . . that you never . . ." His hoarse, stunned voice trailed away, but his palms caught and secured her cheeks and he forced her eyes to his. She read amazement in them, and the still the storm of gray battle was there.

112

"If I had told you, what then?" she whispered. "Would you have let me go?"

"I . . ."

"Would you have believed me?"

"Damn you!" he grated out, and he seemed furious. The tension in his body wound the muscles into hard knots that seemed to embrace her mercilessly. But they could not go back. She could not go back.

"Would you?" she demanded.

"No!" he ground out. "But I—"

"Would have been more tender?" she queried, taunting them both. Dear God, she was on fire. Burning with both pain . . . and something else. The liquid fire he had brought to her body, instilled within her. The need she had so nearly had fulfilled . . .

"Would you have let me go?" she demanded.

His eyes stared down into hers, dark, stormy, passionate, gray. "No!" he informed her, teeth grating, fingers winding into a lock of her. "No, I'd not have let you go, nor can I let you go."

A ragged sob escaped her. Her lashes swept her cheeks. "Damn you, Kendall, I cannot let you go!" he said again, and she didn't know how to tell him that she did not want to be let go. That, even just for this moment, she longed to be loved.

"Put your arms around me," he whispered softly. "Hold me, hold tightly . . . kiss me . . ."

His lips descended upon hers once again. He tasted the salt of her tears. His knuckles caressed her cheek in a gentle flow, and his fingers thread into the length of her hair. His eyes touched hers, held them. Her lashes swept low over her cheeks and she slipped her arms around him, holding tightly.

He felt the pressure of her nails, but knew she didn't mean to hurt him. He began to move, holding back the ravenous hunger, the reckless, desperate desire she evoked. The wild-

113

fire that raged within his loins. Sweet *Jesu,* it was agony to move so slowly, exquisite agony. The tension began to ease from her body, some small sound escaped her lips.

"Kendall?" he whispered her name urgently.

She lowered her head, burrowed against his neck, unable to face him. But her body suddenly seemed to mold to his, to arch, writhe, undulate in rhythm. He felt the silken touch of her breasts, teasing against his hair-roughened chest, felt her fingers clinging to his shoulders once again . . .

She had suddenly given him the freedom to soar.

The passion he had held so powerfully in check exploded. He slid his hands down her back, cradling her buttocks, holding her to him to meet and accept the increasing demand of his driving thrusts. She moved to him instinctively once again, his fire seeming to spread within her as well, to flame and blaze between them, consuming them both, overwhelming the world around them.

For Kendall, there was nothing but the man, and the sensation. The past had faded, her life was gone. She rode the night winds and the darkness and the sweeping hunger that had invaded her, reaching, alive with wonder, knowing that she craved some sweet surcease she could not quite touch . . . enjoying the strange beauty of the exquisite torture and pleasure, dying a bit with the wanting of the end.

It came. A moment of complete rapture; oblivious to everything but the sweet nectar that swept through her body and left her shuddering violently, enwrapped in tiny thrill after thrill, then drifting downward as if through snow-wild clouds into a field of gentle deliciousness.

Brent gave a deep, triumphant cry. She was aware of his body stiffening, driving hard, stiffening . . . Warmth swept through her again, filled her, encompassed her. She trembled violently in his hold . . .

But then that hold eased. Swiftly.

He carefully rolled off her. He did not touch her, but she

114

felt him near her. He leaned on an elbow and stared at her, his curiosity fully aroused now that his passion was sated.

Kendall closed her eyes and tried to roll away from him, crying out in protest when he relentlessly pulled her back. She had wanted him. So desperately. The magic had been beautiful, and she was still in awe of the sensations that led to *the* sensation greater than other . . . rapture.

She wanted to remember. To hide away within herself. To savor the memory while it was fresh, to create a dream with it.

But more than anything, she wanted to crawl into the floor. And die. This had all come about because he had hated her. He had wanted revenge. He had used her. He had finished what she had begun, all that time ago in Charleston.

He would never know just how great his revenge had been, she realized, and the thought was a whole new field of anguish.

She closed her eyes tightly, her lashes long against her cheeks, a barrier she desperately needed. She didn't want to face him, or the questions that would be no less demanding than his heated passions. She didn't want to face the humiliation of them both knowing that he had forced no more than his first touch tonight.

"Kendall—"

"Don't—"

"Kendall—"

"You've had what you wanted, you've had your revenge."

"Oh, no, Mrs. Moore," he said very softly, "I've just begun."

"Brent—"

"Open your eyes, Kendall," he commanded determinedly. "We're going to talk."

Five

If ever in her life Kendall had felt the irresistible urge to burst into tears, it was now. And if ever she had been determined not to, this was also the moment. She closed her eyes and lay stiff within the circle of Brent's arms. "Let go of me," she said tonelessly, adding a quiet "please."

The pressure of his arms increased tautly, but only for a moment. To Kendall's vague surprise and relief, he released his hold. She lay on her back, arms crossed over her chest, one knee rising slightly to rest against the other.

Brent stared down at her, puzzled, and torn between anger that she had again misled him, and guilt because there was obviously far more to the strange and stunning woman—who it seemed was destined to haunt his life—than he had been willing to admit.

A streak of moonlight now fell on the magnolia silk of her flesh. She looked like a painting by a Renaissance master; her protective and alluring posture a picture of innocence that had been stolen. She lay on the floor with her golden hair a wild tangle of curls draping around her shoulders and over her breasts, seeming to enhance the aura of beauty and youth and seductive innocence. Her lashes were thick fans that grazed her cheeks, shadowed to mystery in the thin filter of moonlight. Yet for all its modesty, her pose was shatteringly sensual. Silver moonlight fell on the smooth hollow of her belly, and highlighted the graceful line of a curved hip and long, lean flanks. He wanted to touch her, savor the moon-silver silk of her flesh. Desire, so recently satiated, rose again.

Silently he came to his feet in a smooth, agile motion and padded the few steps to retrieve his breeches. Then he grasped a blanket from the corner of the room and hunched down to balance on the balls of his feet as he cast the covering over her. Blue eyes, shining with the silver of the moon, sprang open wide as she surveyed him with surprise. Then her lashes descended again and she clutched the blanket to her, murmuring a soft thank you.

"Don't thank me," he said curtly. "I want to hear your story."

"What is it that you don't know?" she queried bitterly.

"Are you or aren't you married to that Yankee?"

"I am."

"Why?"

"Because I was sold," she said tonelessly, still refusing to open her eyes and face him. "Just the same as any field hand."

"You were forced to marry him?"

"Yes."

Brent emitted a grunt of impatience. "No one can force another to say yes in the middle of a wedding ceremony."

Her eyes flew open again and fell upon his with a flame of anger. "Perhaps not the way you see it, Captain. But unfortunately we're not all born muscle-hewn men with the power and arrogance to proclaim ourselves sovereign to the world."

"I see," Brent said dryly. "You were beaten and dragged to the altar."

"No," Kendall said coolly. She closed her eyes once more and again attempted to turn away. But he had no intention of leaving her alone. She felt his slight movement as he slid to a cross-legged posture beside her. And she felt his hand on her shoulder, broad palm and long fingers splaying over the blanket she clutched to her.

"Turn around, Kendall. I want to know exactly what you were doing aboard my ship last winter. And I want to know why I just deflowered a virgin who has been married for quite some time."

She spun about so quickly that he tensed, muscles bunching in response to the heated venom in her flashing eyes. "Have you ever loved anyone, Captain?" she demanded coldly. "Not a woman, but a brother, a friend, your mother, perhaps? If you have, Captain, you just might understand. Love can be a greater weapon than any instrument devised by the cleverest armorer. When someone you love is threatened, Captain, you just might discover that you'll do any number of things that are normally against your principles."

His gray eyes narrowed, but his hard, unimpassioned expression didn't alter a hair. "Go on. I'm waiting."

Kendall ground her teeth together and turned her eyes to the ceiling above her. "Waiting for what, Captain? You've heard all I have to tell. My father died. My mother remarried. White trash in an elegant frock coat. Her husband went through the profits of an affluent plantation in a matter of years. He ran out of inanimate objects to sell, and so he turned to flesh-and-blood creatures. I believe the bid on me was higher than it was on my sister. High enough for him to promise me—in writing—that she would remain safe from his avarice if my sale paid the bills."

He was silent for so long that she jerked her head back so that she could face him again.

He sat just like Red Fox, she thought. Spine straight, shoulders broad and square. His chest was still bare, the flesh taut as a drum in quiet, sinewed power. His wrists rested over his knees; only the slow clenching and unclenching of his long callused fingers gave any indication of emotion.

"You still haven't explained yourself," he reminded her, his tone as brutally cold as hers.

"I wouldn't think you'd need an explanation," Kendall said. She had wanted her words to be scornful and biting, but despite all that passed between them, the discussion had come to its inevitable, painful peak. Crimson splashed its way into her cheeks, and her scornful murmur paled to nothing more than a whisper.

"I don't need an explanation for the obvious," he drawled, not allowing her the smallest mercy. "But although I have yet to enjoy the pleasure of meeting your husband while conscious, I've heard enough about him to understand that he cuts a respectable figure. And it strains the bounds of rational belief to discover that a man who has supposedly purchased a bride at an extravagant price has also left her untouched for years . . . I assume."

"Three years, to be precise," Kendall snapped. She clenched her jaw tightly as she saw that her flippant sarcasm hadn't made a dent in his ruthless determination. If anything, he stared at her more grimly . . . more threateningly. She lowered her eyes and noted his hands. His fingers were balled so tightly into his palms that his knuckles appeared white against the dark tan of his flesh. Swallowing, she chewed nervously on her lip, then blurted out the answer he demanded without further prodding on his part.

"John Moore may look fine, but he isn't. He caught a fever several years ago that almost killed him. He has never fully recovered. He suffers from muscle spasms and severe headaches. And from . . . complete impotence."

A flicker of caustic interest at last touched Brent's narrowed eyes. "And so you were deserting the man because of his infirmity?"

For a moment the charge so astonished Kendall that she

could only stare at him blankly. Then fury possessed her like a resurging tide, and the injustice of his callous remark struck a note of wild insanity in her. She sprang upward, forgetting her blanket, forgetting everything in her determination to strike the wry contempt from his cold and arrogant features. With a cry of anguished rage she hurled herself against him, beating her fists against his bare chest, wildly attempting to aim a blow against the strong contour of his jaw. "You are a son of a bitch!" she hissed, yet the vehemence of her whisper faded along with the madness of the action as his arms came around her like bars, crushing her against him as his storm-gray eyes locked with hers. The bare cream-white mounds of her breasts came in naked contact with the tawny-matted hardness of his chest, and she was rudely and painfully reminded of the intimacy she had just shared with the man who scorned her. An intimacy he would not be adverse to repeating . . .

Could this be the same man? she wondered fleetingly. The tender lover of moments past; now the cold, condemning stranger. . . .

She began to struggle again, whimpering slightly as she fought not to inflict pain but merely to put distance between them. He was more ruthless than ever, his mouth grim and barely moving as he spoke, his breath touching her lips as he spoke. "Since you married a Yankee, what were you doing in Charleston on the day the state seceded?"

Kendall managed to press her hands against his chest, but it did little good. His hands slipped down to the small of her back, causing a more disturbing intimacy as he drew her against him, one long limb curved against his knee, the other stretching behind her. The blanket fell down around her hips, and she felt the familiar, frightening vulnerability.

"Kendall!"

He shook her slightly, and her head fell back. She stared up into his eyes, pushing wildly against him to no avail.

She halted, defiance now thrusting her chin high as she met his stare in hostile rebellion.

"I had come home, Captain McClain. Charleston was still my home. I knew South Carolina would secede if Lincoln was elected. I had to be there. With the help of a friend, I had convinced John that I needed to visit my mother, in case hostilities began after the election. I was determined to disappear. I had no idea that he'd followed me."

His brow arched; he smiled with bitter amusement.

"And so you simply stumbled upon me. And elected to use me as an escape from the man you were rightfully married to?"

"Yes! Yes!" Kendall cried out passionately, jerking far enough away in her fury to strike against his chest again, futile blows that he barely noticed as he tightened his hold. "It was no plot."

"You still used me."

"Yes!" she shrieked again. "And don't you dare judge me! I would have used anyone—God himself!—to escape. You don't know what it was like. You don't know what I went through, what . . . what . . ."

Her voice faded, and suddenly her anger failed her. She grasped his shoulders and went limp against him, whispering bitterly against his shoulder, "You are indomitable, Captain McClain. You are raw and exclusive power, able to put others at your mercy. You don't know what it is like to be hated and taunted and abused simply because you are young and healthy . . . and owned."

His hold about her tightened briefly, but Kendall hardly felt the almost imperceptible action. She shivered against him, only barely aware of the heat and security of his body, of the pleasant male scent of his shoulder, slick and bronze beneath her cheek. She shivered, trembled, but still would not allow herself to cry. Nor would she beg him to believe her, plead with him to understand and forgive.

121

Suddenly she did become aware of him; acutely aware of his movement. One hand remained on the curve of her hip. The other . . . shifted. His fingertips lightly grazed up and down her spine. Slowly, gently, caressing her flesh, giving comfort. Kendall didn't dare move. Her breath caught in her throat as he continued his idle motion. Lulling, hypnotizing. How dearly she wanted to wrap her arms around him, find in him the strength that had slipped away from her, find a harbor from the storms of time and the cruel trickery of fate.

No! she cried in silent agony. She was married. Legally tied to a man who fought not a war but a blind battle against God and himself. And the arms that offered this brief comfort were those of a Rebel bent only on revenge. The man she had used had used her in return. Aloof and elusive, an independent power unto himself.

The man who had found his just revenge. On whose behalf she had been kidnapped and dragged into a snake-infested swamp. The strong hand that massaged her now had been the instrument of the humiliating punishment inflicted on her earlier.

She stiffened abruptly in protest to his touch. He had made her his lover, with no love. And she had given to him shamelessly. Responded to his demands with abandoned fever.

Responded sweetly, passionately, hungrily, to a man who had humiliated and abused her! Her senses, dormant so long, had awakened to his touch, and betrayed her heart and mind and pride.

"Please," she murmured tiredly. "I've told you everything. The truth. I did use you, but I didn't intend that you should be harmed. Please let me go."

His motion ceased. His fingers threaded into her hair, but not to hurt or punish. He tugged the gold locks until she faced him again, and for a heartbeat of time that seemed eternal, he stared searchingly into her eyes. "The truth, Kendall?" he demanded rigidly.

"The truth," she whispered. "I swear it."

She didn't know if he believed her or not. The steel gray of his eyes was like a twilight mist that would always hide the soul of the man. His determined jaw would never soften. The strength of his handsome features was equal to that of his tautly muscled form, raw and rugged and hewn with the force of his will and the rough determination of his mind.

Kendall's heart slammed relentlessly against her breast as she stared at him. They were still so ridiculously intimate, though they were hostile strangers. For breathless seconds she was certain that his lips would lower to hers again, that he would demand her with a brutal kiss. And she didn't know what she wanted. To be left alone? To regain her dignity and pride?

Or to experience again the wild beauty of becoming one with a man? The ragged storm of driving, aching need, the fulfillment of the ultimate intimacy.

She closed her eyes, forcing herself to remember that he had taken her only out of his need for revenge. If any other feeling had guided his male demands, that feeling had been base lust. He *had* been able to hurt her. She had opened her soul and allowed him to do so. In a matter of moments, she would be pleading in a torrent of tears that he release her before she could stand no more of the pain and beauty and agonized confusion . . .

He did not bend to kiss her, but eased her down until she lay on the floor again. Mechanically she grasped for the blanket, drawing it over her body like a shield. Only when he drew away did she open her eyes.

He had donned his breeches and was now pulling on his boots. That done, he reached for his shirt and slipped it on, tucking it into the waistband of his breeches without bothering to secure the buttons.

"Are . . . are you leaving?" Kendall heard herself query.

"I'll be back," he said briefly, dipping to retrieve his coat.

123

Kendall shivered convulsively. Was it the blunt conviction of his answer that made her feel both hot and cold, anxious and frightened? Or had she been terrified that he meant to walk out the door and leave her behind—nothing more than a score that had been settled, a debt paid? She didn't know for sure, and the pain of that confusion was horrible and debilitating. She moistened her lips and tried to keep the fright from her voice.

"Where are you going?"

"To check on my men. Some of them are new recruits. I don't want any of the young fools to wake up sleeping with a rattler."

He turned his back on her and strode to the door. She wanted to let him go; she wanted to believe that his leaving didn't matter. But she couldn't stop herself from calling him back, nor could she keep her voice from trembling no matter how coldly and defiantly she spoke. "Captain McClain!"

He paused, hand on the door, and turned to her, his gray eyes smoky slits as he waited expectantly.

"What do you intend to . . . to do with me now?"

He stared at her for several seconds, his features fathomless and as relentless as granite in the pale moonglow.

At long last he spoke, and his reply was dry and curt—and cuttingly blunt. "I don't know yet. I haven't decided."

Kendall winced as the door shut with a decisive snap. And as she stared after him, she felt the heat of temper and rebellion rise within her.

A second sharp scraping of wood sounded. He hadn't decided what to do with her yet, but apparently he had decided one thing. He didn't trust her. And he wasn't ready to let her go—not yet. He had firmly thrown the bolt into place. As thoroughly as ever, she was his prisoner.

She stared at the door for a long time. And then she stared down at her lap, at the blanket that shrouded her nakedness. And she stared at the rough plank floor where she had lost

124

her virginity in a storm of rage and tenderness. She became aware of her own body as she hadn't been when his was near, dominating her mind and senses with his raw and vital masculinity. Aware of the soreness within her. Of the stabbing feeling that had returned to remind her of the tumult. Of knowledge gained, of innocence and pride lost to the storm of desire and revenge.

And she allowed herself the luxury of bursting into tears. She cried until her eyes were drained, and then dry sobs wracked her body. And the pity of it was she did not know exactly what it was she cried for . . .

There were still sounds in the camp as Brent sprang down the steps of the ladder and bent his knees to land silently on the earth. He paused for a moment, his state of dark turmoil somewhat eased as he glanced toward the center of the Indian encampment and saw a number of his men in earnest if somewhat confused conversation with a group of Seminole braves. They had carried some good Kentucky bourbon aboard the *Jenni-Lyn,* and carried it with them when they had left the ship under light guard near the broad mouth of the river. The Rebs and the Indians had obviously been doing some imbibing.

The men did not hear his approach until he was upon them—a very unusual occurrence among the Seminoles and his well-trained sailors. Brent scowled to cover his amusement, and barked out a command that quickly silenced all conversation and brought guilty faces quickly around to his.

"What is this, men? A blindfolded Yank could have made mincemeat out of you!"

The southerners scrambled hastily to their feet, offering wavering salutes. Perplexed, the Seminoles also saluted. Brent had to laugh.

"At ease, men, but let's call it a night, shall we? At dawn the braves come with us to the ship to carry the ammunition to the militia by the bay. And we head out for the Gulf Coast. Trouble is brewing at Fort Pickens, and we've been asked to reinforce the marines. It's going to be hard sailing, and hard fighting."

"Aye-aye, Captain," the men replied sheepishly and in unison. But other than to regretfully hand half-empty bottles to their Indian cronies, his men didn't move. They stared at him as if they expected something more. Blurry eyes held curiosity, a little triumph, and envy.

"Well?" he snapped.

Charlie McPherson stepped forward. "We were wondering about the Yankee spy, Captain. Bet she won't be pulling no more tricks on unsuspecting men, eh, sir?"

Brent's lashes lowered briefly over his eyes. The question could hardly be called out of line or insubordinate. Charlie, Lloyd, Chris Jenkins, and Andrew Scott had all been on deck that night in Charleston. Chris had suffered a concussion from a Yankee gun butt; Andrew, a broken arm. Charlie had seen spots for days, and Lloyd had barely survived a saber wound through the gut.

His men were a close-knit group. They were ardent Confederates, but most had been his crewmen before following him into the makeshift navy. They were a small but powerful dare-devil force, often managing to wreak a havoc with their smooth guerrilla tactics that an army of a thousand men could not.

He owed them an explanation, but he paused a moment, forced to make an instant decision when his soul was still clouded with a brooding uncertainty.

"Men, I think we misjudged the lady."

Brent allowed the words to settle, his eyes narrowing as he scanned their faces. The expressions were all alike—surly. Annoyance slipped into his features; he knew what they were thinking. They had all seen Kendall Moore. And they all bore that slightly pitying look that spoke more clearly than words. She was a stunning woman. Lovely enough to charm her way clear of anything, pretty enough to convince God that the devil was nothing more than a naughty boy.

Someone snickered in the silence of the firelit night. Brent stiffened, but before he could speak, Andrew Scott did so. The young gunner stepped forward.

"I'm ready to listen to your reasons for believing we've misjudged her, Captain." He turned to the men with a laugh. "When have any of you ever seen Captain McClain taken in by the wiles of a woman? The ladies have always flocked to him like flies, but he ain't been taken in by a single one yet!"

A brief silence followed. Surly faces became more curious—and more envious.

"What's the story, Captain?" McPherson demanded.

"It's a simple one, men. Our little lady is a true southerner, born on the outskirts of Charleston. She was forced into a marriage that took her north, and she was desperate to return home. She used us, yes. But not maliciously."

Silence reigned again, feet shuffled.

Robert Cutty spoke up next. He was a planter from south Georgia who hadn't signed up with Brent until after President Davis pressed the *Jenni-Lyn* into service. "So what's to be done with her, Captain?" Robert was a gentleman to the core; he considered the fair women of the South one of the Confederacy's most valuable assets. "Can't return no Charleston lady to a black-hearted Yank."

"But if we're judging wrong," Charlie said quietly, "we can't let no Yank spy loose in any southern city. No telling what a woman like that could do. Wrap a general around her little finger and wind up with him telling her the plans of an entire regiment."

Suddenly everyone was arguing. Brent lifted his hand. "Come to order!"

When silence followed instantly, he stared them down.

"We leave her here. If she is a spy, she can't cause any trouble. And if she isn't . . . well, at least she'll be spared the company of Union troops for the duration of the war. Red Fox has given me his word he will look out for her. And there is no finer guarantee than his word. Now disband, and get some sleep. And for Christ's sake, sleep up on the chickee platforms. I can't afford to lose any of you to a rattler."

Brent watched with his hands on his hips as his men dispersed, seeking the hospitality of the Indians. He heard the soft padding of footsteps on the earth behind him and quickly turned around.

Jimmy Emathla, his dark eyes slightly hazed, as he was unaccustomed to liquor, addressed him.

"What is it, Jimmy Emathla?" Brent asked, switching to the Muskogee tongue. The brave was acquiring a commendable knowledge of English, but out of respect Brent spoke in the Indian's native language.

"We take ten braves to carry the supplies. I lead. Ten men, and five dugouts. Will that do?"

Brent smiled at the solemn Indian, proud in his beads and loose-fitting, multicolored cotton shirt. "That will do fine, Jimmy Emathla. We thank you. The man you will meet at the bay is Harold Armstrong. He wears no uniform. I have told him to make himself visible just as dusk comes. Do not show yourselves until you see him, until you hear the call of a mockingbird. Then you will know that all is clear."

Jimmy Emathla nodded his understanding, then grinned. He raised a half bottle of the bourbon high in his arm and shook it, staring at the amber liquid, fascinated. "This is potent firewater, Night Hawk. We thank you for the gifts you have always brought in friendship to our chief."

Brent smiled, then hesitated, wondering at the shiver of apprehension that gripped him. He accepted the bourbon bottle when Jimmy Emathla pressed it into his hands, and took a long swig, wincing somewhat at the burning sensation that heated his throat and warmed his body abruptly. He gazed at Jimmy Emathla, surprised at the words that suddenly came from his own mouth.

"Jimmy, I am leaving the white woman with your chief. I want to ask a favor of you. Red Fox has many concerns. I would like you to watch out for her, too."

The Indian's teeth flashed a white streak in the shadowed night as he smiled broadly. "I will protect your woman, Night Hawk. No man will touch her."

Brent inclined his head in a silent thank-you.

The Indian suddenly laughed. "The night wanes, my white friend. You leave with the dawn. I will keep you no longer, so that you may enjoy the woman while you can."

Brent shrugged, and raised the bourbon bottle. "I think I'll enjoy a little firewater alone, first." He nodded again to Jimmy Emathla, then turned to gaze into the fire. He sensed the silent padding of the Seminole brave's feet; Indians seemed to respect a man's need for privacy. Alone at last to sort through the tumult of his thoughts, Brent sat before the fire and stared into its warming gold and orange flames.

He should be worrying about the war. Confederate troops were doing well in parts of the Deep South, but it was becoming more and more apparent that Florida was in trouble. The state had seized a number of forts at the onset of the war, but the Union still held the majority of key fortifications. And Union forces invaded the coastline at will. They hadn't yet attempted any successful inland invasions, but it seemed that, as the war progressed, more Florida troops were being called to fight farther to the north. And although the Union Army generals acted like frightened old women in their campaign strategies, the United States Navy had a surprisingly competent man in the main post—Secretary of the Navy Gideon Welles. He acted swiftly and intelligently. So far Brent was managing to run circles around the Union blockades. But how long would the situation last?

He gnawed his inner lip broodingly as he stared at the fire. Jacksonville was so vulnerable to Union attack—and so close to St. Augustine and his home. Florida had relied on the support of the Confederate government in Richmond; instead, the men of Florida were fighting for southern ideals in faraway places.

"What is it with us gallant Rebels?" he demanded softly to the flame. "We are gallant fools. We cannot even touch the ideal that we are fighting to preserve."

Kendall. Even Kendall. Her voice was reverent when she spoke of the South. She might have been a passionate member of the convention who had so heatedly demanded secession . . . or she might be a talented liar.

No. The story she had told him could not have been a lie. He had practically raped a virgin. No, he defended himself, he had not raped her. But he had been determined beyond all denial to have her, and he had seen it through. They both knew he would have brooked no protest.

And all that he had dreamed of touching and feeling had been real. The deep, volatile passion he had sensed was real. She had screamed at the pain of his invasion, but she had been unable to resist the tide of her own sensuality, a tide that eased away hurts, and swelled high to burst upon the shore in a glorious shower of glittering pleasure . . .

He swallowed another draft of bourbon, his muscles constricting as he thought of her. Jimmy Emathla was right. He would have to leave at dawn, and yet he was sitting alone in front of a fire with only a bottle of bourbon for company when she waited not a hundred feet away.

But how did she await him? With loathing and anger? With a longing to experience again the passion she had so recently learned to release? Or was she desperately conniving, wondering if she had tricked him with her bitter story? Maybe the marriage was a fraud, a ruse trumped up by the men who had attacked his ship . . .

130

He squinted until the fire became a shapeless yellow blur. The marriage was real. He had inquired in Charleston and had been told that Kendall Moore was the wife of John Moore, United States Navy.

Brent looked at his bourbon bottle ruefully, then swallowed the remaining contents. He stood and dashed the empty bottle into the fire. Silently he trod across the camp and climbed the ladder to the cabin. His body was a mass of heat and tense knots. However it was that she awaited him, he couldn't stay away from her.

The cabin, with only its two small windows, was dark. He stood just within the doorway and allowed his eyes to adjust. There was no movement in the cabin. He at last saw that she lay in the far corner, swathed in her blanket.

Brent shed his boots and quietly padded across the room. He knelt down beside her warily, wondering if she planned a trick, feigned sleep to take him unaware. But when he gently touched her shoulder, she rolled slightly toward him, and a shuddering sigh escaped her. The black fans of her lashes were closed in shadow over her cheeks. She had fallen into an exhausted sleep. The shuddering little sigh had been the aftermath of a storm of sobs.

Brent stared thoughtfully at her face in repose. The fine, delicate beauty of her features was clear even in the pale moonlight, compelling, touching his soul. The purity of her flawless skin seemed as smooth and enticing as alabaster. He wanted to entangle his hands in the wild spray of glossy gold hair that curled and fanned about her in disarray.

But he did not. He continued to stare at her, bathed as she was in the gentle moonlight. The blanket had slipped when she rolled toward him, and her shoulders and the tempting mounds of her breasts were exposed to his scrutiny. Again he felt the tense constriction of his muscles. The hollows of her slender shoulders, the soft rise of firm young breast,

131

were shattering his control. Yet he was determined to be ruled by his head, not his loins.

War raged within him.

And as he stared at her in the moonlight, he at last realized with surprise that she had not put her dress on. She had not clothed herself in armament against him. Of course, she clutched the blanket like a shield. But in her sleep her grip was lax. Her tense fingers had uncurled. The blanket had slipped. Only her lovely features remained tense. Not even sleep could ease the pain and misery etched into her brow, or dry the tears on her cheeks. How old was she? Brent wondered. Eighteen? Twenty? Twenty-two at most. So very young to appear so anguished.

Brent stood and stripped off his clothes, folding them neatly and meticulously. Desire coursed through him, but he dampened the heat that came unbidden.

It was not determination to remain aloof that made him lie quietly beside her, gently pulling her form to his, not waking her. It was a startling feeling of tenderness.

He lay on his side, his head on an outstretched arm. The other he laced around her, his hand resting lightly on the flatness of her belly. The long, sleek line of her back touched his chest; her flanks were nestled against his hips and thighs. The position elicited a torturous ache deep within him, but he ignored it.

He liked being where he was. He liked the smooth softness of her flesh against his, warm and pliant. He liked the round curve of her buttocks nestled to the hardness of his hip. The instinctive swell of his sex held no danger for her now. It, too, seemed to accept the promise of the feminine comfort unknowingly given.

It had been a long time since he had slept with a woman. A long time since he had rested with soft tendrils of long hair catching and curling about him, with a gentle fragrance wrapping him in lulling comfort.

And he had never slept with a woman who had affected him as this one did. Wracked his body and soul with anger . . . and yearning. Who could fray his temper until it snapped, and stir his passions until he lost all thought and reason . . .

Brent closed his eyes and shifted slightly. She shifted instinctively with him, seeming to fit her body comfortably to his. Nestling more tightly to the natural male hold.

He lightly raised his hand to the deep valley between her breasts. His fingers felt the soft beat of her heart and an aching shudder ran through him. He wanted her; he would have her.

But he could wait. Ease the fever of body and mind with sleep. Hold her with temperance, and hope that the fresh air of night would also bring temperance to his mind and soul and help him discover if his beautiful hostage was part angel as well as vixen . . . or the most treacherous weapon the Union had ever cast down upon the South.

Six

She started to stir because she was cold. Little shivers plagued her body, drawing it from a cocoon of comfortable warmth.

But she was still half asleep when a new sensation aroused her. A soft, stirring touch on her back, gliding lazily over her shoulders, down her spine, circling low and unhurriedly in the hollows just above the roundness of her derriere. Her shivers became little tremors. The gentle touch seemed to create little laps of fire that became an evocative trail of heat against the cold.

The trail rose along her spine again, teased at the nape of her neck. Again moved downward . . . grazing her flesh and igniting flames deep within her that coiled into a low center, then fanned and lapped along her spine once more.

She arched and moaned with the pleasant sensation, yet still basked in the luxury of a twilight sleep.

A hoarse, demanding whisper brushed warmth against her ear. "Wake up, Kendall. It's almost dawn. And I will have you again before I leave . . ."

Instantly brought to full awareness by the sound of his voice, Kendall stiffened and her eyes flew open. She had been cold because the blanket had been drawn from her. And she had been filled with the beginnings of warmth because of the man behind her.

The cabin was no longer illuminated by the silver of the moon; a hazy orange and crimson glow struggled for supremacy over the darkness. As his hand touched her shoulder and firmly drew her to her back, she could clearly see the face of the man, and the smolder in the deep gray eyes that mocked her rigid defiance. His desire was naked and unmasked; as was the determined demand about him that brooked no protest. Kendall closed her eyes against him and swallowed, aware that protest would be ridiculous anyway. She did want him. She had been seduced from sleep, and it was too late to attempt to hide the quivering of her body, the aching response she had already given. How she would have loved to deny him! To lie passive beneath his touch, scornful no matter what he did . . .

But even the rough demand of him excited her. Made her crave again that indescribable sensation of quicksilver longing, reaching, spinning . . .

He was leaving. He had just said that he had awakened her because he was leaving. And he hadn't told her yet what was going to happen to her. She had to remember that he had taken her only out of a desire for vengeance.

She spoke without opening her eyes. "Revenge again, Captain?"

He was silent so long that she opened her eyes to find his in a curious, brooding study of her. But when she looked at him, he smiled and dipped his head low over hers, whispering just above her lips. "No. Not revenge. Desire."

His lips caught hers firmly, persuasively. It was as if he sampled and tested, explored, played teasingly. His tongue rimmed her lips, his teeth caught and nibbled lightly. His mouth widened on hers, forcing admission, and yet when she gave way to the swift ravage of his tongue, he withdrew it and left her searching . . . returning the play, seeking to

135

discover the intimacy of his mouth as he had hers. She was lost to the discovery, aware of his warmth, content and yet hungry for his naked touch, enjoying the strength of his arms about her, the feel of his chest crushed to her breasts.

He drew away from her, and she met his eyes, her own wide with an unhidden query. He shifted and touched her lip with the tip of his finger. "Last night was good, but for you it combined pleasure and pain. This morning will be for the pleasure."

Kendall couldn't draw her eyes from his. The true facts of her situation kept fading from her mind. But those facts were painful, and she vaguely knew that she should fight him still.

Her fight was a soft query. "Why?"

He didn't reply. He brought a knuckle to her cheek and smoothed away a straying lock of hair. His weight settled over hers, yet he did not rush. He made the contact slow, almost lazy. There was time . . . time to savor each subtle touch. Kendall felt him with her whole body, his hair-roughened legs tangled with the softness of hers, his dark, muscled arms about her, strong but giving. His face with its rough, tawny shadow brushed her flesh as his lips sought her forehead, her cheeks, the length of her throat, her breasts.

And she keenly felt his fully aroused desire. A branding pulse against her thighs, threatening, teasing, touching her like a blade of mercury, and bringing new life to the fire that burned low within her. Brief experience had taught her anticipation. And anticipation made her tremble for him. There could be no denial. She wanted him now, wanted him to fill her with the volatile, demanding life that spilt and claimed her and made her totally whole.

She gasped softly as he caught her breast in his mouth and held it, teasing the taut nipple with his tongue. Achingly, slowly. She arched convulsively and dug her fingers into his hair.

He was in no hurry . . . The subtle torture continued, yet the assault on her senses increased. He moved a hand freely along her side, caressing her hips, enjoying the length of her thigh. She was barely aware when he shifted his weight, allowing his masterful touch a greater range. His lips returned to hers, and his palm, rough and callused but light and thrilling, coursed over her belly, circling lower, grazing, drawing patterns down her inner thigh. Kendall shuddered with the sweet impact of soaring sensation. She twisted against him, trying to elude the hand and touch that drained her of all thought, left her a writhing, moaning creature entirely submissive to his will.

She tried to hide her feelings, burying her head against his chest. He would not allow her that concession. He caught her chin between his thumb and forefinger and found her eyes. Then he released her and placed his hand between her breasts. Her heart was thundering. They could both feel it. Her breathing was quick and ragged.

She was trembling from head to toe, wanting him, attuned to him.

"You asked me why," he told her softly. "This . . . this"— his hand firmly molded her shoulder and stroked quickly to her hips and thighs—"is why."

She wanted to speak. Sound refused to form.

He wrapped his arms around her, his eyes closing. "Hold me, Kendall. Touch me. Love me."

Obediently she wrapped her arms around him. Again he carefully balanced himself over her. He shifted, wedged his powerful legs between hers and found no resistance. Her eyes were wide upon his, denying nothing. He watched her as he fluidly brought himself within her, and the tiny sound that escaped her moist and parted lips doubled the erotic pleasure of feminine embrace. Fever raced out of control; restrained passion came unleashed, and he moved inside her with driven need raging a wild, consuming tempo. Again Kendall gasped, her teeth nipped at the muscle of his shoulder, and her fingers moved erratically down his back, clutching, releasing, digging, caressing.

"Hold me," he whispered, "with all of you."

Blindly she obeyed, embracing him with the length of her legs, crying out softly again as the motion brought him even deeper, made him more a part of her. She heard his whisper again, telling her soft things about the way she aroused him. About how very good she made him feel . . .

His face rose above hers, tense with the strain of reaching desire.

"Talk to me, Kendall; tell me what you feel."

She closed her eyes, aware that she arched and writhed to meet each of his powerful thrusts, thrilling again and again as the pleasure soared to unbearable heights. But she couldn't find words. Even in the most intimate lock of their abandoned and beautiful coupling, she still could not speak. Color caressed her cheeks, and she wanted only to hide as she shamelessly, ravenously accepted him.

"Kendall . . ."

"I . . . I can't . . ."

Husky laughter touched the air, a male sound of delighted triumph. "You will, darlin', in time you will."

The laughter and his words abruptly ended as she groaned, and clutched him fervently. She did talk, then. She cried out his name as the sweetness of pure pleasure riddled through her body, grasping her slender form in shudder after delicious shudder.

"Oh, Brent . . . Brent . . ."

He thrust within her once again, hard and rigid; his body stiffened and shuddered and relaxed, and an intoxicating wonder filled her along with the flood of his release, as sweet as the pinnacle of pleasure. There was an awesome power in the loving he had taught her; she seemed to surrender to his

138

will, and yet she triumphed and relished the awareness that she, too, elicited a surrender from him.

His weight shifted, but he did not pull away from her as he had before. His knee remained crooked over her legs; he leaned on one elbow, but a possessive hand rested on her waist. Kendall gazed at him as she struggled to control her breathing, praying that the drugging and heady pleasure and satiation would remain with her. But as sensation ebbed, she was awkwardly aware of circumstances once again. He didn't speak, but just gazed at her, a slight grin tugging at the corner of his lip, his eyes still a smolder of gray.

He moved his hand, idly running his knuckles over her ribs, smoothing a tangle of hair from her shoulder, fitting his long fingers securely over her waist once again.

"And I have to go off to war," he murmured, shaking his head with grave regret, as if it were an astonishing injustice.

Kendall stiffened and lowered her lashes swiftly, then raised her eyes with a defiance that was a desperate bid to hide the fear within her heart.

"At least you know where you're going, Captain McClain."

He arched a single brow, and the rakish line of his grin deepened. "Quite formal, suddenly, aren't we, Mrs. Moore? Although I must admit, since you only deem it proper to use my given name upon occasion, you do choose the right moment. Whispering 'Captain McClain' would do little to increase the delightful rise of passion."

Kendall's eyes flashed dangerously; he saw the tightening of her lips and the clench of her jaw and instinctively shot out his hand to grip her wrist before her palm could connect with his cheek. Fuming fury remained in her eyes even as she knew she was trapped, and he laughed with wry amusement as he pinioned her wrists on either side of her head and bent to brush a brief kiss against her tightly clamped mouth.

"You tell me, Kendall, what should I do with you?"

"You should take me with you," she snapped. "Surely you'll be passing an open Confederate port."

"Surely I will," he agreed pleasantly, smiling at her intermittent attempts to release herself from his hold.

"Then—"

"I can't take you with me, Kendall. I'm headed up the Gulf Coast where they're expecting heavy naval action. It wouldn't be safe."

"But you could drop me somewhere first. Tampa! And then I could arrange transport to Jacksonville or Fernandina—"

The grin of amusement at last left his features, and he spoke with harsh bitterness. "No coastal cities are safe. Jacksonville least of all."

He was surprised to see the color fade entirely from her cheeks, leaving them suddenly ashen. "You . . . you won't send me back to Fort Taylor, will you?"

Brent frowned. "No."

"Oh."

It was emitted as a sigh of relief, but she quickly lowered her lashes away from him. Still he sensed her shudder, and his heartbeat quickened. She did despise the Yankee she was married to, and more than that, she staunchly hid a terror of him.

"Rest easy, Kendall. I would not send you back."

She bit her lower lip, her lashes still downcast, then raised them to stare at him with indigo eyes once more. "Then . . . then, what will you do?"

He chuckled softly, amazed at her perplexity. "You can stay right here," he told her, his grin returning. "Red Fox offered to keep you for me."

"Keep me . . . for you! I'm not a damned ship, Brent McClain! And I don't want to stay here! I implore you as a gentleman—"

140

"Kendall, I distinctly remember telling you the night we met in Charleston that you shouldn't count on my being a gentleman."

Again he saw the flash of anger in her eyes, the tightening of her jaw and stubborn pursing of her lips. Then her lashes fluttered, and she stared at him with sweet innocence. "Captain . . . Brent, don't you understand? There's a war going on! I want to be where I know what's happening—"

"Kendall—" he tried to interrupt.

The sweetness in her voice grew thin as she continued despite his interruption. "I do *not* want to languish in some godforsaken swamp with a bunch of red men and alligators!"

Brent at last eased his hold on her and sat up, staring at the window where the telltale signs of morning were becoming brighter. "Kendall, darlin'," he said tightly, his low drawl heavy with sarcasm, "neither the southern belle act nor an all-out temper tantrum is going to work. You're staying here."

She was silent so long that he at last turned back to look at her. She had pushed herself up to a seated position, shielding her nudity with her arms hugged tightly about her knees. Clouded eyes as deeply blue as a late night sky were upon him; she again chewed furiously on her lip.

"For how long?" she asked in a tense whisper.

His eyes scanned her. Damn her! She could come from a bout of the wildest passion, and just moments later appear like the most provocative of innocents, her wide eyes and her mass of tangled hair enhancing her beauty, which seemed eternally pure . . .

He sighed, relenting. "Until I come back. Until I figure out where to take you, where I'm certain there won't be fighting any time soon."

A slight tremor shook her. Was it relief? He didn't know. She tossed her hair back over her shoulder and stared at him defiantly once more. "If I stay, Captain McClain, I want it

141

understood that I don't grind any more of that damned *koonti* root. And I don't do laundry other than my own!"

Brent chuckled softly, swept her into his arms, and pushed her back down on the floor, the temptation to do so too strong to resist.

"Brent," she protested breathlessly, delicate fingers clasping his shoulders.

But he stared down at her relentlessly. "Listen to me, Kendall. It's important. I want your word that you won't give the Indians any trouble. The swamp can be a haven; it can also be a dangerous hell. And with Yankees cruising the coast all the time, there's even more danger. As a Confederate who has become your lover, I'm not about to return you to a husband you've taken drastic measures to escape. But I guarantee that if you run into any Yanks, they'll return you to John Moore so fast your head will spin. That's nothing against the Federals; it would merely be the honorable thing for them to do."

For the first time he saw tears spring to her eyes; she quickly blinked them away. He wondered with a bitter pain just what kind of a life she had led with John Moore.

"I want your word, Kendall," he said tensely.

She lowered her lashes again. "I won't try to run away from the Indians. I like Red Fox. And Apolka. I . . ." Pain twisted her voice as she paused and then spoke tonelessly once again. "I just wish I could go home. But then, I guess I don't really even have a home anymore. I'd be running in Charleston, too."

It was not a plea for pity; it was a statement of fact. And in that moment, Brent forgave her everything. He tenderly held her cheeks between his palms and gazed deeply into her eyes. "Kendall, the war can't last forever."

She laughed bitterly. "I know. I've heard it from both sides. 'We're gonna whomp the bejesus outa those damn Yanks in a month.' 'Those Johnny Rebs'll hightail it back home in no time.' "

"All right, Kendall. It isn't going to end soon. But it will end. And when it's possible, I'll get you to a southern port. In the meantime, admit that this life isn't so bad. Red Fox is hardly a savage."

"No, but the Night Hawk . . ." she muttered sarcastically.

"Am I?" he queried politely, ignoring the jeer. "So savage?"

"Entirely."

He looked out at the growing crimson morning light seeping through the window. Then he looked back at her. "I'm glad you recognize the nature of the beast, darlin', 'cause I'm getting those savage urges again, and it is going to be a long and dreary war."

She had no thought at all of not wanting him. With a soft sigh she embraced him, welcoming his touch, his quickly aroused desire. Already she was learning him, and the more she learned, the more heady became the intoxication of knowing . . . of anticipating.

And morning was here. Her life, her being, had changed drastically in one night because of this man who had at last become her lover. She had discovered the full and beautiful depths of passion between a man and a woman, and in his arms, she could forget. Forget the tragic winds of the war that ravaged the country. Forget the embittered turmoil that was the reality of her life.

She did not know what he felt for her. She didn't fully comprehend her feelings for him. She only knew that she wanted to cherish him, meet his tempest with a tempest of her own, stamp the memory of him on her body and soul. She wanted to hold fast to her dreams of love and honor in the long nights to come . . .

He held her for a long while, and at last rose. Kendall turned her face into the blanket, not wanting to watch him dress and leave. She couldn't seem to stir herself. She was drained and exhausted, both physically and mentally. So much within her had been stripped bare and laid open. He had played havoc with her emotions, determinedly raped her soul, but then given her a lifeline, which she still grasped hesitantly, but with desperate hope. She was content with the fury of his lovemaking, pleased that he had seemed to need a memory, too, yet incredibly tired from the experience.

It was agony to know that he was leaving. "Night Hawk," she murmured, talking to keep the tears of despair from falling. "Red Fox. And then Apolka. Why Red Fox and Night Hawk? Those are English names."

She sensed his shrug, but didn't dare look his way as he pulled on his shirt and tucked it into his breeches.

"Civilization. The white man, darlin'," he said. "During the Indian wars the whites started giving the red men surnames. And to negotiate with the whites a number of the Seminoles and Mikasukis adopted their own surnames, often from the animals of the forest. Eagle, Possum, Gopher, Gater, and Fox. Now, like the whites, the Indians are beginning to take their fathers' surnames, but it's really a matriarchal society. Red Fox was the son of a squaw named Little Fox. He has a Seminole name; all Seminoles and Mikasukis have a 'real' name, given them at the Green Corn Dance. Red Fox is also Asiyaholo, for his father, Osceola. The whites couldn't pronounce the name correctly."

Kendall heard the thump of his boots on the floor. She felt him approach her and knew that he towered over her. "Then there is the word 'Seminole' itself. The settlers claimed that it meant 'runaway,' because the Indians ran away to the south to escape tribal wars and the whites. But that isn't what it means at all. 'Running free' is the real meaning of the word—and Red Fox runs free. No matter how they have beaten and butchered his people, he runs free . . ." His voice trailed away, and suddenly he knelt beside her, turning her to face him as he held her in a rough grip and spoke tensely, silencing the cry of protest that rose to her lips with the depths of his emotion. "Running free, Kendall. It's all we're really trying to do. Red Fox, you . . . me. Trust in him, Kendall. But if anything ever happens to Red Fox, there is a man at the bay who will help you if you give him my name. He is Harold Armstrong. You can find him at the mouth of the Miami river on the first night of the full moon. The cry of a mockingbird is a signal that all is clear. Understand?"

Kendall stared into his eyes, strenuously fighting tears, and nodded. Bleakly she wondered how he had come to mean so very much to her so quickly. A night . . . only one night had been theirs. And that night had begun with bitter hostility.

"I understand," she at last whispered.

She thought he would kiss her again. A heated fusion before the final parting. But he released her abruptly, stood, and strode to the door. He paused, not daring to turn. His stomach was in knots, a pain seared his chest. He was fighting a war, yet leaving this woman he had so recently wanted to strangle was the hardest thing he had ever had to do. If he saw her again—the blanket draped about her but not hiding the magnolia rise of her breast, her golden hair a wild, tangled cascade, her eyes liquid pools of beguiling indigo, bluer than blue . . .

"I'll see what I can do about the *koonti* grinding," he said harshly.

"Do that," she whispered, her voice almost catching in a sob. She bit her lip and swallowed and managed to speak in a smooth, sarcastic drawl to combat the overwhelming emotion threatening to choke her. "And please, Captain McClain, don't get yourself killed. The swamp can be hospitable, but I'd rather not stay here too long . . ."

Her voice trailed away. He remained still a moment longer;

she stared at his broad back in the gray uniform frock coat and at his tawny head.

Then the door opened, and closed behind him. But the bolt did not slide into place. She heard the fall of his quick steps on the rungs of the ladder, and the soft thud as he leapt the final feet to the ground. The sound of men's voices came to her ears. Orders were snapped out in English and Muskogee. And then she heard a loud chorus of "Dixie"—so incongruous in the primitive Glades. But the sound faded like the fall of the wind, disappearing into the swamp.

She didn't cry. She stared blankly up at the thatched ceiling of her cabin. And in time the sounds of nature overrode the echoes of man. As the sun at last streaked brilliantly through the small windows, she became aware of a symphony of crickets, the screech of a crane, the piglike grunts of a distant 'gator . . .

But it was the chorus of "Dixie" that stayed in her mind. Haunting her. And the broad, gray-clad back of a gray-eyed man. At last she turned into her blanket and again felt her tears take control. She sobbed herself into exhaustion, and then into the oblivion of sleep.

Kendall awoke with a start. She stared about her, trying to decide what had roused her. The cabin was silent and empty.

She frowned, then realized consciously the difference she had sensed. It was not dark, but neither was it brilliantly light. The sun had already fallen low in the west, and dusk was almost upon the camp. She had slept for hours. And the Indians had not disturbed her.

Kendall stood and hugged her arms about herself with a little shiver, closing her eyes. Brent McClain was hours gone, miles away, but she couldn't allow herself to think about the loneliness that would now be hers. How bereft the shining interlude of tempest and splendor would leave her. She had more now than she had had in years. She had hope. She was running free . . .

Kendall slowly smiled. Spinning around, she hurriedly dressed, smoothed out her hair, and approached the door of the cabin. It swung open easily, and she stepped out on the platform and climbed down the ladder.

Life was going on as usual in the encampment. Barefoot children raced about. Cooking fires were flaring. The soft drone of women's voices sounded as they chatted at their domestic tasks, sewing pieces of bright-colored fabric, stringing beads, beginning their preparations for the warriors' meals.

"You have decided to join us, Kendall Moore."

Kendall glanced toward the trail that led through the hammock to the brackish river and mangrove swamps. Red Fox was coming toward her, a young white-tailed deer lolling over his shoulders, an arrow cleanly piercing its neck. The chief had been hunting. He was dressed in the full plumage of a chief; a feathered band adorned his rich black hair; his shirt was ornamented with large silver crescents. He had eschewed the white man's trousers and the brief loincloth he had worn on the ship, and instead he wore a short leather-fringed skirt. Leggings of buckskin protected his calves, and a shot pouch and powder horn hung from straps about his neck, as did his bow and arrows.

"I was sleeping," she murmured, annoyed at the rush of embarrassment that brought a flush to her cheeks. The dark glitter in Red Fox's eyes assured her he understood her need for sleep. He chuckled softly, but didn't taunt her. Instead he touched her elbow, drawing her to walk with him toward his chickee.

"We did not always live in such dwellings, Kendall Moore," he said conversationally. "In the north our villages were made up of fine log cabins, much like that which houses you. But so many times we were burned out. And so many times pushed south. And here, sometimes, the mighty winds that blow and the rains that fall can destroy everything. We have learned to spring back like the roots of the mangrove. We cannot be destroyed, because too quickly we can rebuild." He stopped speaking and walking abruptly, turning to her with an amused grin. "I hear that you no longer wish to grind the *koonti* root."

Again Kendall flushed, aware that her words of anger to Brent must make her seem like an Indian's perfect picture of a lazy and pampered white plantation woman. Not that even the wives of the wealthiest planters led easy lives; usually the larger the plantation, the more work there was for the woman of the house, no matter how many slaves the master owned. "I am not afraid of hard work, Red Fox. I do not mind doing my share, since I am to stay."

Red Fox smiled secretively and started walking again. "Then you have decided, of your free will, to stay with us."

"Yes," Kendall said softly, panting lightly as she strove to keep up with the Indian's long-legged gait.

He paused again, so suddenly that she crashed into his broad back. He was still smiling as he faced her.

"I do not wish you to grind *koonti* root. I wish you to teach my children to speak English."

Kendall stared at him, stunned. "But you speak English fluently yourself, Red Fox."

He waved his broad hands at her impatiently. "I am a man with little time. And I would like Apolka to learn the white man's tongue, also. A man does not always keep his temper with his wife."

Kendall smiled. There were not so many differences between red and white men after all.

"But, Red Fox, I don't speak your language!"

"You will learn a little at a time, as will the children and

Apolka. And already you do speak some Muskogee, Kendall Moore—*Tallahassee.*"

Kendall raised a brow and laughed. "I know only that it is the state capital."

"It means old town," he told her briefly, lowering the deer to the ground before his home and slipping an arm around her as he led her to the chickee. He laughed and pointed toward his cabin, saying with a twinkle in his dark eyes, *"Chuluota*—fox den!"

He spanned his hands abruptly around her waist and hoisted her effortlessly on the platform of the chickee. "And I, Kendall Moore, am going to teach you the swamp. You will learn where the rivers lead when it appears that all is endless saw grass and trees. You will know the color of the snakes that can kill and be aware of the slightest twitch of the rattler's tail. You will know how to hear footsteps in your sleep, and foretell on what days the sky will bring rain by nightfall."

Kendall stared curiously at Red Fox's strong features, and realized he was offering her a friendship few whites would ever receive. A friendship that Brent had long ago been granted and that he cherished and nurtured despite the opinions of his own society. She twisted about to see that Apolka was patiently awaiting her husband and his guest, her pretty mouth formed into a smile, her wide-eyed little boys hanging about her legs on either side, waiting to greet their father and the white woman they had long ago accepted.

Kendall's laughter suddenly rang out like a light melody on the air. She smiled at Apolka, and returned her gaze to Red Fox.

"I will try to please you, Red Fox. I will try very hard—to teach and to learn."

Red Fox nodded, apparently satisfied. He tossed his sheathed hunting knife to Apolka, who caught it smoothly, and inclined his head toward the deer. Again he spoke to Kendall.

"You may start your lessons now, Kendall Moore. Teach, while Apolka prepares our food. In the mornings you will come with me to learn." He paused, dark eyes alight with laughter once more. "You will not need so much rest in the days to come. The Night Hawk will not return for some time. A warrior's woman cannot claim the right to such idleness unless she has used her night hours in offering him comfort and pleasure."

Kendall felt her face grow red instantly; she wasn't sure if she wanted to strike the Indian or laugh. The latter seemed more practical, as Red Fox had already turned away.

She swung around to stand in the chickee, smiling as Apolka urged her children toward Kendall. Kendall stooped to the little boys and hugged them against her, delighting in the warm hugs they returned.

Savages, she thought remorsefully. Just a short time ago she had been ignorantly certain that all Indians were savages. And now she was ridiculously comforted because two little brown-skinned urchins were affectionately cuddling up to her.

She sighed, holding them tight and watching as Apolka hopped down from the chickee to approach the deer. Night was coming to the Glades. The scene was peaceful, the orange sky enwrapping the encampment and the cypress hammock beyond.

It wasn't Charleston. And it wasn't Richmond, Atlanta, or Mobile or New Orleans . . . but it was better than the Union barracks. Ummm, a far better place for a southerner to sit out the war. Maybe things would improve sooner than Brent seemed to think. The South had to win the war. Even the sketchy information Kendall had received made it clear that the Confederacy had superior generals, superior military strategy.

The children hugged her more tightly, demanding her attention. They were so trusting. Truly, it wasn't a bad place to be at all.

A little shiver pierced her heart.

It was, for her, the best place in the world to be. The place to which the Night Hawk would one day return for her . . .

Seven

March 13, 1862

From the bow of the *Jenni-Lyn,* Brent McClain stared southward, searching through the sheltering pines that lined the north Florida river inlet. A tense frown lined his features with strain; his stance was rigid against the sick dread that knifed at his guts.

Half of Jacksonville appeared to be burning.

The war was not going well for the Florida Confederates.

The U.S.S. *Hatteras,* out of Key West, had landed at Cedar Key on January 6, and her sailors and marines had destroyed the railroad wharf and depot, boxcars of military supplies, and the telegraph office. Schooners, sloops, and a ferryboat had been captured. Only twenty-three Confederates had been there to guard the railway terminus; two companies of troops had just been sent north to meet an anticipated attack on Fernandina.

But the troops hadn't been enough. Federals had invaded St. Augustine and Fernandina—and now Jacksonville.

Smoke billowed over the trees, clouding the blue skies, obliterating the brilliance of the sun. Brent closed his eyes and ground his teeth tensely. It was the waiting that was driving him crazy. The total helplessness. He wanted to climb madly through the trees, or strip off his clothing and fling himself into the water and swim—anything to reach the city, to move inland, to see South Seas . . .

He was a captain, he kept telling himself. He couldn't do things rashly; he couldn't risk his ship or his crew or even his own life needlessly. He had to wait until the dinghy returned with information.

"Ahoy, Captain!"

Brent spun about fiercely as Charlie McPherson climbed the rope ladder to the *Jenni-Lyn*'s bow.

"Here, Charlie, quick. Tell me what's happened."

Charlie looked at the tension in Brent's hard features, and lowered his eyes, shaking his head sadly. It was true hell to have to tell one's granite-faced captain that his own hometown had been ransacked beyond recognition.

"Charlie!" Brent snapped.

"The Feds have occupied St. Augustine as well as Jacksonville, Captain. The Fourth New Hampshire are holding it now. The Confederate army had to abandon the city. Most of the damage was done by our own men, and the fires are mostly from the sawmills. Our troops burned them up to keep them from the Feds. And they burned millions of feet of lumber, an iron foundry, and an ironworks. They've scuttled a few ships, too, Captain, so we'll have to watch the river passages."

Brent was silent. Deathly silent. Both St. Augustine and Jacksonville were dangerously close to South Seas. Charlie felt a chill grip his heart as he stared at the rage and sorrow in his captain's eyes.

Charlie cleared his throat and started speaking again. "It's really not as bad as it looks, sir. From what we could see, the homes are still standing. Oh, the Yanks are tearing up a little, but from what Chris and I could gather, they're going easy. A hell of a lot easier than they'll go if'n they ever reach

153

Charleston or Richmond. They think there's a number of Union sympathizers in the city, so they're taking care."

Brent suddenly sprang into action, his mouth a grim line of determination as he turned to stride toward his cabin. The men on deck looked awkwardly at one another as they nervously awaited his reappearance.

It was quick in coming. He had changed from his gold-decorated gray uniform into fawn breeches, white shirt, and blue frock coat. He had stripped off all insignias of his rank in the Confederate Navy. He was tucking his pistol into the waistband of his pants as he strode back to the bow; his hunting knife was strapped high over his calf. His eyes still looked like quick death as they scanned his men.

"I'm going in," he said tersely. "I'd like three of you to come with me, and I'm asking for volunteers. We may need to do some fast talking, and we may wind up shot or spending the remainder of the war in a prison camp. Shot most likely. Out of uniform, we can be taken as spies, and the Feds and Rebs both like to shoot spies and ask questions later."

Andrew Scott, who had accompanied Charlie on the spying mission, stepped forward. "I'm more'n willing to go with you, Captain, and I'm volunteering for duty. But have you thought about this, sir? Both cities are occupied, and the ranking Confederate officer near St. Augustine ordered us back west if we were too late to help out here—"

"To hell with the ranking Confederate Officer," Brent said softly. "On this ship, I am the ranking Confederate Navy officer, and we'll get back to the west coast soon enough!"

Andrew hesitated a moment, a little worried by the reckless fever in his captain's eyes. But as always, Brent McClain appeared calm. Quietly, relentlessly determined, but calm. He would never lead them without a cunning strategy in mind. And weren't they famous because of him? Not only in the South? Just last January, after they had left the abortive Confederate attack on Fort Pickens and sailed into New Orleans, they had been proudly given a New York paper. In it the cartoonist had done an excellent lampoon depicting the Night Raiders of Brent McClain as he slipped through a squadron of Federal ships—right beneath their bows.

McClain was daring, all right. The Feds didn't know yet just how clever.

"I'm your man, Captain," Andrew said.

Half the crew stepped forward instantly. Brent eyed them all with a taut grin and careful assessment. "Chris, Andrew, and—"

Charlie appeared dead square in front of him. "You ain't going in without me, Brent McClain."

Brent pursed his lips against laughter. Charlie was shaking, but he was determined. "All right, Charlie, you're coming. Listen up, the rest of you, because we may have to skedaddle out of here fast. Have the *Jenni-Lyn* at the ready. Keep her out of sight. We can head upriver should we have to, but I'd rather take to the open sea. Our best offense with her has always been defense. We can outrun the Feds. Chris, Andrew, Charlie—get out of your sailors' garb. We've just become merchants—Union sympathizers—fleeing south since we've heard that the Feds have hit the coast."

Despite his frantic worry, Brent waited until nightfall to row the dinghy north of the Jacksonville docks with his three-man crew. The sight of the Union warships in Jacksonville's harbor brought further gut pain wrenching through him. Just five months ago he had brought the *Jenni-Lyn* in to home port for minor repairs. She had been berthed where a Union gunboat now lay at anchor, Stars and Stripes still flying in the night. His heartbeat quickened. Did soldiers now tramp the pine-paneled halls of South Seas? His father and older brother were nowhere near, he knew. Justin and Stirling McClain had joined up with the First Florida Cavalry Regiment; two months ago their troop had been sent north to fight with the Army of Northern Virginia. But his sister Jennifer would be there, and Stirling's wife Patricia and his five-year-old nephew Patrick.

For a brief moment Brent closed his eyes. He was grateful for once that his mother had died in 1858. South Seas had been like another child to her; she had planned each room and decorated every nook and cranny. She had lavished her life and love on two things only, her family, and her home . . . South Seas.

It was possible, just possible, that the Yanks had spared the plantations that lay between St. Augustine and Jacksonville. He could see the haze of lights already as the dinghy lapped quietly through the water. It appeared that the residential and business buildings along the wharf had remained unmolested.

But he had a reputation as a formidable enemy of the North. The McClains were well known. Fine planters, fine sailors, and fine Confederate officers. Would the Yanks leave standing a home that belonged to two Confederate cavalry officers and a notorious naval captain?

"Pull into the little cove up ahead," he ordered quietly, inclining his head to Charlie, who pulled on the oars. "We'll have to go on foot the rest of the way. Split up and convene in town."

They pulled the dinghy high up on a sand spit and covered it with branches. A half-mile separated the beach from the harbor, but as they began to move, Brent motioned for them to crouch down. They could see the Union sentries, dark shadows guarding the docks and wharves. As Brent watched tensely, two soldiers met and paused, lighting up pipes. They appeared relaxed. Why not? he wondered bitterly. The Confederate defenses had left them the city.

"They're not expecting any action," Brent murmured absently to Charlie, who lay flat on the sandy ground beside him. "That's to our advantage." To their advantage for what? He wasn't planning any great military action. All he wanted to do was get hold of a horse and get out to the countryside and reach South Seas. He'd had no right to drag his men into this.

"How about Lil's?" Charlie queried.

Brent knit his brow thoughtfully. Lil ran a tavern on Main Street that was popular with sailors. It was quite possible that Union officers might be imbibing after their victory, and that might make the plan all the better.

"In by the kitchen," he hissed. "Follow the wharf shacks and outbuildings, and move quickly. One by one. Be nimble with your tongues if you're caught."

"Who first?" Andrew queried.

"Me," Brent said. "If I don't make it to that warehouse, you hightail it back to the ship. Chris next, then Andrew, then Charlie."

Brent tensed his body to the ready. He waited until the sentries split and began to divide and walk toward the far sides of the docks. Then he sprang, a darting shadow in the night.

He was breathless when he reached the warehouse and flattened himself against it. He waited tensely a moment, closing his eyes to still the beating of his heart. His breathing at last slowed, and he stared back across the field and far beach, raising a hand, and bringing it down. Instantly a second shadow darted into the darkness. Then a third, and a fourth. At last they all stood pressed against the warehouse, holding to it as if it were a lifeline.

In silence Brent indicated the next building. One by one they moved again, always keeping a wary eye on the sentries.

There were more soldiers milling about the streets, making the rebels' next movements more dangerous. But there were also more obstacles to shield them. Wagons. Supply depots. Trees. Clumps of bushes.

Miraculously, they scurried about undetected, and at last hurdled the picket fence surrounding Lil's tavern.

The sound of revelry within was loud and boisterous. It masked the sounds they made as they vaulted to the rear and again hit the dirt. Brent bolted to the back door and looked into the kitchen.

The large room with its huge stove was empty. Brent carefully tried the door, but signaled for the others to wait. Inside the kitchen he ducked down beside the stove and waited. At long last he saw the wide swishing skirt of a woman swaying through the swinging door to the taproom. He waited until she approached the stove, then leapt quickly behind her to ease his hand over her mouth lest she betray him in surprise.

"It's me, Lil," he said quickly. "Brent McClain."

The rigid form in his arms relaxed; monstrously wide brown eyes closed and reopened with relief. He released the woman who had been hostess to him and his crew on many a drunken evening.

"Brent McClain!" she whispered, hugging him ferociously, then pulling away quickly. "You're mad, Brent! There ain't nothing but Yankees for miles around. Yankees who'd consider you a prize greater than their national treasury. What the fool hell are you doin' here, darlin'?"

Brent shrugged, smiling at the attractive woman. Lil smelled sweetly of lilac perfume; her wide belled skirt rustled with a feminine swish, and her pretty oval face never seemed to age. Her well-endowed figure was tightened to an hourglass shape by her corsets, and her breasts seemed about to spill out from a provocatively low bodice. Warm invitation already filled her eyes, heightened by the sense of dangerous excitement. There had been a time, not too long ago, when he would have been ready to answer that invitation. Lil had warmed him many a night, and he would have been lying to himself if he claimed that she left him unstirred now. But he wasn't planning to prolong this spy mission; he wanted to get to South Seas and then get out. And if he didn't . . .

He wasn't sure he wanted another woman. He wasn't sure

he could even close his eyes and pretend and find any satisfaction . . .

"I have to know what's happened, Lil. I've got three men outside in the bushes. Is it safe out here?"

Lil nodded, and he opened the back door. Andrew, Chris, and Charlie silently moved inside. Lil crept back to the taproom door and carefully looked out. Gracefully she swept back toward them. "Just let me get ol' Pete to keep an eye on the Yanks, and I'll see what I can do to help you fellows." Ol' Pete was a free black. He'd stayed on with Lil long ago when she signed his papers. He was a better watchdog than any coonhound.

The four Confederates stared tensely at one another as they awaited her return. She smiled as she came toward them, but kept her voice low, watching Brent as she spoke.

"Not much of anything has happened yet. Before our boys left, they burned everything that might have been of use to the Yankees. Some of the townspeople fled; a lot of them stayed. The Yanks have done some searching through the city, but they've been all right. There's been a little looting, and a little burning, but nothing too mean. Seems the officers have them under orders to exercise control. They've been polite to the people. They're hoping to find themselves enough Unionists here to hold the city by the townsfolk alone." She followed her speech with a sniff.

"What about the outskirts?" Brent demanded tensely.

A flash of pain appeared in Lil's pretty eyes. "I don't know, Brent, truly I don't. They're confiscating cotton, tobacco, livestock, and food stores, but I don't know what all else. But don't fret none on account of your sister and Stirling's wife. Like I said, honey, these men are on a tight chain. There ain't been no raping or violence against the womenfolk. The town has been occupied real quiet. But, Brent, you'd better get the hell out of here."

"I'm not going anywhere until I've been to South Seas,"

Brent said firmly. "Lil, you still got that hidden storeroom down in the cellar?"

"Yes, but—"

"I need you to get me a horse and tie it up around back. And get these boys down into that cellar until I get back."

"We're not letting you go alone, Captain," Charlie protested.

"Yes, you are. I'm ordering you to stay put. I'm not pulling you into my lunacy. If I don't get back, listen good to anything Lil might be able to find out. Then get back to the *Jenni-Lyn,* and follow orders over to the Gulf. Got it?"

His three men at last nodded unhappily. Lil was more vocal. "You're a damned fool, Brent McClain."

"Yeah," he agreed. "Now, can you get me that horse?"

The back streets of the city were absurdly quiet, although a hint of smoke still hung in the air. But maybe quiet was the only way a city could be when it had just been deserted by one army and occupied by another. All of northern Florida waited breathlessly to see just what repercussions would come its way.

The solemn hush was natural. Those who remained would keep themselves carefully indoors, praying that their homes escaped the wrath of conquering troops. Mothers would be afraid to let their children out for days; stiff, solemn faces would sullenly meet the intruders. . . .

And the Yanks, Brent decided, were handling the victory with downright carelessness. But maybe they just didn't give a damn about Florida. As long as they could steal arms and supplies and ships . . .

As he turned on to the westward pike, he dug his heels into the skinny flanks of the fleabitten gelding Lil had managed to have Pete smuggle to him. He was lucky, he supposed, that Lil had found him anything resembling a four-legged animal; during their retreat, the Confederates had ridden inland on practically anything that could move. Not many horses had been left. Florida's fine cavalry units had taken the horses as well as the men out of the state.

Brent had been certain when he first started out that he had gone mad, and he'd expected to be nabbed by a Union patrol the moment he mounted this sad excuse for a horse. He relaxed his own guard and allowed his mind to drift south.

Don't get yourself killed, Kendall had told him. She had sounded flippant. The charming drawl she could soften at will had been laced with mockery. Yet he had sensed everything that lay hidden beneath it, and he had never been more determined to live. And ever since that day, while he had fought and sailed, her memory had been with him. He dreamed of her . . . coming to him. Her image was so clear. All that had been, and all that hadn't yet happened . . . He planned to rectify that one day.

She was somehow part of his obsession to see his home. South Seas belonged to Justin, but there was plenty of land around the plantation. Acres and acres for a man and a woman to build a home together. Kendall belonged in a home, gracing it, reigning over it, waiting with the magic of her stunning blue eyes to welcome him. A lady in the parlor, a vixen in the bedroom . . . but she was another man's wife.

Brent didn't give a damn. Soon as the war was over there would be a divorce, and he wouldn't care if the scandal knocked the socks off all the old guard. All he had to do was keep her out of Yankee hands until that day.

He smiled suddenly, thinking of her in the swamp. It seemed so long since he had seen her. How were she and Red Fox doing together? He didn't worry so much about Kendall surviving the Indians as he did about the Indians surviving Kendall.

The yearning, wistful smile that had eased his features

suddenly froze. The smell of smoke was thick in the air now. And it wasn't drifting out of the city, but hanging over him.

Brent dug his heels hard into the flanks of his horse. The animal found a sudden spurt of life and bolted into a heavy gallop at his command. Brent flew through the night with the smoke-laden wind, dread again invading his system like shivering sickness.

He raced along the pike heedless of time and space. He came to the southwestern fork and turned without easing his gait. Yet when he came to the curving path that led to the magnolia-bordered trail to South Seas, he jerked the nag to a halt, his body seeming to curdle and freeze as he sat. His eyes were riveted straight ahead.

Without averting his glazed stare, he slipped from the back of the horse and started walking down the trail. Halfway along he started to run. And then again, he came to a dead halt, and slowly sank to his knees.

South Seas was gone. Only three tall Georgian pillars remained. Ghostly sentinels against the smoke-filled night sky. They were absurdly white against the charred rubble that lay about them as they reflected the glow of the high moon.

How long he knelt there—a dull, empty pain numbing all thought—he didn't know. The first conscious reflection that came to him was a soft prayer.

He was grateful that his mother was dead.

Then rage filled him, rage and loss, but he still knelt there, just staring. And then he stiffened as he heard shuffling footsteps on the parched earth behind him.

"Mastuh Brent?" The query was disbelieving, as if he were a phantom in the field. He turned to see a gaunt black man behind him.

"By God! It is you, Mastuh Brent!"

"Hello, Thomas," Brent said softly to the rheumatoid Negro who had served as his father's valet. He gripped the offered black hand firmly and came tiredly to his feet. "Thomas, where's Jennifer? And Patricia and Patrick?"

"Don't fret none, young sir. Miss Patricia and her boy done gone on up to Richmond to stay with her folks. Miss Jenny, now, she didn't want to leave. But your sister's just fine. They didn't burn no slave quarters. Dem Yanks are too busy tryin' to get us coloreds signed up in the Union Army to leave us with no place to stay! Miss Jennifer is back in the cottage with Mammy Lee."

"Can you take me to her, Thomas?" Brent asked wearily.

"Why, yes, sir, I'll be right happy to! But you know, Mastuh Brent, it's right dangerous for you to be wanderin' around these here parts. The Yanks set a big store on pullin' you in as a prisoner."

"Yes, I know, Thomas, thanks. I'll get out soon enough. But I've got to see Jenny."

"Right this way, sir, yes, right this way. Mammy Lee is in the big cottage these days. Afore the Reb army run off, we was taking in sick and wounded soldiers at the ol' manor. Miss Jenny had already moved out to leave more room for the soldiers."

Brent nodded bleakly as they walked past the rubble. He stopped suddenly, stroking his pounding forehead as he stared at the remains of his home.

He exhaled a soft whistle. "They didn't just burn the house down; they took explosives to it!"

"Yes, sir, they did, Mastuh Brent. But you come on now, and get inside 'fore some of them Yankees take a ride on by here."

Brent knew that there were planters who kept their slaves in misery. He knew that some slave quarters were no better than leaky barns, and in his soul, he knew that slavery wasn't right.

But when he stepped into the warm whitewashed cottage of the family cook, it was hard to feel that the McClains had been cruel taskmasters. A fire burned in a neat grate; mocha curtains covered the windows, and an old rug from the manor parlor carpeted the floorboards.

He barely saw thin old Mammy Lee when he first came through the doorway; his eyes instantly lit on the petite blonde in stunning crinolines and frills who dipped her head low over her sewing by the fire.

"Jenny," he said hoarsely.

She looked up at him instantly, lovely smoke-gray eyes like saucers. The sewing flew from her hands and she bolted from the rocker.

"Brent!"

She vaulted into his arms with the force of a hurricane, and hugged him so tightly he staggered. "Oh, Brent! It's so good to see you! But you shouldn't be here!"

He took hold of her slender shoulders and then held her away from him, his lips curling into a smile and his eyes savoring every line of her. "Jenny . . . you look wonderful." Again he hugged her to him, meaning his words, but saddened also by what he hadn't said. She had aged so much in such a short time! She was still several months shy of seventeen, but since he had seen her last, her gamine's face had aged by years. She had been a girl, but now, she was a woman, lovely, shapely, and mature with deep sorrow in her eyes.

"What happened, Jenny?" he asked her tensely, still holding her close. He felt again the inadequacies of war. Older brothers teased sisters, but they protected them; they gave them shoulders to cry on, and they wiped away their tears.

Jenny had been left to stand alone.

And she had done so admirably. Her eyes had saddened, her features hardened. But other than that, she looked like a breath of spring. The little puffed sleeves of her gown were low on her shoulders, making the bodice low and tight. Her waist was slim and pinched, and the skirt of the pale blue gown swayed about her in a graceful bell. The shiny coils of her hair were looped about her head in an attractive array of ringlets and braids.

She was very precious to him, he realized, warmth flooding away some of the coldness in his heart. The destruction of South Seas hurt; it was an anger and a pain that gnawed away at his insides. But South Seas could be rebuilt. Jenny was flesh and blood and irreplaceable.

"What happened, Jenny?" he repeated softly.

She pulled away from him this time and tried to give him a bright smile. "Give Mammy Lee a hug first, Brent, and then come sit. Mammy'll get us some tea. Have you eaten, Brent? Seems to me that soldiers and sailors are always starvin'!"

Brent obediently hugged the old woman who had been a part of his family as far back as he could remember. She crushed him in return, as Jenny had done, wiping tears from her eyes. "You set, Mastuh Brent. I'll git you younguns some tea an' then Thomas and I will leave you alone."

"Thank you mightily, Mammy Lee," Brent said, stilling his impatience to hear what his sister had to say. "And I don't need anything to eat, Jenny. My ship's galley is in good shape."

Moments later he sat cross-legged on the floor, sipping sassafras tea that was strongly laced with brandy. "Have you heard anything from Pa or Stirling?" he asked her first.

"About a month ago I got a letter from Pa signed by them both. They're doing well, but their regiment seems to be committed to the army in Virginia," she replied with a sigh, then smiled. "Pa's so proud of you, Brent. He says they hear all the way up in Virginia about the way you slip through those Union lines!"

Brent grimaced painfully, her words reminding him of the question for which he had to have an answer.

"They did it because of me, didn't they? They burned South Seas in retaliation."

Jenny settled her skirts about her, squirming uncomfortably as she groped for an answer.

"Didn't they, Jenny?"

"Well, yes, Brent. But not just because of you, of course. They did it because of Pa and Justine, too. And Brent, this is going to sound odd to you, but it was like they didn't want to. I was standing at the door with a shotgun when they came. Told them they weren't coming in while I could draw breath. The lieutenant in charge was real nice, though, Brent. They packed explosives around all sides of the house, and he walked right up the steps to stare at me. I know he believed that I would shoot him. But he was more terrified that the fire would start and I wouldn't move. He started telling me how sorry he was to have to ask me to leave my home, but that the orders had come from the top. Brent, when I heard the Yankees were coming, I was terrified. You know, all the stories you hear. I was sure I'd be raped and have my throat slit from ear to ear. But this lieutenant was a real gentleman! He said I could shoot him, but that he just had to move me before I could get hurt. Well, I didn't shoot him. And, Brent, he went into the house after me when he might have been blown to bits. I'd gone back to get the family Bible—Ma did set such a store by that book—and he rushed into the house after me and pulled me out." She fell silent for a minute. "His name is Lieutenant Jacob Halloran. If you ever run into that Yankee, Brent, don't kill him."

Brent was silent for a moment, taking a long sip of his tea. "This is a war, Jenny. You don't often get to know the men you kill."

"There are decent Yanks," Jenny said softly.

Brent raised his cup to her. "And rotten Rebels. War doesn't change men, Jenny. It just brings out the best and the worst in them. A decent man is a decent man. The Mason-Dixon Line can't alter that." He stood up suddenly, handing her his cup. "But it is a war, Jenny. Do you have any idea what they did with the explosives when they were done?"

Jenny shrugged. "They took them out of a supply wagon, I know that. Maybe they took it on over to the Murphy place. They were going to use that house as a headquarters. Why?" Her eyes went wide again as she looked into his, and she jumped to her feet, heedlessly dropping both cups as she grasped his arms. "What are you planning, Brent? You listen to me, big brother. The whole damned Confederate Army fled because there were too many Yanks. What in God's name do you think you can do?"

"A little sabotage, Jenny. A little retaliation of my own."

Her eyes registered her fear. "Brent, I don't think you understand! There's nothin' here but Yanks! Our troops left, Brent. There wasn't even a battle here, just a smooth occupation!"

"Jenny, I understand perfectly."

"South Seas isn't worth your life, Brent McClain!"

"Isn't it?" he demanded. South Seas. The cotton. The port of Jacksonville. Riding out on his own acres. Running their crops to the mills in the North.

Drinking good bourbon before a fire with a book. Hunting on a blooded stallion with a pack of fine foxhounds, following the code of behavior that was all that was left of the Old South.

South Seas . . .

And after all these years, he had found a woman with whom he wanted to share it all. A woman who understood the old way of life . . .

South Seas. A code of honor. A life that might have been.

If he wasn't fighting a war for those things, what the hell was he fighting for?

He smoothed the worried frown from his sister's brow. "I

accepted a commission into the Confederate Navy, Jenny. And I have orders to bring supplies to those who need them—and create havoc upon the Union wherever and whenever I could. Don't fret, Jenny. I have a number of good reasons to go on living. And I'm the Night Hawk, remember? More than a little indomitable. Now, you think they've got supply wagons out at the Murphy place?"

Jenny nodded unhappily. "Just be careful, Brent, will you please? There's a lot of people here who've changed the color of their coats since the invasion. People who are claiming they've been Unionists all along."

"I'll be careful, Jenny. I promise. I told you, I'm sure as hell not harboring any wishes of death."

She looked at him curiously. "Something's different about you, Brent."

He grinned. "I think I'm in love."

"Really?" Her eyes lit up like torches.

"Umm. I'll tell you about it sometime. But right now, I have work to do."

Eight

"I swear to Christ, Brent McClain, you are crazier than a rabid hound!"

Charlie issued the vehement words in a whisper as he and Brent broke the surface of the chilly night water alongside the *Marianna,* a sizable, steam-powered warship berthed in Jacksonville harbor.

Brent ignored the comment as he treaded water and raised a bundle wrapped in waterproof tarpaulins high above his head. "I'm only crazy if the fuses have gotten wet. Remember, Charlie, success can make the difference between insanity and brilliance."

It hadn't been at all difficult to steal a nice supply of explosives from the wagons. The guards had been lax. And why not? The Yankees had walked right into Jacksonville, their only real problems being the destruction left by the fleeing Confederates. Why would they fear sabotage or an attack? Jacksonville was theirs.

Brent's greatest problem had been convincing Jennifer that he wasn't going to behave recklessly because of his rage over South Seas.

He had been reckless—but only at first. Before he had seen that South Seas no longer existed, but knew it within his heart.

Now clear logic had taken control, and he moved carefully. He had filched the explosives and then lain low for the night, watching the Yanks the next day and sending messages to his men through Jenny and Lil. He lay low another night and another day and now . . .

He knew what he was up against. There were guards studiously watching the docks and ships. And that fact necessitated the cold midnight swim in the spring waters. The only way to reach a ship undetected was from the stern.

"How the damn hell we're gonna light matches with wet fingers I'll never know," Charlie grumbled nervously, kicking hard beneath the surface to keep himself afloat.

"Shh!" Brent warned. "You just help me get aboard and then hightail it out of here. I'm going to do the lighting. And get the dinghy back to the ship. I'll swim to shore and make it overland to the river. We won't be coming back this way. They will be after us like a pack of wolves. But they don't have much here they can navigate the river with, and there won't be much they can do till morning anyway. By then I'll be back with you."

Charlie didn't answer; he cursed as he tried to help Brent and dropped a packet of explosive powder into the sea.

"This ain't ever going to work, Brent."

Since they were alone, Charlie had dispensed with all formality. That he had become a first lieutenant in the Confederate States Navy didn't mean a hell of a lot to him. Brent was still his captain, and he was still the first officer. Just like always.

"All we need is one packet, well placed. Then the ship's own armaments and powder can do the rest. Give me a boost, Charlie. I've got to catch hold of her tie line and get to the deck."

Charlie began to spit out a long stream of sailors' oaths as he struggled to assist Brent and remain ready to catch the explosives should Brent lose his grip.

170

"Yep, you're crazier than a damn rabid dog, Brent McClain."

Brent caught a firm hold on the rope with his hands and wrapped his legs around it, shimmying up. He had the long fuse gripped between his teeth, and his progress was smooth. He popped his head over the deck, saw no one about, and signaled Charlie before he leapt silently aboard.

"Go!" he hissed to Charlie.

The head of his first lieutenant disappeared below the water's surface.

Brent lost his first match. It sizzled and went out. He looked anxiously about the massive bow before striking another. The gun deck was right beneath him; if his fire caught hold, the *Marianna* would go up like fireworks on the Fourth of July.

He frowned, wondering if he hadn't made his fuse too long. It would burn forever. Then he shrugged. He wasn't bent on dying. He wanted to give himself plenty of time to get started on the long swim.

He exhaled as the flame of his next match caught the fuse.

Then he stood, shouting out a loud "Ahoy there, Yanks! Your ship is about to blow. Get the hell overboard!"

He grabbed a rigging line and hopped to the gunwale then dived into the water. But before he broke the surface, he heard the sound of scurrying feet; an alarm had been raised.

He felt the strange whiz of a wild shot streaking through the water near his ear—too near his ear. With his lungs about to burst, he jackknifed his body deeper into the water, swimming northward, all the strength he could muster set into his powerful strokes. He passed the studs of the dock and the hulls of a dozen other ships before he allowed his head to break the surface and his aching lungs gasp in great gulps of air.

"Son of a bitch!"

He heard the thundering cry shrill upon the night air; men

began to jump and dive from the ship into the harbor. Brent didn't wait for more. He dived again—and felt the reverberations in the water as the ammunition aboard the *Marianna* began to blow.

And as he had expected, the ship was a floating powder keg. When he broke surface again, the harbor did look like one big Fourth of July celebration. And the Yanks, milling in confusion, were everywhere. It was utter chaos. The water, even at his distance from the burning warship, grew warm.

He plunged again and swam hard, dove again and swam—until he was certain his distance was great enough. The winter chill that still cooled the water kept him moving quickly. And when he swam into a rocky inlet of the shore, he could still see the fire.

He hoped that all of the men aboard the *Marianna* had heeded his warning. He might be fighting a war, but he would never have a stomach for cold-blooded killing.

For a while he lay on the shore, panting. Then he picked himself up and started threading his way through the shoreline trees to the denser forest beyond them, shivering against the damp and the night cold. By dawn he would reach the river where the *Jenni-Lyn* lay hidden in certain shelter.

"Ahoy! Who goes there?"

The demand was barked out to Brent as soon as he set a tired hand on the *Jenni-Lyn*'s ladder. Dripping and chilled with the river's brackish water clinging to him now, Brent was relieved to hear that his lookout was alerted.

"It's Captain McClain!" he shouted.

"Sir! Come aboard! Come aboard!"

He didn't need assistance, but he didn't protest when two pairs of brawny seamen's arms reached over the gunwale and hurled him to the deck with exuberance.

He righted himself quickly and saw that the men who wel-

172

comed him were Chris and Lloyd. "Where's McPherson?" he asked quickly.

"He came aboard half an hour ago, Captain. We poured some brandy into him and packed him off to quarters. Not that we had to strain too hard to get the liquor into ol' Charlie—"

"Ol' Charlie is Lieutenant McPherson, men," Brent said with only light reproach. He and his crew were an anomaly in the Confederate Navy. He had been commissioned a captain, but with certain understandings. His ship had only light guns; she was small in comparison with the frigates and warships designed for heavy battle. Her main function was to hurry supplies where needed with the greatest possible speed. The *Jenni-Lyn* was a blockade runner, but whereas a number of the blockade raiders, playing the game of the hare-and-hound, were privateers not averse to making a profit out of warfare, the *Jenni-Lyn* ran solely for the government in Richmond.

Her crewmen were loyal Confederates, but they sailed without thought of personal gain for one reason only—Brent McClain. And Brent knew that he was in a strange position, carefully teetering on a fence rail. Discipline was always essential aboard ship; but discipline had to be carefully tempered if a crew was expected to play by tight rules. Brent had been offered larger ships; he had tactfully refused, reminding the secretary of the navy that his effectiveness was dependent on his maneuverability.

"Aye-aye, sir!" Lloyd mumbled to Brent's command. "Do we pull her out now, Captain? Upriver, or open sea?"

"Upriver—" Brent began, only to stop short when a warning rang down clear and excited from the crow's nest.

"Yankee flag on the horizon! Schooner, heading in from the mouth, sir!"

"Damn!" Swearing lightly, Brent bolted to the rigging and

173

climbed up to the nest. A schooner, about the same size as the *Jenni-Lyn,* was making the turn into the narrow estuary.

Nothing larger could come after them, Brent was certain. A man had to know the river well or risk being wrecked on the shoals that littered its mouth.

He grasped the glass from his lookout and stared at the ship, trying to decide quickly whether to fight or run. It was possible that they could sink the enemy and thus block the river behind them.

"All hands on deck. Gunners to their stations. At the ready!"

The quiet deck awoke to the scramble of tight-lipped, efficient sailors. Brent shimmied back down the mast and stood beside Lloyd, ready to give the order to fire.

He waited. The ship had to move in close enough to give them a decent shot, but not so close as to be able to fire on them first.

A weary McPherson was at the helm, maneuvering the *Jenni-Lyn* smoothly.

Brent clenched and unclenched his fingers as the schooner moved into the river. Not yet. Not yet. Five, four, three, two . . .

A spout of water suddenly rose to their port like a gusher, and the *Jenni-Lyn* rolled in its wake. The first Federal shot had gone astray.

Brent's waiting game had paid off. Now it was his turn.

"Fire!" he roared out as sea spray rose and fanned over the deck.

"Fire one!" Lloyd bellowed out the order to the four gunners at the first cannon.

The *Jenni-Lyn* shuddered and groaned with the repercussion of the shot. But her crew sent up a cry—a rebel yell of triumph—as the ball tore a hole in the hull of the schooner.

"Reload one, number two at the ready!"

"Reload!"

"Number two at the ready!"

"Hold fire!" Brent commanded, raising a hand as he watched the foundering Union vessel.

Their blow to the enemy craft had been mortal; there was no doubt she would sink. They could blow her out of the water, but the only accomplishment would be a rain of death.

"Captain, look!" Lloyd suddenly pointed toward the wounded ship. "She's sending a boat out, sir. Three men aboard, waving a white flag."

Brent narrowed his eyes as he saw the small boat approach. Two seamen were rowing; an officer stood in the bow of the dinghy, holding the flag. He was a brave man, Brent thought, daring such an approach when it was more than likely that the *Jenni-Lyn*'s guns would roar again.

"Hold all fire," Brent commanded. "We'll see what the Fed captain wants."

"Could be a trick, sir," Lloyd advised.

Brent shook his head. "I don't think so. We've got the advantage; his ship's sinking fast. I think it's a bold move to avoid a slaughter."

"As you say, sir."

"Help 'em aboard. The *Jenni-Lyn* honors a white flag and a noble surrender."

A moment later Brent was facing a young U.S. naval lieutenant with a handsome display of tawny whiskers running from his sideburns and culminating in a neatly clipped goatee. The lieutenant saluted crisply. "Sir, United States Navy Lieutenant Bartholomew Greer."

Brent, concealing with effort a trace of amusement at the man's rigid posture, answered the salute. "Captain Brent McClain, Lieutenant. What's on your mind?"

"Sir, I'm surrendering to you. Applying for mercy on behalf of my crew. Another shot on the *Yorkville* will serve only to take life needlessly. She is no longer any danger to you."

"I can see that, Lieutenant," Brent stated easily. "And I'm

afraid your sacrifice was unnecessary. We didn't intend to fire another shot."

The young man relaxed perceptibly, and Brent was strangely touched. The gallantry of the Yank's gesture was as noble an act as Brent had seen. He thought of his conversation with his sister. Honor did come in both blue and gray.

The lieutenant stiffened again, as if horrified at his momentary display of relief. "I admit, Captain, I counted on your mercy. We know, sir, that you were responsible for the destruction of the *Marianna*. But not a man died, sir."

Brent shrugged, his eyes narrowing. "Killing is a part of war, Yank. But we try to keep it to a minimum."

"Yes, sir," Lieutenant Greer said stiffly. "But I would have blown you out of the water if I could have, Captain."

"That's all right, Lieutenant. I would have blown you sky-high if it had been necessary."

The lieutenant looked about him suddenly—at his own two seamen standing silently, at Brent's crew silently listening to the exchange.

"Sir," he said quietly to Brent, "I'd like to have a word in private with you."

Curiously Brent inclined his head. "My cabin, Lieutenant." He turned to Lloyd and indicated the two Yankee seamen, uncomfortably awaiting their fate. "We move upriver, but take care of our . . . guests. Give them a cup of coffee and some tobacco for their pipes. They might spend the rest of this long war in a prison camp. We can't wait around to pick up any others. If they're any kind of sailors, they can swim to shore."

Ten minutes later Brent was facing the Yankee across his narrow desk. Lieutenant Greer was filling his pipe, a touch of awe in his features. Apparently it had been a while since the men of the *Yorkville* had enjoyed any luxuries. The North was suffering shortages, too.

Brent waited until the Yankee officer had lit his pipe and

exhaled a long plume of smoke. Then he repeated his question. "What's on your mind, Yank?"

The lieutenant stiffened and hesitated, then eyed Brent directly. "Like I said before, Reb, you fight a fair battle. I'm in your debt. I'm going to go off the book a bit and give you a warning."

Brent's eyes narrowed, and he felt his muscles stiffen. He had the same strange sense of dread he had felt when he rode toward South Seas and knew . . .

"Go on, Lieutenant."

The Yank shuffled a bit in his chair. Brent knew he was fighting a little battle of conscience. The rules on one side—a private desire for justice on the other.

"You've got quite a reputation, Captain McClain. I'm sure you're aware of that. Your home was about the only thing we burned between St. Augustine and Jacksonville."

Brent said nothing. He lifted a brow as a signal for the Yankee to continue.

"Some things aren't done quite right on either side," Lieutenant Greer muttered, staring at his pipe and then at Brent again. "It's rumored, Captain, that you're friends with some Indian tribe that's been pushed into the swamp. Some of those Indians stole the wife of a Union officer stationed at Fort Taylor some time back. There are those who say you had something to do with that, since the lady was a southerner. There's another rumor about, Captain. The lady's husband was murderin' mad. I was off the Keys not a week ago, Captain. Seems that Lieutenant Moore is trying to pull orders to go into the swamp after her. He should be able to get them. The captain at Fort Taylor has been advised that the Indians have been running supplies to the lighthouse keepers along the southern coastline. If the Indians have joined the Confederacy, then it won't be out of bounds for the Union to go to war against the Indians."

Brent hadn't said a word during the speech; he hadn't

moved or shifted. He had barely blinked. But he felt his reaction. Cold, savage fear worked its way along his spine and through his limbs. Fear and dread and a terrible certainty.

He would be too late. Too late. Too late. The swamp was a long distance away . . .

He had endangered Red Fox. That realization caused him far greater pain than even the loss of South Seas. Shattering panic and anguish clutched his heart in a vise. Kendall . . . She had been here that first night. Right here in his cabin aboard the *Jenni-Lyn*. He could remember how she had looked. Eyes large and luminous and seductively compelling. He could remember the sound of her voice, how she had moved, how he had touched her and she him . . .

He bolted from his chair and threw open the cabin door. "Charlie! Order the helmsman to go about! We're going to maneuver past the Federals and run the port. Full sail, heading south, Charlie! Call the orders!"

He paused for a moment by the door, listening as Charlie roused the men, unquestioningly repeating his orders.

Then he turned back to the Yankee who was staring at him with naked trepidation in his eyes.

"Don't worry, Yank," Brent said softly. "We'll leave you and your men off somewhere down the coast. You don't deserve to rot or die in a prison, Lieutenant. We can say we dumped you because we couldn't take the time to turn you over to the land authorities."

The lieutenant closed his eyes and shivered almost imperceptibly.

"Thanks, Reb," he whispered.

"Not at all, Yank. I'm much obliged."

Brent left his prisoner in his cabin. There were no secrets of war to be discovered among his charts.

He hurried out on deck. They were going to have to sail through Jacksonville harbor with their guns blazing. And maneuvering past the sunken Federal ship was going to be tricky.

But navigation problems were barely on his mind now. He would do it. He was determined to get through because there was so very much at stake.

Red Fox, a man who lived by a code of ethics more rigorous than that of either North or South, a man who had risked much for the Confederacy. It had been his choice; he would accept no payment or reward for his actions, just as he would accept no consolation if those actions brought him to a tragic conclusion.

But even deeper than his inner cry for the Indian who had taught him the meaning of friendship was the despair that racked his body when he thought of Kendall.

She had touched him so briefly, and yet from her he had learned the meaning of love. She had set down roots that wound about his heart and pulled him back even when he was free to go.

Kendall.

He could see her. Stormy indigo eyes, hair like a cloak of honey to spin about her in splendor and wild disarray.

She was beauty and grace. She held the same intangible spirit as the South. That which they fought to hold and preserve. The evasive soul that bound them, dirt farmer and planter, to fight and best a stronger enemy. It went further than the slavery question. Further than King Cotton. The spirit was perhaps intangible, but Kendall was not. She was alive and vital, and in her warmth and beauty he could touch what he so craved to hold . . .

All that he fought for. A rebel's pride, his honor, his glory, and his boundless, unwavering love.

Nine

" 'Oh, I wish I was in the land of cotton. Old times there are not forgotten. Look away, look away, look away, Dixieland.' " Kendall laughed as she finished her song with its strangely accented chorus, and tugged on little Chicola's hair. "Kah-ton, Chicola. Listen to me. Sounds like kah-ton! And you should see it at harvest time! It stretches forever and forever, like a field of endless clouds!"

"Endless clouds," Hadjo—Chicola's senior by less than a year—repeated solemnly, looking up at the sky and pointing. "Clouds."

"Yes! Perfect. Now, 'Oh, I wish I was in Dixie, away, away. In Dixieland I'll make my stand, to live, to die, in Dixie! Away . . . away . . . away down south in Dixie!' "

The two little children sang along with her, giggling, eyeing her expectantly when the sounds of their voices ebbed away into the high pines from the small, dry clearing where she took them each afternoon to play and learn. They weren't far from the main camp, and often other women besides Apolka would bring their children to the clearing to listen to the strange white woman who seemed so happy in their midst.

And she was happy. Strangely content. She received no news from the outside world, but it was impossible to believe that things could be going badly. And she could spin dreams as endless as the fields of cotton she had envisioned. She would be safe anywhere south of the Mason-Dixon Line once the Yanks had been beaten back. Safe to pursue a divorce and then . . .

Brent McClain.

Her dreams were a bit foolish, she realized in the few rational moments she allowed herself. She'd spent one night of her life with him. And of course that brief hour aboard his ship over a year ago. But she had been dreaming of him ever since then . . . and when the dream came to life in flesh and blood it had shattered her senses. He was constantly on her mind. She was in love with him.

But what of him? He had known she was married. His quest for her had been one of vengeance. He had assured her he would never return her to her husband, and he had promised that he would come back to her. But was that a manifestation of the code of honor that ruled him despite his warnings that he was no gentleman? Or did he plan a future for them? He was a Confederate hero; he was also arrestingly male and very experienced with the opposite sex. It was not just likely but probable that he had a dozen eager women in a dozen ports, some much more suitable than she to be the wife of such a man.

Kendall's eyes clouded for a moment, and she compressed her lips. It was strange, but it didn't seem to matter at the moment. She was married, and she knew that the legal ties binding her didn't mean a thing. All she wanted was to be with Brent McClain. She would be happy with him anywhere.

"Kendall."

A little hand tugged at her skirt, and she gazed down into Chicola's troubled face to realize she had been staring into space, brooding. She smiled warmly and hoisted the little boy to her lap as she sat on a broad tree stump. " 'Dixie,'

181

my little urchin, was written by the son of a northern abolitionist as a minstrel song. And the Confederates picked it
right up. What do you think of that?"

Chicola wrinkled his nose, having no idea what she was
talking about. "Sing more," he told her.

"Not today, little one," she said firmly. "It's time to get
you back home to your chickee. Can't you see that dusk is
falling?"

Two-year-old Chicola and three-year-old Hadjo both nodded at her gravely, and she was about to laugh at their solemn
little faces when a prickling at the base of her spine smoth-
ered the sound before it could come. Someone was behind
her in the trees. She knew it. Just as she kept her part of the
bargain, Red Fox had kept his. She had learned the strange,
meandering waterways of the swamp, just as she had learned
the sounds of all its creatures. And she had learned to listen
with her whole body as well as her ears.

Why the feeling gave her such a sense of fear, she didn't
know. They were close to camp. The Seminole were a protective society, and sometimes even the young braves slipped
quietly into the trees just to see that everything was fine.

The inexplicable chill of fear became raw panic even before she heard the hammock come alive with thrashing feet—
and a mocking chorus of "John Brown's Body Lies
a-Molderin' in the Grave."

Kendall sprang to her feet in terror, screaming out a shrill
warning as she clutched little Chicola tightly in one arm and
hugged Hadjo close to her side with the other.

What had been a peaceful afternoon became in the flash
of an eye a maelstrom of strident discord. The hammock
seemed to be flooded with men, soldiers in blue uniforms
and knee-high boots who thrashed in wave after wave
through the trees. And the soldier with hell and damnation
in his ice-blue eyes who strode toward her with furious pur-

182

pose was the one man she had fervently prayed never to see again.

John Moore.

Kendall screamed again and whirled about, dipping low to clutch little Hadjo more firmly about the waist. Carrying the Indian boys like sacks of grain, she began to run, desperate to reach the camp with her Indian charges before . . .

Before John got hold of her.

She ran blindly and instinctively—foolishly.

The Seminole camp was already a pit of screaming chaos; soldiers were tearing into chickees with bayonets at the ready, searching out the braves who had remained behind when the hunting and scouting parties left for the day. Kendall tore into the middle of the camp and whirled around in mindless panic.

Red Fox! She needed to find him. To find a harbor in his strength. But even as she instinctively thought these things, she knew that Red Fox was not at the camp, and that if he were, there would have been little that he could have done except to die fighting.

"Kendall! Kendall Moore!"

It was Jimmy Emathla. Kendall saw him and ran toward him. He waited to lead her and the children into the forest so that they could disappear into the swamp.

"Jimmy!" she cried frantically, trusting in the proud brave's muscled prowess and proud sense of duty. His dark eyes were upon her, encouraging her to hurry to his side so that she might escape with the sons of his chief.

"No!"

She stopped running, and screamed. Jimmy Emathla fell to the ground as a bayonet ripped through his gut. Tears filled Kendall's eyes; she hadn't even seen the face of the Union soldier who had attacked the Indian. All she saw was a blur of blue . . . and then the red of blood.

An anguished screech brought her whipping around to

face Red Fox's chickee. Apolka had seen her with the children, and was racing toward her, tears streaming down her cheeks, her pretty features distorted with fear.

What followed was a horror that would remain imprinted in Kendall's memory forever. The Indian girl was running as blindly as she. A young soldier, backing away from a confrontation with a brave, did not see that Apolka was only a terrified woman trying to reach her children. He only felt her hurtling toward him where he stood between the chickee and Kendall.

The soldier turned. His bayonet ripped into Apolka. The Indian girl's eyes met Kendall's over the distance briefly. They widened with the shattering pain; they seemed to plead. Apolka's mouth worked open, but no sound came. Her eyes glazed, the dazzling deep brown sheen of love and laughter forever gone, and she fell at the soldier's feet.

Kendall started to scream, huddling to the earth to shield the boys from the sight. And as she screamed, the boys began to cry. War cries, shouts, and the shrieks of panic continued to rise around her. Heavy footsteps padded against the ground; orders were shouted.

Another woman screamed, and even in her shocked agony, Kendall recognized the sound of death. She would never know if the soldiers had thought themselves attacked, or if they had just lost their sense of right in the bloodlust. Maybe the women did attack them, hurtling themselves against the superior strength of the war-trained males in an act of sudden desperation after Apolka's death, preferring to die with honor rather than cowardice.

When Kendall did look up, it was to witness a bloodbath. Women and children were now fleeing into the forest. Some escaped; some were struck down. They had no chance against the white invaders; the majority of the braves had not returned from their hunting trips to distant hammocks. The attack had been made on a encampment of old men, children, and women.

Kendall screamed afresh, this time with pain, as rough fingers threaded into her hair and jerked her to her feet. She was spun about to face the cold, hard eyes of her husband.

He was a tall man, broad-shouldered, dark-haired, and sporting a neatly clipped dark mustache. He might have been attractive, had it not been for the mark of cruelty in his gaunt features and the snow-cold hardness in his eyes. There was no flicker of mercy about him. Nothing human in the unwavering gaze he gave Kendall. His expression didn't alter a hair as he calmly wound her hair more tightly around his fingers, intending to hurt.

"Let go of the brats," he told her curtly.

She saw his rifle clutched in his free hand, the bayonet tip dripping crimson in the dying sunlight.

Despite her own pain she shrieked out, frantically trying to stop the massacre. "Stop! John! Please, I beg you! This is no war, it's murder—"

"Let go of the little Indian bastards."

All around them the screaming and fighting continued. Where was someone she knew? Kendall wondered desperately. One of the Yankees with a sense of kindness and justice. They did exist; she knew they did; she had met many at Fort Taylor.

But not here. John's crew must have been hand-picked. Military men who had fought in the Seminole wars and hated Indians.

"Now, Kendall. Or I'll spear them and spit them right here in front of you."

She couldn't move her head. His hold on her hair was too tight. She tried to think of the Muskogee words she needed, and cried out loudly as she pushed the boys blindly away from her. "Run! Run, little foxes. Run into the trees and hide until the blue men are gone and you see your father!"

185

They refused to move. They were still tightly clutching her skirts in terror. They were too young to understand what had happened.

"Go!" Kendall shrieked, shoving them as hard as she could. She had jerked against John's hold, and instant tears glazed her eyes at the sharp tearing of her scalp, but she felt the little boys at last leave her.

John said nothing else. His thin lips compressed further, disappearing beneath the fashionable droop of his mustache. He used his hold on her to spin her about, tossing her into the arms of a young soldier, a youth of no more than eighteen who wore a sick expression.

"Get her into a boat," John ordered quickly.

The youth nodded blankly. It was apparent that this type of slaughter was not what he had expected of warfare; it was equally apparent that he was too stunned to do anything other than follow orders. But his hold on Kendall wasn't cruel, merely firm. As he dragged her toward the river, she was able to turn back.

A cry rose in her throat; she brought the back of her hand to her mouth in horror and bit into her own flesh, mindless of the pain.

Chicola had obeyed her. She could see him, his little brown legs carrying him from the chaos of the encampment at a steady run. He was already reaching the far line of cypress to the rear of the camp. In a second he would be swallowed up in the trees.

But Hadjo had panicked and run to the warmth and security he had always known. He now clung to his mother's lifeless body. A retreating soldier tripped over the child and turned instinctively to retaliate. As Kendall stared on in numb and impotent horror, the soldier's rifle clubbed the child's head. Hadjo fell on top of his mother.

Kendall started to scream again. Hysterically. Strength

born of her frenzy came to her, and she fought her way to freedom from the startled youth who held her.

"Stop it!" she screeched, racing back to the center of the clearing. "Stop it! Murderers! Bloody murderers! Stop it, stop it, stop it!"

Heedless of her action, she beat against the first blue-coated back she came upon. The face that turned to hers was at first frenzied and angered. But it was not a cruel face. Middle-aged and lined, it was just the face of a man caught in the fever of the fight. As Kendall stared at him with wide, tear-filled eyes, his expression lost its wildness. He looked at the carnage about him, and then back to Kendall.

"Oh, Jesus . . ." he breathed.

Two things happened then, both of which Kendall was barely aware of at first. John Moore came up behind her and gripped her rudely by the shoulders, and the sound of pounding feet was coming toward them from the river.

A shout sounded loud in the now bleakly silent clearing. "What in damnation has gone on here?"

Vaguely, very vaguely at first, Kendall recognized the voice.

Travis.

She saw him, handsome in dress uniform, as he strode to the center of the now still Union soldiers. His company waited in awkward silence as the twenty or so men halted behind him, behind the scene of the fight that was not a battle but a heartless massacre.

Incredulous and horrified, Travis took several steps in several different directions, staring at the corpses of the women and children and old men. Only a few braves lay among the dead, the men Red Fox had left to guard the camp in the swamp, which had known nothing but peace in the remote Everglades . . .

Travis moved in a circle, still staring incredulously. At last he looked with a murderous fury at the other Union soldiers.

"What the hell happened here? Goddamn it, we're not fighting the Indians! We're at war with the Confederate States, not with a bunch of Indian children."

"What's the matter with you, Travis?"

The annoyed question came from John, and his fingers bit into Kendall's shoulders. "We killed a few savages. An Indian pup is still an Indian. It grows up to attack whites."

Travis's face went red with rage, and then white. "I'm the senior officer, John. We were supposed to come in and bargain for Kendall, and warn the chief against dealing with Confederates."

"Lieutenant Moore's right, Commander," a lazy voice drawled out among John's troop. "What's the harm in killing a few Injuns? Twenty years ago we had orders to snuff the lot of 'em out if'n we could."

Travis held silent for a moment, then spoke curtly and cuttingly. "An extra shift of guard duty for a month, soldier. Insubordination. But just for the record, I'm going to tell all of you just what is wrong with slaughtering a few Indians! We are the sailors and marines of the United States Navy. Our immediate job is to preserve our Union. We have been given orders to fight, not to murder. We are the representatives of our country. A country of God-fearing, peace-loving people. We fight for honor. There is no honor in the slaughter of women and children!"

Travis suddenly spun on John, his fury and agitation such that he barely winced at the sight of Kendall. "How the hell could you allow such a thing to happen, Lieutenant Moore?"

John answered between clenched teeth. "The filthy savages kidnapped my wife, Commander. We were ordered to come in—"

"To *deal,* not to murder."

John held silent for a moment. Kendall could feel his explosive anger. "You fight your wars, Travis. I'll fight mine."

The tension that crackled between the two men was as

188

tangible as heat lightning; as explosive as gunpowder. All about them there was dead silence. The air was still; no breeze rustled the trees. No birds called out; not even a cricket chirped.

But then a slight sound could be heard; the buzzing of flies as they closed in on the blood of the dead. Perhaps it was the taunt of that parasitical buzzing, or perhaps it was the slow realization that they were surrounded by their men, but John and Travis both fell silent as they realized this was neither the time nor the place to wage the private battle that had turned friends to enemies.

Travis's eyes touched upon Kendall. They were full of sorrow; they begged forgiveness, and she knew that Travis had come only because he had believed her imprisoned by the Indians. And in his eyes she could see that he already believed she would have preferred being the captive of a tribe of Seminoles—savages or not—to being the captive wife of John Moore.

Travis turned to the men. "Get back to the boats. Now."

A shuffle of feet followed his command. Kendall and John and Travis stood alone in the clearing with only the dead about them.

"We have your wife, John," Travis said with soft reproach. "And she does not appear to have suffered cruelly."

"No?" John demanded. He laughed bitterly. "Maybe she didn't. Maybe she cozied right up to those brown men like a bitch in heat!"

"Goddamn it, John," Travis interrupted, embarrassed for Kendall even after all they had been through together.

"Why protect her, Travis? We both know what my wife is more than willing to do. But then, maybe it isn't the damn savages I need to be worrying about. Maybe you were so eager to come after her because there's been more than friendship going on behind my back."

Travis stiffened like a poker. His face was rigid with his

189

anger; his eyes were ablaze. His hands clenched to fists at his sides. "I won't call you out for that one, John. Because I am your friend. Still. But as your friend, I'm telling you this. You keep up like you're going, and there won't be a man in the world that you can call friend. And if you hurt Kendall in any—"

"Kendall is my wife, Travis, and I'll handle her however I see fit!" John bit out in a thunder of new fury. "You have no right to interfere in a marriage. President Lincoln himself has no damn right to interfere in a man's marriage; neither does goddamn Admiral Farragut!"

Again Travis stiffened, as if he had been struck. "When this war is over, John—"

"Don't you think we should be getting the hell out of here, Travis?" John interrupted coldly. "We could wind up being ambushed by some mighty testy Indians, and if one of them savages takes a knife to your throat, you won't be crying no more over a little spilled blood. You've got yourself a couple of troops of men whose lives depend on you."

Travis swore softly and turned on his heel.

Kendall had stood tensely through the confrontation. Now she closed her eyes, wishing that in doing so she could wipe out the horror around her. Nothing would ever do that for her. She tried to jerk herself from her husband's grasp, but the talons of his fingers on her back were merciless.

"Oh, no, my sweet love," John hissed, switching his hold to the nape of her neck and clasping his fingers almost all the way around it. "It's time to go home—to the Union barracks—and celebrate. Another white woman saved by her loving husband from the barbaric red man." He brought his other hand slowly up and around her neck, squeezing threateningly, slowly releasing, his eyes stone cold and emotionless all the while. She returned his stare, not caring. John could not hurt her. No physical pain could ease the guilt and agony in her heart.

"What a genteel man I plan to be, my love. I plan to accept you back with all loving kindness, ignoring the fact that you've been dirtied and sullied by the Indians. But I do plan to hear all about it. Yeah, I do want to know just why you look so good, Mrs. Moore."

Despair suddenly overwhelmed her. All she could think of was the kindness Red Fox had offered her; and Red Fox would return from his hunting expedition to find his wife and child slain. Because of her. She wished she had died along with the others.

"John," she said quietly, "I suggest that you kill me. Otherwise, one day I'm going to kill you."

The line of his mouth tightened. He released his hold about her neck, only to bring the back of his hand hard against her jaw.

"Try it, bitch," she dimly heard him mutter.

The world faded to black. She didn't feel her husband's cruel grip as he tossed her over his shoulder like a sack.

Kendall tried to lie still and count the knotholes in the beamed ceiling over her head.

She desperately wanted to fall asleep. There was a slim chance that John would remain in the officers' meeting until late into the night and that he would leave her alone if she slept.

He hadn't had much of a chance to confront her yet. She hadn't regained consciousness until the small rowboats taken by the men into the swamp had cleared the maze of rivers and come to a bay. And upon reaching the two schooners they had left at anchor, John Moore had been forced to give all his attention to commanding his vessel. Torrential rains and high winds had descended on them in a fury.

It had taken almost two days to reach Key West. But in that time Kendall had barely seen John. She had been se-

191

questered in a small cabin, and only a young ensign h[...]
come near her, bearing meals and politely asking after h[...]
welfare. He seemed to think she had been rescued from som[...]
terrible ordeal. Kendall hadn't had the energy to dispute hi[...]
She had spent the voyage in alternating numbness and m[...]
ery. When she did sleep, she heard the screams; when s[...]
closed her eyes she saw the image of Apolka just before s[...]
died. When she fell into a restless slumber, she envision[...]
again and again the way Hadjo had run to his mother's corp[...]
and died there on her breast.

God, how grateful she had been for the storms that h[...]
roiled the sea! She had prayed that the ship would found[...]
on the treacherous Florida reefs. She was immune to fe[...]
now. She didn't care what John did to her. She was glad tha[...]
he believed a savage red man had received from her what
he never could or would.

Her dreams had died as sure a death as the Indians in the
camp. She felt as if her soul had been severed from her body.

Upon their return to Fort Taylor, she had been directly
summoned to see Captain Brannen. She had bitterly told him
the truth—that the Indians had offered her no menace and
that the tribe, with mainly young children and women present, had been brutally massacred. But then she had sensed
that she was being grilled for a reason—a reason that had
little to do with the Indians. And she grew nervously silent
because of Brent and his crew of Confederate sailors.

That had been hours ago. Captain Brannen had been
vaguely solicitous; he had agreed with John that Kendall
must have picked up a touch of swamp fever and was merely
behaving hysterically when she begged him to help her escape from her husband. Brannen was basically a kind man.
He had shown distress, patted her head, and told her, "There,
there, now, Mrs. Moore. You've been through a trying experience. Abducted and forced to live with savages. And being
in the midst of bloodshed after living with those . . . people.

You must understand how difficult this is for a man." The captain had shifted his eyes to John, and Kendall had barely constrained herself from breaking into shrill laughter. Everyone assumed that she had been raped by the "savages" and that poor John was holding up admirably, still adoring his wife and trying to behave as if none of it mattered.

Brannen had even put the slaughter down to John's protective feelings for her. Oh, John would be called down. But not disciplined. The Indian action had been "regrettable but understandable."

And Kendall had to bitterly admit to herself that many Confederates would feel no differently. The Seminole Wars were still too fresh in the minds of all white men for more than a few to understand just what had really happened, and to know and appreciate the Indian code of honor.

Kendall couldn't count the knots in the wood. The strange, dark whorls formed faces in her mind. Red Fox's face first. Red Fox returning and witnessing what had been his people, his home, his wife, and his child.

And then she began to see Brent McClain's face, because she was alive, and being alive, she hurt. He had made her so vulnerable, because now she knew that she could be held, cherished, and loved . . .

Even if the words were never spoken.

She would never see him again. She was locked in the cabin. And a guard walked past her door. He was very precise; the coming and going of his footsteps were like clockwork.

Kendall stiffened suddenly, and closed her eyes tightly. Footsteps had just sounded—different from those of the guard's, to which she had become accustomed. Strident, strong steps.

John.

Kendall twisted on the bed and curled into a tight knot with her face curled into her pillow. She tried to make herself

193

breathe slowly and smoothly, but she felt like a cat whose
hackles were rising as she heard the door creak and the
clipped str___ her husband as he moved into the room.

She fe___ pause at the door, then heard him move about
the roo___ pping away the full-dress uniform he had worn
for h___ ing with Captain Brannen. His sword clattered
on t___ wood floor directly beside her head. She opened
her e___ and stared up at him; they both knew she hadn't
b___ eping.

"___ . . ." he began softly. "You became quite friendly with
___ dians who carried you off?"

___ e sensed something in his tone instantly. Warily she
___ sted to her back to keep her eyes on him. She had expected
___ sane anger. It had been obvious when he had come after
her that she preferred life in the swamp to that with him.
But there was something more frightening about the way he
stood before her now than there would be had he walked in
wielding a bullwhip.

"Yes," she said coldly. "The 'savages' you slaughtered
were extremely decent."

"Including the warriors?"

"Yes."

"Ahhh . . ." He nodded, as if they carried on a pleasant
conversation, and sat beside her on the bed. "Tell me, Kendall," he murmured, reaching out to trail stiff, cold fingers
along her cheekbone to her breast, causing her to flinch.
"Tell me," he repeated, smiling at her reaction, "what it was
like. Did you jump like that when the savages touched you?
Or did you welcome them? Was there one special brave that
you slept with? I'm so very interested in hearing the customs.
I understand there were six or seven men in the party that
attacked you and Travis. Did they all have a go at you, my
sweet wife? Or were you clever enough to know from the
beginning who the leader was and charm your way into his
graces?"

She was a fool, but she couldn't help herself. She smiled at him, her eyes glittering with a deep hatred. "Oh, no, John. I didn't select one Indian. I loved all of them. I spent every night going from chickee to chickee, and right from the very beginning I loved it—"

Her words were cut off by the sound of her own scream as his hand caught her viciously across the cheek. She sprang to fight him, but his fingers clamped around her wrists.

"Liar," he told her calmly.

"I don't know what you're talking about!"

"You never touched any braves."

A gnawing apprehension began to tear at her stomach, but she tried to keep staring at him and speak without faltering. "Of course I'm lying. I despise you, John Moore. I'd say anything. There was only one brave—"

Again she cut off her own sentence with a startled and pained cry as he jerked so hard on her wrists that she was certain they would snap.

"Liar," he repeated softly. "And you know exactly what I'm talking about."

"No—"

"You were never touched by any Indian, and you know it. Captain Brannen has informed me of an intelligence report that just came in. The Rebs have been running arms all over south Florida. And a number of the Seminoles a little north of your swampland, around the Okeechobee area, have been raising cattle that mysteriously wind up in Georgia and Louisiana. Do you know why that's happening, Kendall? Sure you do. Because the chief of that particular tribe we just wiped out is a savage called Red Fox. And he's bosom buddies with an Injun-loving Confederate named Brent McClain."

Kendall tried not to move, not to give away any emotion with so much as a flicker of an eyelash.

"You're insane—"

"No. But you're dead, Kendall, if he ever comes near you again. He's a dead man already, Kendall. Marked. I'll find him. And I'll bring him to you on a platter."

She felt the blood drain from her face, but she answered him in a steady whisper. "No, John, you're wrong. You are the dead man. When he discovers what you've done, there won't be a place in the entire world where you'll be able to hide."

"You'd like that, wouldn't you, Kendall?" He was so pleasantly conversational that Kendall's apprehension quickly escalated to a fevered dread. "You have always wished me dead," he said.

"No, you're wrong again. I didn't want to marry you, but I didn't despise you—"

"Until you discovered that you were dealing with half a husband?"

"No, until I discovered that your cruelty is a sickness you don't even attempt to curb."

He smiled again, with frost in the eyes that never appeared warmer than ice. "Cheer up, Kendall. There's a good chance my sickness is about to be cured. We've a new man among us. A doctor who has studied the swamp fluxes and poxes. He has given me medicaments he's been experimenting with for many years—with astounding results. He thinks I have a very good chance of regaining my full health in less than a month, with your help and cooperation, of course."

Kendall shook her head. "It's too late, John. I could never touch you after what happened. All I can see when I look at you is the blood of innocents, of children—"

He laughed and the sound was shattering to her. "Oh, you'll touch me, all right. And soon. You're my wife."

He released her wrists and smiled coldly once more, then stood and deliberately unbuckled his belt. Kendall watched him, once more feeling as if her blood were being drained, sucked away as in a pool of quicksand.

He laughed as he watched her. "Not tonight, my love. Too soon. Tonight you learn a lesson."

His meaning was clear. Knowing she could increase his anger, she spoke in cool fury anyway. "You'd be a fool to beat me here, John. What would your navy friends think?"

"Not a thing, madam. There's not a man out there who wouldn't kill his wife for harboring a Rebel between her thighs."

Kendall stared at him and slowly lifted her chin. "You're sick, John. Really sick. But do you know something? You can't hurt me anymore. And that's part of it, isn't it? You know you can't hurt me so you just keep trying harder."

She gasped and tried to ward him off, flailing and clawing, when he gripped her shoulders and wrenched her over to her stomach.

And she learned that he could hurt her. She screamed when the leather cracked against her flesh for the first time. And she was barely coherent by the time he finished with the tenth whack.

Dimly she heard his satisfied warning as he crawled into the bed beside her. "I promise you, beloved wife, that when the time comes, you will touch me. And give me more than you ever gave the Reb."

"Never"!

She was certain he hadn't heard her. She was turned away from him, and her parched lips could barely form a word.

But she had never meant anything so vehemently in her life.

He could do anything in the world to her, but he would never receive anything from her. Beat her black and blue, break every bone in her body.

And still she would win. Still she would best him.

Because he could never have what she so freely gave Brent. She gave him her love.

But the knowledge of her victory was scant comfort as she wondered how she could ever manage to escape again.

Ten

He'd had a sense of running ever since he began the journey south.

If he could just run fast enough, he could get there. And if he could get there, he could stop whatever horror was coming . . .

And he could find her. Hold her. Protect her . . .

Looking very much like a great caged cat, he paced the deck of the *Jenni-Lyn* as it followed the coastline. Paced and paced. Wanting to hurry, wanting to run. That sense of running held a grip on his body. His muscles were taut and tense and bunched to race.

He knew that Federal ships lined the coast. He didn't care. He would be pleased to blast them clear out of the water. And he knew that he could do so. His determination to reach the swamp was so strong that he had indeed become invincible. The *Jenni-Lyn* had encountered one Union ship three times her size and had maneuvered around her with guns blazing so fiercely that it had been the Union vessel that foundered rather than the smaller Confederate craft.

At long last the *Jenni-Lyn* came to the mouth of the river and cast anchor. Brent and ten of his crewmen set out into the winding maze of the swamp in the dinghies.

But long before they reached the patch of sturdy pine

shore that led to the Seminole encampment, Brent had leapt over the side of his dinghy. The sense of running had become too strong. He swam swiftly through the waist-high water until he reached the land.

And at last he could run. And he did.

Straining muscles that ached to be tested, feeling the beat of dread in his heart.

He ran until he came upon the camp center, and then he stopped short; closing his eyes, opening them again—and discovering that the horror he had found was not an illusion to be blinked away.

The lifeless bodies were strewn everywhere. A brave's arms dangled from a partly leveled chickee. A little girl lay by a now cold fire, her arms clutched around a straw doll with pumpkin-seed eyes.

The eyes of the doll seemed to stare at Brent, as did those of the dead child. Brent forced his feet to move toward the little girl; he stooped and touched the rigid coldness of her face tenderly, closing the lids over dark, sightless eyes.

"Oh, Jesus. Oh, God. Cap'n, look here."

Brent tore his gaze from the child and saw that Charlie had come up behind him and moved onward into the camp. He was kneeling beside the corpse of a woman. Charlie shuddered; his weathered features contorted into a mask of sorrow. He looked at Brent. "It's Apolka, Cap'n. And her little kid."

Brent rose on leaden legs and approached Charlie. He knelt down beside Apolka and the child.

Flies infested the corpses. That seemed the greatest crime; the greatest indignity.

"I want a burial detail put together, quickly," Brent rasped, barely able to give his voice substance. It felt as if wires were being twisted within him. Tighter and tighter. Restricting his breath. Stabbing him, strangling him. Apolka. Lovely and gentle and soft as a young doe. Her life spent in tenderly loving her children, in adoring her husband . . .

Why? It was the most ungodly waste. A sacrilege. What man could kill a creature whose one quest was to love?

Brent barely felt Charlie move away from him to form a work detail as requested. Despite the flies, despite the foul smell of death, he reached down for Apolka and her son, embracing them in his arms as tears suddenly shook his frame. Tears of outrage, of loss, of horror, and of rage. The agony of betrayal. His own. Against Red Fox. Against his friend.

Night was beginning to fall. Beautiful twilight. The time of day that bathed the earth in shades of gold and crimson, yet faded fast to indigo and mauve. The sailors of the *Jenni-Lyn* stood about in the compound silently, paying homage to their captain's grief before attempting to approach him to take away the bodies of Apolka and Hadjo.

His massive shoulders shook as he cradled the bodies. But after the searing cries that had torn from him and ricocheted and echoed throughout pine and cypress, sky and swamp, there had been no sound.

The sun crept ever farther toward the west, yet still he didn't move. Neither did the sailors.

At last there was something upon the breeze; something, for it was not a sound. Charlie McPherson turned first, then one by one the others.

Red Fox stood behind them with a band of braves. They carried not arms, but shovels. Charlie realized with a sickness in his gut that the chief had already been to his camp; that he had returned now to perform the very service Brent had requested of his men.

It would not be a customary burial for the Seminoles. Usually, loved ones were placed within wooden coffins, taken deep into the shade of hammock, and there left with belongings to hasten with them on the journey to the next world.

A warrior's sword would rest beside him, a hunter's bow and arrows. A child's toy. A woman's shawl.

These beloved dead must be buried within the ground. Protected from wild creatures and the flies. The living had to be protected as well as the dead. Red Fox knew this. He had come back to find his family savaged by the white men, and he knew that he would have to bury his wife and child in the white man's way.

For long moments Red Fox stood still on the outskirts of the clearing, staring ahead at the tawny head and bowed, shuddering back of Brent McClain. The Seminole's features were hard, so hard. A sculpture in rock. Bronzed and rigid, they betrayed no pain, and no anger. Time and life and indomitable, inbred pride had given Red Fox a strength and stamina that not even death and agony could break.

It was Red Fox who approached Brent at last. He knelt beside him, easing his son from the white man's grasp. The Seminole stood with the small corpse clutched to his chest, as if the child were only sleeping. Brent at last turned his glazed gray eyes to the dark, fathomless depths of Red Fox.

"I have shed my tears, my friend, as even the strongest man must. Yet they have dried. I have cried out my vengeance to the wind, yet the echo has ceased. In the lonely nights ahead it might be that I shed tears again; and it is a certainty that in time I will seek revenge for this injustice upon my people and life itself. But now, I will give my loved ones to the earth. I will not allow them to remain any longer as carrion for the flies. As storms brew, so will the vengeance of Red Fox. And as they strike with swiftness and cunning, so shall I. Stand up, my friend. And help me with this act for the son of my loins and for Apolka, who held my heart in gentle hands. You loved them, too. This I know well, and the tears of the man who does not cry are comfort to my soul."

Silently Brent stood. Red Fox stretched out his arms, and Brent accepted the cold, still body of the child. Red Fox knelt beside his wife. He laid his knuckles beside her cheek, then traced the still beautiful contours of her face with steady fingers. Then he balanced her body in his arms and stood with smooth grace.

"Come," he told Brent. "We must say goodbye to them."

They buried Apolka with her child in her arms. According to custom, her household items were buried with her.

The high pine hammock became nothing but an encampment for the dead. The Seminole laid their dead loved ones to rest with proper ceremony, and then set the chickees afire. The hammock burned into the night, creating an orange glow in the darkness when the Indians and Rebels at last rowed away.

Red Fox had deserted his encampment to take his people to the nearby encampment of Mikasuki cousins. The high hammock where his cousin's tribe had hewn homes from the swampland was north and east of the blaze that had once been a community of life and laughter for the Seminoles. Red Fox and Brent led their combined men through the river and inlets in the chief's dugout.

For some time they were silent in the night. Then Brent at last spoke his misery. "I have cost you everything. Your home, your wife, your child—"

"You have cost me nothing, Night Hawk," Red Fox interrupted quietly. "Not you, nor your Confederacy. Always we have fought. Always we have died. You did not bring this down upon us. And always, Night Hawk, I have made my own choices. I will choose to fight again."

Brent fell morosely silent again. Then in the near total darkness of the night, he sought out his friend's eyes. "What of Chicola? I did not see . . ."

"His body? No. He lives. He escaped into the woods. Now,

my friend, ask me the question that must gnaw at your belly like worms."

Brent didn't hedge. He met the Indian's eyes openly.

"What happened to her . . . to Kendall?" He could barely force a whisper.

"She fought," Red Fox said with a soft pride and satisfaction. "Not with a pistol or knife, but with her will. Chicola has told me how she tried to protect him. And Jimmy Emathla—who lives now but will probably not see the morning sun—as he lay upon the ground with his mortal wound, heard the words that passed between her and the bluecoat."

Brent felt as if his entire body had become as stiff and rigidly cold as those of the corpses. "What was said?" he asked tensely.

"Jimmy Emathla must tell you himself."

Red Fox was right. Jimmy Emathla would not see another sun. His eyes were already glazed with death when Red Fox brought Brent to the high chickee where the Seminole awaited his demise with courage and certainty.

He appeared glad, however, to welcome Brent. The women who attended him scurried away when Brent knelt beside his pallet.

"Night Hawk," Jimmy Emathla said, closing his eyes as he clutched Brent's hand with a surprisingly powerful grip.

"Emathla," Brent returned, squeezing the hand he held. Pain etched its way into the Indian's features. "Perhaps you should not try to talk," Brent said. "You should preserve your strength."

Emathla shook his head and wet his parched lips. "I die with the night, my friend. This I know. I thank the gods that I have lived to see you. I failed you, Night Hawk. I ask your forgiveness."

"You never failed me—"

"Yes, in my arrogance, I promised to protect the women.

But the men came like the waves of the sea. I was as useless as an old woman."

"No man can combat twenty times his number."

Emathla shrugged his shoulders, hardly able to summon the strength to go on. Eyes that had closed with the strain of movement opened and met Brent's. "You must fight twenty times your number, Night Hawk. She proved herself the equal of any brave in courage. She sought not to save herself, but to save the children of Red Fox. And those who lived did so because she escaped the clutch of a stronger male to race back into the camp and touch upon whatever mercy lay in the souls of those who came. But the one who claimed her . . . she told him that she would kill him. A doe against a panther. There was murder about him. He will kill her, or make her wish that she were dead each day that she lives."

Brent inhaled a ragged breath. "Thank you for telling me these things, Jimmy Emathla."

Emathla inclined his head in a weak nod. His voice was fading so badly when he spoke again that Brent had to place his ear close to the Indian's lips. "There was one among them . . . a white man in blue . . . who did not kill. He might have wept. He raged against the death. And—"

"And?" Brent nodded, his fingers convulsively clutching the light blanket that protected Jimmy Emathla against the evening air.

"Travis . . . they called him Travis. He would . . ."

"Would what, Emathla? Jimmy, think. Talk to me. The man named Travis would what?"

"Help you. I think that he . . . loves the woman. Kendall. She ran for me. She trusted me. Kendall . . ."

Her name was a soft sigh. And the last word that Jimmy Emathla would utter. The sun was encroaching upon the eastern sky when a rattle of death sounded from within the Indian's chest. He shuddered and lay still. Peace composed itself over his features. A troubled world was left behind.

"You pulled off some pretty stunts in Jacksonville, Brent McClain," Charlie McPherson said, shaking a finger at Brent. "But that sure don't mean you can go dancing into Fort Taylor as if you were about to lead the Virginia Reel! That place is tighter than a drum!"

"I wasn't planning on raising a flag and sailing into port!" Brent exploded, running his fingers impatiently through his hair. "And you're forgetting, Charlie—the fort may be held by the Union, but that doesn't mean Key West isn't harboring a number of Confederate citizens!"

"And what're you going to do, Captain?" Charlie inquired dryly. "Ask all the Johnny Rebs to please raise their hands?"

"No, I was planning to use the same tactic we employed in Jacksonville. But this time I'll go in alone."

"Your only chance," Red Fox interrupted firmly, "is the sea."

Brent glanced at the Indian sitting in his open chickee where the three had gathered to talk as the sun rose high into the sky.

Red Fox spoke again. "You may walk into the city, my friend, but what good will that do? Unless you blow up the fort—and again, you will do yourself little good, for Kendall will be inside it. Patience, Night Hawk, must be her salvation. Now she will be kept under lock and key. Well watched. But in time the bluecoat husband will leave again. And the guard will grow lax. It is possible that she will sail with the Yankees once more. That will be your chance."

"We can't sit staring at Fort Taylor!" Charlie protested. "There's a war going on! We're supposed to be patrolling the west coast, then picking up a cotton shipment to take to London to buy arms!"

"I can go for her," Red Fox said quietly.

"No," Brent replied flatly. "Not you again, Red Fox. There is already a hollow in my heart that will remain there all my days—"

"It is unnecessary!" Red Fox snapped, irritably rising and striding across the floor of the open chickee. "I have told you—my choices are my own. And I seek to avenge myself upon these men with more right than you, Night Hawk. I am the man wronged."

"You're an Indian! It is a white war!"

"I have made it my war!"

Brent stared at Red Fox, his temper rising. It appeared as if the two would collide in an explosion of tension and rage.

Brent exhaled slowly, regaining control of his anger.

"Red Fox, they will be expecting an Indian attack. I'm willing to bet they'll be watching for your rigs with a hell of a lot more care than they do the blockade runners for the time being."

Charlie interjected nervously, "A red man would be dead in Yankee waters, and we can't go waving the Stars and Bars. So where does that leave us?"

"With a Yankee . . ." Brent said softly.

"What?" Charlie and Red Fox demanded in unison.

"A Yankee. Name of Travis. Jimmy Emathla spoke of him right before he died."

Brent suddenly snapped his fingers and faced Charlie—the captain in command again. "Charlie, we've got to get to the mouth of the river and find Harold Armstrong. See what he knows, and see what he might have picked up off the telegraph. The Yanks have Cedar Key, but Harold should know what's going on anyway. We have to find out just who this Travis fellow is. And get Harold to give us a contact on the island of Key West so we can find out when John Moore embarks on one of his sailing trips. We are going to pull your tactic, Red Fox. We'll exercise patience." He paused, clenching his jaw. Patience. When the Yank could be killing her, might have killed her already? No. Moore wasn't going to harm her. Not in the sense of breaking bones. She was some kind of a prize to him, like a trophy.

Brent swallowed and kept talking. "Red Fox, if you choose, you will sail with us. We're going to gamble on a Yankee called Travis."

The full moon rose high in the indigo sky. A dark silhouette appeared on the shore.

The call of a mockingbird broke the stillness of the night.

Still the men were quiet as they slipped from the trees and convened on the shore. Not until Harold Armstrong laughed out loud and boisterously shook Brent's hand and patted him enthusiastically on the shoulder did they relax.

"You slippery scoundrel!" Harold declared. "Feels like a month of Sundays since I've seen you, Captain McClain. But things have been moving like clockwork here. I haven't wanted for a thing, nor have any of the other settlers down here. The Indians have kept things coming just fine. But come on up to the cabin, boys. I'll fill you in on the latest while I fill you up with some fine beef and homemade cider!"

"Sounds fine, Harry," Brent agreed. "We need to know what's happening. Especially at Fort Taylor."

"I'll do my best. Now tell your troops to be careful here. Ain't too many rattlers on the high ground here, but I found a few coral snakes nesting a mite too close to the cabin the other night. Come on, now."

Brent motioned to his crew. They all fell into step behind him.

He followed Harold's graying head through a thick pine forest to the small settlement of heartily loyal Confederates eking out a living along the bay. On the river, not too far away, Union soldiers were holding a small fort that had once been used in the Indian wars. But there weren't more than a handful of whites in this virgin region of the state—nothing worth bothering about. The Union soldiers left the people alone, unaware that the rugged men and women who had hewn homes along the sea on the edge of a savage swamp were the stuff of which victory was made.

Not much later Brent and Red Fox and Charlie McPherson were grouped together again around Armstrong's table, listening avidly as Harold spoke while feeding them fine hunks of fresh beef his wife Amy had prepared before leaving the men to their talk.

"It's going to go on getting tighter and tighter, yes sir. 'Specially on the seas. Ever since they sailed that ironclad outta Virginia t'other day—"

"The what?" Charlie McPherson demanded.

"Ironclad, sailor—ironclad. The Rebs raised the old *Merrimack* from the harbor where the Yanks had sunk her. Plated her all up in iron and renamed her the *Virginia*." Harold's light eyes misted with envy. "Wish I could have seen her. Seems she plowed right into the Feds! Sank a score of them. And not a shell could harm her. Cannonballs bounced right off."

"Damnation!" Charlie exclaimed, his face glowing. "I knew we'd get them damn Yanks on the sea!"

"Whoa, boys," Harold warned them, shaking his head sorrowfully as he poured tin mugs of cider. "The victory didn't last long. The Yanks had their own ironclad ready to meet her the next day. They battled it out for hours and hours, the biggest damn naval battle a man could hope to see! The *Monitor* and the *Virginia* both backed out at last. You have been out of touch! The entire world will hear about it soon. I'm telling you, boys, warfare will never be the same again. Those two ships proved that everything we've got has been outmoded!"

Brent should have cared. He should have been fascinated by the genius of the Rebel shipbuilders.

He could only care about one thing.

"You got any good contacts on Key West, Harry?" he asked. "I need to find out a few things going on at Fort Taylor."

"Sure, I got contacts on Key West! What kind of an intelligence man do you think I am, Captain McClain?"

Brent grinned at the rebuke from the grizzled old man. "A damned good one, Harry."

Harry pulled out a chair and sat, watching Brent curiously. "Well sure, but I'm telling you, Captain, you can't get into Fort Taylor. That Yank lieutenant was mad as all hell about the Indians making off with his wife. Got her back now, I hear."

"We know that, Harry."

"Oh, yeah." Harold Armstrong gazed curiously at Red Fox, but Brent offered no further information.

"What do you know about Lieutenant Moore, Harry?"

"He's like a cat on the prowl, spends half his life hoping to catch up with you, Captain, from what I hear."

"Can you find out when he sails again?"

"Sure."

"And I need to find out whatever I can about a Union officer name of Travis something-or-other."

"Deland," Harold supplied quickly.

Brent glanced at him with surprise, and Armstrong hastily continued. "United States Navy Commander Travis Deland. He's right beneath the captain they got stationed there."

"Has he got any kind of a reputation around here?"

Harold shrugged. "Yeah, seems he gets along good enough with the folks in Key West. Real gentlemanly sort. Firm, but nice and polite. Why?"

"Because I'm going to try to talk to him." Brent stood up and stretched and gave Charlie McPherson an impatient pat on the back. "Get the crew back together. We're going out tonight."

"Ah, hell!" Charlie muttered, draining the last of his cider and pushing back his chair. "Chris and Lloyd found themselves a couple of pretty girls in this backwoods hellhole, and now you're asking me to tell them fellers we're pulling out!"

Harold Armstrong laughed. "Good thing you're going to pull them young fellows out! You must be talking about the Beler girls. Their pa's the preacher here—and a mean man with a shotgun. He's got himself a passel of daughters, from age three on up, and he's just as protective of those girls as a big old watch dog might be! Now, I'm certain your boys are with the older girls, and that the older girls are just as happy as punch, but it's a darn good thing you're pulling out! Beler has raised them girls to be real little ladies, he has. He wouldn't take to any young sailors trifling with their affections, if you do take to my meaning."

"Hell!" Charlie muttered again.

And that was that.

An hour later, the *Jenni-Lyn* was pulling from the river to the open sea.

If Brent had started out just minutes later—or if a black-puffed thundercloud hadn't covered the moon at just that time—the crew might not have missed the small, battered dinghy that sidled past them, precariously close.

But as it was, the *Jenni-Lyn* was far out into the bay when Harold—watching from a sandy shore—saw the dinghy and warily hobbled down to investigate.

He was amazed to see a set of long delicate fingers curl over the gunwale, then slide weakly away. He trained a lamp within the dinghy and exhaled a long whistle.

There was a girl in the dinghy. Her face was as pale as

211

the moon, yet as beautiful as its ethereal light, and framed in a cloak of golden hair that spilled about her where she lay on the baseboards. As he stared at her, her eyes flickered open, and he wasn't sure if their color was black, or so blue that they became the indigo of the night sea. She tried to dampen parched lips and speak. She failed, then tried again. To hear her, Harold bent low beside her, awed by the beautiful woman who had appeared from the sea.

"What is it, girl?" he demanded gently.

Her hand rose again, reaching toward him. It fell back to her side. She hadn't the strength to hold it up.

"Help me," she mouthed at first, and then her voice found substance and a parched whisper sounded in the night. "Help me. Oh, please, help me."

"Now, now! of course old Harry Armstrong is going to help you, girl. Don't you fret. Just take it easy. I'm going to take you to my cabin and feed you and set you before a fire."

"Harry?" she queried urgently. "Harold Armstrong?"

"Yes, ma'am. Harry Armstrong, at your service."

"Thank God. My name is Kendall Moore. Brent . . . Captain McClain said I should come . . . to you. You will help me? You'll keep me from the Yanks?"

"Ain't no Yanks going to find my cabin, ma'am. And there ain't no friend of Brent McClain's going to suffer none near me. You just hang on, ma'am. You're all right now. You're safe."

"Oh, thank you. Thank you . . ."

Her whisper faded away. Her eyes fell shut.

The comfort of relief had taken away her fragile grasp on consciousness and allowed her to sink into welcome oblivion.

Harold looked at the girl—no, woman—more closely, then scratched his head and stared out to the sea.

She had to be the wife of the Yank. The woman the Indians had stolen. The reason Captain McClain was sailing for Key West right now . . .

The captain had just missed her, Harold thought sorrowfully. Missed her by a matter of moments . . .

Harry reached into the dinghy and lifted her slender body into his arms. He started back past the sand and the pines and set up the trail that led to his cabin, his mind plagued with confusion.

What had happened with the Indians, Captain McClain, and this Yank's wife who spoke like a southern magnolia? And how in hell and tarnation had she gotten here? All the way up here from Key West in a beaten old dinghy. A sea-rotten rowboat?

Eleven

Her sleep was clouded with nightmares, and in her dream world she heard the voices again and again. Her voice. Shrill and strident. And then Travis's . . . gentle, calming, pleading.

"I swear to you, Kendall, I'll think of something. Listen, John has been assigned to the *Mississippi*. He's not coming back again for a long time."

"I can't stay here, Travis, I can't! Not after what happened."

"Kendall, I cannot let you walk out of here. I know John hurt you; that's why I came. But if you give me time, I'll come up with something. Give me time to work on Brannen. Right now he believes he's harboring a Confederate spy in his midst."

"I am a Confederate! I've never denied it! And it's not what happened to me that upsets me, Travis. It was the Indians. He ordered that slaughter! Oh, Travis, I'll never be able to forget what happened! Never, as long as I live. And I'll hate the Yankees—"

"Kendall?" Very quietly. "Kendall, I'm a Yankee. Do you hate me?"

"Oh, Travis, no! of course not. You know I care for you! But please, Travis, understand. I can't help being what I am and I'll never forget what John did in the name of the Union."

"That isn't fair, Kendall."

"And the men here, Travis! They all act as if I should be hanged! I can't bear it."

"Kendall, we're at war! They know you were with one of the greatest enemies the Union Navy will ever know. Oh, Kendall! I do understand. *My* men didn't behave like that. You have more friends than you know, Kendall. You just won't give them a chance."

"I can't give them a chance. John thinks he's getting well. And I couldn't stand it, Travis! I would always feel as if he touched me with blood on his hands, I would hear the screams . . ."

Kendall tossed in her sleep because the dream was so real, so vivid. She could see Travis, all his love and care and concern in his eyes, holding her close. "Kendall, give me time to find a way to get you out. And to find a place where you'll be safe."

That was when she had stared at the open door beyond him. And as he had gently whispered promises, she had grasped the heavy blue water pitcher on the bedside table and cracked it over his head with all her strength.

Forgive me, Travis!

Kendall moaned softly and thrashed about. Something cool was placed on her forehead, and she was no longer in the barracks, but in a small fishing shack on the western shore of the island.

"God go with you, young lady. God go with you."

The woman who spoke looked old, but she wasn't so very old. She had lost her oldest son at the First Battle of Manassas. And she had lost her second son at Second Manassas. They had chosen different sides. One died in blue; one in gray. The woman was forty, she told Kendall. She looked sixty.

But the journey had been harder than Kendall had expected it to be. So quickly she ran out of water! And the heat of the day, and the water chill at night. Things had begun to blur . . .

Kendall woke up with a start, amazed to awaken in such soft comfort. She lay on cool sheets, and her throat no longer felt parched and dry.

She opened her eyes to see that she faced a window with the shutters thrown wide open. Dazzling sunlight streamed in on her. Glorious green vines curled around the frame of the window, and just outside she could see beautiful purple flowers. Orchids.

"Back with us, are you, dearie?"

Kendall turned to see a buxom woman with iron-gray hair twisted into a neat chignon and bright blue eyes that twinkled like diamonds sitting in an upright chair beside the bed. She was dressed quite simply in homespun cotton, but she sat straight like a perfect lady, and her voice was soft and cultured. Kendall smiled shyly, confusion riddling her mind.

"I'm Amy Armstrong, young lady. You washed up on shore last night. Harry says you're Kendall Moore, a friend of Brent's."

Kendall nodded. Her nightmare had been a reality past. Past. It was over. She had escaped. She had found a safe harbor. Harold Armstrong really and truly existed, and as Brent had told her, she had been able to come to him for help . . .

"I did find the right place, then," Kendall murmured with a sigh.

"That you did, young lady!" Amy Armstrong said cheerfully, rising from her chair to plump Kendall's pillow and straighten the sheets about her. "Now you just sit tight, and I'll bring you something to eat. You must be half starved. How you survived in that dinghy I'll never know, much less how you managed to navigate. You must be quite a competent sailor, Kendall Moore!"

Was she? Kendall wondered. She had tried to follow the

islands and then the sun, and then the stars. Travis had taught her so much about the sea. And then Red Fox had taught her to read the skies and the breezes.

But she had barely made it. If she hadn't reached the river when she had, and if Harry Armstrong hadn't been there, she would have died.

"I'm not a great sailor, Mrs. Armstrong," she said softly. "I was just very desperate." She bit her lip and then offered the friendly matron a strong smile. "I want to thank you, Mrs. Armstrong. You and your husband, of course. I don't know anything about you—I'm not even sure exactly where I am—but I bless you for helping me, and I don't want you getting me anything. I'll get up and help you with whatever I can."

"Don't be silly now, girl!" Amy Armstrong protested, her buxom body moving crisply toward the door. "You stay right there in bed! You suffered some severe exposure. You may not want to admit it, but believe me, missy, your body is weak. Any friend of Brent's—"

"I'm not sure I'm really his friend, Mrs. Armstrong."

"Of course you are, dearie!" Amy Armstrong proclaimed, continuing on to the door. She gripped the handle and turned back to Kendall with a grimace. "We know exactly who you are, young lady. And we know just about everything that's happened. If that Seminole Red Fox thinks you're worth dying for—that's good enough for me. And Brent—well, he's half crazy worried about you! I don't mind saying that I love Brent McClain, and seein' how he feels about you—well, it just seems natural that I'm going to love you, too! So don't think a thing about your situation. This isn't Charleston, I'm afraid. It's not even Jacksonville. The old guard just isn't around to watch our morality!" She shook her head sadly. "I'm wondering if there is an old guard anymore."

A sigh escaped her, but then she sternly shook away her

217

melancholy. "Today, young lady, you're going to stay in bed. Tomorrow I'll let you up."

"Oh, wait, please!" Kendall begged, kneeling on the bed to stop the woman. "Did you say Brent—"

"You won't get another word out of me, young lady, until you eat well and get some rest!"

Amy Armstrong walked out of the room and firmly closed the door behind her.

And no matter how Kendall pleaded when she returned with a full tray of food, Amy staunchly refused to talk. "When you wake up in the morning, Kendall, we'll talk."

"But I just woke up!"

"And you're as weak as a newborn foal! Now get some more sleep, and tomorrow you'll have a nice bath in steamy hot water and a walk in the garden."

"The garden?"

"Oh, yes! We have a beautiful garden. Harry is a horticulturalist. Or he was before the war. I work with the plants now, and Harry keeps himself busy scouting for information to pass on to stray Rebs. Now you settle down for a nap."

"I'll never sleep!" Kendall protested.

But she did, and her sleep was long and restful, undisturbed by dreams. And in the morning she helped Amy carry huge pots of hot water to a big iron tub and she sank into the oblivion of a steamy bath. She closed her eyes with the luxury, and therefore didn't see the horror or fury in those of her hostess when they lit upon the welts that still marred the smooth cream of her back.

But Amy pursed her lips and kept her silence.

"Julie Smith, one of the local girls, gave me a lovely gown for you. I think it will just fit. You're both tall and slender. You're a little thinner, which will be just fine since we don't have an extra corset for you."

The gown was beautiful. Kendall hadn't worn anything like it in months. It was pale peach with a white center bodice, and Amy even produced a peach ribbon to tie about her throat. "Petticoats! You must have a crinoline for that skirt. I've one in the trunk."

Kendall laughed. "Mrs. Armstrong, you are so very kind! I feel as if I ought to be attending a ball with a barbecue and fiddlers and dancing into the night!"

"Amy, dearie! Call me Amy. And, oh, yes, I do remember being as young as you. We're Charlestonians too, Kendall, did I tell you that? Originally, I mean. We've been living here for almost twenty years now."

"All alone?"

"Oh, no. There are about a hundred of us sprawled along the coastline. And it is a beautiful place. Hot, of course. But so very beautiful. Orchids grow divinely! Come, I'll show you!"

The Armstrongs' cabin stood in a fairy-tale setting. It was secluded on three sides by a wall of high pines. A vegetable garden grew in the rear, but the boardwalk in front was surrounded by colorful flowers. Hibiscus, orchids, and more exotic flowers that Amy named as they passed them. "Down that little trail is the barn. We have two cows, two mules, and three pretty little thoroughbred fillies. You're welcome to ride, of course, but only around the paddock. It's easy to get lost around here unless you know where you're going!"

Kendall smiled, then frowned and caught Amy's arm. "Amy, please—now will you tell me about Brent? Have you seen him? Do you know where he is?"

Amy hesitated unhappily, then forced her cheerful smile back to her worn but lovely features. "Why, I suspect he should be back any time now."

"But you do know where he is?"

"Yes."

"Where, Amy? Oh, please, tell me!"

Amy sighed. "All right, Kendall. He went to look for you."

"Oh, no!" Kendall gasped. "He'll be caught. He'll be killed!"

"Now, stop that!" Amy ordered firmly. "Brent is no fool. He won't rush in without knowing what he's doing. He's planning on searching out a man named Travis."

"Oh, no!" Kendall gasped again. Brent and Travis. She loved them both, and they were both so full of honor and pride. A loyal Unionist, and a loyal Confederate. Both so stubborn and loyal to their causes. They'd wind up killing each other, and it would be her fault just as the massacre at the camp had been her fault . . .

"Get ahold of yourself, my girl!" Amy commanded staunchly. "Red Fox and Brent are together, and I don't think the whole Union army would be a match for those two. You'll see. And rest time is over. We've no slaves around here, Kendall. You can come and help me in the garden. And walk the chicken feed through the trail out back. I hate the creatures too close to the house. They get loose and wreck everything in sight. And Harry will come home mighty hungry tonight because he's busy helping a privateer do some repairs on his sloop. Let us get going now."

Kendall mechanically followed Amy. She was more than happy to fill her hands with work. But no matter how Amy chattered, she couldn't busy her mind.

She was crazy with fear. Brent—and Travis. What would happen when they met? Travis had the forces. Brent had his sheer strength and indomitable willpower. And he would have rage and revenge in his heart because he obviously knew what had happened . . .

And then there was Red Fox. He would be insane with anger and pain. He would kill anyone who wore Union blue. Red Fox . . . How would she ever face him again? He had given her so very much, and she had cost him everything.

She didn't think she could bear any more loss. Not on her behalf. It would have been better had John Moore killed her.

The Yankees, Brent decided, squinting beneath the sun, seemed perpetually determined to act like fools. It was frightening the way they let things slip by them. If he didn't watch himself, he would grow careless simply because they were so damned unalert!

If the Rebel armies had as many men as the Yanks did, and if there had been some cannon factories south of the Mason-Dixon Line, the war might have ended in a matter of months, he thought.

Brent had learned from Harry's informant that Lieutenant Moore was not at Fort Taylor; he had been sent north up the Gulf Coast to serve with the fleet under Admiral Farragut.

And Brent had learned that Commander Travis Deland would be heading a routine scouting party out around the lower Keys on his ship, the *Lady Blue*, a schooner with six guns.

Brent had sailed the *Jenni-Lyn* beneath the *Lady Blue*'s nose, then run hard before the wind on a run through the reefs to hide behind the growth of a tiny mangrove island too small to appear on the charts of any but the most meticulous cartographers.

All he had to do now was wait. The *Lady Blue* was following him at full speed. It seemed that no matter how long the Unionists had been stationed in the Keys, they hadn't learned the dangers of the reefs. At her present direction and speed, the Federal schooner would pile up on the coral rocks at any minute. Then the *Jenni-Lyn* would only need to sweep by and pluck the Yankees from the water. He'd have his hands on Travis Deland.

"Captain," Charlie, standing beside him on deck, said uneasily. "Look at her. She's veering. That's one damn Federal that's gonna clear the rocks!"

Brent's brow furrowed as he saw that the *Lady Blue* was

indeed veering. She was maintaining her speed smoothly, but maneuvering to the starboard. Her captain was aware of the reefs.

"We can't afford to receive a shot, Captain. Or to welcome a boarding party. That Federal is probably carrying a crew of forty, and we're only twenty."

"Twenty-five," Brent corrected. "Red Fox and four of his braves are aboard, Charlie. But I don't want to get shot up. We're in Federal waters; we can't afford to limp through here. We're going to have to give the *Lady Blue* a shot. Charlie, get Lloyd to rouse the gunners to the ready. Fast!"

"Battle stations! Now!"

The deck of the *Jenni-Lyn* resounded with the clatter of running feet.

"Load cannon number one."

"Load one!"

"Take her with a single shot," Brent commanded. "One clean shot dead on her bow as soon as we move the *Jenni* into position!"

Charlie, at the wheel, steered them clear of their island cover just as the Federal schooner completely cleared the reefs and raced toward them in swift pursuit.

"Fire!" Brent ordered.

The cannon boomed. A second later the schooner staggered and heeled hard to starboard, her bow a wall of flames. The chaotic ruckus aboard could be heard across the water. "Get me the glass, Charlie," Brent ordered.

He stared ahead at the wounded schooner, through the spyglass. Men were running about the burning deck. Some were plunging into the sea. Suddenly a shout rang out, and the panic subsided. Sailors raced to the bow to fight the blaze.

"Move in before her gunners have a chance to get into action," Brent ordered quietly.

The *Jenni-Lyn* glided smoothly to the scene of the struggling vessel. But before they came in too close, Brent sent a signal man to the mast to ask for the Federal's surrender.

Any officer should capitulate, Brent knew. The schooner couldn't take another shot, especially at this close range. A ship's captain would be consigning his men to hell were he to refuse terms.

As Brent stared at the *Lady Blue*, a white flag was hoisted up her mast.

The *Jenni-Lyn* went about to meet with the Federal, her grim-faced crew ready to hurl their grappling hooks. Brent saw a tall man in a commander's crisp uniform standing rigidly on deck to meet him, two line officers at his sides.

Brent started suddenly as he stared at the young commander with the intelligent brown eyes and the strong, gaunt features.

He had known Travis Deland all along. The Union officer he faced was the man who had pulled him from death in Charleston harbor.

"We meet again, Yankee," Brent said quietly.

"Yes, we meet again."

"Don't make it a slaughter, Commander. Order your men to hold all fire."

"Terms of surrender, Captain McClain?" Deland inquired crisply.

"I want a moment of your time, Commander," Brent replied dryly. He turned his head slightly as he heard Red Fox move quietly to take a place behind him. "And I want whoever aboard your ship took part in the massacre in the swamp. Give me those men—for a fair fight with the Indians whose homes and families they destroyed. The rest of you will go free. The southern prison camps are getting mean, Commander. No malicious intent—some of our armies are fighting on the same rations already."

The men aboard the Federal ship were silent for a moment. Then Travis Deland spoke up.

223

"My men were not in on that raid, Captain McClain. I give you my word as a gentleman, sir, that I would not have taken part in such a massacre of the innocent."

"I do not accuse you, Commander Deland. But you carry more than your company aboard your ship. I feel it safe to assume that you have men beneath you now who did do murder under the auspices of the Union Navy and Lieutenant John Moore."

A man suddenly broke from the Federals' rank, ripping a shot packet open with his teeth. "Storm the Rebs, Commander! Storm them! We've got the numbers!"

A shot rang out from the *Jenni-Lyn* just as the Yankee raised his loaded rifle. Brent didn't need to turn to know that Chris—a crack shot—had picked off the seaman from the crow's nest atop the mainmast.

Travis Deland watched the man fall without betraying emotion. He stared at Brent. "I can't turn my men over to you to be tortured and executed."

"No one will be tortured or executed. They will engage in fair fights. Your brave gallants in blue were happy to draw Indian blood before. Why not now?"

Travis didn't take his eyes from Brent's. "Seamen Crocker, Haines, Dunphrey, and Holmes. Front and center!"

"No! Commander, those savages will—" a man began to protest.

"Coward!" Travis bellowed. He spun on the three seamen. "You made the war with the Indians. Now you will fight it—and fight it with courage!"

"A man for a man," Brent said softly, his voice still carrying to the deck of the *Lady Blue*. He nodded toward Red Fox. The Indian and three of his braves bolted over the rails with swift agility and boarded the *Lady Blue* to face their Union counterparts.

"All other small arms overboard!" Brent ordered.

Travis didn't blink. "Small arms overboard!"

"There will be no interference on either side," Brent said smoothly. He pointed toward the crow's nest. "Chris will pick off the first man to move against an Indian—or a Yank. A fair fight."

Travis Deland nodded his agreement.

A savage war whoop sounded, and Red Fox jumped for one of the men in Union blue. The sailors responded to the frenzy of the fight, drawing the very weapons they had used against the women and children of the Seminole encampment.

It was a fair fight, but quickly terminated. Red Fox and his men fought with vengeance. They saw their slain wives and bloodied infants in their minds as they charged.

All four of the Yankees died swiftly. Silence reigned again. Travis moved a hand, and his crew moved to enshroud the bodies of the dead.

"Now, Commander, if you'll be so good as to step aboard the *Jenni-Lyn* for a few moments, we'll shortly part company."

"Don't do it, Commander!" a gunner sang out. "It's a rebel trick!"

"Don't be absurd," Travis answered tiredly. "It's no trick. He could have blown us to kingdom come had he wished."

Without a flicker of expression, Travis smoothly boarded the *Jenni-Lyn*.

Brent inclined his head slightly. "My cabin, if you will, Commander. I believe you know the way."

"Sit, Commander," Brent said shortly after they had entered the captain's cabin and Travis stood rigidly at attention. Brent slipped a slender cheroot from a teakwood stand atop his desk and lit it, inhaling deeply. He perched on a corner of his desk, then offered the stand of cigars to the Yankee. A knot of jealousy encircled his heart. John Moore might be a hell-sent bastard, but if Brent was any judge of people, Travis Deland was a man of strong and noble character. He

225

apparently knew Kendall well—and loved her, according to the dying words of Jimmy Emathla. What did Kendall think of Deland? What did she feel for him?

Travis accepted a cigar, and the match Brent offered. "You want Kendall, don't you, Captain?" Travis inquired softly.

Brent nodded. "I can't attack the fort, Commander. I haven't the weapons or the men—and it's hardly likely the Confederacy would spare them to me. I'm afraid we've other objectives more important than taking Fort Taylor." Brent hesitated a moment and then continued. "The Indians at the encampment weren't all dead. One of the survivors witnessed a scene between you and Moore—and Kendall. And then he heard some things that passed between Kendall and her . . . husband. Deland, that man means to kill her. The Indian said that you were a man of honor. Commander Deland, I want you to help me. I do want Kendall. But I can't free her without your assistance."

Travis Deland exhaled a long sigh. Then his dark eyes fell steadily on Brent. "It should seem strange to me, Captain, that the famous Night Hawk has taken time out from his war to seek a woman in the Florida Keys. But it doesn't seem strange at all, because you see, I love Kendall very much myself. But I can't help you. Kendall has already escaped."

"What?" Brent's body stiffened like a mast.

Travis hesitated, and Brent saw pain darken the man's eyes. "Kendall was with me when the Indians abducted her. That brave with you today led the party. I thought she was being held by savages against her will, so I did follow John into the Glades, but I caught up with him too late. Too late I realized that Kendall was happy there. Anyway, soon after we returned to the barracks, we found out that a suspected alliance between the Rebs and certain Seminoles was fact. John knew that Kendall had been with you." He paused again, his facial muscles showing the strain of his tale.

"I heard her screaming the night we returned to the fort.

226

I heard her halfway across the barracks. No one would do anything about it, Captain. You must surely understand that Yanks aren't going to feel a lot of pity for a woman who has not only cuckolded her husband, but has done so with a Reb naval captain. Don't think too badly of them, McClain. They all think John taught her a little lesson—and that he'll forgive her now and go on as before. But I . . . I know John. As soon as he left, I went to see her. I promised her I'd get her out somehow. But she was hysterical. Said something about John getting better and she wasn't going to wait. She pretended to listen to me for a while. Then she cracked me over the head with a water pitcher. When I came to, I discovered she had escaped from the fort on foot. I went into town and at last found out that she had sailed off in a little dinghy. She's already gone, Captain. Been gone a couple of days."

So where the hell was she now? The question shrieked in Brent's mind, but he stood silently and walked to the cabin door. "You're free to go, Commander Deland."

Travis stood awkwardly and moved toward the door.

"Maybe you should know, though, Deland," Brent said softly, "that I intend to find John Moore one day. And when I do, I'm going to kill him."

Travis hesitated, curling his cap in his fingers. "There may come a day, Captain, when I kill him myself."

He moved past Brent and then paused a moment longer. "In case you haven't heard, Captain, New Orleans fell to Admiral Farragut yesterday."

A shudder of doom gripped Brent's gut. New Orleans. The largest city in the South . . .

"Thank you for telling me. Good day, Commander. I hope we meet again when this war is over."

"So do I," Travis muttered, "so do I . . . Captain?"

"Yes?"

"Look for her. Search for Kendall until you find her. She's a fair sailor, but she's alone. The only advantage she has is

227

that John is in New Orleans right now. But I don't know where she was headed. Find her."

"I will find her."

The words were quiet. Low. In the steel-gray eyes that observed him astutely, Travis could find no reason to doubt their intensity.

"And tell her for me . . . tell her that I love her."

McClain didn't reply. He saluted sardonically. "Good day, Commander Deland."

"Good day, Captain."

The men of the *Jenni-Lyn* removed the grappling hooks as soon as the Yankee commander had boarded his own ship.

They were sailing back around the tip of the island when Brent reappeared on deck, striding toward Charlie at the wheel.

"I'm going to spend half this damned war in the pursuit of one fool female!" he thundered. "Keep her headed north, Charlie. Follow the chain. Double the man in the crow's nest, and keep a spyglass on the islands. We're looking for . . . anything that sails. Fool female!" he spat out again, pounding on the wheel with a fury.

Charlie wasn't fooled for a second. He knew that Brent was worried sick. But he couldn't worry about Brent for long because Lloyd was suddenly shouting from the crow's nest, "Sloop ahead, Captain. Starboard side!"

"What flag is she flying?" Brent demanded tensely.

"No flag, sir. Should I lower our colors?"

The Stars and Bars flew proudly from the *Jenni-Lyn*'s mast. Brent shook his head and then called out, "No, leave them flying. We should be a match for any sloop. Keep your eyes trained for a flag."

"They're raising one, sir. It's the Stars and Bars, sir! She's a Confederate. And she's signaling for a rendezvous."

"We'll meet aside her then, sailor. But get the men to battle stations just in case. We're still in Yankee waters."

But they needn't have worried. The sloop was a privateer out of Richmond, heading for the Bahamas. The young captain told Brent he hadn't dared raise his own colors until he had seen Brent's.

"But I was hoping to catch ya, Captain McClain," the young runner told him. "We pulled into Biscayne real carefully, 'cause we'd heard the Rebs had a man there to kind of help us along, you know. I had some repairs to make on the hull—caught a cannonball a few days ago. Anyway this old man—Harold Armstrong, he said his name was—said I might catch up with you out here. Said to tell you that he's got the woman. Didn't say anything else, Captain, just that."

Brent silently exhaled a long sigh of relief. "Thanks, Captain. You've just saved us a hell of a lot of time."

"You've heard about New Orleans?" the privateer asked quietly.

"Yeah, I just heard."

" 'Damn the torpedoes—full speed ahead.' "

"What?"

"Oh, just something that Union Admiral Farragut said when he swept past the forts. The Yanks are quoting him all over the place. The Union is piling on more and more ships. We just don't seem to be able to keep up."

"No, we don't," Brent said. "Well, thanks again. And watch out—you're in Yankee territory here, as you know. The blockade gets tight as hell a little farther south. They know we're pulling in supplies from the Bahamas."

"I'll be careful. Oh—and thank you, sir."

"For what?"

"Never thought I'd get to meet the Night Hawk. You have quite a number of admirers up Richmond way, sir. And, I might add, quite a few enemies up Washington way."

"I know. But that's war, sir." He saluted the privateer cap-

229

tain then turned to Charlie. "Charlie, we've one stop to make, and then we'll return to the damned war!"

He shook his head with aggravation and turned away from Charlie. "I'm going to catch up on a little sleep. Tell Red Fox that Kendall is with Harry. Damn woman!" he muttered. "Thinks she can take on not only the Yanks, but the whole damn sea. She's driving me crazy. I'm going to kill her!"

Twelve

"You mark my words, Kendall," Harold Armstrong said, securing a clump of dirt around a freshly transplanted bougainvillea, "the day will come when this place will be busier than Richmond!"

He sat back on his heels and dusted the dirt from his hands as he smiled at Kendall. "You'll find plants here that are native to South America—and North America! You see the trade winds carried pollen. The Glades are unique, young lady. Wild. And when they're bordered by this glorious stretch of beach . . ." He sighed, a man completely replete with bounty for life.

Kendall laughed. "Yes, Harry, your place is very beautiful." The smile faded from her features. "And of course, I saw the beauty of the Everglades when I was with Red Fox . . . but I don't know if I have enough of the pioneer spirit to live there! It's also lonely. And beauty can harbor quicksand and snakes and—"

She stopped short as Harry chortled out a gleeful laugh. "You're gonna tell me, girl, that you haven't got the pioneer spirit! You sailed all that distance in a little dinghy? You're pioneer enough for me, girl."

Kendall shook her head with a sigh. "I dream of home all the time, Harry." When she wasn't worrying about Brent and

231

Travis and Red Fox and everything that could be happening while she waited, she added silently. "I dream that the war will end. That the Yankees will at last grow tired of trying to subdue us and leave us to live as we please. And one day I will go back to Charleston. I'll find a way to defeat my stepfather, and I'll restore Cresthaven to its former grandeur. Oh, Harry! Pa built his plantation with so much grace! The grand staircase appears to stretch forever, and when we had a party, the house was filled with women in beautiful gowns and rustling crinolines and men in the most handsome attire! Pa was considered to be quite a theologian; the debates that filled the drawing room were wonderfully exciting!"

Harry smiled vaguely, wondering why it hurt so to hear her speak about her home. Plants were his love, now that his children were dead. He had made his move to Florida with contented purpose in his heart. But although the slavery question had meant little to him and Amy in their wilderness retreat, he was a born South Carolinian, and when his state seceded—and then his adopted land followed suit—he'd known he would have to become involved in the conflict, at least in some small way.

And when Kendall spoke, he could see things through her beautiful blue eyes. Days of grace. Of easy, dignified living. A code of behavior so dignified and gallant and held dear to every heart with no rules on a piece of paper to make them so.

But that was over. He didn't know why he felt it was gone; the South appeared to be winning the war. Except that New Orleans was already under Yankee rule, and he knew full well that the South was suffering severe shortages. He didn't want to tell Kendall that, though. Just as the young woman had captured his wife's heart, so had she captured his.

And he loved to see her smile. To hear her laugh.

"Yes, yes," he murmured, catching one of her delicate

hands to pat absently. "How about helping me prune back the tomatoes?"

"Of course, Harry"

Harry Armstrong started to amble around the cabin toward the vegetable garden in the rear, but he stopped suddenly as a long, mournful note sounded in the air. He gazed easterly, toward the beach, and a broad smile broke out on his features.

"Harry?" Kendall queried in confusion. "What was that?"

He laughed heartily, and his warm eyes twinkled out his pleasure. "A signal, girl! Billy McGretter's down at the beach blowing out a signal on a conch shell."

"What does it mean?"

"It means, young lady, that Captain McClain is back!"

"Oh!"

He had made it! Kendall's hand fluttered to her throat. Shivers of delight and fearful anticipation seemed to race all along her limbs, making her feel dreadfully weak. She wanted to see him so badly! She ached for him, longed for him . . . and he was here. But what should she do? Should she stand here and coolly await him? Or give in to her heart and fly down the path to the beach where the river met the ocean to watch him come ashore and then throw herself into his arms, heedless of all but the wonder of seeing him?

She closed her eyes for a quivery moment. What if he hated her for all the tragedy she had brought about? What if he had only thought to save her because he was, whatever his denials, a gentleman. A cavalier of the highest order, unable to leave her in the hands of the enemy.

Her dilemma was solved as Amy suddenly came running out of the cabin, allowing the door to swing shut behind her as she anxiously wiped her floured hands upon her apron. "They're here!" she cried joyously. "What's keeping you two? Let's give our boys in gray a proper welcome!"

Kendall's feet found life when Amy rushed past her, her ample bosom heaving with the exertion. The trail through

233

the pines seemed to stretch forever, and as she ran, Kendall was tortured with doubt. Was the bond that existed between them real? Or had she conjured it up in her mind out of her own desperate need for him? Could he possibly be as magnificent as she had created him in memory?

The pines began to thin out as she neared the beach. The earth beneath her feet slowly changed from dirt to dusky sand. Then suddenly she was clear of the trees altogether; only tenacious bushes grew sporadically along the edge of the brackish water.

And then, just as her legs had carried her without conscious command, they ceased to move, bringing her to a breathless halt far from the river's edge.

The *Jenni-Lyn* had been anchored within the inlet. The crewmen were eschewing the dinghies and hopping into the water to swim to shore. The men laughed and splashed one another and whooped out loud, triumphant Rebel yells. Kendall wondered vaguely if they all knew that, for this brief time, they were sheltered from the war. But she couldn't share their enjoyment of the safe harbor; she was too busy searching for one certain Rebel. Her breath was ragged from more than the run; her heart was pounding out the beat of a thousand cannons as she stood still, paralyzed when at last she saw him.

He was dressed in his gray captain's frock coat with the gold trim, much as she had last seen him. His boots were almost knee-high, but as he thrashed to the shoreline with his long strides, they didn't protect his fitted gray trousers from being drenched. Like his men, he didn't seem to care much about being drenched. His movement was too full of hurry and purpose.

He had grown a mustache and beard, which he kept neatly clipped, Kendall noted. And they were quite becoming. He was, she thought—love and pride sending through her body

234

a rush of thrills—the epitome of the cavalier. Imagination could never outdo reality . . .

"Brent! Oh, Brent!"

She forgot fear, she forgot protocol—and she completely forgot that a lady in her circumstance chanced all hope for respectability as she again found wings within her feet to run. She gave no thought to her gown, nor to any of the onlookers, as she rushed in headlong toward him, splashing heedlessly through the water.

His gray eyes at last touched upon her. A dry grin cut across his features, and he waited.

And when she was at last right before him, he stretched his arms to catch her to him, holding her close. She wanted to weep with the joy of feeling him. Of being held against his male warmth and strength. His iron grip about her caused no pain, only a delirious happiness.

"Oh, Brent!"

He at last held her away and lifted a wicked brow. "You almost make me forget that I'm ready to strangle you."

"Strangle me?" Kendall demanded, her eyes hungrily devouring his features. She wanted to touch them one by one, explore the fullness of his lips beneath the handsome curve of his mustache, ease away the lines of strain about his eyes, smooth the tautness of his brow . . .

"Yes, ma'am, strangle you," he said sternly, and she was quickly reminded of how piercingly his steel gaze could cut into her. "When I met with your Commander Deland—"

"Travis!" Kendall murmured, horrified. "Oh, Brent, you didn't kill Travis, did you?"

She was too worried to feel the rigid stiffening of his body so close to hers. She wasn't even aware of the strict tightening of his jaw. He blinked, and then said caustically, "No, I didn't kill him. Your Yank friend is just fine."

"Oh, thank God," Kendall murmured. But when she broke free of his hold, only to throw her arms around his neck once more, she saw that Red Fox, his features as fathomless and proud as ever, stood right behind Brent. Tears sprang to her eyes, and she broke from Brent with a wild strength to reach the Indian, clasping his hands and falling to her knees in the shallow water before him.

"Oh, dear God, Red Fox! I'm so sorry. So very, very, sorry. Forgive me!"

"Get up, Kendall," Red Fox commanded, kneeling to bring her up beside him. His dark eyes met hers gently. "Do not ask to be forgiven for the cruelty of others."

"Red Fox . . ." Her lips quivered as she whispered his name, and then she was hugging him, clinging to him, trying somehow to give back what had been taken from him, to offer her sorrow in understanding of his. His arms awkwardly came around her; his hand patted her back.

"We will endure, Kendall," he whispered in Muskogee, and her mind took several seconds to make the translation to English. Then she pulled back to meet his eyes again, her own still filled with tears. "Your son Chicola ran into the trees—"

"He lives. He is safe with his mother's people."

"Oh, thank God!"

Red Fox gazed past her silken head, cradled against his bare chest. Brent McClain was staring at them, and for a moment the steel of his eyes had become as light and vulnerable as a silver mist. Then Brent stiffened perceptibly. Impenetrable steel fell with ruthless control over the silver mist. He raised a brow.

"Shall we get out of the water, Mrs. Moore? Boots are difficult to replace these days."

His voice seemed to crack against Kendall like a lash, and she wondered what she had done when she turned from Red Fox to face him. She felt as if her heart were stretched like a bowstring, so tautly it might snap. Why was he so cruelly reminding her that she was a Yankee's wife? Was it a warning? A taunt so that she wouldn't forget that legal ties bound her to another, and that he was free? He might enjoy her— but, then, society did not decree that a man should not enjoy a lusty vitality. Along with southern gentility, Kendall thought with sudden fury and resentment, came southern arrogance. He felt it his due to claim her whenever he chose; he would probably never feel it his due to marry her, even if she were free.

It was Amy Armstrong who saw the hurt, confusion, and then anger flicker across Kendall's expressive eyes. She stepped forward, carefully staying just out of reach of the water's edge. "Y'all come on up to the cabin, now, Brent McClain. Bring those wild boys of yours with you! We've got a whole side of beef ready to cook on a spit!"

"Thank you, Amy," Brent murmured distractedly. He sloshed out of the water and turned back to his men, who were still half in and half out of the water. "Liberty for all except the guard crew. And for Chrissake, Lloyd, Chris, remember you're officers in the Confederate States Navy when you visit the preacher's daughters!"

"Yes, sir!"

"Yes, sir!"

Despite the respectful replies, the two young sailors gave one another joyful glances before wading ashore to freedom. Brent slipped an arm around Amy's stout shoulders and murmured something that made her laugh like a girl.

Kendall, standing in the river with the water up to her knees, froze rigidly as she watched Brent walk to the trail. His men walked past her, yet she was barely aware of the surprising respect they offered her as they doffed their hats.

"Come, Kendall."

When all had gone on by, she felt Red Fox place his hand gently on her shoulder.

She stared into his dark eyes with bewilderment.

"What did I do, Red Fox?"

"You did nothing, Kendall."

"Then why—"

"The Night Hawk is a strong man; he can deal with many things. He is not afraid to face battle, or death. But he is now beset by something new to him. He is learning fear."

"Fear? Brent is not afraid of me!"

"He is afraid of what he feels for you. He is discovering what jealousy is. Now, come. It is a good lesson, but should not be pushed. I enjoy teaching him, but he is my friend, and friends should be taught gently."

Together, Red Fox and Kendall trailed behind the others to reach the high ground and the welcoming cabin of the Armstrongs.

Although Kendall hadn't quite figured out where the other settlers had built their homes, a number of Brent's crew had. Given liberty, the men had sought their own diversions. There were obviously more young ladies around than the preacher's girls, because the sailors had disappeared almost to a man. Amy told Kendall with assurance that they would all be back when her meal was cooked—and that they'd probably have a few extra guests on their arms!

And so as she stood in the cabin's kitchen cleaning fresh vegetables to drop into a pot of seasoned broth, only Brent, Red Fox, Charlie McPherson, and Harry sat about in the adjoining parlor. Charlie and Harry puffed pleasurably on pipes while Brent lit up a cheroot. The foursome drank brandy while they discussed the war.

"There's gonna be trouble all along the Mississippi! Real trouble—more'n we had with Farragut taking New Orleans!" Harry advised dourly. "They've even got a general out on that western front that seems to know what he's doing, name of Grant."

Brent, leaning against the coral rock mantel, grunted. Kendall gazed up from the potbellied stove to find his eyes broodingly upon her. He didn't look away when he met and captured her gaze, and it seemed that he grew angry just from staring at her.

"I don't think we need to worry about no Grant when we got Jeb Stuart and ol' Stonewall Jackson and Robert E. Lee with the Army of Northern Virginia," Charlie declared solidly.

Harry grimaced, then gazed at Brent, frowning until he had followed the Confederate captain's eyes to the kitchen and Kendall. Then he grinned and asked, "What about you, now, Brent McClain?"

Brent at last turned his eyes to Harry.

"What?"

"Where are you and your crew of roughnecks heading, Captain?"

"Oh . . . uh, west. We've got to get some things in and out of the Gulf area. Then we're going to make a run to London. Sell some cotton, and make a few deals to purchase arms. We'll take Kendall to London. Get her a place under an assumed name—"

"What?" Kendall suddenly screeched, dropping an unsliced carrot into the pot.

"I said I'm taking you to London," Brent repeated with sharp aggravation.

"No, you're not! I don't want to go to London!"

"Oh?" Still leaning with apparent nonchalance against the mantel, he lifted his brandy snifter along with a caustic brow. "You'd rather return to Fort Taylor?"

Kendall set down her knife and placed her hands on her hips. "No, Captain McClain, I wouldn't. But I'm not going to London when the war and everything I love is here!"

"I can't watch over you through a whole damn war, Kendall!"

"You don't need to watch over me at all!" Kendall protested furiously.

"The hell I don't!" Brent growled, his fingers growing white-knuckle tight around his snifter. "You need to be watched every damn second!"

Kendall forgot that they had an avid audience in the other three men. She stalked to Brent where he stood at the mantel, her eyes blazing a static blue fire.

"No one is asking you to watch me, Brent McClain. And I'm not one of your slaves, a piece of property to be safeguarded for later use! I am not going to London. I can stay here with Harry and Amy. And if I prove to be a burden on them, I'll return with Red Fox to his people. And don't you dare tell me that I'll endanger them again. The captain at Fort Taylor was furious when he heard about the massacre. He won't allow any of his men near the Indians again!"

The line of Brent's lips compressed until it almost disappeared between mustache and neatly clipped beard. He set his glass down on the mantel with such a sharp click that Kendall was amazed it didn't break. He tossed his cheroot into the fire, then dipped a low bow to the other men. "Will you excuse Mrs. Moore and me, gentlemen? I'd just as soon not paddle some sense into her in front of spectators!"

His hand clamped down on her arm before she could protest, and he jerked her so roughly that she lost her breath. No help came from the other men in the cabin; as she was dragged in seconds flat to the door, she could hear their gruff and amused laughter.

"Stop it!" she finally gasped in protest, trying to grab at the door frame. "Brent McClain, stop it! Let me go. Amy's soup is going to be ruined."

"Don't fret none, Kendall. I can watch the soup!" Harold promised cheerfully.

"Now, you can come along like a lady," Brent hissed in

her ear, "or you can come along over my shoulder. But you're coming with me!"

"No! Brent—"

The combustible anger in him really frightened her now. She had waited for him so long, aching to feel his touch. But now it seemed that nothing could really be right between them, and it all should have been so beautiful. Tears sprang to her eyes when she saw that she could elicit such violence in the man she loved—the man she also resented and feared.

"Brent, wait! Listen—"

"Over the shoulder is fine with me," he said impatiently, and her grip on the doorframe was broken as he brought action to follow his words. There was nothing gentle about his broad hands and powerful arms as he swept her cleanly off her feet and threw her over his shoulder. Her midriff landed hard on his shoulder, and once again protest was knocked from her along with her breath.

Where was Amy, Kendall wondered, when she needed a woman's help so badly?

That answer came quickly to her. Amy was in front of the cabin, beyond the flower garden, turning the huge side of beef on its charred pine spit.

"We're off for a walk and a bit of a talk, Amy," Brent said pleasantly enough as they passed her by.

Kendall strained against his back with her fists and tried to plead with the woman.

"Amy . . . Mrs. Armstrong—"

"Have a nice time, dears!" Amy called, waving a large napkin cheerily after them.

Kendall at last saw the barn with its paddocks as Brent stalked on by it with her. He kept on going, through another slender trail in the pines. "Kendall, it's time you learned you're nothing but a woman," he said as she struggled wildly against him, anger gripping his voice.

241

"Only a woman?" she raged. "What is that supposed to mean?"

"You can't fight a male! You really don't understand that. And since you need to learn, I might as well teach you."

"What are you talking about?"

Her words were cut off as he finally came to a halt and set her down. Kendall gazed about her in confusion for a moment. They had come upon water again. But here the sand was white, and the small beach was flanked by thick trees and bushes. She stared at Brent and saw that he smiled grimly with his hands once more firmly set on his hips.

"Oh, we're alone, Mrs. Moore. Quite alone. You can scream and rage your head off, and not a soul will hear you or see you."

Her heart began to thump and squeeze painfully as she surveyed him standing there, so rigid that his muscles visibly bunched and a pulse ticked in his cheek. His gaze was hard, and as cold as a deep winter snow. There was certainly no love in his eyes. No tenderness. Only anger, barely restrained.

Kendall planted her own hands on her hips and tossed back her mane of hair. "I don't begin to understand you, Captain McClain. You didn't bring me here! I got here all by myself. I may be just a woman, I grant you, but I did arrive—"

"And you might have killed yourself! With no need. Your friend Travis had promised to get you out, but oh, no, you had to set off like a little idiot—"

"I couldn't wait!" Kendall protested, feeling a squirm of discomfort. Just how well had he come to know Travis? "And I'd like to know just how the famous Night Hawk, the king of Confederates, happened to extract all that information from a Yankee! Are you playing two sides of a field, Captain McClain? Are you really such a great war hero? Or are you running the blockade just for profit like the others?"

She backed away when the words were out of her mouth.

His expression hadn't really changed, but he had taken a step toward her and there was something so menacing in his step that she was forced to realize just how badly she had goaded him.

"I would kill a man for less than that," he said quietly. "But then you're not a man, are you? And that's the point of this conversation." His hand shot out suddenly, his fingers gripping her wrist, jerking her hard against his body. Then before she could gasp an outraged protest, she felt herself being spun about and backed to a tree. He moved his form against hers so that there was no space between them, and placed his hands on either side of her head, entangling her hair in his fingers.

"Now," he murmured, his tone more conversational but his muscles still taut with restrained tension, "tell me, Kendall, what do you do? You can't move. You're a prisoner. It's a sad fact, my sweet, but the male of the species is stronger. I can do anything I choose—and you can't do a thing about it."

"So what is this supposed to prove, you insolent—"

His lips fell upon hers with a savage hunger that stole both words and breath. She wanted to protest the ruthless violation, yet even as she tried to rebel, treacherous longings arose. It had been many long months since she had seen him last; months made up of endless days spent yearning so vividly for his touch that she could not deny it now, no matter how brutally bestowed. With all the need and sweet thirst of her heart and soul she returned his kiss, her response as wild and demanding as his assault.

His lips moved from hers at long last and he drew a ragged breath before brushing soft kisses over her brow, her eyelids, and her cheeks. A soft sob escaped her as she met his storm-cloud eyes again, met them with a plea for understanding and all the naked emotion that she could never attempt to deny him.

243

"Kendall, damn you, you've got to learn—"

"Learn what, Brent?" she cried in sharp interruption. "What would you teach me? That the world is dangerous, that life can be cruel?" Tears started to well in her eyes and she blinked them back in a fury. "Dear God, don't you think that I know that? I've lived through the worst horror imaginable since I saw you last! I wasn't even sure at times that I really wanted to survive. Every waking moment was a nightmare and the only good dreams I ever had were—"

She broke off abruptly, staring at him. The world did stretch between them. Their time together seemed destined to be filled with action and emotion, anger and passion. Yet no matter how very little time it was they managed to share, it was the magic of her life. He had become her reason for living, and she didn't want it to be a dream.

His eyes were on her so intently then, seeming to stake and hold her where she stood, reach into her soul. She had thought at first that he would hold her. That he would envelop her in his arms, for the tempest she had lived through had been a knife within his heart as well. Other things seared his mind and soul as well, she knew. Battles she never saw, private wars he fought alone. So much between them. But he didn't hold her. He watched her with a gleam of fire within his eyes. When he spoke then his voice was hoarse, so deep, almost shattering in its demand. "The only good dreams were what, Kendall?"

She held her breath. Stared at him in return. She had given away so much of herself, of her heart. A strange fear simmered within her. A fear that he couldn't have longed for her as she had longed for him. For a moment, she couldn't speak herself. But then the very cruelty of the life that surrounded them touched something within her, and she knew that she could only be honest, give her heart, and pray that he would take it gently.

"You," she whispered. She inhaled, and felt the breeze.

The palms swayed around her. She heard the cry of a seabird, and still felt the power of his eyes as he stared at her.

"You!" she whispered again. "Dreams are you, life is you, waiting is . . . you. I—I love you, Brent."

"Oh, God!" he exclaimed. "Little fool! I've forgotten war, life, death, and honor—because I love you!" he told her with somewhat of a pained and bitter twist to his words. Then his hands were on her shoulders, hard, taut, fingers biting into her. "That's why you've got to pay me heed, it's why you have to listen to me!"

"Oh, please, Brent! I don't understand you, and I do love you, and the time we have together is so infrequent and so terribly brief! Please, Brent, please . . ."

"Kendall," he murmured huskily, dragging her into his tender embrace. "What can't you understand? I'm frightened to death to leave you here again! You can't fight alone. John Moore could come back here, and you would be as powerless as you were before. I can't protect you from him and fight a war—"

"Brent! You couldn't have protected me in the swamp! There were too many of them! A bullet can kill a man as easily as it can kill a woman. I swear to you, Brent—"

"We'll discuss it later," he interrupted her suddenly. "I can't stand it anymore."

"What?" Kendall murmured in confusion, putting her slender hands against his chest to stare into his eyes.

"Love me, Kendall," he murmured huskily.

"I do love you, Brent," she replied in all innocence.

He groaned softly and pressed her to him again while holding her eyes captive with his smoldering gray ones. The imprint of his body suddenly seemed branded upon hers despite their clothing. A bolt of heat shot through her with a flash of fevered excitement and exhilarating danger. A rose blush splashed across her cheeks.

"Here?"

He lifted a finger and brushed a straying lock of hair from her face. "Umm-hmmm."

She suddenly felt as if she were going to fall. He sensed her shivery weakness and swept her into his arms, then lowered them both to the sand. His hands caressed her lovingly as he kissed her mouth again, slowly, lingeringly. They were such powerful hands, she thought vaguely. However he touched her, she thrilled at the strength of him.

"Brent?" she whispered against his lips.

"Hmm?"

"What if someone comes?"

"No one will come." Long fingers found the hooks at the back of her dress.

"Brent?"

"Hmm?"

"What about the Armstrongs? What will they think? We'll be missed."

"They'll think we found a beautiful spot along the shore and that we're making love."

"Brent!" Her dress slipped from her shoulders, and his lips pressed against her naked flesh. She moaned at the contact, and lay limply against him with no further protest.

He lowered her down on the sand and stared at her with passion and tenderness, his eyes darkening to a charcoal that held her transfixed with wanting him. He stripped away his coat, and lifted her head to place it on the gray cloth, spreading the tendrils of her hair in a fan about it, watching each touch of his fingers on her with a yearning fascination. His shirt went next, and when she saw the bare bronze breadth of his chest she could remain passive no longer. With a little cry she bolted against him, burying her face in the crisp, tawny curls that roughened that expanse of male flesh. "I cannot bear to be away from you," she murmured with a little sob.

He didn't reply. He massaged the nape of her neck with

the palm of his hand, then reached for the hem of her skirt to pull the garment over her head. The rich length of her hair fell back in a riot of sleek waves to curl about her breast, and he had barely tossed the garment aside before he uttered a hoarse cry and enveloped her in his arms, his hands making a thorough exploration of the naked mounds and valley before him. He kissed her throat, her lips, her breasts, lavishing a passionate hunger on each that made her strain to him, made her forget that they lay on a bed of sand, and that the sun-streaked blue of the sky was their ceiling. Sweetness swept through her. Unbearably sweet fire. And a need to touch in return. She threaded her fingers through his hair, kneaded his back with her palms. Touched with love and need and tenderness every part of him that she could reach.

She felt his fingers slip beneath the band of her pantalettes and teasingly graze her belly. Like a kitten she arched to his touch, losing all inhibition in the wild beauty of the sheltered cove. Something as primitive as the beach welled within her, a longing to please the man who could so masterfully draw her into the maelstrom of his consuming passion.

He sat back on his haunches, and leisurely tugged the drawstring of her pantalettes, watching his movement. Then he placed his hands on her hips, arching them upward as he eased the cotton fabric from her body. But he did so slowly, stooping to kiss each new expanse of silken flesh bared to his pleasure. His mustache teased her flesh, his lips and tongue stroked it with a damp, tantalizing heat that drew a riot of convulsive shudders from her. Still he continued his sensual torture, seeking a complete intimacy that drove her wild and left her quivering and calling out his name.

He at last rose from her and removed his scabbard and sword and boots, but when he began to touch his breeches, she was there, kneeling before him, seeking to do the service herself. And she understood his need to touch her so thoroughly for the wildfires flaming within her blazed ever higher as she loved him, knowing the strength of his thighs, the smooth flatness of his belly, the full potency of his masculinity.

He sank to his knees to meet her in the sand and eclipsed her with his arms, finding her lips again, running his hands along her back, caressing her spine, cradling her buttocks and drawing her to him tightly to savor the simple pleasure of their naked bodies melding. Then again she felt herself lifted, and laid on the sand. And he was above her, tense in features and form as he parted her thighs to wield himself within her in a passionate, explosive drive that was itself a shattering wonder. The heat touched all the way through her, riddling her with wonderful little shocks of glory, and she luxuriated in it, embracing him as he filled her.

Hovering over her, he stared into her eyes, and she looped her arms around his neck, not fearing to meet his eyes in the wonder of sensation. The waves beat a gentle pulse beyond them, and the pines swayed softly. The sand was warm upon her back. All these things she knew, yet they were but a subtle enhancement of the primal delight of having him take her, of having him so fully within her, making her so totally his for that spellbound moment of time.

"I love you, Brent," she whispered. "I love you so very much."

He smiled, and replied against her lips, "I love you, too, little Reb. I love you, too . . ."

He kissed her, then held himself slightly above her, watching her as he began to move. Tenderness gave way to flaming hunger, hunger to deep thrusting demand. Slim hips arched to his with mounting, writhing fever, and the supple, giving beauty of the woman drove his passion to raging bounds that seemed to know no end. And yet there was. He heard her shivering cry of sweet fulfillment, and his seed burst from him in a moment of shuddering glory. So volatile, so complete . . .

He held on to her in contented silence, then shifted his weight and stared up at the sun as he idly stroked the damp flesh of her arm. The pines shaded them from the direct glare, and all he could think was that everything was so beautiful. She lay with him unafraid in the golden daylight, and her form was as naturally beautiful as the sun and sea.

For a long while they remained silent, savoring the time together, the gentle touching that followed the explosion of mutual desires appeased again after so many nights of dreams. It was Brent who spoke at last.

"I do love you, Kendall," he said softly. "That's why I'm always half crazy. Frightened silly of what might happen to you."

She leaned on an elbow and gazed at him, her eyes beautifully languorous and sultry, crystalline with the heady drug of his masterful seduction. "How long will we have?" she asked huskily.

He winced. "Tonight. Tomorrow. Tomorrow night."

She leaned over him, and the golden satin tendrils of her hair teased his flesh. "Then let's not waste time," she murmured, and her lips fell to his chest, her kisses searing its expanse.

His passion flared quickly as she showered him with her love. He gripped her shoulders and pressed her to the sand, almost angry with the intensity of ardor and emotion she could so easily evoke.

"No—we'll not waste time," he responded heatedly.

And again he loved her with a shattering passion.

And again and again as the sun sank and the cove was filled with the golden glow of twilight.

Thirteen

Amy's barbecue was a wonderful success. The settlers who lived on the high ground at the juncture of bay and river inlet gathered to greet their Confederate heroes. Fiddles and flutes provided a merry entertainment, and children played along the garden paths. The men discussed horses, crops, and the war; the women exchanged recipes and sighed over the pictures in a copy of *Godey's Lady's Book,* which Brent had thoughtfully confiscated from a Federal sloop in late December.

The full moon was still out, riding high above the revelry. Like the boisterous musicians of the group, that silver orb seemed to illuminate the festivities defiantly. It was difficult to believe that the Yankees were very near, in control of the outdated Fort Dallas up the Miami River. But the men of the nearly defunct fort never bothered with the bay settlers; their numbers were insufficient, and they could never control what was still a winding wilderness on the borders of a savage swamp. They were oblivious to the fact that the seemingly worthless settlement provided a harbor for some of the greatest enemies to the Union cause.

Kendall, too, was oblivious—to everything but the moment. She was very grateful to Amy and Harold Armstrong. They had accepted her without question; in turn, a very moral society had straightened its spine, cast its chin in the air, and decided that she would be accepted with dogged loyalty. She, poor creature, had been a victim of northern tyranny—just like the South. And it was so obvious that the dashing hero Captain McClain was in love with her. Kendall's own love and devotion to her Reb gave her a certain respectability; it was innocently fierce and beautiful, and it gave her an aura of ethereal loveliness that no one could resist. By the time she and Brent had returned to the festivities surrounding the cabin in the woods and eaten and danced with the others for less than an hour, there wasn't a woman left among the settlers who regarded her as anything other than the gentlest of well-born ladies.

And Amy—blessed Amy! That staunchest of honorable and ethical ladies treated the situation with the smoothest of aplomb. When the partying had all died down and Brent's sailors had all been invited to bed down in different homes, she had merely procured an extra pillow, stuffed it into Brent's hands, then wished them both a pleasant night without a flicker of judgment in her rosy features.

Harry, however, hadn't been able to resist an amused wink.

Kendall spent the night in the splendor of her lover's arms. It was so good just to sleep beside him, to find sweet security and warmth in the strong shelter of his body. She slept well not only because he had exhausted her, but because her contentment was drugging and overwhelming.

But when she awoke in the morning she was surprised and troubled to lift her head from his chest and discover that he was staring pensively at the ceiling. He knew she had awakened, yet he did not bring his gaze to meet hers.

"I am taking you to London," he stated firmly.

"No!" Kendall protested, leaning her torso over his chest and placing her hands on either side of his face to bring his eyes to her. "No, Brent!" she pleaded. "That's foolish. You say I'm in danger here, but what if the *Jenni-Lyn* is taken at sea? What a disaster that could prove to be! And you have to travel up the Gulf before you go to London; I know you're not planning on taking me there. Please, Brent, don't be foolish. You'd come back and take me over to Europe, and then I'll never see you at all, because you'll always be called back to fight! This is where you come, Brent. This is where I can believe that you will always return. Please, I beg of you . . ."

"You have no protection here!" Brent declared heatedly. He stared into her eyes, as liquid and shimmeringly blue as all the vastness of ocean and sky. He felt her against him. The plush softness of her breast crushed against his chest with the passion of her plea. He threaded his fingers suddenly into her hair and pulled her against him, cradling the nape of her neck and tenderly massaging her hair and scalp. "If I take you to London," he murmured, "we'll be together for a long ocean voyage."

"And then I may never see you again," she replied brokenly. "Brent, no one can come in and massacre a hundred white settlers. The Yanks don't bother with anyone here. And if they did, Brent, I am becoming very self-sufficient. Red Fox—"

"Red Fox will return to the swamp," Brent interrupted sharply.

"But I know how to find him!" Kendall exclaimed, tearing from his grasp to place her hands on his chest and hover over him, staring into his eyes once more. "Truly, Brent! He has taught me so much. I can probably follow the maze of rivers and canals better than most white *men!* And he will never be taken by surprise again, Brent. You know that as well as I do—oh, I know you do, Brent!"

Brent frowned and a little nervous chill swept over his face like a cold wave as his smoky gray eyes narrowed to smoldering slits. "Tell me," he murmured, his arms lacing tightly about the small of her back and jerking her abruptly closer, "do you insist on staying here because it is my place of safe harbor—or because Red Fox is close?"

Her eyes widened incredulously, and then a subtle smile curved her lips. "Can you truly be jealous of a man who loves you as he does his own people? If so, my daring Rebel, you are a blind fool. I will freely tell you that I love him—as the brother he has been to me on your behalf." Kendall dipped her face to his, whispering kisses against the taut corners of his mouth, teasing her own lips with the tawny brush of his mustache. Purposely she pressed herself against him, sensually brushing her breasts along his torso. She lifted herself once more, her palms firmly pressed against his shoulders as she shook him slightly. "I love you, Brent. Wherever I am, I am alone without you. Yet when I live with the belief that I will see you again, I can go through the days and months with a certain courage and contentment. Please don't mistrust the love that is all I can give you—and don't doubt a friendship that is both noble and pure."

Heavy lids with their thick golden lashes fell over his eyes, then rose once more. His eyes appeared charcoal as he searched out her features, then tenderly grazed her cheek with his knuckle. "You are beautiful, Kendall," he murmured. He didn't need to say more; his understanding was given her by the proud warmth in his eyes and in the reverence of his touch. Kendall fell against him, relishing his powerful embrace. Yet she felt she could not give enough. She nipped the tendons of his shoulder, then teased the light marks of her gentle bite with the tip of her tongue.

"It is you," she murmured, "that I love." Shimmying down his length, she continued to bathe him with her kisses, her mutterings becoming incoherent as his body's response to her touch grew heatedly evident and ignited a frenzied excitement within her.

"It is you that I need . . . you that I want . . ."

She was not afraid to touch him intimately, to glory in the

sexual beauty of her love. Nor was she alarmed when he moved and his hands closed powerfully around her waist, lifting her and bringing her on top of him once more. Pride as pure as the light of the sun illuminated her eyes to glistening pools of liquid enchantment as they met his. Her love made each subtle movement, every soft breath, an enticing enchantment.

He would love her, Brent thought, far beyond the realm of death.

He shuddered suddenly, thinking that their time together was brief, and so very precious. It must be cherished to the fullest extent.

He smiled, his eyes growing deceptively slumberous.

And then he brought them together with an explosive thrust of passion, bringing them both quickly to a heated crest of quivering pleasure. And when he held his well-bred tempest in his arms in the aftermath of that wild rage of pleasure, he could not help but touch her again, running his fingers leisurely along her back . . .

Suddenly he stiffened rigidly and bolted up in the bed, twisting her to lie flat on her stomach so abruptly that she emitted a startled cry. Brent ignored her and ran a single finger over the faded welts on her back.

The marks were already pale, the swelling barely perceptible when probed, yet he was amazed that it had taken him until now to see them. But he had been so fevered yesterday simply by seeing her, knowing she was safe, holding her in his arms . . .

His desire had drugged his mind, but now that he had seen the telltale lines that marred the pure beauty of her flesh, he was livid with rage. He had never felt such an intense hatred in his life.

"*He* did that to you?" Brent's voice was so low and tense that Kendall started shivering.

"It's over, Brent," she said softly.

But it wasn't. She knew that as he continued to graze his fingers along her shoulderblades and spine.

"I will never rest while that man is alive."

The raw conviction of the threat set her shivering again, but now Brent didn't seem to notice.

"Brent, please, don't do anything rash."

"I never do anything rash," he told her quietly. She was sure that he didn't. She was equally sure that he would carefully plot and plan and that one day he would search out John Moore.

But somehow the thought left a cold feeling within her heart. There was so much hatred in the low, heated tone of Brent's voice, a passionate fury barely bridled. And she was frightened somehow of the extent of that hatred. She despised John Moore; hated him herself with a true intensity. But more than anything, she wanted to forget him. He had no place here. He was coming between her and Brent, and she couldn't bear that. Hate could cloud and overwhelm the simple beauty of the love they had been granted just moments to share.

"Brent?" she murmured.

"What?" Even the question was harsh.

"Please, Brent—please don't let him come between us now. Please?"

He rolled onto his back and stared at the ceiling, lacing his fingers beneath his head.

"Brent?" she pleaded.

His eyes at last met hers. "I am going to find him, Kendall. Not today, and maybe not tomorrow. But someday. I will find him. And he will pay for Apolka and Emathla and Red Fox's son and all the innocents who died because of his brutal cruelty. And he will pay for all that he has inflicted upon you."

Kendall buried her head against his shoulder, fighting tears. She could not deny that John deserved punishment.

Yet for some strange reason, she didn't want Brent to kill him.

She knew that Brent killed men. A cannon went off—and men died. But that was warfare. The tragedy of battle could never be good, yet it existed because of men's beliefs, and she was quite certain that few soldiers killed with either gladness or hatred in their hearts. Warfare could be so impersonal. Men marching from one line to kill the men who held another line. And the blood of the fallen was the unfortunate mark of victory.

Yet if Brent were to find John Moore, death would not be impersonal. John's death would be murder.

And she wondered what it would do to the soul of the man she loved. A man raised to uphold a strict code of honor . . .

"Brent," she whispered, "please, please, come back to me. Don't let him win, don't let him create this barrier between us now. It is taking you away from me and it is too soon that you will truly have to leave me."

He watched her, and the glitter of murderous revenge at last left his eyes. "Come here, darlin'," he murmured, ruffling her hair and drawing her close. He squeezed her tightly to him for a moment, and she felt the tension slowly ebb from his muscles. It was still there, she was certain, locked deep within him. But he did not intend to allow it to intrude upon the time that was theirs.

"I already wasted half an afternoon being jealous of a redskinned 'savage' who is truly one of my best friends. Foolish, huh?"

"Oh, definitely."

"Oh, yeah? Then what about Deland?" he demanded with feigned aggravation.

"Travis?" she inquired innocently.

"Travis—with his message of love."

She grew suddenly serious. "I love Travis, too. As a very

dear friend. He is a good man, Brent. He is made of heart and soul, and many times his kindness made my life bearable."

He did not taunt her again, but watched her instead with gentle amusement. He kissed her forehead.

"It's a pity the man is dressed in blue. He would have made a fine Rebel! Seriously, my love, I would not want you to deny the devotion you give Red Fox or Deland. Your passion and loyalty are part of the lovely web that has entirely entranced me. I will just have to adapt to the fact that the woman I love draws adoration just as flowers draw bees. I suppose I shall manage." Grinning ruefully, he kissed the tip of her nose.

It would not be possible, Kendall was certain, to know greater joy or happiness than she did at that moment in his arms.

They spent the day together, taking the Armstrongs' Arabian fillies for windswept races along the beach. Brent taught her the trails through the pines and foliage. He showed her secluded beaches, and he teased her until she stripped and bolted into the warm spring water along with him, enjoying the surf and sand and golden sun. Paradise surrounded them, and paradise was within them. But as the glory of the sun's gold extended to crimson then faded to mauve, they grew quiet and solemn. Time was their enemy, slipping away too quickly. Only the night hours remained for them. And only gnawing hunger and the promise of those last hours together sent them back to the Armstrongs' cabin.

They were startled to find another party in progress. An amused Harry informed them that they had just missed a wedding.

Lloyd had decided to marry up with the preacher's girl— and the preacher had given in to Lloyd's determination.

Where he had first scoffed at a sailor for a son-in-law, he had come around to decide that an officer aboard the famous *Jenni-Lyn* was quite a catch. Lloyd had promised that after the war was over he would put his energies into making a port of the harbor in the bay.

Brent watched Kendall as she received the news. He watched her as she offered joyous and enthusiastic congratulations to the newly married pair. Even as he met and congratulated his sailor himself, he watched her from the corner of his eye, a worried frown at last furrowing his brow.

Kendall had eaten; she had insisted on helping Amy clean up along with the other women. And then she had quietly and discreetly disappeared into the cabin.

Excusing himself from his celebrating crew, Brent strode after her. The cabin's parlor was empty; he stalked toward the small bedroom Kendall had been given and pushed open the door without knocking.

She lay on her back, staring blankly upward with her hair a curling web of disarray that aureoled her fair features. Her hands were folded over her waist; her skirts fell gracefully about her.

Silent tears streamed down her cheeks.

"Kendall!"

He approached her quickly and sat at her side, scooping her into his embrace. She didn't resist him, but locked her arms around his neck and sobbed into his shoulder.

"What is it, my love?" he demanded gently.

"Oh, Brent. I'm so happy for them. Truly I am."

"You don't sound very happy," he remarked dryly, trying to draw a chuckle from her. She cried harder.

"Kendall, please, sweetheart, what is it?"

"Oh, Brent! I can never marry you! We can never be together as we should be. A couple before God and man. And it didn't hurt so badly when I could ignore it, but now—"

"Kendall! Ssshh. Darlin', don't cry like this, please." It

258

didn't occur to him that he hadn't ever mentioned marriage; what lay between them had become so deep that such a commitment would have been assumed under normal circumstances.

He opened his mouth to tell her that he didn't intend for John Moore to still be breathing when the war was over. Then he closed it abruptly. He knew that she worried feverishly on that score. And he didn't believe it was because she feared John might be the victor in a hand-to-hand combat— or because she could possibly mourn her husband for a moment.

It was something far more serious than that. Something that he didn't quite understand, but intended to respect—verbally, at least.

"Kendall . . ." He smoothed back her hair with all the love and tenderness in him. "Kendall, the war will end. And you will be able to get a divorce."

She stiffened suddenly in his arms, and her words were a whisper. "What . . . what if the Yankees should win?"

It was a question that most southerners wouldn't think of breathing in the spring of 1862. Only a few military men and civilians with foresight—men well aware that the blockade would grow tighter and tighter and that the South couldn't produce the arms it would need to fight—even gave such a supposition any grave thought.

Brent wanted to shout that the Confederates couldn't possibly lose the war. Day after day he waged battle, watched men die, heard the statistics as the death toll rose.

Until this moment, he hadn't realized that he couldn't accept the fact that it might all be for nothing.

"We won't lose," he murmured, but even as he spoke he felt a frightening chill of apprehension.

"I said, 'what *if,*' Brent," Kendall pleaded tearfully.

"We will still manage. You lived in New York for a while, Kendall. You know the Yanks are flesh-and-blood people.

There will be northern mothers to weep for the death of southern sons. If we lose, the South will face a period of punishment. Things will change forever, irrevocably. But we will still be dealing with people. I have friends in the northern ports, too, Kendall. Washington, Baltimore, Boston. They didn't turn into monsters because of the war. One way or another, when the fighting is over, we'll see that you get a divorce. Please don't cry so, Kendall." He hesitated a moment. "Kendall, we both know that Travis would help you in court—if the word of a Confederate officer should come to mean nothing."

She bit her lip and closed her eyes tightly, nodding briefly, then restlessly raised her lashes once more. "But what about your family? What about your home?" she asked.

"My home is a pile of rubble, and my family will love you—whether you previously had one husband or twenty. Don't insult them, Kendall. They will not judge you; they will take pleasure in our happiness. Now, how is that?"

"Oh, no, Brent! Your home—"

"Jacksonville was invaded," he said briefly, then added, "the Confederate Army caused most of the destruction, but I'm afraid the McClains aren't popular among the Federals. It was just a house, Kendall. My sister was fine, and I learned that my father and brother were fine the last she had heard. Houses can be rebuilt. I learned just how little South Seas meant when I reached Red Fox and truly learned what loss was. Kendall, believe me, we are lucky. So much tragedy surrounds us. Yet we have one another to cling to; we have dreams to see us through the night. We will make it to a happier time."

He drew away and gazed deeply into her eyes. She tried to smile at him, but the effort was ludicrous. Bursting into tears again she hurled herself against his shoulder once more.

"What now?" he demanded, both exasperated and amused.

"You're going to leave," she sobbed. "You're going to sail away in the morning . . . and I'm so frightened for you, Brent. So terribly frightened. So many men have died . . . so many more will die . . ."

"I promise you I won't die," he swore ridiculously, massaging away the pain and tension along her shoulder blades as he held her tight. "I promise you, I won't die."

"I cannot bear that you are going away."

He had no reply for that; no rational answer to make it all easier.

He thought of what a fighter she was; of all that she had endured with dignity and pride. He thought about the stripes on her back and how much abuse she had suffered and still held her chin proudly high; her slender back straight and her slim shoulders squared.

And he was glad that she had finally given way to her deluge of tears. He was glad that he was with her, able to give her at least his shoulder to cry on when he could offer little else except vague promises.

"Brent?"

"What, my love?"

"Promise me that you will hold me all night, that you won't let go for a single moment."

He lay beside her, cradling her against the length of his form and holding her tightly. "I promise," he whispered.

It was one promise he could keep.

By morning she had regained her poise. They made love fiercely, then she assisted him with his frock coat, tying his gold sash about his waist with deft fingers. She stood silently by while he buckled on his scabbard and sword, and handed him his slouch hat with its defiant plume. They clung together in a long embrace, ignoring the dawn as they hungrily savored a last kiss.

Then it was Kendall who opened the door, and calmly slipped an arm through his to escort him to the *Jenni-Lyn*.

The men of the *Jenni-Lyn* bade respectful goodbyes to the Armstrongs and the settlers who had come to see them off. And then each man came to Kendall, cheerfully boasting that their ship could best anything at sea and that it would, quickly. Even Lloyd kissed her after he had passionately done so to his wife; Charlie McPherson gallantly kissed both her hands—then blushed all the way to the *Jenni-Lyn*.

At last she felt the touch of Brent's lips against her cheeks as his gloved hands wrapped around hers. She didn't dare look at him, but stared ahead at the ship silently.

He squeezed her hands briefly and released them, then turned and stalked toward the *Jenni-Lyn*.

She would never forget the way he looked as he left that morning, the epitome of both chivalry and authority in his captain's uniform, his hat angled slightly over a brow, his mustache and beard freshly clipped. His shoulders seemed incredibly broad, his form entirely lithe and agile and yet stalwart as he swung aboard his ship.

His eyes met hers briefly across the water. He saluted her, offering a dry grimace. She returned his salute with a wave, and forced a brilliant smile to her face.

Kendall kept that smile rigidly set into her features until the *Jenni-Lyn* sailed from the bay.

Then slowly it faded away until the *Jenni-Lyn* became a speck on the horizon.

"Come on back to the cabin now, honey."

Kendall felt a gentle touch on her shoulder and turned to see Amy Armstrong staring at her with deep compassion etched in her endearingly plump features.

It seemed strange, but the sight of Amy's matronly face tugged on Kendall's heartstrings. A yearning swept her to go home to Charleston.

She wanted to see her mother and Lolly. There had been a time when her mother had been loving and supportive; a time when she had cuddled her daughters to her and given tremendous comfort.

But Kendall couldn't go home. And she had more comfort than she might have ever hoped for in Amy Armstrong.

Yet it wasn't the same. And she had to learn to stand alone.

"I'll be along soon, Amy," Kendall promised, managing another assuring smile. "I promise. You run along. And when I come back up, I promise I'll make up for all the chores I haven't done!"

Amy didn't look particularly happy, but she acquiesced to Kendall's wishes. "All right, child, but don't stay down here alone for too long now."

"I won't."

Amy left her. Kendall stared past the inlet's mouth to the bay, feeling the breeze, hearing the sounds of the forest.

There was a subtle change in the air. Kendall turned swiftly to see that Red Fox stood behind her.

"Time passes, Kendall," he said quietly.

"I know."

"As surely as the setting sun."

Kendall nodded.

Red Fox stretched out a hand to her. She took it with both of her own.

"I am leaving," he said softly, "but I will always be near you. You know that, don't you?"

"Yes." She lifted her head, and at last was able to smile from the heart. "And I also know that I shall be able to find you."

Red Fox removed his hand from hers. Much as Brent might, he reached to smooth a straying lock of hair from her cheek. "I will see you soon," he murmured. She nodded, and he silently turned to disappear into the trees.

She wondered suddenly if Brent could ever truly under-

Fourteen

June 1862

The greatest travail of the war for those left behind was the anxiety of waiting and the tedium of day-to-day life.

Kendall had taken to spending the mornings helping Amy with the livestock and gardens, and the afternoons riding the trails and beaches.

Summer was hot, unbearably so, but in the numerous coves and strips of palm-shaded white sand, the sea breezes could be cooling. And she liked haunting the shores of the bay; somehow it made her feel closer to Brent.

It had been a shattering disappointment when he had not returned after his assignment to the Gulf. All the more bitter because he had accomplished nothing. New Orleans had been closed up tighter than a drum, and Pensacola remained in Federal hands. Brent had carried desperately needed Florida salt into the wilds of the Louisiana bayous, and could only hope that the militia had managed to disperse the precious substance to the slaughter yards where it could be used to preserve meat for the fighting forces of the Deep South.

Brent had been sent on to London where a shipment of morphine had been promised him. There hadn't even been an extra afternoon that he might have given her. As the war raged on, not even the numerous Confederate victories could brighten the plight of the wounded soldiers. With the blockade winding ever tighter, the Confederate armies suffered ever more severely from lack of supplies. In the letter Brent had sent her he had spoken with an eloquent despair about the fate of the wounded. One of his gunners had taken a shell in the leg at the mouth of the Mississippi. There hadn't been a drop of anesthetic to give him, not even a drop of brandy or bourbon to ease his pain when the limb had been amputated. He could only imagine the plight of the soldiers on the field.

Morphine was vital.

Kendall understood, but still the waiting was hard. She read and reread every precious newspaper that made its way to the settlement, and gloried along with Harry at news of the southern victories. General McClellan's hesitant tactics had made something of a disaster of his Peninsula campaign; Stonewall Jackson, Jeb Stuart, Old Jubal Early, and the dignified Robert E. Lee were running their troops ragged with sheer audacity and, as always, superior strategy. McClellan was such a procrastinator, Harry told Kendall, that Abe Lincoln had made a number of dry witticisms at his general's expense—one being, "If McClellan is not using the army, I should like to borrow it for a while."

McClellan, it was assumed by both sides, would shortly be replaced. But for the time being, his army was taking no great victories.

But no matter whether North or South took the day, death took its toll. And there were injured to suffer the stark agony of battle wounds.

Kendall halted her filly on the sand of the cove where Brent had taken her that day so long ago. She tethered the mare to a seagrape, stripped off her shoes and stockings, and tucked her skirts about her to run her toes through the sand and surf.

A frown knitted her brow. Although the armies on the

eastern front were doing well, the Confederates in the western arena had suffered a number of serious blows, the loss of New Orleans among them. General U. S. Grant was fighting battles in Tennessee, Kentucky, and along the Mississippi. He had led successful campaigns against Fort Henry and Fort Donelson in western Tennessee, and although the Union had suffered very heavy losses at Shiloh, the Confederates had been forced to withdraw. Another of Lincoln's famous quotations referred to Grant: "I can't spare this man—he fights."

The question that had plagued her since she had first voiced it to Brent came back to pierce her mind.

What if the Union wins the war?

Kendall pressed her hands over her eyes. She couldn't bear the thought. Something, some vague thing that was irreplaceable would be lost. Forever.

She pulled her hands from her face and stared out over the water and frowned again, then placed her hand over her eyes to shield them from the sun's glare. Her heart seemed to catch in her throat for a moment as she saw a ship heeling lightly before the wind—not five hundred yards out.

It was a schooner, well supplied with guns. Four that she could see on the port side, like those on many of the ships she had seen at Fort Taylor.

And the Stars and Stripes waved from the mizzenmast.

In panic Kendall started to run from the surf, but then she paused, turning back to stare at the ship again.

The schooner wasn't at anchor. And its movement was erratic, as if the vessel were unmanned, a ghost ship playing upon the surf.

It would shortly run aground, Kendall surmised shrewdly. Straining her eyes still further, she saw that the masts were charred and the sails tattered.

It is a deserted ship, Kendall thought with a little thrill.

Harry . . . she had to run and get Harold Armstrong, Kendall thought logically. But again she paused. Although grievously wounded, the schooner still appeared to be maneuverable. And it wasn't far away. In fact, it had been veering closer and closer.

Kendall bit her lip and stared back to the seagrape where the filly was contentedly searching out the few clumps of grass that grew from the sand. She stared back at the ship.

If the schooner wasn't quickly steered into the deeper water of the channel, it would definitely run aground, and possibly be wrecked on an underwater rock near the shore. It was a large schooner and certainly couldn't be sailed by one person alone for any distance. But the weather was fair; the breeze light. There was enough canvas left to a number of the ragged sails to catch the wind . . .

I have to be mad, Kendall thought. Maybe the ship only appeared to be deserted. If she swam out, she could be plunging into disaster. Asking to be raped or murdered or, at the very least, captured.

She waited, as seconds ticked by. But then a heady excitement gripped her with the potency of a drug. All she ever did was wait. Wait—endlessly. And here was a chance to do something.

She was always dictated to by the whims of men. John Moore. And even those who loved her sought to direct her. Travis, Red Fox—and Brent. When Brent was with her, he assumed full command. And when he left, it was as if he could calmly place her into a cubicle of his mind, assured that she would be where he had left her while he turned his thoughts to the war.

Kendall glanced hurriedly about her, then waited no more. She tore her gown over her head and dropped her single crinoline to the sand. Standing in pantalettes and chemise only, she took one deep breath and flung herself into the water.

She wasn't an experienced swimmer; she had learned to keep herself afloat, however, while she lived with the Indians. And as she moved to the bluer depths of the bay, she suffered stabs of fear, which she fought furiously. Sharks sometimes plagued these waters. And there were all sorts of other vicious little sea creatures. Devilfish, jellyfish, barracuda . . .

And there might be creatures even more vicious aboard the schooner. Men. She would be vulnerable indeed when she rose dripping from the sea clad only in sheer white cotton.

Kendall kicked more vigorously against the warm surf. Her arms began to flail at the water and she was suddenly gulping for breath. She was panicking, she realized.

She halted, treading water and drawing in a long breath. A wave came to lift her and shower droplets over her head, but she didn't go under. And when it had passed, she had calmed herself. If she met with trouble, she would meet with trouble—but she would be damned if she would allow herself to foolishly drown because she was a coward.

Kendall made her strokes sure and smooth. In just minutes she reached the schooner. Once there, however, she faced another problem. How to get aboard. She forgot that the bay might be host to hungry sharks as she swam around the schooner in perplexity. But at last, along the bow, she discovered a spot where the hull had been severely damaged. Planking was ripped away almost to the water line. By gripping the starboard gunwale, she could hurtle herself upward and onto the deck.

For a moment she paused there, feeling the sun beat down on her sea-salty flesh. Dizziness swept through her as she blinked furiously. Had she truly been an idiot? What had happened to the schooner's crew? What if they had died from disease? Was she now contaminated?

She clutched the gunwale to steady herself, and then winced as a splinter tore into her palm. Mechanically bringing her hand to her mouth to bite down on the injury, she looked about her.

The schooner wasn't as large as the *Jenni-Lyn,* but she was graceful and compact. Across the deck Kendall saw a lifeboat suspended from the rigging with the name of the schooner painted on its stern in black: U.S.S. *New England Pride*.

"All right, *New England Pride*," Kendall murmured, moving slowly across the deck. "Let's see if we can make you the C.S.S.—something!"

As she gingerly walked to the wheel, Kendall became more and more convinced that, for whatever reason, the ship had been deserted. Possibly it had been engaged in a battle, and its crew had simply left her.

But the schooner hadn't sunk, and relentless currents had carried it here.

Kendall strained and puffed to take the schooner about, and she almost gave up in despair and frustration as her strength didn't seem to be equal to the task. But just as she cried out in fury against her own helplessness and buried her face against a sweaty arm on the wheel, the wind gave a sudden shift—and with it the schooner gave in to her command.

Once the ship had submitted to Kendall's handling, it became as docile as a lamb. The ragged sails took the wind, and the vessel floated across the bay. But as she neared the mouth of the deep-water inlet, Kendall suddenly realized that she was approaching a secret harbor where Rebel ships sought shelter—and she was flying the Union flag! Praying that the ship would hold the course, Kendall scrambled around to the mizzenmast and fumbled with the knot in the rigging that worked as a pulley for the flag. She turned her teeth to the task, and at last the weathered knot began to give. Heedlessly Kendall kept working at it, wearing the flesh of her fingers raw as she tugged at the hemp with teeth and hands. At last it gave, and a sturdy jerk pulled the Stars and Stripes from their proud whip in the wind.

But the schooner began to heel dangerously to port, and Kendall made another mad dash back to the helm. The ship responded to her touch this time as sweetly as a kitten.

"If I could only be in two places at once," Kendall mur-

270

mured to the ship, "I think I would actually have a good chance with you on the open sea!"

But she couldn't be two places at once—and just as she had realized she was sailing into a settlement with the Union flag flying, she remembered that she was sitting at the wheel with her chemise and pantalettes plastered against her. She might just as well be naked.

"Damn!" she murmured.

Again she leapt from her place at the wheel, hurrying to bring down the tattered sails. The task was a labored one; weathered and scorched rigging battled her fiercely. But at last she brought down all but the jib, then scampered about the deck as she sought out the anchor crank. Miraculously, it was in decent shape. Too late she realized that it would be far easier to cast anchor than to weigh it. But despite all the humiliation she had already endured in her life, she had been raised with a keen sense of propriety. She hadn't minded stripping to save the ship, but she certainly wasn't going to greet society practically naked. There had to be some piece of clothing in the crew's quarters. And although she wasn't exactly in the inlet yet, she was beyond the first stand of mangroves, hidden from any other ship that might wander into the bay.

Despite her determination to garb herself, Kendall felt a sweep of fear once again as she approached the steps to go below deck. It was like stepping into a void of the unknown, and her hands trembled as she touched the rail. But the sun was shining through a multitude of portholes, and Kendall shook off her fear. If there were any Yankees aboard the ghost vessel, they would have appeared by now.

Still she hesitated in the narrow hallway that apparently led to the officers' cabins. Horrible visions of cruel, leering deserters filled her mind. Impatiently, she forced herself to move forward and approach a door. If she was such a pathetic

271

coward, she should have never swum out to the ship. As it was, she had to do something.

Kendall breathed a sigh of relief as she pushed the door in and found the dim cabin empty. Her assumptions about the crew deserting had to be correct. The *Pride* was definitely empty.

She discovered quickly that she had stumbled into the captain's cabin. A ship's log lay open on a desk, and a navy frock coat with a captain's bars lay tossed over the chair before it. Curiously Kendall ran her fingers over the last page of the log, reading the words written in a handsome and flourishing script:

31 May '62
0700 hours
Frigate on the horizon; flying no colors. No doubt that she is CSN. We are swifter; she is stronger. We will make no move to attack, but will hope to pass her by.

1100 hours
Commander Briggs read her name. She is the CSS *Okeechopee;* Seaman Turner tells me she is a Florida-based privateer. No other U.S. ships in sight; we will maneuver to starboard to avoid the Confederate.

1300 hours
She moves in to do battle. We cannot avoid her guns. I close here to command the battle. Dearest God our father, protect us all, your sons. Yet as we commit fratricide, pit brother against brother, I wonder if you, in your divine wisdom, can look down upon us with grace.
Forgive us our sins.

Captain Julian Cuspis Smith
U.S.S. *New England Pride*

Tears stung Kendall's eyes. The page didn't read at all as a ship's log should—not after 1300 hours. It was not blunt fact. Not just a chronicle of happenings.

She would like to have known Captain Julian Cuspis Smith. He was a man incapable of being a war machine.

Kendall breathed a silent prayer that the captain had lived as she flipped through the previous pages of the log. The *New England Pride* had been commissioned into the U.S. Navy in June of 1860. Her keel had been laid in Boston the previous year. She had been involved in the blockade of Charleston, and had recently been ordered to join a patrol outside Mobile.

Nothing really worth knowing, Kendall thought pensively. Still, she would carry the log ashore and turn it over to Harry.

Kendall picked up the captain's blue frock coat and the log and left the cabin, closing the door behind her. She slipped the frock coat over her shoulders as she climbed to the deck once more, pensively chewing at her lower lip as her mind clouded with the tragedy of war. She walked up to the deck with a suddenly weary heart. She wished she had not read the log; she wished that she had never known Travis. War was so much easier to endure when you could hate the enemy without question.

"Well, well, well. What have we here?"

Kendall started violently and stared across the deck. A man stood by the helm. His short-waisted cavalry coat was of an indiscriminate color—possibly because of fading or possibly because of dirt. His trousers were blue, but that told her nothing, for many Rebels wore blue pants beneath gray or butternut jackets.

He was of medium height and stocky build. His hair was dark, his beard rough and matted with the stains of chewing tobacco. A leer spread across his features.

"My, my, my, what do we have here!" he breathed again, walking toward her.

Kendall clutched the log tightly against her chest for whatever protection it might offer.

"Who are you?" she snapped with a forced bravado. "How did you get aboard this ship?"

He paused, obviously surprised by her angry demand. But he merely hiked up shaggy brows and laughed. "Little Reb's got a bit of fight in her, huh? That's all right, honey, I like my women with spirit."

Kendall ignored his insinuation, staring him down while she desperately wracked her mind for a course of action.

"Are you a Yankee, then?" she demanded, not able to pinpoint his accent or his clothing.

"Reb—Yank—what's the difference. The army ain't no place for old Zeb."

"You're a deserter."

"Nah, honey. Just a sharp man." His black button eyes narrowed shrewdly upon her. "And I'm going to take this ship and hightail it outta here, little lady. It's shore gonna be mighty nice to have you along with me honey. Yeah, mighty nice."

He took another step toward her, and Kendall noticed that he had a pair of smooth-bore pistols crossed into the waistband of his pants. A leather thong tied about his thick girth held a leather case with a long and lethal Bowie knife. The closer he came, the yellower his teeth appeared to be, the more loathsome his odor.

"This is my ship," she stated flatly, coldly. "And you aren't taking it anywhere."

"Whoo-whee! Little lady! Old Zeb is gonna have a good time with you! Now hand the book over, baby, and let old Zeb hold you in his arms."

If she retreated, she would fall down the companionway. If he touched her, she would pass out with the horror.

But he held three weapons while she had nothing but a book.

274

He snatched the log out of her hands. The captain's coat she had taken from the cabin fell to the deck, and she stood before the man with her damp undergarments hiding little from his imagination.

"Oh, Lordy, Lordy . . ." he murmured.

She felt herself crushed against him, and at first she did have to fight an overwhelming dizziness as his scent and cruel touch assailed her simultaneously.

She had to think, had to do something . . .

She forced herself to touch him as he nuzzled his coarse beard against the flesh of her throat, greedy lips planting wet smacking kisses on her. She willed herself not to foolishly pit her fists against him in a frenzy.

And she allowed her hands to wander down his back until she found the leather thong . . . and then the case . . . and then the hilt of his Bowie knife.

Once her hand closed over that handle, she couldn't allow herself to think anymore. In a quick slash of her arm, she brought all her strength into play to drive the blade deep between his shoulder blades.

A bellow of amazement and pain raged from him. He cast her brutally away to claw in a frenzy at his own back, his face turning a mottled purple, his features contorted with stunned fury.

"Bitch! Southern bitch!"

Kendall had fallen to the deck. Hurriedly she jumped to her feet and nervously backed away as he once more came toward her with staggering steps. She screamed when his hand—blunt and squat, the fingernails black with dirt—reached for her, catching the lace of her chemise and ripping it open.

She had failed. And the filthy monster was going to make her wish she were dead a hundred times over before she really was.

She screamed again in primal rage and despair as his hand clawed for the bare flesh of her breasts.

But he never touched her. Suddenly he stopped and stood straight; his eyes widening, his mouth forming an O of disbelief. For countless seconds he simply stood there, suspended. Then he crashed to a heap at Kendall's feet.

She stared down at him in shock and amazement.

And then realized that another knife had joined hers in his back.

Slowly, her shock seeped through her and rendered her mind and body incapable of normal action. She looked across the deck.

Red Fox, silent and dripping wet, balanced on the gunwale. He barely glanced at Kendall, then silently hopped to the deck and approached the fallen man. He pulled his knife from the bloodied, lifeless back and wiped it clean on the sleeves of the man's short cavalry coat. He repeated the action with the Bowie knife, tucking both into a band about his calf.

Kendall was so transfixed by the Seminole chief's appearance that she couldn't even think to pull her torn bodice together. He stood, and his dark eyes flickered over her briefly. He padded silently on bare feet to the fallen navy frock coat and brought it to Kendall, slipping it around her shoulders.

His touch brought her back to life. She hurled herself against him, shuddering, tears streaking down her cheeks.

"Red Fox . . . bless you . . . how . . . where did you come from?"

He held her a moment, then set her away and squatted to pick up the dead man's legs and drag him toward the railing. Then he stooped again, and heaved the corpse overboard.

He watched as the water accepted the body as it might a sacrifice, whirling, seeming to suck the man under. He would come afloat again, but for now he was food for the fishes. Then he turned back to Kendall.

"I am often near," he said simply. "I saw you swim for the ship, and I watched as you brought her around. I came to the inlet by land, and so it took some time. I saw that white trash pull a canoe from the trees and approach. I swam."

Kendall was amazed and touched to realize that Red Fox had been keeping an eye on her from a safe distance.

"Thank you," she said quietly.

"You did well," he said, ignoring her words. "The wound you inflicted on him was deep, but not mortal. You have more to learn, Kendall."

She nodded in silent agreement. "Will you teach me, Red Fox?"

He shrugged. "In time. You should *not* have come aboard the ship, Kendall."

She hesitated a moment, lowering her eyes. "But I—we—have her now, Red Fox. She is battered, but she could be made seaworthy."

Red Fox lifted one eyebrow sardonically. "We have her? And for what?"

"I don't know . . . yet," Kendall faltered. But then she felt a defiant determination. An idea that had been a vague cloud in her mind now found full formation. "This ship is mine," she said. "I found her. I saved her from grounding. She is ours if you wish—but she is most definitely mine."

Red Fox emitted a growl of impatient irritation. "I ask again—for what?"

"To fight," Kendall said softly.

Red Fox threw up his hands in exasperation and stalked across the deck once more to set his hands and muscled biceps on the anchor crank. Kendall scampered across the deck, following him.

"Red Fox, listen to me—"

"No!"

"We could do something, we could have a purpose!"

He spun around to face her, dark eyes blazing. "Fool woman! I seek to protect you, but you wish to hurl yourself into danger and possible death."

"Red Fox, I can't stand the waiting."

"The Night Hawk would be furious."

"The hell with the Night Hawk!" Kendall exclaimed, startled by her own declaration yet determined that the Indian would not see her falter. "Red Fox, Brent comes so briefly. Then he sails away. I love him, Red Fox, yet still he is easily able to forget me and turn his heart to the war. He risks his life daily, yet that is expected. I am not property, Red Fox. I am not a slave. My life is my own, as is his. Please, Red Fox, please, listen to me. We could do some good with very little risk. Slip out of the inlet at night and seek out small Yankee blockade ships. We could—"

"Without a crew?" Red Fox demanded skeptically.

"We can find a crew."

Red Fox sniffed. "Where, Kendall? The men left in the settlement are boys and old grandfathers."

"Old doesn't mean worthless. And you have braves, Red Fox."

"Whites do not fight alongside Indians. They use them in alliance, yes, but they do not fight beside them. And it does not matter. What you suggest is"—for once, Kendall saw Red Fox struggle for a word in English—"ridiculous!" he at last exploded.

Kendall turned her back on him. "I told you, Red Fox, this is my ship. And I will sail her—with or without your help."

He broke into a fit of what she assumed to be cursing—but he spoke in his own tongue too swiftly and vehemently for her to understand his words. At the end of his tirade she heard him mention Brent's name again, and she spun around to face him once more, her eyes alight with pleading.

"Red Fox, Brent will never know! He won't be back for months! We can slip in and out of harbors and give all the ammunition and ships we seize to the Confederacy. Red Fox, I even know something about these cannons. I was"—she hesitated a moment, the brilliance of her eyes clouding—"I was at Fort Taylor long enough to learn something about artillery. These are Parrotts," she said, gesturing toward the guns mounted on the schooner's deck. "And if we're lucky, the shot will still be good. Oh won't you listen, Red Fox? Can't you see? We'll repaint this boat and rename her *Rebel's Pride!* We wouldn't need a crew of more than twenty—ten whites, ten Indians! And—"

"One woman?" Red Fox queried with doleful skepticism.

"Yes," Kendall said quietly. "I *am* a good sailor, Red Fox. I proved that when I made it here in a rowboat! We'll be careful. We'll test our wings thoroughly before we fly! Red Fox, women on both sides have been spies. They have even donned men's garb and joined the armies. I'm a Confederate, Red Fox. I have to fight this war!"

"Do you seek to fight a war—or to exact revenge?"

"Does it matter?"

"If you are captured, you know what will happen."

She met his eyes without flinching. "Yes, I know."

The anchor thudded into place, and Red Fox spoke again. "I cannot do this to the only white man I can truly call my friend."

"Then I will do it without you," Kendall vowed staunchly.

Red Fox released a weary sigh. Apolka's death had not been mentioned between them, yet Kendall knew that he thought of his slain wife and son.

"The Armstrongs will stop you. They will never agree to this foolhardy plan of yours."

Kendall lowered her eyes to hide a smile. She knew she

had Red Fox convinced. And if she could convince an Indian with a heart and will of steel, she could convince anyone.

The *New England Pride* was about to become the *Rebel's Pride*. They would paint the schooner gray and sail for the Confederacy.

Brent wouldn't be pleased if he found out, but Kendall hoped he never would.

And she couldn't afford to think about Brent. Just as she couldn't dwell on the fact that she had stabbed a man and that Red Fox had finished him off with cold detachment. And she couldn't allow herself to wonder if she wasn't anxious to come upon John Moore.

Neither Red Fox nor Brent would ever understand that she needed to fight her own battle with the man who had made her life a hell before there ever was a war.

And Brent had been gone so long. In the endless days and sleepless nights, it was sometimes hard to believe that he had ever held her.

Love was not a tangible substance. And in the present chaos of fraternal bloodshed, she often wondered if she could ever really reach out and grasp it tightly . . .

Fifteen

September 1862

The *Jenni-Lyn* limped into Norfolk and up the James River to Richmond Harbor. She had taken five shots, yet still she sailed, battered and bruised, her precious cargo safe in the hold.

Brent was glad to step onto dry land, yet as soon as he did, he was greeted by navy officers. He suffered enthusiastic congratulations and was then informed that President Davis and Secretary of the Navy Mallory were waiting to see him.

He ordered Charlie to see to the ship's repairs and Chris to see to the unloading and dispersement of the cargo. He then climbed into a buckboard and traveled through the streets of the Confederacy's capital.

How ragged Richmond looked after London.

There was no lack of silk or satin in England. Smiling women in the height of fashion, well attuned to the latest French styles, graced the manors and markets in their finery, unaware of the stench of poverty beneath their noses—or of a foolish war being fought across the ocean.

A foolish war . . .

Richmond was pathetic.

Few people walked the streets. Those who did appeared tense and pinched. And thin.

A neatly attired Negro greeted him cordially at the president's home, and led him to a small informal parlor.

As Brent accepted Davis's hand in a firm shake, he thought the president had aged a great deal in just the little more than a year since he had seen him last. Mallory wasn't looking healthy, either.

The black valet poured them brandy and offered Brent a cheroot. Brent accepted it, savoring the fine tobacco. They just didn't know how to roll a decent cigar in Britain.

"You were shot up quite a bit coming in, I hear," Jefferson Davis said thoughtfully.

"Yes, sir. Two frigates gave us a run as soon as they saw our colors."

"But you made it." Davis shook his graying head. "You're quite an anomaly, Captain. One the men of which our gallant South is made," he added softly, more to himself than to Brent. Then he offered his official guest a dry smile. "You'll notice, Captain McClain," Davis said cordially as he sat across from Brent on a slender settee, "that we're a bit informal here today." He hesitated, his expression pained. "The fighting just north of us has been very severe, and we've sent many of our womenfolk south for safety, including my wife, Varina."

Brent nodded, Watching the president's face. It was ironic that Jeff Davis should be sitting there at all, leading the Confederacy. He had been against secession—until Lincoln declared that he was absolutely opposed to slave states or territories. Davis had served in the U.S. Senate and had been secretary of war under President Franklin Pierce—and then returned to the Senate. He was a dignified man, tall, slender, and straight, yet he was often plagued by illness. Known to have a hot temper, he quarreled frequently with his generals—Robert E. Lee, an old friend from West Point, being the exception.

"I noticed that the streets are somewhat deserted, sir," Brent responded.

"Not that I truly expect any danger to our capital," Davis assured Brent hastily. "Not when we have men such as Jackson and Lee heading up our fine Army of Northern Virginia!" His eyes narrowed as he stared at Brent. "But then you have kin in one of General Lee's regiments, don't you, son?"

"My father and my brother, sir, Florida Cavalry. I've been away a long time. I've been hoping to hear some word of them and of the war efforts, especially in Florida. I'm afraid I'm quite out of touch."

Davis rose restlessly and strode to the cold fireplace. Florida was a point of discomfort to him. He raised his brandy glass to Brent. "Your ship is going to be laid up for about two weeks, I imagine. You're welcome to use that time to ride out and join with the army. Find your father and brother and ride with them a day or two. As to the war . . . I don't think we have ever been closer to glory. If only we can keep supplies coming in . . ." The president let the words hang; then he smiled. "As long as we have men such as you, Captain, we shall rise to triumph. Too often those who brave the Union gunboats do so only for profit. Ah, well . . ."

"What about Florida, sir?" Brent persisted quietly.

Jefferson Davis sighed. "We have not taken any of our forts from the Federals, Captain McClain. But neither have they been able to move inland. They remain in St. Augustine and Fernandina, and they have deserted and retaken Jacksonville. If you refer to a certain bay, sir, far south where the settlers aid our cause, then I can assure you that all is well." He paused. "Mrs. Moore is still living safely under their care."

Despite himself, Brent felt a blush tint his sun-darkened

features. Did the whole damn world know about him and Kendall?

Secretary Mallory, who had been silent during the conversation, spoke up tactfully. "We make it our business, Captain McClain, to see to the concerns of those who serve the Confederacy when they embark upon dangerous journeys for her cause."

"Thank you," Brent said tightly. Maybe it was a good thing that everybody seemed to know his business. He'd been worried sick about Kendall the entire voyage. He had dreamed of her repeatedly and so intensely that he had awakened himself with his groans and tossing. And too often dreams had turned into nightmares, nightmares in which he had returned to find Kendall gone, and a Union sloop sailing away with her a prisoner in chains on board. And always John Moore would be in that dream, taunting him "My wife, Reb! My wife. Mine. The woman you want belongs to a Yankee and you have lost."

He clenched his jaw and swallowed. God, how he wanted to get back to Florida. Forget the whole damn war and rush back and see for himself that she waited, alive and well and beautiful, smiling and free.

There wasn't even a slim possibility of his getting back—not until his ship was seaworthy. The Confederacy couldn't afford to provide him with another ship; he'd just have to wait for the *Jenni-Lyn*. And then he'd have another lousy night and he'd be leaving again. A wave of despair washed through him, and he fought it bitterly. Would the war ever be over? Would life ever be normal again?

He didn't want to think of the answers. Richmond was an answer in itself. Nothing would ever be the same.

"Well . . ." Davis cleared his throat. "When your ship is in order, Captain, I need you to sail down to the Bahamas for an arms shipment. You'll be given the particulars. Then you'll, ah, be needed to take your cargo up the Mississippi."

284

"The Mississippi?" Brent queried thickly. "Isn't New Orleans still held by—"

"The Yankees, yes. They're trying to cut us in half, Captain, by ruling the river. We mustn't let them. You must slip through, and bring ammunitions to Vicksburg. I'm afraid that city will be a target for the Federals." Davis was quick to pass over the fact that he was asking Brent to do the impossible. "But, until then, Captain, why don't you search out your family? We'll provide you with a decent mount. And a map of the roads that we consider safe. Lee's beginning an offensive now. He's sent Jackson to take Harpers Ferry; then they will meet in Maryland. We do give you our heartiest gratitude, Captain. I can't tell you what that morphine and laudanum will do for our brave men on the field."

Davis didn't need to tell him, Brent thought grimly. But he stood and shook the president's hand, and then listened intently to all that Secretary Mallory had to say.

His men were elated to be given two weeks' leave in Richmond town. The naval engineers promised that the *Jenni-Lyn* would be as good as new within the fourteen days. Aware that the taverns and whorehouses of the Confederacy's capital would be lively well into the night and that his crew would receive a well-deserved rest, Brent became anxious to get on the road. He hadn't seen his father or Justin in more than a year, and given the opportunity to do so, he damn well didn't want to waste any time.

Following the Army of Northern Virginia wasn't an easy task, even when one had knowledge of that army's movements. As Brent traveled the Virginia countryside—bursting with late summer beauty—he could well understand why the Federal generals had such a difficult time keeping up with Lee.

And even he had a hard time remembering the blood that

had already bathed Virginia. Birds sang along the trails; the grass and foliage were lush. The first shades of warm fall colors were just coming to the trees, and everything spoke of beauty—and of life.

Yet he couldn't allow himself to be lulled. Virginia was a battleground. He was aware that he might run into Union troops almost anywhere outside of Richmond, and that awareness made him constantly alert as he traveled in a circular route along the pike around Washington, westward, following in the wake of the Army of Northern Virginia.

Brent traveled for three days, avoiding farmhouses and towns and spending his time in solitude. Nights camping out in the open beneath the canopy of the sky were peaceful and filled with yearning. Living with the simple bounty of nature reminded him of seasons in the Glades with Red Fox. He longed for the virgin wilderness that composed so much of his state. He wanted to go home, then remembered that he no longer had a home. But it didn't really matter when he lay at night beneath the stars with his saddle beneath his head. He could share the beauty of the night sky with a certain woman. He knew he would be at home wherever she was.

On his fourth day out he ran into an army scout—luckily, a Confederate, as the men almost literally collided in a copse and would have shot each other had they not been too startled to draw weapons. Brent learned that Stonewall Jackson—commanding six divisions of Lee's Army of Northern Virginia—had just taken Harpers Ferry. Lee was awaiting Jackson's divisions, which were to rejoin the main army at the town of Sharpsburg by a little stream called Antietam Creek. Brent should have no problem finding the army soon if he just stayed on the road.

"But I'll warn you, Captain," the gaunt scout warned him, "Lee's already met up with McClellan's forces. There's one big battle about to go on. T'aint really the time for a friendly visit. You navy fellers aren't much for fighting on land, are you?"

Brent shrugged. "If the Florida Cavalry is fighting, I'll fight alongside them."

The scout narrowed his eyes at Brent, then nodded. "Guess so, Cap'n. You got kin with the cavalry?"

"Under Stuart," Brent replied. "My father and my brother."

"Stuart's cavalry covered Longstreet from South Mountain. Most of the big generals are all gathering already. You'll find Jeb's cavalry at Sharpsburg, all right, if'n you're sure you want to."

"Yeah, I want to."

"Guess so. Well, Lee's set up headquarters in a grove off the Shepherdstown road right outside of Sharpsburg. Don't mind tellin' you he was expecting some sympathy from Maryland—a welcome, kinda. Ain't been what he was hoping for. I won't hold you up anymore; like as not you'll want to find your kin while they're still living. Another couple hours and you should make Lee's headquarters."

The scout doffed his hat. Brent continued onward.

Within two hours he came face-to-face with the three men who were the heart of the Confederate forces: Robert E. Lee, Thomas Jonathan Jackson, and James Ewell Brown Stuart. Lee appeared both surprised and amused to be welcoming a naval captain into his headquarters tent, but his humor was brief. The situation of his army was too tense for levity. Brent had never met Lee before, yet he quickly saw that all he had heard about the brilliant man with the quiet dignity was true.

No matter what the situation, Lee was a gentleman. He hid his surprise and amusement and introduced Brent to Stonewall Jackson and Jeb Stuart.

"There's a battle already happening, Captain McClain. The first shots were exchanged this afternoon. We're not at sea, sir. You're not under my command, and I can only warn you that this engagement will be harsh. As usual, the numbers of the Federals far exceed our own."

"Yes, sir, I understand," Brent said quietly but firmly. "But you've a company of Florida Cavalry here that is composed of men I grew up with. My father, my brother, and a dozen other Jacksonville gentlemen. I rode with them in peace, and I can ride with them in war. I'm a sharpshooter, sir. I won't be in the way."

"Jeb?" Lee, his strategy plans laid before him, raised his eyes to Stuart. "Cavalry's yours. You know anything about this young man's family?"

"Sure do," Stuart replied. "Captain Justin McClain and Lieutenant Stirling McClain. You'll find them camped about a quarter of a mile down—the farthest tents."

Brent saluted sharply and turned to leave the command tent. Lee called him back, blue eyes momentarily twinkling despite the hardships of fighting a war.

"Don't get yourself killed, young man. I understand you're invaluable to the navy."

Brent saw the horses, tethered for the evening, before he spotted the men of the Second Florida Cavalry. And a look at the horses was frightening. They were too thin and ragged looking to proudly carry a noble cavalry into battle.

He felt his stomach tighten and sink as he approached a group of men gathered around a campfire beneath the dark sky that promised rain.

The men were more tattered than the horses. Several were bootless, with scraps of material wrapped about their feet.

Their uniforms were piecemeal, ragged and worn, and like the army scout he had encountered earlier, they all appeared gaunt.

Before he reached the fire one of the tattered scarecrows stood.

"Brent! By God, Stirling! It's Brent!"

The scarecrow rushed toward him and nearly knocked him off his feet, exerting tremendous force for such a scrawny creature. But Brent didn't mind. He hugged the enthusiastic man, not objecting to the thunderous pounding upon his back. At last the man pulled away, and Brent stared into deep gray eyes amazingly similar to his own.

"Pa! Damn, it's good to find you! I've been afraid—"

"Afraid I might have taken a bullet and you hadn't heard?" Justin McClain queried sardonically. "Not yet, son. The old bones may be brittle, and the old head quite gray, but the soldier has life in him yet!"

"Brent!"

Brent turned from his father to embrace his brother—another ragged scarecrow. He pulled away from Stirling with an awkward smile.

"No offense meant, but you both look like hell."

Stirling shrugged. "That's one of the reasons we're moving into Maryland. Virginia's been raped, Brent. Lee can't clothe us or feed us properly because the countryside has been bloodied, pillaged, and burned. We're hoping to pick up some Yank supplies."

"You look great, son," Justin said proudly.

Brent grimaced. "I just came from London."

"You haven't been home?" Justin demanded anxiously.

"Not since early spring. Why?

"I get letters from your sister, but I worry about her just the same. She says things are just fine. The Yanks come in and out, but they leave the townfolk alone."

Brent felt a tremor constrict his throat. Obviously Jennifer hadn't mentioned that South Seas was nothing more than a past glory.

"Jennifer looked fine when I saw her, Pa. Pretty as a picture."

He couldn't see any reason to tell his father or brother

about South Seas. Not when they were about to engage in battle.

"What the hell are you doing here, little brother?" Stirling demanded with a broad grin. "Not enough action on the seas, huh? Or in London? Don't that beat all, Pa? We've been running our asses ragged out here while Brent's been partying in London. We should have joined the navy, Pa, not the cavalry!" Stirling laughed loudly as he clapped Brent's shoulder. "Well, brother, you want a little action, and you'll see it tomorrow. McClellan's arranging his whole damned army to meet us tomorrow."

"From what I hear," Justin interjected with the same good humor his elder son had offered, "Brent's seen a might of action already on the seas. But what are you doing here?"

Brent shrugged. "The *Jenni-Lyn* was all shot up. She's being fixed at the naval yard in Richmond. I had a couple of weeks to wait. Jeff Davis himself suggested I come out and find you two."

"That was right nice of him." Stirling approved. "Well, come on then, Brent, and say hello to the boys. You know Cliff Deerfield, Craig Hampton, and a few of the others. Old man Reilly was killed at Second Manassas, but we're still a damned good troop."

With Justin in the middle, the three McClain men linked arms and joined the group about the fire.

The flames had died down; the encampment, except for the pickets, had bedded down for a restless night.

Stirling McClain, staring silently at the frame of his tent, nudged his brother. "Brent."

"Yeah?" Brent replied softly in the darkness.

"What's this rumor about you stealing some Yankee's wife?"

Brent stiffened, instantly awake and alert. "It isn't a rumor,

290

Stirling. It's more or less true. Only I didn't steal her; Red Fox did. Then the Yankee stole her back, and then she escaped from him and came back to me."

Stirling exhaled a soft whistle. "All those years when no girl seemed to do for you! And now you've got yourself messed up with a married woman."

"Her husband's a brute, Stirling." Brent was silent for a moment. "And she's worth anything I have to go through to keep her, brother. I'm going to marry her, Stirling, as soon as we can get her a divorce." Again Brent hesitated uncomfortably. "If you've heard about this, Stirling, I guess Pa has, too."

"Yeah."

"There's nothing dishonorable about it, Stirling. I love her. And I don't care if we're talked about from here to kingdom come. I just hope Pa's sense of pride isn't wounded."

A voice suddenly broke in on them from the darkness. "Your pa's sense of honor ain't tinged in the least, son. I trust *your* sense of honor. You just do what's right by that girl, you hear?"

Brent smiled in the blackness of the night. "Yeah, Pa, I hear you."

"Now, will you two please hush up and let an old man get some sleep. I swear you're worse than a pack of belles at a tea party." He hesitated, then added gravely, "And tomorrow isn't going to be any tea party, sons. Get some sleep."

September 17 dawned gray and drizzly.

Jeb Stuart's cavalrymen were ordered to cover Jackson's flank and the mile between Jackson and the Potomac. The horse artillerymen were to hold their line and create the illusion that that line was solidly held by shifting gun positions between bursts of fire.

By seven o'clock the battle was raging in full. And death could be seen all around.

The men had fought in a cornfield, the ears golden for picking, the stalks green. But there was no longer any corn. No tall green stalks. So much artillery had blasted through the fields from both sides that the cornstalks had been sheared off just above the ground.

All that was visible was a sea of bodies. Where the corn had been now lay a field of tangled corpses clad in blue and gray.

The cavalry held off Union General Doubleday when he tried to move in on the Hagerstown road; they riddled the fields about them with artillery. Stonewall Jackson held his line with tenacity, yet the loss of life around those still standing to fight was awesome and devastating.

Brent worked alongside his father and brother, loading a Parrott cannon. It took six men to load and fire the cannon, and if one was picked off by sharpshooting advance troops, another man was called in to take his place. Constantly they shifted the guns under his father's command.

Stirling tried to sing and joke during the endless morning hours when the battle raged before them, the bodies piling high in the vast expanse of the cornfield. Blue and gray. Blue and gray.

Brent's hands were black with powder; his muscles were strained. He learned something about the Army of Northern Virginia that day: it didn't quit. Its men were fighters. Its generals survived on tenacity and audacity and they could encounter a foe with far superior numbers and still fight on with nothing but willpower.

It was difficult to tell who was winning the battle. From seven to twelve the intense fighting continued through the cornfield to a tiny little Dunkard church. And by noon the reports were that the Confederates had lost about six thousand men, the Federals about seven thousand. Staggering statistics. But they were more than statistics. They were the tangled heap of men who lay where there had once been corn.

"What are we doing here, Brent?" Stirling asked tiredly, wiping sweat from his brow and leaving his face marked with black powder.

"We're fighting for the Confederacy," Brent replied tonelessly.

Stirling laughed dryly. "The Confederacy. Brent, we started this war mainly to preserve states' rights. Sure, slavery was the right in question, but we all wanted states' rights. And here I am in Maryland watching men drop beside me while my home has been invaded and I'm nowhere near to protect it."

"Watch it, Stirling!" Brent rasped as a cannonball went flying over their heads with a warning whistle and exploded just feet behind them. Brent felt as if he'd been picked up by strong, hot hands and literally tossed into the air like a leaf. He crashed heavily to the ground. For seconds he lay still, gasping in the heated, wet air. Then he moved. Nothing broken. But there was so much powder in the air that he couldn't see a thing. He got to his knees and began to crawl about blindly, hearing the agonized cries of wounded men from every direction.

"Stirling? Pa?"

He found his brother when the smoke began to clear. A thin line of blood trailed from Stirling's mouth. But it wasn't that blood which terrified Brent; it was the pool that congealed around a hole his brother gripped with his hands at his middle.

"Brent?"

"I'm here, Stirling. Don't try to talk, I'm going to get you out of here."

Stirling emitted a short laugh that quickly became a choke. "Remember the magnolias, Brent? How they dipped low over the drive? I always loved to ride along the drive, racing until I could see South Seas rising above the trees . . . don't you remember, Brent?"

"Yes, Stirling, I remember. Quit talking. I'm going to patch you up."

Stirling screamed as Brent lifted him to wrap his coat tightly around his middle. He had to get Stirling off the field. He had to find a surgeon. Dear God, where did one find a surgeon in this melee of blue and gray bodies?

Beyond them stood the West Woods. Across from the woods, battle had been raging at the Dunkard church. Who held the church? Brent wondered. Could he get help?

He dragged his brother from the range of artillery fire and found a cool clearing in the woods. Stirling opened his eyes.

"Take care of South Seas, Brent. And Patricia and Patrick . . ."

"Quiet, Stirling," Brent said, trying to hide his anxiety with exasperation. "Just lie still and breathe slow."

"Stretcher!"

Brent swung about as he heard the cry come from nearby. He couldn't see much of anything because of the smoke in the woods.

"Stretcher!" he called out himself. There did seem to be medical help in the vicinity.

"I'm coming . . . Call out again so I can find you!"

The voice that responded to his was low and calm and full of reassuring authority. Brent stood to stare through the smoke and foliage—then froze as a man stepped into view.

He was in blue. A Yankee captain, Brent saw from the gold insignia on his sleeves. His sandy hair was short, his brown eyes wide, warm, and sharply intelligent. The man was about his own age, and he returned the same startled stare.

For long moments the two stood, tensely and warily locked

in that stare. Then the captain's eyes wavered down to Stirling.

"Gut shot, is he?"

"I think," Brent said tersely.

The Union captain knelt down beside Stirling and moved Brent's improvised bandage. "It may not be that bad," he muttered as he ripped away Stirling's cavalry jacket and shirt and bared the flesh.

"I need to get him out of here," Brent said thickly. It was obvious that the Yanks were controlling the Dunkard church and the woods.

The Yankee captain turned to Brent. "You can't move him without assistance. You could kill him."

Brent swallowed against a thickness in his throat.

"I can't leave him," he barely whispered.

The Yank captain stood, gnawing at his lower lip. "Listen to me, Reb. All that you might have heard about Yankee surgeons killing more Rebs than our artillery isn't exactly true. I'm a doctor, sir. And I believe in my oath to save lives—and my oath doesn't say a damn thing about saving only lives in blue coats. Leave him with me. It's his only chance. This land is already swimming in death. Thousands have died already, and more will do so. Don't make him be one of them."

Stirling suddenly groaned in a shuddering agony. Brent knelt down beside him "Stirling, can you hear me? This is Captain . . . uh—"

"Captain Durbin, Medical Corps," the Yank supplied, kneeling again at Stirling's other side across from Brent.

"I met Durbin before the war in New York," Brent lied. "He's going to take care of you."

"No—no, don't leave me to die with the Yanks."

"You're not going to die, Stirling. I never did want to run South Seas. You have to live to do so. Stirling! The Yanks are the only ones with supplies! The only ones with—"

A hand touched Brent's arm. He stared into the army captain's eyes. Durbin said, "He's passed out. You don't need to keep talking. He may die, but I give you my word that I'll do my best to save him. But you'd better get the hell out of here if you can. A prison isn't the nicest place in the world to be. Tell me where to reach you. I'll write about his condition as soon as I can."

Brent hesitated only a second. "Jennifer McClain, Jacksonville. If he dies, our sister will notify his wife . . . and son."

The Yankee nodded. "Go, Reb. Get out of here before you get me court-martialed."

Brent stood and ran back through the woods.

Through the afternoon the fighting continued. General Hood tried valiantly to hold a line in a pitted alley along one side of the field, but there were too many Federals. The bodies piled in the path were three and four deep, and already the soldiers were calling it Bloody Lane.

Lee made the decision to cross back over the Potomac to western Virginia, and McClellan made no move to stop him.

The bloodiest single day's battle in the Civil War had been fought.

Brent spent the night listening to the cries of the wounded and searching for his father.

Captain Justin McClain, Second Florida Cavalry, was among the missing.

Brent left the Army of Northern Virginia the following dawn, riding for Richmond. He skirted the buildings of the capital and made straight for his ship. His men were not aboard as they were still on leave. But Brent wasn't interested in company. He spent the next four days in solitude, staring at the paneling above him as he lay on his bunk and listened to the hammering of the shipbuilders.

Charlie McPherson was the first to return. He had heard about Brent's father and brother, and respected his captain's privacy. But as the crew began to drift back, Charlie appeared at Brent's door.

"Won't disturb you long, Captain, till we set out of here, that is. But we've been hearing some strange rumors in the taverns. I thought you might want to know about them."

"What is it, Charlie?" Brent asked wearily.

"Seems we have some competition on the blockade. A Confederate schooner has been appearing from nowhere with no commissioned officers. The Yankees are saying she's commanded by an Indian—and a woman. She's blown four Union sloops, three schooners, and two frigates out of the water. All down in the South Florida waters. She's bearing the name *Rebel's Pride.*"

Brent had been lying on his bunk. His feet suddenly slammed to the floor. "What?" he hissed.

"Rumor's got to be true, Captain. The old tars at the tavern were quoting right out of the Yank newspapers. And the Yanks are a little bit in awe—and mighty upset. There's a hell of a bounty out on that ship. Perty near as high as the one on ours!"

"Son of a bitch!" Brent thundered. "That little idiot! I don't believe her! She has no conception of what warfare is all about. Where the hell did she get a ship? Or a crew? An Indian, huh? Damn Red Fox!"

Charlie stood back in silence, wishing he hadn't felt honor-bound to be the bearer of such tidings. Brent McClain seldom lost control of his temper, but when he did, all hell raged.

Captain McClain paced the confines of the cabin, his gray eyes as fierce as a smoldering fire about to explode into blazing heat.

Suddenly he stopped before his desk. "Are we ready to sail?"

"Yes, sir. Crew's all aboard. We were supposed to go out with the dawn—"

Brent strode determinedly past Charlie.

"We're sailing now. Dusk is a good time to run the blockade." Halfway out of the door, Brent suddenly paused and slammed a fist into the paneling.

"I'm going to kill her. Damn—I'm going to strangle her. She's got to learn that she isn't invincible and can't run around like a damned fool—if I have to put her in chains to prove it!"

Brent stalked out on deck, shouting orders.

Charlie followed along, but he wasn't about to remind Brent that he was a bit of a fool himself—joining up with the Army of Northern Virginia for a lethal battle and then storming through a Federal blockade as if it were a yacht race.

Fools, Charlie thought. Fools and heroes. They were much the same.

Sixteen

October 1862

"She's gone, Kendall! The *Rebel's Pride* is gone! He's taken her!"

Kendall's eyes flew open, she stared numbly at Amy Armstrong who had burst open her bedroom door and brought her to a startled and confused awareness. Amy wrung her hands nervously while Kendall tried to blink the sleep from her eyes and comprehend the words being shouted at her.

She had been dreaming, and in her pleasant dreams the war had been over; life had again become what it once was . . . long ago, so long ago. Cresthaven was the focus of her dream; the grand plantation house had loomed majestically beyond the miles and miles of cotton ready for harvest.

In the dream she had walked along a trail with Brent, arm in arm, and though they bemoaned the lost past, it was with a soft nostalgia for the pain endured by both North and South. Their own future loomed beautifully before them.

The glorious cause had become a reality; the Confederate States of America had survived. And she had been a part of it. Small, perhaps. But her determination to put to sea the abandoned Yankee schooner had been an important contribution to the war effort . . .

"Gone!" Kendall gasped incredulously, throwing her covers from her and wrenching her mind away from the dream. "The ship is gone? Amy, what are you talking about? How could she just be gone? We have lookouts to guard her!"

Amy opened her mouth to speak as Kendall stood up next to the bed, but she gasped instead as a man's broad bronzed hands fell on her shoulders and firmly moved her out of the way. Kendall's jaw dropped as Brent stepped into view and bodily removed Amy from the room.

"I'll explain the situation, if you don't mind, Amy," he murmured politely. Much too politely . . .

He looked wonderful; just seeing him, hearing the low drawl of his voice made Kendall feel as if her blood heated, as if her entire form quivered inside and out. He was always on her mind, day in, day out. She lived for the few precious times when he would appear before her. She wanted to fly to him, throw her arms around him and hug and hold him and assure herself that he was real, cherish him.

Instead, she froze where she stood, feeling as if the heat in her veins had suddenly been replaced by ice water.

She had never seen him stare at her so coldly—or so furiously. And it was all the more terrible because it wasn't a fit of sudden rage. He was calm, perfectly calm. And perfectly controlled. Yet she felt that if she touched him, he would feel like rock, cold and rigid.

"Brent," she murmured, trying to keep her voice from quivering, forcing herself to remain still and not back away from the calculated fury that hovered like an aura about him.

Apparently Amy had decided to obey Brent—and desert Kendall. At any rate, she was gone.

Brent stepped into the room and closed the door behind him.

Kendall didn't want to admit it, but she was frightened of him. Truly frightened, as she had been when she had seen him

300

in the swamp for the first time after the disaster in Charleston. More so, perhaps, because she knew him now.

Knew him, and yet didn't know him. What was the war doing to all of them? Did her own eyes ever mirror that look of pain beyond description? His eyes were so cold that she felt as if her heart had stopped.

His anger was dispassionate, yet raw . . . and ruthless.

Physically he hadn't changed. He still wore his gray frock coat with the gold insignia and decoration with the same handsome cavalier effect. His mustache and beard needed a trim. The rugged angles and planes of his face appeared a little more gaunt than when she had last seen him. His lips were tightly compressed, but then she reflected sadly that she had more often seen him in anger than in laughter.

No, her heart cried out. He loved her, she knew that he loved her. And when they had been together last her world had been full of splendor despite the war that raged.

He hadn't spoken yet, he was just staring at her, and as always, he had that explosive vitality about him, even as he stood still. In movement he exuded agility and power. Even immobile he still seemed to radiate an overwhelming passion.

And she couldn't move. All she could do was stand there and return his stare, and vaguely and sickly think that this wasn't the way she had dreamed of seeing him again . . .

At last she did move. Her fingers fluttered nervously to the throat of her high-collared white nightgown. And at last, through the shock of seeing him so, her mind began to function. Amy had been shouting about the *Rebel's Pride* being gone, and now here was Brent, staring at her as if he were a king about to order an execution.

Kendall shook off the fear that had gripped her and narrowed her eyes upon him. This was to be no tender reunion. And she'd be damned if she'd let him put her on the defensive with this unwarranted attack.

"What did you do with my ship?" she demanded crisply.

It was the spark that was needed to ignite all the smoldering fear and anger he had been burying beneath a calm facade all the way from Richmond.

Maybe, if he had never been at Sharpsburg, never seen the blood flow in the water of Antietam Creek . . . Maybe, if he hadn't seen his brother torn with shot, if he hadn't been forced to leave Stirling with the Yankee surgeon, if his father hadn't been among the missing . . .

Maybe he could have behaved differently. Perhaps then he could have taken her into his arms and explained that he had already lost almost everything that he loved, and he couldn't go on living if he were to lose her, too.

He was shaking as he stalked across the room, his control shattered by the defiant toss of her head and the coolness of her question. And he knew he hurt her when he gripped her arms, but he couldn't ease his hold. He shook her as his eyes tore into the rebellious blue that met them, wanting to hurt, wanting to strip away the proud composure that could all too easily be her undoing on some distant day when he was too far away to fight for her.

"You reckless little wench!" he hissed at her through clenched teeth. "If you want to get yourself killed, do so on your own! You've no right to kill old men and more Indians and a bunch of children in the process!"

His grip on her was painful. Kendall's first thought was self-preservation and escape. She brought her free hand against him, clawing at the fingers that ripped into her like iron talons. "Brent, stop it. Let go of me!"

He did so, hurtling her from him with a force that sent her sprawling onto the bed. As she floundered to regain her balance, he paced toward the door again, stopping there and sweeping his hat from his head to rake his fingers through his hair. Kendall didn't try to stand again. She fumbled against the material of her gown to come to her knees and back herself against the simply carved headboard of the bed.

When he turned again she was ready to spring and run—or fight.

"Do you ever," he demanded heatedly, "stop to think of what you are doing?"

Suddenly everything seemed to well up inside her—the waiting, the striving, the fighting . . . the dreaming. He was her world. He and a vague, intangible fantasy that faded daily—the South.

Without them, there was no future. Only the bleak ashes of a burned-out existence.

She had been compelled to fight the Yankees. As wonderful a man as Travis was—and she knew many other decent men who wore blue—she had to fight. Because she could never forgive all that had been done to her. The lash marks on her back had slowly vanished, but they would never disappear from her heart. Nor would she ever, as long as she lived, forget Apolka's screams . . . or how helplessly she had stood as children died all around her.

"I know precisely what I'm doing, Captain McClain!" she enunciated with crisp, slow wrath. "And I ask you again, what have you done with my ship?"

He offered her a dry, grim smile, crossing his arms over his chest and leaning a shoulder nonchalantly against the door. "So you do admit it's your ship?"

Kendall hesitated. "I don't captain her, if that's what you mean. But she is mine. I found her, and I saved her."

"And you sail aboard her?"

"Not always. Only when we stay close by and pick off the enemies who stumble into the area. Harry and Red Fox sometimes take her farther out, and Harry is officially her captain. Damn you, Brent! You act as if I were fighting for the other side."

"I see," he interrupted smoothly. "It's all for the war effort."

"Of course, you idiot, what did you think?"

He lifted a brow; the muscles about his jaw constricted, but he made no reference to the name she had called him. "Then," he said smoothly, striding toward her, "you certainly shouldn't mind that the ship is being officially turned over to the Confederacy?"

The color drained from her face as she realized exactly what he had done. Then a fury like a brush fire seemed to take hold of her. He was always gone. Always. And he had the nerve to sail back in and interfere with her life without even speaking to her first.

"Yes, I do mind!" she hissed, not caring that he came ever closer to her. "I mind tremendously! I mind that—Brent! Stop—"

His hands had clamped over her shoulders, wrenching her from her rigid pose against the headboard and swinging her onto her back, across his body, so that her hips lay on his lap and he was pressing her shoulders to the bed while leaning over her to deliver a staccato lecture.

"When will you ever think, Kendall? When will you ever learn? What the hell do you think will happen to you if the Yankees catch you? They'll crucify you, Kendall. And Red Fox. If they catch an Indian sinking Federal ships . . . but Red Fox is a man, at least. And a warrior. He knows what might happen to him. But you, you little fool—"

"Don't!" Kendall shrieked, unable to break his hold, but determined to be heard. "Don't tell me about Red Fox being a man! And don't tell me I don't know. I was there, Brent! I was there when the Seminoles were all but eradicated! Do you think a woman can die any less than a man? Where do *you* get the right to risk your life constantly? Where does the difference lie? You are barely ever with me, and when you are, your mind leaves well before your body. You put

me up on a shelf while you plan your warfare, then sail away. A woman is for entertainment only—expected to wait idly and anxiously for a man's next return! Wrong, Brent! I cannot simply wait and worry!"

She wasn't sure what impression her passionate speech had made on him; he continued to glare at her. So many nights she had dreamed about his arms around her, and now that he held her, she was torn in two. The feel of him was good. The heat, the muscled vibrancy. Yet she wanted so badly to cast him from her, to prove that she was strong and capable and—equal.

"Kendall," he said quietly, his lips coming close, his grip on her shoulders intensifying as he bent ever lower over her until his torso brushed hers, "pay attention to what I am saying. It's all been pointed out to you before. If the Yankees catch you, they'll return you to John Moore. But there's a good chance they'll consider you fair game first. They know you've been sleeping with a Rebel, and that you've been sabotaging their war efforts, whether you captain that ship or not. If you think life with John Moore was bad before, wait until you're returned to him a second time—that is, if you have a mind left after the Yanks have finished with you."

His words were so cold . . . like pellets of ice thrown on her one by one.

Did he care about her at all? It had been months since she had seen him. He had been in London where there was no war, where the ladies dressed in silks and maintained creamy complexions and a gentle, feminine demeanor. Had he been with another woman? With other women? She closed her eyes suddenly, wanting to touch him, wanting to feel that he was hers.

He wasn't hers. He was the Night Hawk. Coming and then leaving her to darkness . . . always. Like the wind he whirled into her life, and when the tempest was gone, there was the funnel of emptiness.

Could he begin to understand how she felt?

"Brent," she said softly, "did you know that women have donned uniforms and disguised themselves as men to join the front lines of battle? Harry got ahold of a Washington newspaper, and there was an article on the northern women, comparing them to their southern counterparts. Of course the author of the article admitted he had no southern statistics—"

"Kendall—"

"Listen to me, Brent. I swear it's all true. The article was written because there was this tremendous battle at a place in Maryland called Sharpsburg and one of the Union wounded was a girl—"

"Stop it, Kendall!" Brent raged. "Just keep quiet! I don't want to hear it, and none of it matters. If you can't sit still by yourself, I swear I'll turn you over to the Yanks myself. At least you'll stay alive that way."

"Alive! The female heart can stop a bullet as easily as the male—"

"Kendall, I swear to God, if you open your mouth again, I'll close it for you."

"You will not! You'll listen—"

A sharp crack ended her sentence—his palm against her cheek. He saw the pain in her eyes, the reproach—and then the hostility. He wanted to apologize—but couldn't bring himself to do so, and that tugged at his heart and the turmoil in his mind still further.

He tried to tell himself later that her mention of Sharpsburg had triggered his anger. He tried to find any number of other excuses.

But there was no excuse. And the guilt that plagued him even as she clawed out at him in a furious retaliation kept him fighting her.

"You see," he taunted, the cruelty in his voice a hoarse cover for his longing to beg her forgiveness. He caught her

306

flailing arms as she tried desperately to free herself from his hold. "You cannot escape. It's a lesson we've been through before, but you can't seem to get it right, can you? You can't win, Kendall, so don't fight me."

"Let go of me," she said, miserably trying to fight her tears. She couldn't believe that he had actually struck her. Or that it had meant nothing to him to do so. A gentleman never struck a lady . . . but then, Brent probably didn't consider her a lady. She was a Yankee's wife, and nothing that she ever had with Brent could be truly right. He had whispered beautiful, impassioned words of love, yet she wondered if he had whispered those words for expediency's sake.

No! No, he did love her. She believed it, she had to believe it . . .

But he had slapped her, and now he taunted her, deliberately provoked her.

She ceased struggling and stared at him with cool, narrowed eyes. "Captain McClain, you're not my father, and you're not my husband. There are times when I truly doubt that you're my friend. Let go of me. And take your lessons and opinions elsewhere. I don't want to be slapped, abused, taught—or touched—by you."

"You're acting like a child, Kendall, a spoiled little girl."

"Oh, God!" she groaned, her teeth gritting with fury and aggravation. "I mean it, Brent, I—"

"Do you?" he interrupted, suddenly rigidly still and tense as he stared at her. And as she returned his stormy gaze, she knew that she didn't. She wanted to go back; she wanted to close her eyes and open them again and discover that their argument had been a dream and that Brent was smiling at her, offering her his embrace.

What did he want from her? she wondered, wishing fervently that she didn't love him, didn't feel cherished, warmed, and comforted by his muscular touch.

She closed her eyes. "No," she whispered.

"Kendall . . ." he murmured.

She didn't know if he uttered her name with love or with a fevered desire. But it didn't matter, because just as she couldn't deny him, she couldn't deny the response of her flesh to his. Yet what she felt wasn't desire; the tempest of their anger had left her feeling as if she had been battered against the rocks, and all she sought was a safe harbor.

Tenderness, a gentle touch, to feel that he did love her, even if love was only an illusion.

The arms that had forced her down suddenly embraced her. Lips that had been held taut in a bitter line softened to touch hers. Like a breeze at first, and then hungrily . . . in an ardor that left no room for tenderness.

Kendall clung to him, as if weathering a storm. She did not fight the winds, but rather rode with them. She reexperienced the taste and touch and sensation, the scent of him, the masculine feel of his commanding lips on hers . . .

Familiar, missed, longed for . . .

Kendall looped her arms around his neck, glad to hold him, to inhale the sun and sea and male strength of him. But even as she held him and felt the touch of his lips and teeth and tongue, the shivery brush of his mustache and beard, the warmth of his sinewed arms, she fought the raw power of his male strength.

She was tired of learning the lessons.

He deserved to learn a few. Brent McClain always called the shots. Anger on his terms; love on his terms . . .

He broke away from her at last, and she couldn't read the expression in the smoke of his gaze. A slight trembling shook her; it was so hard to think when he was so close. The heady potency of his touch was like a drug that overwhelmed her senses, and hence her mind. But she had to hold her own, and she felt that for her sanity she must prove her point.

She offered him a dazzling smile. "I've missed you so

much, Brent," she whispered, and the husky tremor of her voice was real.

He didn't speak, and she reached out a tremulous hand to touch his cheek, loving the soft touch of his beard and the smooth bronze flesh. Had there ever been anyone, she wondered, more the epitome of the cavalier than he? A gentleman always, heartbreakingly handsome, yet as rugged and determined as the ever-changing land.

A sadness touched her as she smiled. Perhaps Brent couldn't understand, because she was fighting a part of the very ideal for which they waged war—southern womanhood. Ahh, but they were supposed to be sheltered ladies, gentle flowers for men to valiantly protect. The ideal was beautiful and courtly and truly a dream.

But the men had never understood that the South bred strong women; from the wives of the poor farmers to the belles who married and ran the great plantations, they were expected to handle a rugged lot.

Yet Brent would defend the honor of a woman to his dying breath. As he would defend her life, always above his own. The code, the ideal, the dream; it was a part of him.

"You've taken my ship," she said softly. "What more trouble can I get into?"

"Why?" he responded to her question with another. "Why did you risk it, Kendall?"

"It is my war, too, Brent."

He shook his head. "No, Kendall. You don't understand war. You gambled everything in the wild hope that you might kill John Moore."

"No. You're wrong, Brent. And I never took unnecessary risks. Red Fox and Harry ran the *Rebel's Pride,* and they took a number of ships. Red Fox did not seek revenge; he did not slaughter the Yanks. I was behind it all, yes, and I was aboard once when they sank a frigate. And yes, Brent, I felt a wonderful power, a great surge of victory. It felt good

309

to fight. But I was never hoping to kill John. If I could ever forget the things that happened, I could pity John. He has been dead a long time—in his heart." Kendall ran her fingers through his hair, and luxuriated in the touch of the tawny gold. She smiled again. His hair was growing well over his collar. Then her smile faded. "You look thin," she commented softly.

He straightened, and freed from his restraint, Kendall slid from his lap and walked idly around the bed to sit on the other side and eye the tiny bedside table with its squat gate legs. In the drawer was the knife Red Fox had taught her to use after she came so close to disaster aboard the schooner. Deftly she opened the drawer, slid the knife out, and slipped it unobtrusively beneath her thigh.

"Did things go badly in London?" she queried.

"No. Everything went well."

Then why are you like this? she wanted to shout. It seemed that an unbreachable wall was growing between them, and what she was about to do would make it worse.

"Have you . . . have you spoken with Red Fox?" she asked.

"Yes."

"He knows you've taken the ship?"

"Of course."

And no doubt, Kendall thought bitterly, Red Fox was glad to see the *Rebel's Pride* go. Relieved to be freed from the responsibility of constantly worrying about her . . .

Kendall tensed as she heard Brent stand and slowly walk around the bed. He removed his scabbard and sword and idly opened the buttons of his frock coat, tossing it aside before standing in front of her and cupping her chin caressingly in his long fingers to bring her eyes to his.

"Kendall," he said thickly. "The fighting is over for you. Please, listen to me, because I sincerely mean what I say. If I hear of any more of your exploits, I will find you. And I'll take you forcibly to another country to wait out the war. Do you understand me?"

"Brent—"

She barely saw him move, heard only a whisper of air—but suddenly he had dropped to one knee and drawn his knife from its strap about his calf.

And he held his knife against her breast.

His mouth was a line against the hardness of his jaw as she stared at him in startled confusion.

"What if I were a Yank, Kendall? There wouldn't be a thing that you could do. My blade is at your breast."

He slid the blade so that it slipped between the buttons of her gown, kissing her flesh, teasing it with coldness, threatening it, but not drawing a scratch. Her eyes were melded to his, it was hypnotism, it was anger. She clenched her own jaw, saying nothing as he slit the buttons one by one. Her own blade was hidden beneath the fabric of her gown, yet she didn't move for it. Timing was her weapon.

"What would you do if I were a Yankee, Kendall?" he repeated.

She held her chin high. "Not all Yanks are cruel rapists, Brent."

"No, they're not. Nor should you ever count on all southern men being the essence of gentility. Do you see your position, Kendall?"

"Yes," she snapped out bitterly.

He stood and sheathed his knife, then removed the band from about his calf and turned from her as he pulled the tails of his shirt from his breeches.

"I haven't much time," he told her with his back still turned to her.

"You never do," she commented dryly.

He spun back around. "I can't help that, Kendall."

"Ummm," she murmured, lowering her lashes. "The gallant male must rush to the line of the fire."

"Stop it, Kendall."

She sat perfectly still, listening to the slight rustle as he removed his clothing.

"It's morning, you know," she said hollowly.

"So?"

So you walk in to toss me about, dictate your orders, and then hop into bed. And God help me, I still love you, still want you. But you'll walk right out with the bed still warm and sail away to fight without another thought of me until you're ready to return.

"I realize I haven't much of a reputation left, Brent, but Amy is probably still in the cabin."

"Kendall," he growled impatiently, kneeling on the bed beside her. "I have been away for a long, long time. Your reputation is hardly relevant here. Our circumstances are unique. I'm quite sure that the Armstrongs will expect us to want to be together."

She didn't want to feel the sensual pull of his naked body against hers. She didn't dare raise her lashes, or turn to him. Her body was already thrilling to the touch of his, blood seeming to heat, limbs to weaken, heart to thud in sweet anticipation. He lifted her hair from her neck and pressed his lips to the nape, nipping the flesh gently, caressing it with his lips . . . and the tip of his tongue. Heat seeped through her, liquefying and intensifying with each tender, taunting touch.

She couldn't give in . . .

She faced him at last as he placed his hands on her shoulders and pressed her down to the bed. His eyes held hers as his hands pushed aside the fabric split by his blade, baring her breasts. He brought his weight alongside her, and gazed at one firm mound while he cradled it and raised the nipple to a peak with a graze of his thumb. Then he lowered his head to allow his lips to savor the fullness.

Kendall threaded her fingers into his hair, trying not to

think of the pain of wanting him. A fire of longing and aching need rose from a center deep within her.

His hand slipped beneath the hem of her gown and ran a course of exotic heat from her calf to her inner thigh where he began to tantalize her vulnerable flesh with lazy circles. He paused for a moment, murmuring against her breast as he tugged at the gown.

"Let's get rid of this," he said huskily.

She swallowed and stiffened. "Kiss me, Brent."

"I am."

"My lips, Brent. Please, kiss me."

He shifted obligingly and slowly lowered his lips to hers. She reached swiftly beneath her and brought forth her blade, flattening it against his throat with the blade threatening at the vein.

Surprise leapt into his eyes, then a fury that turned them from a smoldering gray to a shade of black.

She spoke quickly. "What do you do now, Brent? One move . . . the slightest movement, and I could sever your jugular."

He swore softly, his tone dead and menacing. Kendall swallowed again, forcing her eyes to stay on his without wavering.

"We are all vulnerable, Brent. We can all die. Your life means more to me than my own, yet you must risk it. And you don't even ask if I understand."

"That's different, Kendall."

"How so?" she edged the blade slightly closer, drawing a thin trickle of blood. "I am a woman. And yes, you are far stronger. Yet I could end your life here."

He smiled at her. She kept her eyes wide upon his, yet when he subtly, smoothly moved his hand to hers, enveloping it and crushing it until she gasped and released her hold on the weapon, she could not move against him. He picked the

313

knife up from the pillow and furiously tossed it across the room.

"I took your knife, Kendall."

"Only because I allowed you."

"You were able to bring it against my throat—only because I allowed you. And because you're a woman, you allowed me to take it."

"That had nothing to do with my being a woman! It had to do with the fact that I love you."

"You have lost the argument, Kendall."

"I lost when I fell in love with you," she said bitterly.

"You love me—yet you pressed a knife against my throat?"

Kendall closed her eyes. They flew open again as his fingers wound tightly into her hair. He kissed her again, angrily, demanding and devouring. There were tears in her eyes, but she could not fight him, nor could she understand the depths of his heated fury.

He didn't speak to her, didn't whisper encouragement with loving tenderness. Powerful hands that trembled with impatience ripped the remainder of the gown's seam; it landed in a discarded heap on the floor.

He made love to her voraciously, consuming, overwhelming, invading every part of her. Longing allowed her to match his passion, to burn in response to the devil that possessed him.

The morning passed in a blur of fevered tempest. Sweet satiation came, and the fires were kindled anew. And still no words passed between them; no promises of peace.

At last, physically exhausted despite the noon hour, Kendall fell into a restless doze beside him, her legs entwined with his, her slender hand and arm draped over his chest.

When she awoke, the sun was still blazing . . . but Brent was gone. Kendall stared about the room, searching for some sign of him. But there wasn't a trace. No sword, no plumed hat. Nothing to indicate that Brent McClain was near.

She started to leap from the bed, only to emit a soft moan as she realized how sore and bruised she was. She winced, then moved more carefully as she rose and hurriedly washed and dressed.

Kendall found Amy in the garden cutting roses. She hesitated before approaching the gentle matron, smoothing her hair, and praying that she showed no sign of the intimate moments just past.

"Amy," she murmured, keeping her eyes downcast, "where's Brent?"

She at last raised her lashes as Amy paused long before making a reply.

Amy appeared confused and upset. "Why, he's gone on, dear. He spoke with Harry and Red Fox before taking the ship, then came to you. We . . . uh . . . all understood. You two young people have so little time. And he's had a rough time of it, you know. What with his father missing and his brother so bad off and in the hands of the Yankees."

"Amy, what are you talking about?"

"Well, if I understand it right, his ship was laid up for repairs in Richmond before he could come here. He went off to see his pa and brother who are with Lee's army. He was with them for that dreadful battle at Sharpsburg, and his brother was badly wounded—and taken by the Yanks. His father was simply among the missing."

"Oh, God," Kendall groaned.

"Harry was upset that I spoke to you before Brent did, but . . . well, I didn't know about everything then, and I thought you had a right to know about the ship," Amy continued. "I still don't understand why Brent left without telling you!"

"Maybe I do," Kendall whispered bleakly, turning to leave the garden before Amy could see the tears form in her eyes.

"Kendall—"

"I'm all right, Amy. I just . . . want to be alone."

She raced down the trail to the stables and then to the cove blindly, finding her way by instinct alone. When she reached the shore, she sank down to her knees and cried.

Brent himself was wounded. In the heart, and in the soul. She should have been able to help. Instead . . .

He must have been angrier than she had realized. Furious enough to wash his hands of her. She hadn't tried to understand what was driving him, and she had taunted and cornered him. And she had truly lost . . .

Kendall stayed at the cove until the sun set. At last she ran out of tears and wearily returned to the cabin.

Seventeen

June 1863
Vicksburg, Mississippi

Dearest Amy,

I have, of course, no idea of how or when this letter will reach you, but I write with the prayer that it will get through. We are too busy here at the hospital to truly form friendships, and so I hope you will bear with me as I put my thoughts on paper. The hope that you will read them and understand is a great comfort to me.

The situation here grows more perilous daily. Living under siege is, at best, devastating. And, dear Amy, I mean no reproach by that! None of us knew what it would be when you helped me leave Florida to come and assist Harry's brother at the hospital. I am strangely content. I suffer terribly for the men brought here in tatters and pieces, yet I am so very pleased to be helping! I am useful, Amy. And that is, to me, so very, very important. And I am busy from dawn to dusk, which keeps me from thinking about Brent and brooding and crying and—

* * *

The shattering sound of a shell explosion close by startled Kendall. She jerked her hand away from the paper and held her breath for a moment. The oil lamp on her rough wood desk rattled. The walls about her seemed to groan and shiver.

But then there was nothing more. She exhaled a long and shaky sigh. Vicksburg had been under siege for over two months now, and she was still trying to accustom herself to the sounds of the shells that continually poured into the city. The hospital, situated far from the river, was generally safe, although several shells had shattered two wards, killing the men who rested in them.

Kendall paused a moment and listened, but no more fire whistled through the air. The Yanks had called it quits for the night. She looked at the letter she had been writing, and then slowly ripped it to shreds.

She was insane to be writing about Brent. Insane to be thinking about Brent. She hadn't seen or heard from him in nine months. Not since he had left her without so much as a whispered good-bye.

She had heard *of* him, of course. Captain Brent McClain was still a Confederate hero. The southern papers claimed that he alone kept a fifth of the Rebel armies eating, and said that he was responsible for taking or destroying fifty Federal ships.

Where was he now? Kendall idly tapped her quill on the desk. Had he ever returned to the bay? Had he ever cared enough to wonder if she was all right? She hadn't heard from Amy since February, not long after she had made the move to Vicksburg.

It had simply been impossible to stay by the bay after Brent left that last time. The *Rebel's Pride* had been taken from her. And she had been certain that Brent would never return.

Not to her.

She hadn't dared return to Charleston; as long as there

was breath in his body, she would never trust her stepfather. And although it made her a bit nervous to know that John Moore was serving under Farragut somewhere along the Mississippi, no one had believed that the Yanks could beat back the Rebel armies opposing them on the western front. Vicksburg was impregnable, surrounded by mountains and facing the river. In February, when Kendall had made her decision to assist David Armstrong at the hospital, no one had even imagined that Vicksburg could come under a siege such as this.

No one in the South, at least. The Confederates, from the very beginning, had little to fight with except courage and bravado. But no matter how courageous the men, their willpower alone could not withstand the strength and number of Yankee guns concentrated on them.

Kendall stood and stretched, placing her hands low on her sore back as she did so. She was so tired. Yet no matter how she pushed herself, she couldn't forget Brent. Somehow it had been bearable—hard but bearable—to be away from him when she could believe he would come to her again. When she could allow herself to dream of sharing a future with him.

But the dream was as dead as the eloquent grace that had once been Vicksburg. Memory did not dim, but plagued her daily. Even after all this time, she would see his face when she tried to grab a restless hour's sleep. And it was the laughter that she remembered. The cavalier smile that rakishly cut across his rugged features, gray eyes that could smolder to a summer heat with more power to warm than the sun.

Kendall winced and bit firmly into her lower lip. If she was going to remember Brent at all, she would be wise to remember that his temper had a bite like a pronged whip, that he could be insolent, arrogant, and irritatingly superior. *He* was the fool who was determined to get himself killed.

Why wasn't it possible, she wondered bitterly, to run away

from love? Red Fox had told her she could never do so . . . and time and distance were proving him right. He had tried so hard to dissuade her from leaving. She was acting like a child, he had said impatiently—just as Brent had told her. Brent would be back; he would expect to find her.

But she couldn't believe that Brent *wanted* to find her . . .

She missed Red Fox. He was the closest friend she'd ever had. She missed his quiet words, his presence, the calm and stoic beauty of his spirit.

And she missed him because he was a tangible link to Brent . . .

She had to forget Brent, bury herself in work until exhaustion overwhelmed her and cleared her mind of the dreams.

She worked from dawn to dusk. The siege was flooding the hospital with so many wounded soldiers that it was sometimes difficult to maneuver between the stretchers.

The Confederate General John Pemberton was trying desperately and valiantly to hold the city, but the Union's General Grant was a determined man. And the people of the old southern city had been strong and resolute, adapting stalwartly to hardship.

But as the weary weeks wore on, courage and gallantry were fading to obscurity along with the food supply. Horses, dogs, and cats found their way to dinner tables. And as the supply of those beasts dwindled, roast rat sometimes became the evening meal.

There was a tap on the door of her tiny room. "Yes?" Kendall called out quickly, glad to be jolted from her morose state.

"I need you, Kendall. That last shell caught several men. They're bringing them in now."

"Coming, Dr. Armstrong!" Kendall called quickly. She smoothed her hands over the skirt of her dress and mechanically glanced in the tarnished mirror above the simple washstand. Something in her own reflection caught her attention, and she paused with a wince, running a finger over the hollows under her cheekbones.

She looked terrible. Purple shadows lurked beneath her eyes and she thought she resembled a skeleton—all eyes and bone. Sighing, she tucked a straying lock of hair back into her chignon and resolutely turned away from the mirror.

Dying men probably didn't care too much what she looked like, as long as she had a gentle touch and offered water for their parched throats.

David Armstrong was much like his brother—a strong and gentle man, an indefatigable worker. Kendall had grown as attached to him as she had to Amy and Harry. She met him in the hallway where he was rolling up his sleeves and strolling toward a washstand.

"Down the hall, Kendall, we've three amputations."

Kendall paled visibly, but nodded. She hated this part of her work more than any other. The men screamed and fought. They cried and pleaded and begged for mercy.

But gangrene was one of the worst enemies of the war for either side. The rotting infection could kill where shots left off.

"Have we any anesthetic?"

Dr. Armstrong leveled his eyes to hers unhappily. "No."

Again Kendall nodded, fighting nausea.

"Come along," Dr. Armstrong said crisply.

Kendall followed.

She could not save the poor young soldier from losing his leg, but she knew she was invaluable to Dr. Armstrong. Most of the South's able-bodied men were on the front line in the defense of the city and could not be spared for hospital work. She knew Dr. Armstrong well now; she had his saws and other instruments ready before he could ask for them. And she was there with the dressings for the stumps, and with soothing words for the patients and a gentle touch. Yet still she feared she would be sick each time she attended in surgery, causing further distress for the already agonized patient.

Dr. Armstrong worked quickly, expertly, and methodically. At last the third man was taken away; the echoes of his screams faded from the hallways. A male orderly wrapped the human refuse of torn and severed flesh and took it away. Kendall stared numbly after him.

Dr. Armstrong slipped an arm around her shoulder. "Do you know," he murmured softly, "the hardest thing for me is the birds. All this carnage goes on, yet the birds see only that spring is changing to summer. And the flowers . . . they continue to grow. Ah, well. Life will always go on, Kendall. A time to sow, a time to reap."

Kendall glanced at him, startled by his fancy. He was always so busy—kind, but direct.

He smiled at her. "Kendall, you should be dressed in beautiful silks and muslins and flirting with all the fine youths at a ball. I can just imagine you, child, as you should be. So lovely. Carefree again, with no anxieties. This is not, I'm afraid, much of a place for a fine young lady."

Kendall grimaced. "Dr. Armstrong, I'm not terribly sure that I ever *was* a fine young lady."

He shook his gray head sagely. "My girl, you will always be the finest of ladies. And you're strong. You will survive all of this suffering. Many, I'm afraid, will not."

Kendall felt a tug at her heart. "Do you believe that we . . . that we will lose Vicksburg?"

"Kendall, it's not a matter of belief. Look about you. We're all starving to death. Vicksburg is already a shell. Its citizens scurry to seek shelters in caves and in the basements of haunted remnants of homes. And every day there are more and more Federals. General Pemberton is making a valiant stand, but how long can a tattered, barefoot, and starving army hold off men who are well fed and well supplied and twice their number? Yes, unless a miracle occurs, Vicksburg will fall. Just as the South—"

He cut off his words hurriedly, seeing her stricken expression. "Don't pay any attention to me, Kendall. I'm just a tired old workhorse, worn out before my time!" She still appeared stricken, and vulnerable. Again Dr. David Armstrong sought to undo the pain he had so obviously caused her. "We should receive some morphine tomorrow," he said cheerfully. "We've sent a man across the river to steal through the Union lines to a contact. We'll meet him together, tomorrow night."

Kendall smiled vaguely. "Morphine," she murmured. "That will be wonderful." Tomorrow they could chop up men who wouldn't scream quite so loud. What a pathetic blessing.

"Go on to bed now, Kendall. Get some sleep."

She went to bed, and she slept. But her sleep was plagued with horrible nightmares. A man in gray screamed on the operating table. And when she turned to see him, it was Brent.

She woke up shaking, then forced herself to seek sleep again. But she saw the operating table again. And there was another man lying on it. His flesh was copper-bronze, and he bled from numerous wounds. He turned to her and whispered, "Revenge!"

It was Red Fox.

Then he bolted from the table, and she saw that he was chasing her. She ran, but before her loomed Brent, covered in blood, his handsome gray frock coat tattered and ripped, his feet bare. His eyes accused her.

She was trapped between them. And she covered her face with her hands and sank to her knees, screaming. They were the men who had once loved her, had once cared for her. And she had brought them to the greatest agony . . . and in her dream, she was afraid.

She awoke again—her scream drowned out by the sound of a bursting shell. It was morning. Kendall struggled up and washed her face. She raised her eyes to the mirror and noticed that the dark circles beneath her eyes seemed to have darkened overnight.

She reminded herself again that the wounded men would hardly care what she looked like as long as she tended to their needs.

The day seemed to stretch on forever. Grant was bombarding them from land; Admiral Porter bombarded them from the river. Along with the wounded soldiers came injured civilians—old men, women, and children—caught in the line of fire. Seeing the children hurt Kendall the most. Gaunt, ragged little scarecrows, they didn't understand anything about the war. They only knew that they hurt.

At last the shelling ceased for the day. Doctors who slept during the day awoke to work through the night. Kendall retreated to her cubicle of a room in the hospital and studiously tried to wash the stench of death and decay from her body.

"Kendall!"

She heard Dr. Armstrong's voice along with his tap on the door. "Yes?"

"Are you coming with me?"

"Oh!" The morphine, yes! He had asked her to come along. "Yes, yes, I'm coming, right now!"

Hurriedly she donned pantalettes and a simple cotton gown and threw open the door. Dr. Armstrong offered her his arm gallantly. "Come, my dear," he said with a twinkle in his eye. "I'll escort you through the streets!"

It should have been depressing to walk through the haunted streets. To view the burnt-out shells of once grand homes. But as they walked through the darkness and the silence, David Armstrong talked, pointing out the various homes and telling her amusing anecdotes about the people who had once resided in them.

And summer was in the air. The freshness of the river breeze was a vast improvement over the stench of death that clung to the hospital.

They turned left, away from the city and the Rebel batteries. A soft whistle sounded on the air, and Dr. Armstrong halted, holding her arm tensely. But a young boy scampered from a clump of bushes to meet them.

"Doc Armstrong, I don't know what's gone wrong. I can see the boat, but she's not coming in. Look out yonder. You can see her driftin' on the water? When the moon comes out from the clouds—see? There. Why isn't he bringing her in? Billy should be through the lines!"

Dr. Armstrong was silent as he stared out at the river. "I don't know," he murmured at last. "But the current is going to take that little rowboat away real soon. I wonder if he got the morphine?"

Kendall looked from the boy, who couldn't have been more than thirteen, to the aging doctor. As if reading her thoughts, the boy started speaking again, a little catch hoarsening his voice. "I'd try to get her, but I can't swim, Dr. Armstrong. Ma was always sayin' she'd tan our hides if she ever caught us in the river or the creek."

"I can go get her," Kendall volunteered.

Dr. Armstrong stared at her as if she had gone insane.

"No, Kendall, I can't send a woman out—"

"Certainly you can!" Kendall insisted with annoyance. "This boy can't swim, and—sorry, Dr. Armstrong, but you're too old. Besides, the wounded in that hospital simply couldn't afford to lose you."

As she spoke, Kendall began to rip at the seam of her dress. She was going to have to get rid of the bulk of the material, or she would drown herself. She didn't dare tell Dr.

325

Armstrong that she was scared silly. She still wasn't a *strong* swimmer. And she tried to convince herself that as long as she didn't panic, she would be fine. The boat wasn't far away, but it was drifting farther.

"Kendall, we'll go for someone else."

"There isn't time. The morphine will drift out to the Yanks, and I'm quite certain they won't gift wrap it and send it back!"

She tossed off her shoes, then noticed that the young boy was staring at her. She laughed to ease the tension. "Listen," she murmured, looking down at her pantalettes and her short, ripped bodice, "I do realize this can't be the latest from *Godey's,* but we can consider it the costume for lady swimmers."

"Kendall," Dr. Armstrong began to protest uneasily. But she didn't wait to be stopped. She plunged through the weeds at the river's edge. The water was cool at night, and she gritted her teeth as she mentally braced herself against it—and the worry over what creatures might be lurking there. She quickly stretched out her arms to swim, loath to keep her feet on the muddy bottom any longer than necessary. For several strokes she cut through the water, then paused, kicking furiously, to search for the small, drifting rowboat. Dismay chilled her heart as she saw that it was still several hundred feet away. She should turn back . . .

But memory of the men screaming in the operating room kept her going. She took a deep breath and began to swim again, trying to maintain slow, easy strokes. She paused, eyeing her objective once more. It was so far! Again she took a deep breath, reminding herself it was safer to keep going than to allow her limbs to grow too chilled.

She began to swim again, forcing herself to be as methodical as Dr. Armstrong. She glanced up. Just a little farther . . . just a little farther.

And at last, she was upon the rowboat. She reached for

the gunwale and gripped it, then leaned her cheek against the wooden hull, breathing deeply and resting before trying to haul herself from the water into the boat.

A feeling of pride and happiness enveloped her. She had been frightened, but she had managed to get the boat. And because of it, so many men would find solace from pain . . .

Suddenly a scream tore from her throat as hands clamped over hers, rough hands, strong hands, tugging at her. "Come aboard, spy!" a voice invited cheerfully.

"No!" Kendall screeched, fighting the hands in raw panic. But she was dragged from the water and deposited on the middle thwart of the boat.

"I'll be damned, Sergeant! It's a woman."

"I won't argue with you there, Private Walker," a pleasant male voice responded lightly. "It certainly is a woman."

Kendall stared with wide-eyed desperation from the blue-clad man in the bow to the blue-clad man at the stern, now calmly rowing them along with steady strokes to the opposite shore.

"Wait!" she pleaded, suddenly certain that the sergeant was a decent sort from the gentle quality of his voice. "Wait, please! We need the morphine!"

"What morphine?" the sergeant demanded, his leathery face frowning into a thousand wrinkles. "There was never any morphine aboard this boat, lady. Just small arms. We took her from a man trying to smuggle arms into Vicksburg."

"But I don't understand—" Kendall began.

The sergeant laughed. "Sorry, lady, your man was no philanthropist. He probably decided he could make more money with weapons than he could with medicines. But don't worry, ma'am—he's going to sit out the rest of this war in a Union prison."

Prison . . . dear God, Kendall thought belatedly. These men were Yankees, and they were taking her to the Union line. She was sitting before two Yankees in nothing but her

327

bodice and pantalettes—dripping wet—and they were taking her to the Union line.

She leapt to her feet, causing the boat to wobble precariously. But before she could dive back into the water, the sergeant flung his arms around her legs, and she crashed down hard on the midship thwart.

"Sorry, ma'am," he muttered, "but we've come up with a number of pretty spies, you know. You're going to come with us to see the lieutenant."

Kendall didn't feel the bruises on her ribs where she had fallen. She closed her eyes, her mind suddenly gone blank with terror.

She would never be able to say that they weren't kind to her. As soon as they reached the shore, the soldiers gave her a blanket to drape about herself. Any man who offered her so much as a licentious stare was harshly reprimanded.

She was taken over a half mile of shoreline to a spot where Yankee tents were pitched in abundance. Thousands of men in blue sat around campfires, yet they merely paused in their evening meal to watch the procession as she was led through their midst.

At last they stopped before a large tent. The sergeant slipped beneath the flap quickly—and just as swiftly slipped back out to hold it high, indicating that she should enter.

She stood still, her hair dripping and clinging to her face as she stared at the young lieutenant who sat behind a field desk.

She was surprised when he instantly and politely rose. He smiled, and she saw that he was even younger than she had first thought, his features merely worn by the ravages of battle. His eyes were a golden hazel, alert, yet tired. His manner was quietly authoritative.

"So you're our Confederate spy," he murmured.

"I'm not a spy," Kendall replied, more tired than nervous. She met his gaze boldly and defiantly. "We needed morphine. I swam out to get it."

"We found that rowboat filled with arms."

"So I heard."

"Did you? Then did you hear that once we had taken it, we used the boat as bait to discover who has been slipping into our ranks to steal arms?"

"No."

"What is your name, ma'am?"

She hesitated. "Kendall," she murmured. "Kendall . . . Armstrong."

"Have you eaten, Miss Armstrong?"

"I . . ."

"Foolish question. No one in Vicksburg has eaten well for quite some time."

The lieutenant strode past her to the tent flap. "Private Green! Fetch some rations for our Rebel guest—pronto!"

"Yes, sir!"

He smiled at Kendall again as he came back into the tent, sweeping his arm politely to indicate that she should take the squat folding chair across from his field desk. With little choice, Kendall sat.

"Lieutenant," Kendall murmured, "I assure you I'm not a spy. It would be rather useless to be one at this point, don't you think, sir? Vicksburg is in a desperate plight. Yet there is no information that could really save the city, is there?"

"Save it—no," the lieutenant replied. "But prolong this misery, yes. We know that the arms carrier had contacts on the shore. Ah . . . here is your meal. Please, eat."

She would have liked to turn up her nose at the food; she could not. There was fresh beef on the plate. And bread—with no mold. Summer corn swimming in creamy butter . . .

"Thank you," she said shakily, practically attacking the food as the delicious aromas assailed her.

"Eat slowly," the Yankee lieutenant advised her, not unkindly, as he returned to his own chair and surveyed her. He plucked a dark liquor bottle from beneath the desk and set it on the table.

"Do southern ladies accept a swig of whiskey?" he queried almost whimsically.

"This one does," Kendall said softly.

He rummaged through a drawer until he found a glass. Kendall tossed down the liquor offered her in a single swallow. It stung her throat, but it warmed her. She turned her attention back to the most delicious meal she had ever consumed. She barely noticed that he silently stared at her.

"I'm not really sure what to do with you," he said at last. "For tonight we'll put you in the tent next to mine—under heavy guard, of course. By tomorrow morning my men should be able to scrounge up some clothing for you. And I'll speak with the general."

Kendall at last set down her fork and sat with her hands in her lap, eyes downcast. She wasn't about to argue with this man. She didn't think that he really believed her to be a spy. And it seemed likely that he would eventually release her.

Private Green was called back. She was led to another tent with a clean cot—and rough, but warm blankets.

She assumed she would toss restlessly, and nervously, all night, but she didn't. Amazingly, sleep overwhelmed all thoughts of fear and anxiety. She slept deeply—and dreamlessly.

She awoke to the sound of bugles—reveille—and then the cacophony of clanks and rustles as thousands of soldiers fell into ranks.

She pulled her blanket about her as she listened to the

sounds of the Yankee camp, closed her eyes tightly once more, and prayed.

"Dear God—please! Please make these people release me before they discover that I'm the missing wife of a Federal naval lieutenant."

"Miss Armstrong, I'm tossing a gown in to you. Please dress immediately. Private Green will be waiting to bring you to my tent."

Kendall held her breath as a deep russet cotton gown was tossed into her tent. It was the lieutenant who had spoken—as polite as he had been last night. Yet there had been something different about his voice . . .

She didn't want to crawl out of the cot. She was suddenly terrified to face the day.

Brent McClain! she wailed in silent, furious reproach. You took my ship and demanded that I play a safe role—a woman's role—in this war. On the ship I could have fought. Here I cannot. I am helpless. You arrogant bastard, you have done this to me!

But that wasn't really true. He had wanted her to stay in Florida, in the safe harbor . . . but she had gone to Vicksburg and innocently determined to catch a drifting rowboat.

She couldn't have done differently, she thought with a sigh. And she forced herself to rise—and don the russet gown.

Her suspicion that something had changed overnight became positive knowledge as she entered the tent of the young lieutenant.

He was not alone. Two older and very severe-looking officers were seated on either side of him.

The lieutenant didn't rise. Nor did he indicate that she should sit. He stared at her with cold accusation.

"To my left, madam, is Quartermaster Jordan of the United States Navy. I'm sure you're aware that our assault on Vicksburg has been a combined effort of army and navy.

Quartermaster Jordan recently transferred to our front from a short stint at Key West. He saw you come in last night. And he's quite certain that he recognizes you. He says you were aboard a Confederate schooner that blew a Union ship straight to hell. What do you say to the charge, ma'am?"

"I deny it, of course," Kendall murmured, trying to speak with conviction and still the tremors that shook her.

"Furthermore," the lieutenant continued as if she hadn't spoken, "he tells me it was rumored that the woman taking our Federal ships was the wife of a fellow naval officer. Your name is Kendall Moore, madam, not Armstrong."

They had her—and they knew that they had her. She felt as if the entire world were slipping away from beneath her feet—but she was determined that they not know it.

She stiffened her spine, squared her shoulders, and slightly lifted her chin.

The lieutenant pushed back his chair and stood and approached her.

"You are guilty, madam, of acts of sabotage against the United States armed forces. The penalties for that are grave, Mrs. Moore. Under normal circumstances, we would be forced by law to send you to a prisoner-of-war camp. I would thank God, if I were you, Mrs. Moore, that I was married to a naval officer. We will place you in your husband's custody—"

"No!" Kendall interrupted sharply—icily.

"What?" The young lieutenant appeared confused.

"I said no. I do not want to be placed in my husband's custody."

"I don't think you understand. The alternative is prison."

"I understand perfectly," Kendall said with cool dignity. "I prefer prison."

The young lieutenant stared at her, noting the stark purpose and determination in her beautiful clear blue eyes. Seconds ticked by.

At last he threw up his arms in exasperation. He strode around to sit behind his desk and scrawl on a piece of paper.

"This grieves me," he said huskily. "I never thought I would have to condemn a woman to such a fate. Mrs. Moore, won't you please reconsider? Your husband will certainly be angry, but as you're his wife in the sight of God—"

"No, Lieutenant," Kendall interrupted firmly. "I will not reconsider."

The young man winced. He scrawled his signature on an official paper.

"Private Green!" he called sharply, never taking his eyes from Kendall.

The private appeared quickly in the tent, saluting. The lieutenant rolled and bound his order and handed it to the private. "Arrange an escort. Sergeant Matling can be in charge. Mrs. Moore is to be taken to Camp Douglas in Chicago. She is to be held there for the duration of the war."

Camp Douglas. Kendall felt her heart sink. It was reputed to be the Andersonville of the North; a place riddled with lice and disease and famine . . .

Her lips started to quiver; she pressed them firmly together, forcing herself to keep her chin high. Even Camp Douglas would be preferable to John Moore . . .

Or so she thought until she reached the prison four days later. Hell couldn't have been worse than Camp Douglas.

Eighteen

Kendall didn't think she would forget the stench of Camp Douglas as long as she lived—or even after death.

She had been warned by the young men charged with her transport that the commander of the camp was a tyrant—a man who believed that dissenting Rebels should suffer. Yet conditions inside the camp guaranteed suffering without any assistance.

As soon as she set eyes on the camp with its seemingly endless walls and stark rows of buildings, a feeling of sickness seemed to rob her muscles of strength and her bones of substance.

She arrived in midafternoon, and after the gates had opened to afford them entrance, she saw a number of the prisoners taking exercise in the vast center field. They looked worse than scarecrows, she thought. Thin as rails, tattered, dirty—and tragic.

She didn't have long to stare; she was led into the commander's office.

He barely glanced up as he looked over her papers. "Throw her in with the Georgians," he said briefly.

"Sir," Private Green protested, nervously clearing his throat, "the prisoner is *Mrs.* Moore!"

"She wanted to fight with her Rebel friends—let her rot

with them." He at last looked up with a sneer cutting across his heavily bearded features. "Seems to me she prefers the company of Rebel trash to a Yankee husband. Go on. Take her. Let her discover just how gallant that Confederate rabble can be. Most of those men haven't seen anything remotely female in at least a year. Let's see how filled with Rebel fever she is after a few nights with that chivalrous filth."

It wasn't Private Green who led her away, but the Yankee commander's assistant. Kendall jerked her arm from his grasp to turn back to the man at the desk.

"Captain?" she said sweetly.

"What?" He glanced up and surveyed her slowly.

Kendall spit on the floor. "I'd rather be raped by a thousand Rebs than touched by a single Yankee."

"Get her out of here," the commander snapped. "She'll change her tune soon enough."

Perhaps she would, Kendall thought sickly only moments later.

She was led down a long row of identical buildings; then a door was unlocked and pushed open—and she was shoved in.

It took her eyes a few moments to adjust to the dimness after the brilliance of the sunlight. But when they did, she visibly cringed.

There were about three dozen men cramped into the small quarters. Dirty, ragged, gaunt, unshaven, and filthy. The smell of privy buckets was overwhelming; in a far corner, there was a pool of rancid water from a leak in the ceiling.

The men who returned her scrutiny hardly resembled soldiers of the grand Confederate Army. Whatever uniforms they had once possessed were so worn and ragged as to be unrecognizable.

And they all looked like ferrets. She felt as if their eyes bored into her like those of a thousand voracious rodents. One soldier, looking like a mass of disjointed bones, pushed

335

himself up from the floor and advanced toward her. "I'll be damned—I will! It's a woman!"

He kept coming at her, then circled around her, his lifeless yellowed eyes awakening to a glitter with his interest.

Kendall backed herself to the door that had been slammed and bolted behind her. She braced herself against it, warily returning his astonished and rapt stare.

The man was about her own age, she thought bitterly. Maybe even handsome when not so skeletally thin. And when not encrusted with filth from his matted hair to his shoeless feet.

"Oh, honey," he breathed, bracing his hands on either side of her head against the heavy oak door, "it's been a long, long time since I've seen somebody soft and curved . . ."

He moved to touch her and Kendall instantly snapped out of the feeling of sympathy that had gripped her when she heard the wistfulness of his tone. She screamed and sank to the floor, covering her face with her hands. "Please . . . oh, please . . . don't . . . don't . . ."

There was an abrupt and total silence in the room as the pathetic wail of her voice died away. Then suddenly there was a shuffling of feet and a stir in the fetid air as another man came forward. He knelt down beside her and gently smoothed her hair, then stood and turned to his comrades, a proud and defiant figure despite the blisters on his feet and the rag-tag state of his mud-encrusted body and clothing.

"We *are*," he stated commandingly, dignity ringing clear in his tone, "still soldiers in the Confederate States Army. We are a proud and chivalrous breed, men. Not a band of licentious rapists! This lady has apparently fought the enemy as we have—and thus been given a spot in this hellhole. We will not, men, I emphasize, *we will not* aid the enemy by inflicting further misery on this poor girl. We will prove ourselves the last of the cavaliers—gentlemen, my friends, to the bitter end."

Again he bent to Kendall. She met a pair of warm brown eyes set with sensitivity and warmth in an aging and weathered but kindly face. "I'm Major Beau Randall of the Twenty-Second Georgia Regulars. I've not much to offer, ma'am, but I am at your service."

His kindness was more than she could bear. Kendall began to cry, and he took her in his arms to soothe her.

Beau Randall had—from that very first day—set the tone for the behavior toward Kendall.

She liked to think that her presence among them somewhat improved their dreary existence. All thirty men longed for a lover; she could be lover to none, but she could offer her heart in friendship to them all. And in the presence of the Twenty-Second Georgia Regulars, she felt a great deal of faith in the human spirit return to her. Men were not so terribly different in their emotions from women. The married men spoke wistfully of their wives and daughters; the single men spoke of their dreams, and of the fiancées and lady friends they had left behind.

Kendall was certain that she kept them mindful of their manners—and that was good for their pride. They were able to remember that they were men, not caged animals.

But there were times when even she could not shake off the misery of prison life. Half the men were suffering from dysentery and scurvy. Rations were so lean that few had the strength to shake off illness when it struck. The death toll was horrendous.

At six o'clock each morning, the buglers sounded reveille. The prisoners were lined up in the yard and roll was called. No one dared move out of line; sick or weak prisoners were held up by their friends. Infractions of the rules were harshly punished. An unwary word could sentence a man to hours astride a "Morgan's mule"—a large sawhorse set behind the barracks. The guards also used solitary confinement and ration-cutting, which could be fatal, to punish offenders.

Although the commander of Camp Douglas was known to be a cruel man, the majority of the Yankee guards were not. They were forced to run the place by their commander's rules, yet it was not true brutality on their part that created misery for the prisoners. The true misery resulted from the overcrowding, the hunger, and the rampant disease.

After roll call, the prisoners were generally left alone. The kinder jailors sometimes brought them newspapers and, occasionally, letters from home. Kendall spent many of her days avidly reading and rereading the papers. She read them aloud to the few Georgia Regulars who had never learned to read. By the time she had been in the prison for a month, she had become their official reader. Each time a paper became available, the men would form a crescent about her, and all of them would listen as she read.

The end of July brought them sad news. Kendall's voice trembled as she read to her fellows that Vicksburg had fallen. Pemberton had officially surrendered to Grant on the Fourth of July. And worse than that, the Fourth of July had marked the end of another battle—a battle in a tiny little town in south-central Pennsylvania called Gettysburg. General Robert E. Lee had been forced back. Both Rebels and Yankees had suffered terrible death tolls during the battles that raged from the first to the fourth.

An ironic Independence Day for both nations . . .

Everyone was solemn when Kendall's voice at last faded away, the final word of print having been read. Silently they broke their cluster, ambling in different directions to find what solitude they could within their own minds.

Kendall sat against the wall with her knees hugged to her body. She rested her head on her arm and tried to understand the numbness that assailed her. She wanted to feel . . . she wanted to hurt for all the thousands who had died at Gettysburg.

But she couldn't seem to feel anything at all. The war was numbing her heart to tragedy.

She felt a presence near her and lifted her head as Beau Randall sank down beside her. "You all right?" he asked gently.

She nodded.

"Sure?"

Kendall grimaced. "I think I have lice."

Beau laughed. "Probably. If you don't, it's a miracle—living with us as you are. We're all infested!"

Kendall smiled for a moment, then frowned. "Beau, aren't the two sides exchanging prisoners anymore? Is there any hope that we'll get out of here?"

He sighed. "I'm afraid there's very little hope. General Grant is afraid we'd all wind up right back in the front line and that he'd have to eradicate the entire southern population to win the war. He knows his own boys are suffering badly in our prisons. Hell, he even knows a lot of them will die. But he can reinforce his ranks without calling in released prisoners; Robert E. Lee can't do that."

"Then there's no hope," Kendall whispered.

"There *is* hope, Kendall. There's always hope. A lot of these Yanks are human; they're not fond of seeing us sicken and starve. I'd be willing to bet a number of them could be bribed—if any of us had anything to bribe them with. I . . ."

Beau's sentence trailed away as they both turned to the door of their barracks. They could hear the heavy lock grating. Curiously they glanced at the Union soldier who entered.

"Mrs. Moore!" His eyes ran across the lethargic prisoners until they came to rest on Kendall. "Note for you, Mrs. Moore."

Frowning, Kendall stood and took the note from the Federal guard. He spun on his heel to leave the second she had it in her hand.

Beau stood beside her. "What is it?"

"I . . . I don't know," she murmured, slitting the envelope. Dizziness swept through her as she saw her husband's precise scrawl:

> *Hell has just begun. I'll be in Chicago to take you into my custody on September first. Our kindly President, Mr. Lincoln, was horrified to hear that a lady was being kept at Camp Douglas. Think of Mr. Lincoln in your prayers, Kendall.*
>
> *Your ever devoted husband,*
> *John*

"What is it?" Beau demanded again as he saw Kendall's complexion turn as pale as snow. She sagged against him, and he grasped the paper from her fingers. Quickly his eyes scanned the words. "Kendall, you're going to get out of here. This is wonderful."

She shook her head, unable to speak. "You . . . you don't understand," she at last murmured. "He'll . . . he'll kill me!"

"No, Kendall, no man could be angry enough to kill you! Surely he understands your feelings. Brothers have fought brothers in this war. Sons have fought their own fathers."

Kendall shook her head. "John is no ordinary man. He doesn't understand the meaning of the word 'mercy.' "

Suddenly she was crying on his shoulder again, and as he tried to soothe her, she discovered herself pouring out her life story. She told him about her flight to Charleston—so long ago now!—and she told him about Red Fox and the Indians—and all about Brent.

"Brent McClain?" Beau asked a little incredulously.

Kendall didn't notice the tone of his voice. She nodded.

"By reputation," Beau murmured, "he's quite a man.

340

And"—his voice softened—"it sounds as if he's very much in love with you."

Kendall laughed bitterly through her tears. "Not so much in love, Beau. He walked out on me."

"Kendall, he's a naval officer. He had to follow orders." Beau hesitated a moment, frowning. "McClain . . . There's a McClain here. Lieutenant Stirling McClain."

"It must be his brother," Kendall murmured, glad to hear that he was alive—for the time being, at least. "He was wounded very seriously at Sharpsburg last year."

"Well, he looks all right—as all right as any of us," Beau added with a grimace. "I've spoken to him a few times. They send the Georgia and Florida boys out to exercise together occasionally."

"I'm glad he's well," Kendall whispered. "A . . . a friend told me he was wounded . . . and she also told me that their father was reported missing. Assumed dead, I imagine. I'm so glad Stirling recovered."

Beau placed his hands on her shoulders and stared into her eyes. "Kendall, you told me that Brent left you shortly after he returned from Sharpsburg. Honey, don't you know how he must have felt just then? I can tell you what he was thinking."

"What?" Kendall asked listlessly.

"Brent had just lost his father, and his brother. He couldn't bear the thought of you being killed, too—or captured, as you have been. Sharpsburg was a horrible battle, Kendall. A bloodbath. It's no wonder he was furious with you for taking so many risks. He couldn't stand to lose you, too. He left because he did love you—but couldn't guarantee that you wouldn't throw yourself back into the fray."

Kendall shrugged. "I doubt it. It's been almost a year since I've seen him. I doubt if he still remembers what I look like. Hah! I doubt if he'd recognize me now. Even my mother wouldn't know me now." She sniffed with bitterness. "He never came back . . . and I didn't try to throw myself into the fray again. I became a nurse—behind the lines, like a good female. It was pure chance that gave me to the Yankees . . . Oh, what does it matter?" she sighed tonelessly. Her tears had made her so tired that she couldn't seem to care about anything. She leaned against Beau's shoulder, and closed her eyes. At least," she whispered, "you understand now why John will . . . kill me."

"Don't give up hope, Kendall," he whispered vaguely, staring blankly across the room. "Never give up hope. We'll think of something. I promise."

"It doesn't really matter," she said. And as she leaned against him in her despair, it didn't. War and hunger and disease were her only reality. And John . . . John as dangerous as war and hunger . . . and disease. There was nothing for her.

Once there had been. A silver time of hope and happiness . . .

Brent. She could still see him in her mind's eye so clearly . . . so painfully, agonizingly clearly. And she still loved him. With all her heart and soul—but she was certain she would never see him again.

John Moore was coming for her. And she was suddenly praying that her days at Camp Douglas could go on forever.

"I'm so tired, Beau. So tired."

"Rest," he told her softly. Beau Randall didn't say anything else. He let her fall asleep against his shoulder.

When she was in a sound, exhausted slumber, he gently lowered her head to the floor. He found the note, which had fluttered to the floor, then inquired softly among the men for a piece of graphite. He didn't have much space to write, so he chose his words carefully.

When he had completed the task to his satisfaction, he ran his fingers in a nimble search over his shirt. Sewn into the lining of a tiny pocket he found what he sought. His last gold piece. Holding it carefully in the palm of his hand, he sat and stared at the door, waiting for the night guard. He was the kindest of the jailors, and the father of six; he was always in need of money. And if a lot more could be promised, Beau reckoned, his note stood a good chance of getting through.

He could only pray that it got through in time. Yet even if it did, he asked himself, what good could it do? Brent McClain was a naval genius—but not a magician. How in heaven and earth could McClain possibly get Kendall out of a Union prison? The Yankees would probably shoot him on sight.

The Florida Keys
August 18, 1863

The schooner was running with the wind, heeling hard to the starboard and disappearing rapidly behind the island.

Travis Deland cursed his luck as he stared at the spot of blue ocean and blue sky where the vessel had been.

He sensed a trap. He hadn't had a chance to see the ship's name, and she hadn't been flying a flag. If he had any sense, he'd turn back.

He sighed. The orders had been adamant: Stop the blockade runners—at all costs.

If all supplies could be kept out of the starving South, the North could win the war. But too many daring captains were running past the Union ships among the miles and miles of islands and the wild coastline of Florida. And Florida was now supplying the Confederate armies with most of their beef and salt.

"Commander?" Lieutenant Hanson, at the wheel, queried.

Travis shook his head, then sighed deeply a second time.

"Chase the schooner, Lieutenant. What the hell! At worst we'll all be killed. But God forbid we let the enemy escape."

Travis stood tensely as they took the vessel about and set off in the wake of the schooner. He could too clearly remember another day like this. A day when he had fallen right into a trap set by Brent McClain . . .

They rounded the tip of the island. Immediately he saw the schooner dead ahead. And just as immediately, he felt the shuddering grate as his keel scraped over a coral reef.

Damn! he thought furiously. He had let the Rebel captain lure him into another trap. He barked an order to his crew and stared across the water at the elusive schooner.

She was flying a white flag. Travis frowned and squinted against the bright summer sun. The name of the schooner had been painted over, and she was flying no flag except the white one. Surely not for surrender!

Truce? He studied the lines of the ship, and his heart began to beat heavily within his chest. It had to be the *Jenni-Lyn*. McClain's ship.

"Lower a boat," he rasped out quickly.

"Yes, sir. Shall I accompany you, sir?" Hanson asked.

"No, I'll go alone."

"Sir, it could be a dangerous privateer."

Travis laughed dryly. "The captain of that ship is the most dangerous man I know, Lieutenant. But not to me—not at this moment."

Fifteen minutes later he was facing Brent McClain.

The southerner was shirtless—bronzed and lean and wire-muscled. The deepening lines around his steel-gray eyes were the only visible ravages of the war he fought.

McClain's men stood silently by as Travis climbed aboard the ship. Brent McClain offered his hand to Travis as he boarded. Ridiculously, Travis felt as if he were greeting an old friend.

"Come to my cabin," Brent said briefly. Then he turned

quickly—not so much to lead the way as to control the sudden shaking that had gripped him.

He had been terrified that he wouldn't be able to find Deland in time.

The message from Camp Douglas hadn't reached him until the tenth of August. Mercifully he had just come back into Richmond. God! What would have happened if he'd been in London or in the Bahamas or somewhere out in the Gulf? He didn't want to think about it. He had been in Richmond. And he had made the Keys in three days' time with the Federals breathing down his neck all the way. It had taken him another five days of sweating worry that bordered on panic to seek out and corner Travis Deland . . . and this was just the beginning. He couldn't panic. Everything had to move as smoothly as clockwork.

He almost took his cabin door off the hinges as he opened it. Then he forced himself to take a deep breath and step inside.

When they were seated, Brent astounded Travis by tossing him a crumpled, dirty, and often folded note. Travis frowned as he tried to decipher the scrawls on it. He stiffened as he saw John's handwriting—and read the words. Then his brow furrowed as he read the message that had been added in another hand:

Kendall is here. Also Sterling McC. Situation desperate. Moore coming on 1st Sept. If you've any Yank friends, use them.

> B. Randall
> Camp Douglas

Travis threw the note on the table, shaken. "When did you get that?" he demanded hoarsely. "I'd heard that Kendall was in Vicksburg. They didn't take prisoners when the city surrendered."

"From what I understand," Brent said flatly, "she was taken before the surrender. A Dr. Armstrong was expecting some morphine to be smuggled in. They saw the boat they expected, but no one was rowing it." He shrugged and exhaled slowly. "You know Kendall. She swam out to get it. And two Yank soldiers were aboard."

Travis picked up the note and stared at it again. He swallowed. "Maybe John has changed. I haven't seen him in nearly a year. He's been assigned to the Mississippi—"

Brent McClain interrupted him with a sharp and explosive expletive. "You know as well as I do that he'll kill her—or worse—if he gets hold of her again."

Travis made no denial. "This note says that your brother is in Camp Douglas, too."

"Yes."

Travis exhaled a long breath. "I'm not sure what I can do. This may come as a surprise to you, but Abe Lincoln is a kind and gentle man. He visited Capital Prison in Washington and was horrified. I'm sure he believes he's doing Kendall a favor by ordering she be released to her husband. I have no authority whatsoever over John. There would be no way for me to secure her release when—"

"I don't want you to secure her release. I want you to take me into Camp Douglas as your prisoner."

"What? You're crazy, McClain. How will that help? You'll be in prison, and John will be able to walk off with Kendall—"

"Getting out will be my problem," Brent interjected smoothly. "Just get me into the right place. And lend me a handful of gold coins; my Confederate money is worthless. I'll manage the rest. I'll come with you now. Charlie McPherson will sail my ship away."

"But, McClain, I'm not the senior officer at Fort Taylor. The captain might decide to send you to another prison."

Brent raised a sardonic brow. "Aren't the Yankees also trying to prove their honor."

Travis stiffened. "The captain is an honorable man."

"Then he will surely understand that you gave me your word when I surrendered that I would be sent to Fort Douglas—to join my brother."

"I just hope someone doesn't shoot you on the way," Travis muttered.

Brent laughed. "I think I have more faith in Union civility than you do, Deland. Let's get out of here. We haven't much time."

Kendall sat in a corner of the yard, staring at the men as they walked for exercise, but not seeing them.

Despite Beau's determination to cheer her, she couldn't rouse herself to even a semblance of energy.

She simply didn't care anymore. There was no way out of Fort Douglas; she was doomed. As each day passed, the time came nearer when John Moore would appear and take her . . .

So many men had died in the war. *Why not John?*

She despised the fact that she could wish for a man to die. But she did. Just as she cringed each time the barracks door swung open and booted feet entered. Just as she shivered when anyone, even Beau, came near her.

"Kendall? Excuse me, but you must be Mrs. Moore."

Kendall saw that the dusty feet by her side were bare. She looked from the feet up the legs and torso of the man and swallowed with a start. His hair was dark, and he was pathetically lean—but there was one feature that was heart-wrenchingly familiar.

Gray eyes . . . No, they were blue, but with that touch of storm clouds in them . . .

"I'm sorry," the man murmured hastily, bending down to her. Stirling McClain was alarmed at the pallor in the woman's fragile features. She looked like a madwoman to him at first—red-blond hair a wild tangle to her waist, the color dull and lifeless, her dress ragged and worn, her complexion parchment frail.

But beneath the prison dirt and tattered rags, he could now see a delicate and stunning beauty. He saw it in the teal-blue eyes that stared at him with alarm. He saw it beneath the smudges of dirt on her high cheekbones, and in her petal-soft lips.

"I'm sorry," Stirling repeated. "I didn't mean to startle you. I'm Stirling McClain."

"I know," she said softly. "You . . . you look like Brent."

Stirling smiled. "No, he looks like me. I'm the older."

He was pleased to see a smile curve her lips. She was truly beautiful.

Stirling cleared his throat. "Major Randall has been talking to me about you. He's mighty worried about you, ma'am. We . . . uh . . . we all are. I guess I'm just trying to talk some sense into you. The major says you've hardly eaten in a week. He says it's as if you're hoping to die. Don't do that, Kendall. One way or another, this war will end. There will be people to help you. And . . . well, Kendall, my brother loves you very much."

"I haven't seen your brother in almost a year," Kendall said quietly.

"That doesn't change anything, Kendall. I know Brent."

Did she truly know him? Kendall wondered. Despair settled over her again. What did it matter? She would never see him again . . . but she tried to smile for Stirling McClain. "Please don't worry about me. I'll . . . I'll be fine. I haven't had much of an appetite, that's all." She tried to laugh, but the sound was more like a croak. "You must admit that the meals are hardly appetizing!"

"Keep up your strength," Stirling insisted earnestly. "None of us ever knows what the future—"

His words suddenly broke off. Curiously Kendall looked at his strained features. Puzzlement knitted his brow as he stared at the center of the yard. Then amazement lightened the tension in his gaunt face. He stood and began to walk across the yard, limping slightly. Then he wasn't walking, but running, his limp becoming more pronounced.

Kendall watched him for a moment, then shrugged as she saw that he had merely raced away to greet another prisoner. The August sun was in her eyes, so all she saw was another body in tattered gray. Despondency settled over her again, and she stared sightlessly at the dirt.

A moment later, a shadow fell across the sunlight. A pair of feet were before her again. These wore boots. Her heart quickened as she feared that the Yanks had come to tell her that John . . .

Her fear died as her eyes followed the boots upward to gray trouser legs. This prisoner was obviously new. Far healthier than most. Still composed of sinew and muscle and—

"Oh, God!" She began to tremble.

Gray eyes were staring down at her. Steel-gray with no hint of blue. Her incredulous gaze fell on a face as familiar to her as the sun, and as powerful, as full of heated, radiating strength. Brent . . . She blinked, but he was real, flesh and blood, standing before her, as ruggedly handsome and assured as ever.

How many endless nights had she longed for him, ached for just a glimpse of him? And now he was here . . .

And she looked like death. Gaunt, pinched, and filthy. There were hollows above her breasts, her figure was skeletal. Her hair was a mass of snarled, tangled knots; her flesh was deathly pale.

"Brent?" she whispered aloud. "No . . . oh, no!"

Kendall struggled to her feet, bracing herself against the barracks wall. She covered her face with her hands as tears rose to her eyes and sobs rose in her throat. "No!" she cried in horror again, and her limbs found sudden flight as she tried to run past him.

He caught her arm and swung her back around, pulling her to his chest. "Kendall . . ." he murmured. He didn't see the dirt smudges on her face, nor did he care that the golden sheen was gone from her hair. He didn't notice that her gown was ragged and filthy, or that she was gaunt and thin. He saw only the woman he loved . . . and had almost lost.

"Kendall . . ." he repeated, cherishing her with his reverent touch, cradling her head to his shoulder, caressing the nape of her neck.

"Forgive me, my love," he whispered. "Forgive me."

A shrill whistle sounded. Their brief exercise period was over. Brent pulled away from her and anxiously searched out her eyes. "We're going to get out of here," he promised.

"How? And how did you get here? Oh, Brent, it's impossible."

"Trust me. I haven't time to tell you now. I'm in with the Florida Cavalry. Just be ready to move. Understand me?"

Kendall nodded. "I love you, Brent."

"I know," he told her, his lips curling in a semblance of a rakish grin. "I love you. Now go—before they see us together."

He gave her a little shove toward the Georgia Regulars' barracks, then turned abruptly and hurriedly joined the Floridians who listlessly shuffled toward their own building.

Kendall seemed unable to move. She vaguely saw Beau coming toward her, felt his hand on her arm as he gripped it. Beau led her along. Her feet moved with his, but her eyes remained riveted on Brent. She watched him until he disappeared behind the other door. Then she allowed Beau to lead her into the barracks. She heard Beau's excited words.

"He came! And he's got a hell of a plan, Kendall. We're all going to get out of here!"

"All?" Kendall murmured. She was elated—and yet she felt drugged. Stunned, unable to function or think.

"Well, the Florida Cavalry and us, at least. Dear God in heaven, the Night Hawk has come. His name is the password Kendall—Night Hawk. Keep your ears sharp. Keep listening."

She smiled distantly. She would keep listening for the Night Hawk, keep waiting. Always . . .

Nineteen

"Night Hawk!"

The whispered words were spoken by one of the Yankee guards, who had come into the room and closed the door behind him.

Kendall had been dozing. One of the benefits of malnutrition was that sleep came easily to weak and worn bodies no matter what the excitement or turmoil of the mind. But she heard the words so quietly stated.

Kendall hopped tensely to her feet, her eyes flashing from the Yank to Beau.

"You've got to give me a good crack over the head," the Yankee said. "I don't want to be court-martialed or shot." He handed Beau an army-issue revolver as he spoke.

Beau nodded. "I'll see that you're sound out. Is everything all set?"

The Yankee nodded. "Just move quietly in the courtyard. They've already got more'n half the guards knocked out and trussed up in the old storage bin. The man on the gate has been well paid, but the rest of us won't get the other half of our gold until you're clear of the place. Go out one by one— and watch for signs of activity. If the wrong parties are alerted, we'll all be in trouble. Now move, Major."

Kendall watched wide-eyed as Beau nodded. Then he

swiftly swung his arm and brought the butt of the pistol down hard on the Yank's head. The man sank to the floor without a sound.

Beau looked about at the grim, gaunt faces staring his way. "Kendall goes first. Then the rest of you will line up. Y'all heard the Yankee—move quiet."

"Where do we go?" Kendall asked as she stared at Beau.

"Out to west field beyond the exercise yard. To the coffins."

"To the—?" Kendall began, but Beau pulled open the door, shoved her out, and pulled it closed once more. Kendall swallowed the rising panic that clamped her throat. She had to be calm, had to act quickly and quietly . . .

Kendall looked about for a guard who might try to stop her. There was none. She hurried through the dark and silent building to the exercise yard, and then froze.

No guards awaited her there—only a heavy wagon hitched to four sturdy draft horses. And littering the ground around it were a score of coffins.

A hand suddenly clamped over her mouth from behind. Terror shot along her veins. She tried to scream.

"Kendall, it's me, Brent. Come on. Quickly."

Her eyes widened, but she said nothing as she saw him. He was dressed in the blue coat of a Union Army captain.

He saw the fear in her eyes as he hurried her toward the wagon. "One of us has to drive out of here," he told her softly.

He gave her no time to protest. She was breathless when they reached the coffins. Fear seized her again as she saw two more men in blue working among the pine boxes. Brent must have felt her tension as he whispered to her again. "It's just Stirling and one of his sergeants. Move, Kendall—quick!"

"In here!"

The direction came from Stirling McClain. He had opened

353

the lid of one of the coffins and indicated that she was to lie down inside it.

"I . . . I can't," she gasped, horrified.

"Get in, Kendall!" Brent commanded.

"The only way out is as a corpse," Stirling said, trying to keep his voice light. Kendall nervously glanced into the shadow of the barracks. Two other men were piling something there.

The real corpses, she realized, the men who had died that day in Camp Douglas.

"Oh, God," she murmured sickly. "We're desecrating our own dead."

Brent emitted an impatient oath. Stirling spoke quickly to reassure her. "Kendall, they are just that—dead. They were brave Confederates all. They would applaud our efforts to survive. Now—"

"Get in the coffin!" Brent hissed. "We've got another twenty Georgia Regulars to go."

Kendall crawled into the box. When the lid closed over her, she had to knot her fingers together and clench her teeth to keep from screaming. There was total darkness and a horrible feeling of suffocating. Her fear increased as she felt the men lift the coffin and shove it into the wagon. A moment later she shuddered as another box was set over hers with a thud.

Don't scream, don't cry, don't panic, she warned herself. Another jolt shook her. The horses were moving, pulling the wagon.

The wagon stopped, and Kendall realized that they had reached the gate. She heard Brent's voice, muffled and low, as if it were far away.

"Nothing but dead Rebs! We're going to ship them back south for burial!"

"Open the gates! Death detail leaving."

Kendall held her breath. It seemed as if eons passed. Eons

in the terrible, claustrophobic coffin. The darkness overwhelmed her as did the cramped quarters. She wanted to scream and scream and beat her fists against the wooden coffin that reeked of death.

Suddenly, abruptly, the wagon began to move again. Kendall braced herself as best as she could against the sides of her pine box. An eternity seemed to pass—an eternity of misery. She was tossed about, bruised and scraped, exhausted from trying to keep herself from being flung hard against the wood as the horses' movement threw the wagon's cargo about.

At last the horses came to a halt. Kendall heard wood rasping against wood as the coffins were dragged from the wagon. Tears of relief sprang to her eyes as she felt her own coffin being dragged, and then hefted, down.

The lid lifted. Brent's eyes, steel-hard and anxious, were on her. He reached for her hands to help her out.

"Oh, Brent!" she gasped, ready to throw herself against him.

He clasped her to his chest for the briefest moment, then almost tossed her into his brother's arms. "We've got to keep moving," he said with cool authority. With her shoulders assuringly held by Stirling, Kendall stared about her. They were in a large forest, their only light that of a benevolent moon. She recognized the Georgia Regulars who were hurriedly helping the last of the "corpses" from the coffins. She also recognized a few of the Floridians in Stirling's command from chance meetings in the exercise yard.

"There are almost fifty of us," Brent said quietly to the men who had gathered around him. "Split into groups no larger than ten. Stick to the dirt roads, live off the land. Move south as quickly as you can, and never, never forget that you are in enemy territory."

"God go with us all," Beau murmured.

"Amen!"

The chorus arose softly among the men, along with hurried thank-yous to Brent. Kendall felt Stirling push her ahead of him. "Start walking, Kendall," he said quietly.

"Brent—"

"He'll catch up with us. Come on!"

He gripped her hand, and together they began to run. She heard footsteps behind them, but a quick glance at Stirling's calm, moon-shadowed face assured her that it was only the rest of their party.

The woods rustled with life as the human invasion brought alarm to the night creatures. The trail that Stirling had chosen grew narrower and narrower. Leaves and branches slapped at Kendall's arms; roots and rocks threatened to trip her. A screech owl startled them both as it flew above them with an angry shriek, but they kept on running, the moon's pale light filtering through the trees to guide them.

At last Kendall felt that she would die if she ran another step. Her legs ached as if knives had pierced her calves; her heart had begun to hammer and her lungs threatened to explode. Gasping, she jerked back on Stirling's hand and clung to an oak for support.

"Stirling, I can't . . ."

"Just a way farther, Kendall. I'll carry you."

"No!" She couldn't allow a starved and emaciated man to bear her weight. "I . . . I'm all right."

She forced herself to run until they reached a clearing that was shielded by a vast circle of strong old oaks and dense foliage. In its center was a shabby, weathered cabin, barely visible among the trees.

Stirling emitted a soft bird call—the muted cry of a night hawk. It was answered from inside the cabin. He gripped her hand and pulled her toward the rickety steps. Instinctively she cringed as he threw open the door, but they were greeted by Beau and three of the Georgia Regulars who had reached the cabin before them.

"You all right, Kendall?" Beau asked anxiously. "Jake, get Kendall some water."

Private Jacob Turner instantly did as the major commanded, drawing a dipperful of water from an inside pump that loomed against the rear wall. "No rust," Turner assured her.

She drank half of the water greedily, then handed the dipper to Stirling.

"Where are we?" Kendall asked nervously. "And where is Brent?"

"He and four of the Florida boys had to send the horses and wagon back to Camp Douglas, so the Yanks wouldn't get suspicious. This cabin belongs to a friend of yours—some Yank. That's all Brent would say. He arranged to have some clothes waiting here for us. As soon as he gets here, we'll start moving again," Beau said. "Lieutenant McClain," he addressed Stirling, "I suggest you get out of that Yankee coat. It might draw too much attention if we're seen as we pass through the countryside."

Stirling nodded and hastily shed his coat. Kendall noted that the tattered gray coats Beau and his men had been wearing had been replaced by nondescript brown and beige civilian clothing.

"There's something for you, too, Kendall," Beau said. "We'll just step outside until you're ready."

Quietly, gallantly, the men filed out of the cabin. Curiously Kendall stepped toward the gown draped over a rocking chair.

Tears stung her eyes as she realized it was one of her own. A simple day dress of light cotton with a high neck and long sleeves that puffed at the shoulders. She had often worn it around Fort Taylor.

Travis . . . Dear Travis. Along with Brent, he had gone through great risk to free her.

"Kendall?"

It was Stirling's voice. Polite, inquiring.

"Almost ready," she returned softly, hurriedly shedding her prison rags to don the fresh gown. She needed a bath. She had become accustomed to filth in Camp Douglas, but now . . .

Now there was Brent. And he had said that he loved her even though she was thin and haggard—and probably smellier than an old shoe.

But the luxury of bathing would have to wait. She resolutely hooked her gown and threw open the cabin door just in time to see Brent approaching the cabin with four Florida cavalrymen behind him. Her heart seemed to stop; she wanted to rush to him and hold him—yet she also wanted to shrink away. She knew that they were still in a desperate situation, and that survival was the top priority. Still she couldn't bear to have Brent see her as she was—emaciated, strained, a far cry from the fashionable creature he had met on the Battery in Charleston a lifetime ago.

His gray eyes searched for and found her, but then they turned to Beau. "Were the coats here?"

"Yes, we've got yours."

"Water?"

"Yes, the pipes were clear."

"Food?"

"Not edible. Someone tried to leave supplies, but raccoons or something got in. There was only a little maggot-infested beef."

"Damn!" Brent muttered. He swiveled to address the men behind him. "Get some water, and change your coats. And look around quickly. My friend promised shoes. Stirling, see what we've got to carry water in. And let's get going. The faster we get away from here the happier I'll feel. Let's move!"

* * *

They walked through the night. Brent took the lead, leaving Beau or Stirling beside Kendall. But when the morning sun began to creep into the sky, Brent decreed that they should rest in the cool shadows of the forest until night fell again. Kendall curled up beneath a gnarled oak, turning her back to the men.

But there was no hiding from Brent. He lay down behind her and slipped an arm around her, pulling her to his chest. Silent tears streamed down her cheeks, and despite her efforts to hide her feelings, her shoulders trembled with her sobs. In the harsh light of the morning sun he turned her to face him, gravely studying her features. "What is it?"

"Please don't touch me," she murmured. "Not . . . not when I'm like this. Oh, please, Brent, not when I'm so horrible. You . . . you won't be able to love me. I'm as thin as a rail, and my face—"

He placed his forefinger on her lips, hushing her. Then he traced the fragile lines of her cheeks and jaw.

"Your face, Kendall, has never been more beautiful to me. There are new lines, yes. There are shadows and pallor. Those things will fade with time, Kendall, but not the courage and dignity that put them there. Kendall, I need to hold you. Don't shrink away from me. I won't make love to you—not because you are any less beguiling than you ever were, but because you're half starved and weak." He crushed her slender length hard against his. "Kendall, I love you. I can't ask you to forgive me for leaving you the way I did. I'm not sure I can forgive myself. I thought that if I left you, I could forget you. You seemed so hell-bent on killing yourself. I've tried to understand what drives you, and I know that we're much alike, you and I. But I've seen so much death and suffering. My father . . . my father disappeared in a deluge of blood and death so horrible that, with all I've seen, I'll never forget it. I needed you to be waiting for me, Kendall. I needed to know that I was fighting for something. That when it was all over, someone I loved would be waiting at home. Then it would all have made more sense."

"I was so afraid you didn't love me . . . couldn't love me, after what I did."

"Pulling the knife on me?" he queried softly. "I was irritated. You outfoxed me, love. And you did prove a point, I have to admit, it didn't do much for my pride. But it didn't stop the love I felt for you. Nothing could do that. I was afraid, and I was selfish. I couldn't be there to protect you." He paused, caressing her hair as he cradled her head against his chest and shoulder. "Kendall," he said at last, his tone low and grave, "we're in great danger now. We've a long, long way to go before we reach home."

Home . . . He meant Florida, but Kendall didn't protest. Charleston was no longer her home. Charleston was a lifetime ago. So was New York. Vicksburg had just been a place to escape to.

"How will we go?" she murmured.

"South through Illinois. Then we'll follow the Kentucky-Tennessee border roads to Virginia. The Union holds most of Kentucky now, but the people are still in sympathy with the Confederacy. But it will all be risky. We're going to have to walk most of the way, staying off the main roads. Keep in mind, Kendall, that anyone you meet might want to kill you for a Rebel or turn you over to the Federal authorities."

Walk . . . from Illinois to Virginia. She couldn't believe they would ever make it, never . . . but she would never have believed she could escape from Camp Douglas in a coffin, either.

"Brent?"

"Hmm?"

"Did Travis help you get into Camp Douglas?"

He hesitated a long time, and then replied. "Yes. We lured him out of a cove in the Keys. Then I turned my ship over

360

to Charlie and myself over to Travis Deland. I had to get myself captured."

Kendall felt a little thrill ripple through her. The sun seemed to warm her with a brilliant, radiating heat, yet she was sure the source of that heat was his touch . . . his softly spoken words.

He had left his ship, his men, the Confederacy—to come for her.

"Thank you, Brent," she murmured, clutching the hand that rested around her waist and bringing it to her lips. "Thank you so very much."

She felt his whispered words against her hair and ear. "I had to come for you," he told her. "I love you."

Tears suddenly rose in her eyes again. "Oh, Brent, you shouldn't hold me. You shouldn't be so close. You might get lice!"

He laughed, gently, teasingly, putting her fears to rest. "Kendall, I love you, even with lice. Stop crying. We'll get some good strong lye soap, and you'll be fine. Now get some rest, my love. We're going to have to travel quickly when darkness comes. John Moore will have half the Illinois militia after us when he discovers what's happened."

John . . . he was so distant in time and in her mind, yet she had almost given up on life because of him. And now, in the midst of war and bloodshed, she was so happy. She lay filthy and tattered in a northern forest, but the warmth of the sun had never been so beautiful, and she had never felt so content merely to lie on the grass and feel a man's arms about her.

No matter what happened in the days to come, she had this moment . . . and the knowledge that Brent had risked everything to have her at his side.

"Kendall?"

"Yes, Brent?"

"We owe our freedom to your friend Deland."

"I know." Kendall settled against his shoulder. "Brent, if this war ever ends, I'd like you to be his friend."

"The war will end, Kendall. Now go to sleep."

Kendall closed her eyes. There was still so much she wanted to talk about. She wanted to tell him she was so sorry about his father—and so happy that his brother was well and with them. She wanted to know how Amy and Harold Armstrong were, and she wanted to hear about Red Fox and the Seminoles and Mikasukis. But she was bone weary, and painfully aware that they would need to move quickly with the night to escape any traps John might set.

There would be days and days in which to talk. And sometime in the future she could begin to dream again. Dream of a time when she would be clean and strong enough to reach out and touch him with her love.

For now, she could find a respite from war and fear in the power of his arms and the shadow of his love.

Brent set a harsh schedule for them—one that would have done any Confederate general proud. Twenty miles a day was the goal they strove to achieve. It was of utmost importance that they leave Union territory, especially Illinois, behind them.

Kendall had never imagined that a state could be so vast. Walking by night, resting by day, it seemed that nothing ever changed. They took circuitous routes to avoid cities and towns; they even walked extra miles to avoid farmhouses.

Each morning when dawn broke she was exhausted, falling quickly into a heavy sleep. Brent worried over the ill health of his group, but he also knew they had to drive southward relentlessly.

No one broke. Each day their muscles found new strength. Their food was meager. Despite the lush summer growth, they seldom dared steal from the farm fields, and they hadn't enough ammunition to hunt forest creatures. Thanks to his time with Red Fox, Brent was adept at fashioning bows and arrows from branches and flint, and all the southerners were fine shots, but they had to hunt and cook their food discreetly and quietly. It was better than the prison ration, but they still went to sleep hungry.

The many streams along the way provided an ample supply of water. To Kendall, the greatest luxury of all was bathing. Yet the sight of her own nudity was appalling; she still resembled a bean pole. She was glad they had companions on the journey home; she would have been truly horrified for Brent to see her pathetically thin body in the raw. Beau or Stirling always waited for her near the stream when she bathed, and she was grateful that Brent was always too busy to come near her. They had formed a strange relationship that enabled them to endure the long days. They were friends, not lovers. He barely spoke to her as they traveled by night, but he always held her tight when they slept.

Sometimes Kendall worried about his restraint. Brent appeared as robustly healthy as always. His powerful frame was accustomed to exertion. As the weeks passed, he lost some weight, but only appeared to be more tightly sinewed. Lusty, vital, vibrant . . .

And she grew more afraid. He was more tender than he had ever been, when he wasn't being the blunt Captain McClain. But even his kindness sometimes frightened her; she didn't want to be pitied. She wanted to be boldly, passionately loved, yet she wondered if that tempestuous love still existed within her. The war had left its scars on her.

Summer turned to fall as they at last left Illinois behind them. They celebrated jubilantly on the October day when they crossed the state line. Beau and his Georgians broke into ecstatic Rebel yells; Stirling quietly reminded them all that wherever the people's sympathies lay, Kentucky was largely in Union hands.

Brent tolerantly allowed a time of rejoicing, not joining in the wild revelry, but watching as he leaned against a tree.

"Gents, we should save this till we reach Tennessee," he said quietly. "If we keep a steady move on, we'll reach safety soon enough."

But nothing could stop the lightness of heart that had come to all of them. They were, at least, out of Illinois. It was quite a victory—especially since they realized the Yankees had surely combed the state for them.

Late on the second afternoon in Kentucky, Kendall was awakened by whispering. She twisted about to realize that Brent was no longer beside her. Startled, she sat up and saw him speaking in hushed tones to Beau. Curiously she brushed her hair from her forehead and pushed herself to her feet and approached them.

"I'm telling you, Brent, she's an old farm woman all alone. And I'm telling you she's a Reb."

"How the hell can you guarantee that, Beau?" Brent demanded skeptically.

"Well, what can she do to us if she isn't a Reb? Nine men and a young woman against one old hag? She's offered us a decent meal, Brent. Hot cooked bread, cooked vegetables. Ham and grits and black-eyed peas—"

Brent chuckled suddenly at the longing in Beau's voice. "I guess I can't blame you much, Major, for a hearty appetite. All right. We'll stop at the old woman's farm. But we'll keep a couple of lookouts posted at all times."

Kendall at last stepped toward them. "What's going on?" she asked them, her brow knitting in perplexity.

"Beau went out scrounging something to eat and met an old woman in a cornfield. Seems she's asked us all to Sunday dinner. I'm not sure I approve, but . . ."

Kendall could almost smell home-cooked food. She threw her arms around Brent and tilted back her head to meet his eyes pleadingly. "Brent, what harm could an old woman do to us? Oh, please—"

"The major has already used that argument, Kendall." Brent shrugged; his eyes met hers with an indolent twinkle. "Seems there's a creek nearby, too—and the woman has offered us all a bar of her best lye. Sounds like our evening is set."

Soap . . . what a luxury! "What are we waiting for?" Kendall queried anxiously.

Again Brent shrugged, but he didn't seem entirely pleased.

"We go!" Kendall replied happily. She spun away from Brent. "I'll wake the others," she called over her shoulder.

Minutes later Beau was leading them through a ragged cornfield to a weatherbeaten farmhouse. The countryside was still and autumn-beautiful, and they didn't see a soul until they approached the house, the front door swung open and a tall, slender woman with iron-gray hair welcomed them with a broad smile.

"Glad to see you again, Beau. These your friends?"

"Yes, ma'am," Beau replied. "I warned you, we're a bit of a crowd."

Her colorless eyes surveyed the group, but the old woman's smile remained friendly and welcoming. "It's so nice to see people these days; the more the merrier. Come in, y'all come on in. I've been cookin' and bakin' all morning with the greatest pleasure!"

"Thank you, that was right kind of you, ma'am."

"Name's Miz Hunt, young man. Hannah Hunt."

In return, Beau pointed along their group calling out names. Hannah Hunt nodded to each introduction, then moved away from the door, indicating they should all come in. Beau started to walk up the entry steps, then hesitated, speaking softly. "Private Tanner, Sergeant Marshall, you two draw first watch. Hudson and Lowell will spell you shortly."

The aromas coming from the house were driving Kendall

half crazy with hunger. Yet when she started to follow in Beau's footsteps, a sixth sense made her stop and turn around. Brent was staring at the house, a puzzled look darkening his eyes and tautening his features.

"Brent, what is it?" she asked.

He shook himself slightly, as if startled by her question, then shrugged. "I don't know . . . just nervous I guess."

"Captain," Bill Tanner, one of Beau's Georgians, said quietly, having heard Brent's words, "believe me, sir, the sergeant and I know how to keep a sharp watch."

"I don't doubt that," Brent acknowledged. He shrugged once more, then slipped an arm around Kendall's shoulders. "Let's eat, Kendall, shall we?"

"Definitely!" Kendall agreed with sparkling eyes. She was worried about Brent, and watched him carefully as they all sat around a large, rough wood table in Hannah Hunt's huge farmhouse kitchen. She offered to help, but Hannah insisted she sit. And as huge platters of ham swimming in country gravy were passed around, Kendall relaxed as she saw Brent do the same. Compliments flowed from the table. Kendall was certain that it was the best meal she had ever eaten. Hannah kept up her side of the conversation, bemoaning the war.

"I used to have ten hands to feed every day, till they all upped and joined the army. Some Yanks, some Rebs. And now all's I gots is the armies threshing through my fields, robbing me blind. First those southern generals, Kirby-Smith and Braxton Bragg, stole everything in sight for their men. And now the Union men are back—" She broke off suddenly. "Dear me, how I do run on. And I baked you a great big blueberry pie."

Kendall couldn't touch the pie. Her stomach had become too small, and she had already overstuffed it with ham and bread and vegetables. But she didn't want to hurt the old woman's feelings so she slid her piece onto the plate of the sergeant who was sitting to her right, winking as she did so. He returned her wink and consumed the pie with pleasure.

A chair scraped, and she saw Brent rise. He moved about the table and whispered in Hannah Hunt's ear. She laughed, and handed him something from a cabinet. A second later he was standing behind Kendall's chair, and she glanced up at him curiously. She noticed that the tension had entirely left his features. There was a slight curl to his lip, and his eyes were an unfathomable smolder. He bent low to whisper against he ear. "Let's take a walk."

He pulled out her chair, and she stood, wondering what he was up to. Brent excused them politely and took her hand.

"Hudson and Lowell will be right out," Brent told Marshall and Tanner as they passed by them.

"It's all right, Captain," Bill Tanner called. "That nice Mrs. Hunt brought us out some pie."

"Yeah," Jo Marshall guffawed. "And Tanner here ate the whole damned thing. Didn't leave me a bite."

"You said you didn't want to eat pie until you had some ham!" Bill protested.

Kendall laughed at the two of them. They were both two years younger than she, yet they had become hardened soldiers. It was so pleasant to see them joking after such a painful and dangerous time.

"Where are you going, Captain?" Tanner asked.

"For a walk beyond the house," Brent replied. "I want to enjoy the sunset with a full stomach for a change."

"Where are we really going?" Kendall asked a moment later as they entered a field of pines beyond the house.

He gazed down at her and squeezed her hand as they walked. "To see the sunset."

Almost as he spoke, they came upon a brook, its bubbling flow providing light and pleasant music in the cool of the evening. Pines swayed about them, and the sun cast a ripple of gold over the running water.

"Oh, Brent! How beautiful," Kendall breathed, breaking away from him to rush to the water and shiver with delight as she cupped its coolness in her hands and dashed it against her face.

"Yep," he murmured softly. "I imagined it would be."

Kendall heard the husky timbre of his voice and turned around uneasily. His features were again tense; his eyes were dark as they lingered over her, following her form with subtle insinuation. He smiled as he caught her startled gaze and came to squat down beside her and pull something from his pocket. He presented it to her, slowly opening his fingers. On his palm sat a bar of soap. "How about a twilight bath, my love?"

Kendall stared from the soap to his eyes, fighting a ridiculous fear of what lay ahead. "It's cold, Brent. We'll both catch pneumonia."

"It isn't cold; it's cool. And I'll keep you warm."

Kendall stared back at the soap, held so lightly in his powerful hand.

"Kendall," he caught her chin with his free hand and gently forced her to meet his eyes. "I wanted to give you time to heal a little. Time to know me again. To trust me. But have mercy, darlin'. I'm going mad sleeping beside you night after night."

"I . . . I'm afraid," she whispered.

"Of me?"

"Not of you. Because of you."

"Because of me?" he repeated, amusement and puzzlement playing in the smoky depths of his eyes. He sat down and drew her against him. "Mind explaining that one, my love?" His voice was soft as he ran his fingers along the nape of her neck to her shoulder.

"You're always . . . strong, Brent. Nothing changes you; nothing can break you. We're half starving, yet it seems you become more powerful. Oh, Brent—"

"Kendall," he interrupted firmly, straightening her so that she sat facing the water. She felt his fingers working the hooks at the back of her dress, yet when she nervously clutched at them, he caught her hands and pushed them away. "I have a growth of unkempt whiskers that looks like an untamed forest. Neither of us is fit for washed society."

"Brent, please. don't. I—"

"You are beautiful."

"No, I'm not. You can count every rib—"

"Kendall, I'm dying to count every rib."

His voice was a whisper, husky, heated, caressing the lobe of her ear as his fingers tightened over her shoulders and he moved close behind her. "Kendall, I feel like a brushfire. I want you so badly that it's consuming my thoughts. As I walk along daily, I forget where I am, where I'm trying to go, because I'm watching you and remembering what it was like to feel you naked against me, to touch your breasts with my lips, to have you move against me. My love, it's an ache, a yearning, a fever. Don't you ever feel it, Kendall? The need . . . the hunger . . ."

Kendall swallowed and moistened her lips, shivering. She did—oh, yes, she did, now, with his words and touch igniting a trembling desire within her. But she was still afraid . . . of failure, of not being able to please him, of finding that she could not soar again . . .

"Brent, sometimes all I can remember is the cries of the men in Camp Douglas. The misery, the filth. I can't remember the things that were beautiful and—"

"I'll make you remember," he told her. His words were firm but gentle, and then he was standing and drawing her to her feet. He turned her around and finished undoing the hooks. His hands slipped beneath the fabric and eased the gown off her shoulders. It fell in a cloud about her feet.

She couldn't turn, couldn't move, as she heard him discard his clothing behind her. She barely breathed as his hands spanned her waist. He held her tight as he discarded her shoes and threadbare pantalettes. Kendall leaned her head against his shoulder and shivered in the evening air as he lifted her in his arms and waded slowly into the clear water of the brook.

"It's freezing!" she protested.

"No. The sun has warmed the water."

A moment later he set her down. Twilight was upon them as she met the slow burning fire in the dark gray recesses of his eyes. It was cold in the water, yet where he touched her, her skin warmed. The sharp, pungent scent of the lye soap was between them, yet as his hands began to lave her shoulders, the cleanliness was as delicious as the callused brush of his fingertips. She could not draw her gaze from his. The water about her glittered with the final ripples of golden daylight, and was reflected in the hypnotic gray embers of his eyes.

Brent paused for a moment, holding the soap against her shoulder as he reached with his free thumb to follow the line of her cheekbone to her jaw. He brushed his fingers over her throat, and along her collarbone. She was still too thin, but none of her perfection of form had surrendered to the ravishes of hunger. It was as if the beautiful lines of her body had been sharply delineated by an artist's brush. And he wanted to touch her, to kiss the hollow shadows and the feminine curves that had defied the destiny which had imprisoned a nation.

He began to wash her again, savoring the soft feel of her flesh. His hands cupped her breasts, his palms found her nipples. A slight sound escaped her, her lips parted as she drew her breath in sharply. But still her eyes were upon him, eternally blue, indigo with the coming of night. His palms slid down over her ribs, and he discovered that he could easily count them. Her waist had become minuscule, but beneath it her hips still flared invitingly under his touch.

He emitted a hoarse groan and crushed her against him, now feverishly exploring the supple length of her back, discovering the dip at its base and then the enticing swell of her buttocks. His desire was hard against her, throbbing with need and a raw male potency he couldn't restrain. His body strained with the tension of longing . . . and loving.

"Can you remember now?" he hissed throatily, gripping her hair to arch her throat and bring her eyes once more to his. "Now . . . this. Do you remember, my love? The beauty, the longing, welling up inside you, begging to be stroked, caressed, nurtured, and then freed. Tell me, my love, do you remember?"

Remember? Yes . . . no . . . yes . . . but it wasn't a memory, it was now. Heat and fusion . . . fire. Circling, spiraling, flickering through her. Rendering her weak, then giving her strength. Sweet fire, tearing through her veins, causing her to quiver at his touch, to arch nearer, to seek . . .

"Kendall!"

He shook her slightly, and she felt the raw pounding of his heart, the sinewed strength of his muscles, the wonderfully hot, naked male flesh brushing against her own. She felt his masculinity, pulsingly alive and vital, a brand of searing heat low against her abdomen. She moistened her lips . . . and touched him, feeling a new shudder of pleasure rip through her as he groaned and then carried her to the edge of the stream.

He made love to her with both their lengths half in and half out of the water. The tide that surged through him was a rage of hunger and passion too powerful for him to control. And yet as it thundered and stormed its course, he savored the shuddering pleasure of her fevered embrace. Her supple legs were wrapped around him; her feminine hips rose to fuse with his demanding thrusts.

Wild, erotic, beautiful. A sunburst in the deepening twilight . . .

There was no other woman like her. He could sail a thousand seas, search a million ports. But always he could come back to her.

He held her, shuddering with the aftermath of the ultimate eruption of their love and pleasure.

And she lay beside him, softly sighing out, curling into him.

They lay in contented silence, until he felt her shiver. "We'd better dress," he said softly.

She shook her head. "No, Brent. I want to wash my hair. And then . . ."

"And then?"

"I want to make love again. We won't have much time alone until we get home."

He laughed softly and rose, helping her to her feet. "I hope I've completely restored your memory."

"Oh, quite completely," she murmured, midnight lashes sweeping her cheeks as she blushed. She turned from him, trying to hurry back to the water. He caught her arm and stopped her. She kept her eyes lowered, her blush increasing as she knew he scrutinized her from head to toe.

"Kendall," he told her. "You are beautiful. Don't try to hide from me. Give me what little we can have."

She flung herself against him, encircling his chest with her arms, resting her cheek against his muscled and hair-roughened breast. "Oh, Brent, I love you so." She held him tightly for a moment, then broke away and dashed back into the water.

Smiling, he followed her, helped her thoroughly wash her hair, and then demanded that she help him.

And then they made love again, slowly, luxuriously, exploring one another with heated kisses rediscovering all the pleasurable nuances and deep intimacies of unashamed and unrestrained love. The heat of their ardor kept them warm beneath the autumn moon; the fires of love burned brightly against the darkness of the night.

Brent was so content that he almost dozed. Then with a sigh he nudged her. "Come, my love. We really *will* get pneumonia soon if we don't go back. I want to move the men into the protection of the forest."

Lazily, Kendall stirred. She smiled with rueful regret, but rose with his assistance and indolently allowed him to help her dress. When she had buttoned his coat, she slipped her arm around his waist and leaned against him as he led her through the darkness.

An aura of contentment and understanding embraced them as they walked. A wonderful interlude of shared splendor and peace. Kendall knew that she could endure any hardship as long as Brent lived and breathed . . .

The wonder of the night was abruptly and completely shattered as an agonized cry reached them. "Oh, God! God in heaven, help!" And then footsteps sounded, thrashing, running crazily through the pines.

"Brent! Where are you? Come quickly. Oh, Jesus! Brent!"

"I'm coming!" Brent shouted. Kendall felt his body grow rigid with tension. His hand clutched hers, and they were running through the pines, fear flooding their veins.

Twenty

Jo Marshall nearly collided with them as they broke from the woods.

"It's Tanner, Captain. Something's real wrong. The major's with him now. And some of the other boys are gettin' sick."

Brent's grip on Kendall's hand tensed unintentionally as he dragged her past Marshall.

They returned to the farmhouse in time to see Tanner writhing on the steps. Brent released Kendall's hand and knelt beside the convulsively twisting man. Another scream ripped from Tanner's mouth, and he called out to God in a blood-chilling agony.

"Tanner," Brent began, trying to still the contorting limbs of the suffering soldier. But Tanner suddenly screamed again, then went still. Dead still. Brent and Beau both stared at the dead man with disbelief. Then Beau closed the lids over glazed eyes that mirrored the final agony of life even as death ended all mortal pain.

"Sweet Jesus, what the hell—" Beau began, but was interrupted by new screams, coming from inside the house. Stunned, Kendall followed Brent, Beau, and Jo Marshall into the parlor.

Stirling McClain was trying to administer to both Hudson

and Lowell, who were showing Tanner's symptoms. "Lowell, try to speak to me! What is it? What hurts?"

"My insides, it's like a shell burst—God in heaven! God—"

A scream cut off Lowell's reply. He buckled to the floor, gripping his stomach. A trickle of blood escaped from his lips. Then suddenly he contorted again—and lay still.

Beau, Stirling, and Brent stared at one another, shocked, and seeking an explanation none could give. Suddenly Beau turned and raced back into the kitchen where the planked table still carried the remains of their meal. His two cavalrymen were still seated at the table, their heads lying on it. He touched his sergeant's face and found the flesh cold. The man was stone dead.

Kendall raced to the doorway and stared at Beau. Brent and Stirling came in behind her. Brent brushed past her and walked to the table, his eyes as dark and hard as a steel blade as he rummaged through the remains of the food, touching the bread, smelling the meat.

"The pie," Stirling said suddenly. "Brent, Beau, did you eat pie?"

"No," they replied in unison.

"Kendall?"

"No."

"Jo?"

"No, sir."

Brent found a plate with some pie on it. He plunged his fingers into the blueberries and rubbed the substance between his fingers.

"Poison," he said.

"Poison?" Kendall repeated stupidly.

"That woman put poison berries in the pie." He halted for a moment, then stared at Beau. "Where the hell is she?"

"I . . . I don't know. She made coffee. I was dozing in the parlor when Tanner started to scream."

"Stirling?" Brent queried tensely.

"I was with Beau, but I heard a door swing and slam in the back."

"She's probably heading out to find some Union soldiers. Let's go."

They brushed past Kendall, leaving her alone with the dead men who had been her family for months.

"Wait!" she screamed suddenly. She had been chilled at the expressions on their faces—Beau, Stirling, Jo Marshall, and especially Brent. They were going to kill the old woman.

She spun about and chased after them, tripping and falling in her haste over Tanner's body. She recoiled from the dead man, her heart and mind a tumult of confusion. Six men had died in unspeakable agony, but she couldn't allow Brent and the others to retaliate in the heat of sick fury. She wasn't sure why, she didn't entirely understand herself, but if they savagely murdered an old woman . . .

"Wait!" she shrieked again, stumbling to her feet and racing after them. "Wait!"

She saw them across the cornfield—the old woman riding a broken-down gray mare, Brent, his brother, Beau, and Jo Marshall trying to corner her and cut her off. Kendall started running through the stalks of corn, stumbling and falling often in the darkness of the night, so dimly illuminated by the moon.

She reached them in time to hear Hannah Hunt shouting viciously, "You all deserve to die. *You* caused this war! You and your slavery!"

Jo Marshall shouted in return, tears streaming down his cheeks. "Bill Tanner never owned a slave in his life. God! How could you listen to those screams?"

Jo lunged toward Hannah, pulling at her scrawny leg where it hung over the mare's side. Kendall glanced from Beau to Stirling to Brent. All three had set faces and eyes that glittered like ice on the moon's glow.

"No!" Kendall shrieked. She threw herself on Jo Marshall's back. The impetus of her action sent them both crashing to the ground. As she rolled, stunned, Kendall heard Brent issue a loud curse as muffled hoofbeats sounded on the earth. She dimly realized that Hannah Hunt had escaped.

"Get her!" Stirling shouted.

"Kendall Moore, what the hell is wrong with you?" Jo raged furiously, disentangling himself and staring down at her. Before she could reply, Brent rudely hauled her to her feet. He was staring at her with an icy rage in his eyes.

"What were you doing?" he shouted, shaking her with little control over his temper.

Kendall fell limp beneath the overwhelming power of his red-hot anger. Her teeth chattered, and she shivered. His rage could be as stormy and passionate as his love.

"It would have been murder," she ground out tonelessly.

"Murder! Justice! Are you blind? Didn't you watch those men die? Now she's going to report the rest of us to the Yanks. You idiot! You should have been chained in a cage when this war broke out! What do you think the Yankees would have done if they had caught you blowing their friends into bits and pieces? And this was worse—cold, calculated, cruel, and bloody murder. I'd like to—"

"Beat me?" Kendall interrupted, her own temper rising beneath his brutal grip and tongue lashing. "Then do it—but spare me your lectures! You were acting like a mob! You can't take the law into your own hands!"

"And what would you suggest? Should we call in the Yankee judges? Kendall, you were in prison with those men! They've been your friends, closer than blood, for months!"

"Brent, I don't need to be reminded of how horrible—"

"We've got to get the hell out of here," Beau suddenly interrupted, rushing toward them in the darkness. "She got away. We could have a whole regiment after us in a matter of minutes!"

Brent shoved Kendall away from him with such force that

she collided with Stirling. He clutched her shoulders to steady her, but his touch was as cold and harsh as his brother's. Brent swore viciously beneath his breath. "You're right, Beau. Let's move."

"We've got to bury Tanner and the others," Jo Marshall insisted, not ashamed of the tears that coursed down his young face.

Brent clamped a hand over his shoulder. "We haven't time, Marshall. Tanner was a good soldier. He would have understood."

Brent reached for Kendall's hand, jerking her away from Stirling. "I hope your energy is at a high level, Mrs. Moore. Thanks to you, we're going to have to run like the wind all night."

Kendall swallowed a reply, glancing covertly from Brent to Jo Marshall to Stirling to Beau.

They all looked as if they would readily murder her instead of the old woman who had escaped him. Not even Beau's eyes offered her the briefest flicker of understanding.

When Brent called her by her married title, she knew his rage went far deeper than the surface. Had she truly betrayed them all? No, she was right. If she had to do it all over again, she would have done the same. She couldn't allow them to become savages.

A time would come to live again, and when that time came, humanity would return. But there could only be a future if there were men like Beau and Brent—and Travis Deland. Like Abe Lincoln, the Union President who died a little bit with each of his men on the battlefield and objected to a woman's being kept in a prison camp.

Kendall cried out softly as Brent wrenched her arm and dragged her back through the cornfield. He didn't understand her. Perhaps he never would. But surely he hadn't ceased loving her . . . or had he?

It seemed that she hadn't a friend in the world.

Stirling ran abreast of his brother. "We've got to stop at the house quickly. Tanner was carrying a Colt pistol, and Lowell had a carbine rifle. We might need them."

"Right," Brent puffed out. "We'd best get into those trees—and cross through the brook just in case they bring dogs out after us. We need to get across into Tennessee—and pray to God that we can hook up with a Rebel regiment."

Stirling nodded and turned back to Beau and Jo, running close on their heels. "Come on, y'all. We'll make a quick stop, then run like hell."

They left Kendall on the steps while they procured weapons. Moments later they were running back through the trees, then splashing across the brook. She closed her eyes as Brent pulled her along behind him. She couldn't believe he could be so cold and cruel when less than an hour ago he had loved her tenderly and intimately in the very spot they now left behind at a breathless pace.

Their group of five barely spoke through the long night. When day at last broke, they found shelter in a cave along a stretch of mountains. They sank down to the cool floor in exhaustion.

Kendall slept alone. Brent was far from her.

In the days and nights that followed, Stirling, Beau, and even Jo Marshall gradually seemed to forgive her. At least they behaved courteously toward her and asked after her concerns. The first winter snowfall came on the night they walked into Tennessee, and Beau put his arm around her to offer her warmth.

But Brent remained as cold as the winter snow.

They were in a harsh region, and the severe weather slowed down their progress. Food became more and more scarce. Yet none of the hardships tore Kendall apart as did the constant pain within her.

She might have apologized. She might have gone to Brent's side and begged his forgiveness, begging him to understand that she was just a woman, with a woman's heart.

But she couldn't do that. She had been right. And the months that they had been together had taught her a lesson about love. A lasting relationship could not develop only from nights of sweet, delirious passion. It had to go much deeper. And as much as she loved him, as much as she suffered from the cold, silent war they fought, she staunchly believed that he owed *her* an apology.

Beau and Brent were wary of farmhouses, even after they had crossed the border, and so they kept plodding along through the mountains and valleys, determined not to stop until they reached a sizable town. They did come upon one deserted old shack that Brent and Stirling investigated with an Indian's stealth. The find provided them with two pair of fairly new boots, some flour, and a precious casket full of needles. Kendall was able to fashion them some warm cloaks from curtains and bedspreads taken from the shack, and to trim them with rabbit pelts. Still, as they moved by night, winter seemed bitter cold.

On Christmas day, as she lay down wearily to sleep, Brent came to her at last. She started when his hand touched her shoulder; her back instinctively stiffened as she spun about to face him, her eyes narrow and sparkling dangerously.

He brought a finger to his lips and whispered a "shhh," indicating the sleeping men behind him, curled beside a low-burning fire. Then he reached out a hand and drew her to her feet, leading her more deeply into the cave where a rock formation provided a secluded chamber.

Kendall opened her mouth to speak, but she was able to whisper no more than his name before his lips touched hers and his arms melded her form tightly to his.

How easily she was seduced, she was to marvel later. Yet as his strong, demanding hands expertly removed her cloth-

380

ing, his demandingly provocative kisses stripped her of thought and reason. Her flesh tingled against his, the pleasure of feeling his nakedness against her was intoxicating. And her heart told her that he had come to her . . . and that in so doing he had offered his apology. She was more than ready to forgive him and welcome his touch . . . the flame of love. When he brought himself inside her she felt as if she had become liquid heat, so much a part of him that he could mold her pliant form at will, pull the strings of her limbs and heart as if he were a master puppeteer. He whispered commands, and she obeyed, turning, twisting, arching, embracing, totally submissive and eager to meet his demands. He brought her to a pinnacle of pleasure, withdrew, and showered her with kisses, turning her at his whim, sending her into a sighing delirium as his moist lips trailed along her spine and the small of her back to her buttocks. And then he was a part of her again, sweeping her once more into heated fever, and then to the sweet, explosive crest of passion.

She lay beside him, pulling her gown about her as a cover as she became aware of the cold that his touch had dispelled. "Brent," she murmured lazily, nuzzling her cheek against his chest and entwining her fingers in the rough, damp mat of hair, "I'm so glad that you see now I was right. I hated being—"

"What?" he interrupted sharply.

She lifted her head to stare at him, her eyes brilliant blue in her trusting innocence. "I accept your apology—"

"What apology?" he exploded, smoke-gray eyes narrowing sharply. "I'd still be glad to take a switch to you—"

"What?" She interrupted this time, her voice sharp.

"You might have killed us all. You did act like a fool, and every time I think about it I feel my blood start to boil. Don't bring it up again."

"Don't bring it up! Why you insolent son of a bitch! What possessed you to make love to such a fool!"

Kendall watched the smoke-gray of his eyes become hard and cold as his tawny lashes half closed over them. She could see a tick of anger in his cheek beneath the thick golden growth of his beard.

"Certain needs," he grated out, "have little to do with a woman's idiot mind."

Kendall braced herself, stiffening as new fury surged through her. She couldn't control her explosive temper, and her teeth clamped hard together as she instinctively attempted to strike him. He caught her wrists, but not quickly enough to keep her nails from raking his cheek.

She found herself jerked fully on top of him, staring into his eyes. "Kendall," he hissed softly, warningly, "don't go into battle without any weapons. Don't ever give what you're not willing to get."

"Captain McClain," she said icily, struggling against his hold, "I've decided I agree with you. I have been a complete idiot—where you're concerned. I'm not some food that exists to appease your hunger. I'm afraid my idiot mind really is a part of my female body."

"Kendall, you're a sensual woman. I can't believe that our basic dispute made our being together any less pleasurable for you."

"Fine! Brent, you're absolutely right. Making love is just like eating, right? No matter what is happening, we all crave food and water. I hadn't thought of it that way before. I was a fool. I loved you. But if I'm sensual—if I have needs—then *I'm* the one with a choice. There are three other male bodies out there."

"Stop talking like a whore!"

"And Beau is far more pleasant to be around. Why should I—"

His fingers jerked painfully into her hair. "What is it now,

Kendall? The war isn't enough for you? Are you so anxious to see Beau and me at each other's throats?"

Kendall shook her head and closed her eyes. "No," she whispered.

He released her hair and embraced her with a trembling tenderness. "I'm sorry, Kendall. I didn't mean what I said. It hurt when you called me a son of a bitch, and I retaliated."

She wanted to cry. It was so good to feel his tenderness, to reach his soul. To hear his whispered words . . .

"If you would just learn to stay out of things that don't concern you," he murmured absently. "When you don't know what you're doing, Kendall, you do behave foolishly."

Kendall pulled away from him, hardening in her resolve. "Brent," she said coolly, "I am concerned with everything that happens to us, and I did not act foolishly. I never have. Many things I've done have had dire consequences—and yes, I've needed help many times. But I couldn't have changed any of them. If you can't accept that—"

He bolted into a sitting position, gripping her shoulders and halting her, his eyes smoldering intensely. "What I can accept, Kendall, is you trusting me once in a while. I don't want to argue with you. I grant that you are quick and bright—and certainly courageous. But, Kendall, you cannot change the course of the war. That old woman murdered five men. If ever there was a candidate for hanging, it was Hannah Hunt. Your allowing her to escape might have gotten us all captured. I would have probably been hanged or shot, and you would have been returned to John Moore. Now I'm telling you, madam, as soon as I'm able, I'm going to pack you off to safety. And if you budge from where I send you, I'll find you—come war, or doomsday. I hope you understand me, Kendall."

"Wait a minute!" Kendall protested angrily. "That isn't fair, and you must surely know it! You walked out on me. That's why I went to Vicksburg."

"I didn't exactly walk out on you. I am bound to fight this war. You are not."

"No more. You were a prisoner—"

"Kendall, I have to take command of my ship again. Stirling will have to rejoin the Army of Northern Virginia. And Beau and Jo will have to rejoin their regiment."

"And I'll have to sit in my cage like a good girl?" she asked acidly.

"That's right, my love."

"Brent—"

"Kendall, don't you ever listen?" He stood impatiently and began donning his clothing. Kendall hurriedly picked up her gown, determined to be the one to walk away. "Brent—" she began.

"Kendall," he interrupted. "I love you."

Tears stung her eyes. "You can't love me, Brent, and call me an idiot."

A grin touched the corners of his lips. "Yes, I can," he said softly.

"Not to my mind," she murmured. "And if you tell me that my mind doesn't matter, I will find the strength to rip you ragged!"

He laughed suddenly and reached for her hand, pulling her to her feet and helping her with the hooks on her gown despite her squirming protest. "Madam, we can have all this out one day. A full-scale brawl, if you choose. But not now. For now we have to survive. Let's get some sleep. I don't want the others to wake and find us gone."

Kendall opened her mouth and then closed it, still angry that nothing seemed resolved. But he was right; they had to survive.

They returned to the place where the other men lay sleeping. She lay down beside Brent near the fire, but not until she succumbed to sleep did the rigidity of her spine disappear and allow her to accept comfort and warmth from his arms.

That night they hid in the mountain foliage as campfires in the distance warned them that they had at last stumbled upon a troop of soldiers. Brent and Stirling volunteered to act as scouts, and silently, stealthily disappeared into the night. They were back quickly, joyously announcing that they had indeed found a Rebel regiment.

It was Christmas . . . And it was wonderful to feel that they had really reached their homeland. Wonderful to share the meager rations with the soldiers on the field, to sing carols as they gathered around the fires.

But it was frightening, too. The Rebel division didn't look much better than they did. Many of the men had bound their feet with strips of material because they had no shoes. Their uniforms were tattered and threadbare. Some wore blue coats they had stolen from the Yankee dead.

Kendall sat at Brent's side and sipped watery coffee, vaguely hearing the Christmas carols and subdued conversations of the men. Someone was telling Beau that half the camp was down with dysentery; an epidemic of fever had cost them twenty-four men just last month. Kendall was certain she would burst into tears. Then, just as surely, she felt a cold calm settle over her.

The South was going to lose the war. She was certain of it, just as she was certain that many of the men in the Tennessee regiment knew it, too. Proud, brooding eyes told her so.

They would fight on to the bitter end, but already they were backed to the wall, dodging the enemy blows . . .

"Kendall, did you hear me?"

"What?" She turned to meet Brent's brooding gray stare.

"They've a wagon moving east tomorrow. Some of the amputees and other wounded men are being taken to Richmond to form a last-ditch defense troop for the city if it's needed. They can take you with them. You won't mind helping some of the men who are still recovering, will you?"

"Of course I wouldn't mind helping. But what about you and—"

"They only have room for you. We'll have to keep going on foot; they can't even spare us a horse. But we should reach Virginia soon enough."

"I—"

"You're going, Kendall. They tell me the threat to Richmond has diminished recently and that President Davis's wife is back in residence. She's an old friend of mine, and she'll watch—she'll be glad to have you as a guest until I can get there and find out where Charlie has taken the *Jenni-Lyn.*"

"And then?"

"And then, if I can, I'll take you home."

"Where is home, Brent?" she asked softly.

The question gave him pause. South Seas no longer existed. But home was still farther south than Tennessee. "Back to Amy's," he answered wearily. "Kendall, I'm too tired to fight with you."

Kendall sighed softly. "I'm not fighting you, Brent. I was just asking."

Nor did she fight him when he led her to the small tent they had been offered for the night.

She was glad to lie beside him, glad to accept his love-making time and time again, even if the only words that passed between them were the urgent whispers of passion. Parting had become a way of life during the sad years of war.

In the morning he saw her to the wagon that would bear her to Richmond. He was silent as he climbed into the buckboard with her, barely finding space to stand in front of her as she found a seat between two old corporals. He leaned down to whisper to her. "Be there, Kendall. Wait for me in Richmond—exactly where I'm sending you."

She smiled dryly at him. "Where else would I be, Brent?"

"I never know—and that's what always worries me."

Kendall lowered her lashes. "I will be there, Brent. I promise."

A whip cracked, and the buckboard jolted as the horses started moving in a slow, choppy trot. His whisper brushed huskily against her ear. "I do love you, Kendall." He stood back to stare at her and saw that her blue eyes were taking on an indigo glaze as they shimmered with tears. "Even if you are a fool woman," he added with a wicked grin.

She tried to smile, but the effort failed.

"And I love you, even if you are an insolent son of a bitch."

He kissed her, savoring the last tender expression of love with the soft fullness of her mouth. Then he jumped with a smooth agility to the ground despite the erratic movement of the wagon. Her eyes were on him. Beautifully blue. Sad and resigned. Yet ever promising love . . . and a spirit that would live forever.

He watched the buckboard until it disappeared beneath the shimmer of the brilliant morning sun.

Twenty-one

March 1864

Brent did not immediately return to Richmond. Kendall was somewhat bitter, but not completely surprised. She was at last coming to know Brent very well, and when intelligence reports warned that the Yankees were planning an invasion inland from Jacksonville, Florida, to try to take the state's capital, it seemed almost normal to Kendall that Brent, a Confederate Navy captain, should leave the sea and hurry south with Stirling to fight a land battle.

If she didn't love him so much—and worry continually that a bullet would find its way to his valiant heart—she could have truly understood what drove him to fight when he was not even called upon by honor and rank to do so.

He had been fighting a war for over three years, yet he had seldom been in a position to help his own ravaged state. He and Stirling had been given special permission to join the Olustee battle, and when Kendall saw the newspapers following the Rebel victory, she was pleased for Brent's sake. Tallahassee had been saved, and when the Rebel forces were being beaten back in many places, the Floridians had brought about a thrilling triumph. How satisfied Brent must have been, she thought, and she felt very close to him, for she knew what it was to fight from the heart.

And she did have his letters. Her lot was no worse than that of any other woman in the Confederacy; some wives hadn't seen their husbands since the war began . . . and some wives would never see their husbands again.

And at least she was in Richmond. Varina Davis, the Confederacy's first lady, had been unfailingly kind to Kendall. She had taken her under her wing the night she reached Richmond. Kendall had luxuriated in a long, hot bath. Then she had enjoyed a savory fish dinner and basked in the warmth of the fire and a glass of fine vintage brandy. Varina had arranged that Kendall be given rooms in an old inn nearby, and she frequently invited Kendall to join her for meals—or merely for tea so that she could keep her informed regarding the progress of the war, and of Captain Brent McClain.

Kendall admired Varina Davis tremendously. The First Lady of the South was soft spoken with a quiet dignity. She was a mother who had lost a beloved son during the war, not a soldier, but a toddler, for her little boy had fallen from the porch of their home in Richmond, the White House of the Confederacy. Kendall heard very sad stories about that day, about how the child had died in his father's arms, and of how his mother had had to force the war letters and decisions to come to a halt for just hours—the only time granted to two such parents to grieve. Thinking of Varina's son made her think of another little one who had died, Red Fox's boy, and she knew that though none of them would ever forget most of the horror they had witnessed, they would carry the anguish over the children they had lost until death and beyond. But Varina did not allow herself to dwell on sorrow. She had other children to raise, and Kendall found herself delighted with the still-large Jefferson brood. She realized that she did dearly love little ones, and longed for one herself. She was in no position to be a mother, she knew—

being a "scarlet" woman, the despised wife of one man, the mistress to another. And still . . .

Her landlady was the widowed mother of two daughters, one five, one fourteen, and Kendall spent what spare time she had in their company, sewing, reading, playing.

Wishing the world could be what it was not, missing Brent. And dreaming of a real home life. One day. Fearing that she couldn't bear children, fearing equally that there could never really be a family life for her and Brent.

But perhaps it wasn't all as bad as it seemed.

Kendall had learned from Varina that—far from being ostracized by her countrymen, as she assumed she would be—she had a small reputation as a heroine. She had fled a Yankee husband for her native land, and she had captured a Federal vessel and put it to use for the South. She had been taken prisoner at Vicksburg while trying to procure medicaments for a Rebel hospital, and that, too, embellished the legends being spun about her. That she was known to be the mistress of the famed and idolized Captain McClain only made her story more romantic and enchanting—especially to the young ladies of Richmond.

Kendall found it all a bit ironic, because she knew she was still in a precarious position. Although hundreds and thousands of good men had died on both sides, John Moore was still alive and unharmed. She had been labeled a spy by the Union, and although she would have never spoken her thoughts aloud to the still determined South, she was convinced that the war could have only one ending. And when the Federals were again in charge . . .

She should be planning an escape. She hadn't seen her husband now in over two years, but just as she knew Brent, she knew John Moore. She knew that as soon as he could, he would find her. Even if the war dragged on another five years, or ten.

She should flee. Escape to Europe perhaps . . . but she

knew she could never leave—not while she waited for Brent. And she knew that Brent would fight to the bitter end.

So she filled her days by working in the hospital in Richmond, suffering with the wounded soldiers, but never running away from their stench or their pain. The war had hardened her, and Vicksburg had given her experience. She was a welcomed assistant to the doctors; she never blanched or paled at the sight of a maggot-filled wound, and she never fainted during an amputation. That alone made her invaluable.

The work drained her strength, but the men revived her spirit. Some days she saw familiar faces—men she had grown up with in Charleston. Helping them, easing their pain, writing their letters seemed to bring back a part of her life she had lost. Old-timers spoke about her father; her younger patients could wistfully recall the barbecues, the hunts, and the balls . . . and she could remember being young herself.

At the end of March, Varina Davis gave her a letter from Brent. He had written it at the end of February, and in it she could sense his triumph and elation at having helped the Rebels expel the Yankees from inland Florida at the Battle of Olustee. He told her that he and Stirling were going to try to slip into Jacksonville and see their sister, then start back north to Richmond. Stirling hoped to visit his wife and son along the way. He hadn't seen them since the winter of 1861. Stirling was due to be back with Jeb Stuart's cavalry by the end of April, and Brent assumed that Charlie McPherson—who had taken the *Jenni-Lyn* on another run to England for supplies—would be back in a Confederate harbor by April or May.

It was not an eloquent letter; it was brief and factual, written on the back of an old procurement order. But it was signed "With all my love, Brent," and those few little words warmed her heart and gave her strength.

And yet, something about the letter nagged at her, and she didn't realize what it was until several weeks later when she discovered another familiar face in the Richmond hospital.

Stooping to pour water for a feverish private, Kendall felt a tug on her skirt from behind. Sweeping a stray lock of hair from her forehead, she turned to see a strangely familiar countenance. The soldier's face was dirty, and his beard had grown thick and bushy. But when she met a pair of delighted hazel eyes, she realized she was staring at her brother-in-law.

"Gene! Gene McIntosh! Oh, my Lord, how are you? How stupid of me! You're lying in a hospital and—"

"And I'm going to be fine, Kendall. Caught a ball in my shoulder last week from a Yankee picket when I was out scouting, that's all. They were able to remove it clean. I'll be heading back out in a day or so. Kendall, we've worried about you now for years. Lolly never writes that she doesn't mention how she prays that you're all right."

Kendall lowered her lashes and bit her lip. "Oh, Gene! I should have written to Mother and Lolly, but I'm still afraid of what my stepfather is capable of conniving."

"Kendall," Gene interrupted her, seemingly surprised, "your stepfather is dead."

"He was killed in the war?" Kendall queried with amazement.

"No," Gene chuckled. "Mean George choked to death trying to eat up all his beef before our own army could ask him for it."

Kendall knew she shouldn't take pleasure in hearing of a man's death. But she couldn't help being glad that there did seem to be some justice in the world.

"How are Lolly and my mother?" Kendall asked. "Have you seen them?"

"Had a furlough night before Christmas time," Gene told her. "You don't even know you're an aunt, do you, Kendall? Lolly and I had a baby girl—born last summer. She's pretty as a picture, Kendall. Eyes as blue as the sky, and hair so gold it looks like sunlight."

"How wonderful, Gene! I'm an aunt! And Lolly and the baby and Mother—they're all doing well?"

"Right as rain, Kendall. I get a little anxious about them sometimes; they say the Yanks will rip up South Carolina if they get in there, on accounta them thinkin' it was us who caused the war."

"Oh, my God—"

"Now don't fret, Kendall. I shouldn't have said that. We've got the best damn soldiers and generals in the world. The Yanks will never get to Charleston."

Yes, they will, Kendall thought, but she didn't press her opinion on Gene.

"Kendall, why don't you go home and see them?"

Gene's question made her realize what had bothered her about Brent's letter. Family. He loved her, but he was still beholden to his brother and sister . . . and she hadn't seen her own mother since the day Charleston seceded from the Union.

"Gene, I will. It will have to be a quick trip, but I am going back." She gave her brother-in-law a quick kiss on the forehead and spun around, determined to speak with the chief surgeon right away. But she turned back first. "Gene, are you sure you're going to be all right?"

"I'm positive," Gene assured her, smiling broadly.

The news of Gene's death reached Lolly in Charleston on the afternoon of Kendall's arrival.

The sisters had enjoyed two hours of an ecstatically happy reunion. Then a soldier had come to the door with a letter from Gene's commanding officer. He had died of an infection following surgery.

Kendall was more than ever glad that she had come. Lolly

had grown stronger with the war, but her marriage had been a true love match, and a part of Lolly died that day. Kendall was glad to be there to hold her, to help her past the initial bitter pain and trauma.

She had dreamed of spending days chatting with her sister, laughing and chuckling over the antics of her lovely little niece.

Instead Kendall was left to plan a wake and hold Lolly's slender, sobbing form as Gene was laid to rest in the family plot with full military honors.

Her mother was bedridden with a bad cold.

But at least she was able to hug and kiss her despite the maternal chastisements that she would make herself sick.

"I don't care if I'm sick for a month, Mother! It will be worth it to have kissed you."

Her mother cried and held her. It had been so long since she had seen her elder daughter.

"Mother scares me," Lolly admitted to Kendall quite frankly, trying to dry her tears long enough to nurse the baby girl who would never know her father. "She catches these colds so frequently. She has no strength, and I feel as if I'm about to break half the time myself. And I just can't handle both plantations. Kendall, can't you stay here? Cresthaven will be yours, you know."

"No, Lolly," Kendall said sorrowfully in response to her sister's plea. "I have to get back to Richmond. But I'm going to find a nurse for Mother, and I'll hire some good people to help you."

"Who?" Lolly demanded bitterly. "All of the good men are in the army."

"Some are already home," Kendall said assuredly.

In the week that followed, she found a free black woman who had a wonderful way with her mother and two good men, men she trusted, to take over as foremen for the plantations. Lolly seemed skeptical when she realized that Kendall had hired amputees sent home from the army, but then she had listlessly shrugged. Kendall knew she couldn't expect her sister's spirit to heal for a long time.

Despite the men she had hired, Kendall spoke truthfully to Lolly before she left. "Lolly, Charleston won't be safe if—"

"If the Yankees win the war?" Lolly asked dryly.

"Yes," Kendall said softly.

"What do you suggest?" Lolly inquired tonelessly.

"I'm not sure yet, but I think I know a place where there will be few repercussions. I'll let you know soon."

Kendall broke off as she saw her sister's dry smile. "Kendall, we haven't heard from you since the war started. When you say *soon*—"

"That's not fair! I couldn't come to Charleston, and you know it."

"You could have written to me. Kendall, do you resent the fact that you were sold to John Moore instead of me?"

"No!" Kendall exclaimed, horrified. She vehemently shook her head. "Lolly, I never resented you in any way. I was older, and I was the stronger. Our stepfather thought I would fetch a higher price."

Lolly laughed, and the radiance of her blond beauty glowed for a moment despite the recent tragedy. "Kendall, I'm still not strong. I'm worn out. I could not have begun to endure the tragedies you've lived through—marriage to John, the prison camp, running all over the country. I'm just dyin' to meet your Captain McClain. Why, the two of you have been the talk of the war!"

"There will be no 'two of us' if I don't get back to Richmond," Kendall murmured.

Kendall's mother cried when it was time for her to leave, but she believed her older daughter would take care of them, come back for them when it was time to move. She was too weak to leave her bed, and so it was Lolly to whom Kendall said her final goodbyes.

And Kendall and Lolly, finding that the war had created a stronger bond between them, hugged each other tightly. Then Kendall kissed the baby, marveling again at the perfect new life, and tried to murmur her farewell cheerfully.

"Kendall," Lolly said softly.

"Yes?"

"It's ironic, isn't it, that Gene should die—and not John."

"Yes, it is ironic. Lolly, I will see you soon," Kendall added.

Lolly smiled and waved.

Kendall's mind was so full of her family that she thought of little else as she took the train back to Richmond. She barely noticed that nervous soldiers hovered at various points along the way.

Despite her pessimism regarding the war, she didn't realize that anything was amiss until she returned to the inn and discovered that Varina Davis had been trying to contact her. She freshened up and rushed to see the First Lady of the Confederacy.

Kendall was greeted by a black butler, who led her to Varina's music room. She sipped mint tea as she waited.

"Oh, Kendall, dear!" Varina said as she swept into the room. Her voice, as always, was soft and well modulated. But then, Varina's voice would be soft and cultured whether she was saying that it was a delightful day or that the Yankees had just taken Richmond. She was a truly beautiful woman in every sense of the word, gracious and courteous and kind and completely dignified.

"What's wrong, Varina?" Kendall asked.

Varina didn't answer right away. She smiled and walked over to Kendall, her crinoline rustling beneath the bell of her pearl silk morning dress. "First of all, my dear, I'm leaving the city again. That terrible General Grant is closing in on us. And I do have something to tell you that I'm afraid will cause you pain. Captain McClain was here in your absence. He was hoping to find you and to pick up his ship, but Lieutenant McPherson hasn't returned with her yet. He was sent to London again. Oh, if the British would just step in and offer us their support! But that's neither here nor there. Captain McClain has gone back to join his brother's unit, and I think it might be best if you were to leave Richmond with me."

"Oh, no!" Kendall interrupted at last, feeling the blood drain from her features, leaving them as pale as the snow. "Oh, no! Brent was here, and I wasn't—"

"It's quite all right, dear. He went to the hospital and learned that you had gone to see your family—"

Varina broke off as Kendall hopped to her feet. "You don't understand! I promised that I would be here."

"Kendall, we're in the middle of a war. I'm sure the captain understands."

Kendall shook her head vigorously. "I have to find him. Do you know where he went?"

"North along the pike to join General Lee's army. You can't go after him, Kendall. The countryside is crawling with the enemy."

"I have to go! I have to! Please, Varina! If you can help me, do so. One way or another, I must catch up with him!"

Varina sighed. "President Davis would be most displeased! But all right, I'll find out when the next messenger is leaving and arrange for you to go along. But, Kendall, you'll have to travel rough roads quickly; it's imperative that all letters from my husband reach General Lee as soon as possible."

"Believe me, Mrs. Davis, I am well acquainted with rough roads and hazardous travel!"

* * *

Kendall and Captain Melbourne—the messenger entrusted with carrying letters between the South's president and its leading general—reached the army camp in two days. Kendall was struck again by the ragged appearance of the starving men.

But the appearance of the men was not her major concern at the moment. Her heart had been pounding for the entire journey; she had been living with fear and dread.

Brent had told her to stay in Richmond, and whether his ultimatum had been fair or not, her promise to him seemed to make her absence a betrayal. And their time together was always so brief . . . and so precious. She wanted to see him so badly, but she was afraid of his reaction to seeing her. She practiced the words she would say to him over and over as Captain Melbourne delivered her to the cavalry . . .

She saw Brent first. He was leaning casually against a grazing roan, sipping coffee from a tin and listening to the conversation around him. His gray eyes seemed intense as a low murmured comment passed. Then he laughed and the hint of a grin curled his lips.

He looked far different from when she had seen him last. His beard and mustache were neatly clipped. His hair curled over his collar, but the cut was neat and fashionable. His coat was as tattered as those of the men about him, but somehow he was the perfect picture of the southern officer, masculine and correct, arrogant and gallant.

She wanted to call him; his name formed on her lips, but she couldn't say it. Suddenly a long whistle sounded. One of the men had seen her and expressed his surprise and wistful admiration.

Brent's gray eyes turned to her and widened in amazement. Her heart seemed to cease its beat as she waited for his reaction. Anger, dismissal, denial . . .

But he smiled, and she feared she would pass out with the sheer joy of relief. He came to her, long strides eating the distance between them, and then she felt the thrill of his arms about her, his powerful fingers in her hair. His arms crushed her to him. And then, before all his comrades, he kissed her, lovingly, passionately, tenderly. Tears sprang to her eyes with the sweet caress of his mouth, with the scent and feel of him. For long moments she forgot the war, forgot the world, as the earth and sky spun about her.

But then he was whispering to her, his words confused, his tone an anguished demand.

"Kendall . . . what are you doing here?"

"I . . . I had to see you, I promised to be in Richmond—"

"Kendall, we're about to encounter all of Grant's army!"

"But I—"

"Wait!" Brent murmured, holding her hands but drawing away from her. A brilliant twinkle of fire burned in the hazy gray depths of his eyes as he indicated the audience of cheering Rebs behind them. "I think we need to find a bit of privacy."

Someone cleared his throat, then laughed. "There's a little tavern not far from here, brother. I hardly think this camp is the place for a lady."

Kendall turned to the speaker. "Stirling!" she exclaimed, joyously hugging him. He swept her around in a circle and ignored his scowling brother. "Kendall, you look lovely! All these poor soldiers must think they've seen an angel! But this isn't a safe place for you. Brent"—he turned to his brother—"you've got to get her out of here."

"I know. But—"

"I'll clear you through Stuart. Hell, Brent, you're navy. You don't have to be here at all."

"I'll be back at dawn," Brent promised. Then he saw that the entire regiment was staring at the three of them. He raised Kendall's slender hand in his. "Kendall, meet the boys of the Second Florida Cavalry. Boys, meet Kendall Moore. Say hello and goodbye quickly, darlin'."

Kendall blushed as the men cheered—but she wasn't embarrassed for long, because she found herself swept up on Brent's roan in front of him. He turned the horse and started out of the encampment at a brisk trot. They were challenged several times, but Brent informed the pickets that he was escorting a lady to safety, and they were allowed to go on.

They didn't speak until they reached a run-down tavern. After tethering the roan, Brent swung her down and led her inside, holding her hand firmly while he procured the only available room from the harried innkeeper, who immediately noted Brent's uniform and demanded to know what was going on at the camp.

Brent didn't lie. "Battle will rage soon, sir. And, yes, it will be nearby."

"You're not a deserter, are you, Captain?"

"No, sir, I'm just spending a few hours with my . . . wife. Then I'll return to the front."

And then, at last, they were inside the shabby room. Brent looked about dryly, then shrugged and pulled her into his arms.

"I'm sorry I couldn't do any better."

Kendall smiled. "If you'll recall, sir, I've spent many a night in a cave. This will do right nicely—as long as you're with me."

"I'm with you," he murmured huskily.

"Brent," Kendall began, "I'm sorry I wasn't in Richmond. I gave you my promise—but I wasn't expecting you and—"

"Tell me later, Kendall . . . much, much . . . later." His words were interspersed with the moist and heated touch of his lips on hers, on her throat, the lobe of her ear, and the nape of her neck. Brushfires of longing swept through her in wave after shuddering wave, and she clung to him, arching

400

her throat to meet his steel-gray eyes with a brilliant blue shimmer in her own.

"Later," she agreed, "much later . . ."

And it was a long while later, when the sun had set and the moon had begun to rise, that they nestled together in satiated contentment and began to talk.

Brent had one elbow crooked beneath his head as he stared up at the ceiling. His other arm was around Kendall. His fingers idly smoothed her hair as she rested her cheek against the dampness of his bare chest.

"Kendall, I wasn't angry. I'm glad to see you, but I wish you hadn't come. This place is going to come alive tomorrow. Lee's planning to meet Grant in the Wilderness, hoping to take advantage of the forest terrain. We're outnumbered atrociously."

Kendall ran her fingers over his chest. "Brent, you don't have to be here. Please don't fight in this battle. I'm frightened."

He was silent for a moment. "Kendall, I've wanted to throttle you half a dozen times, at least, but in the last few months I've had time to think about things. In a way, I have been unfair. I love you, Kendall—truly love you—and I've tried to understand you. I can't stop loving you, Kendall. The war and time and distance can't change my heart. Yet I know you can't be broken. I only hope you can be tamed. A bit, at any rate. Kendall, I have to fight this battle. The Confederacy needs every man it can get."

Kendall fought back tears, but her voice was taut with choked sobs when she spoke. "I don't understand you, Brent. There's no reason—"

He interrupted softly, "There's every reason, Kendall. There's the South, there's you, there's me—there's us."

"The South is doomed, Brent."

"Don't say that, Kendall," he snapped harshly.

"It's true, and you know it, Brent. You knew it the night

401

we met, the night South Carolina seceded from the Union. I was the one with the dreams back then."

"Kendall, I don't know anything, except that I've got to fight tomorrow. All we really have, Kendall, is fighting spirit—and tenacity." Suddenly he shifted, bringing his weight over hers and locking her fingers with his own against the bed as he hovered over her. "Kendall, we can't always know right from wrong because the world isn't black and white. There are always shades of gray in between. We can only do what we feel to be right. You're a married woman, Kendall, but the love we share is right—no matter where it takes us. And back in Kentucky, when we fought over that old woman, the consequences of your actions might have made them very wrong. But you did what you felt was right, Kendall. I think I can understand that now. Ah, Kendall . . . you'll always be a pain in the neck."

"Brent!"

"But I love you because of it. I love you because you're proud and determined, and no man will ever break you, not even me. I'm asking you to understand that I have to go into this battle. And I'm also asking you to make me a promise."

"What?" she asked huskily, torn between a desire to slap him for calling her a pain and a need to wrap him so tightly in her arms that he could never leave her again.

"I want you to go home as soon as possible. I mean home to Harold and Amy's place. Richmond isn't going to be safe."

Kendall parted her lips to protest, but he closed them with a gentle kiss.

"As soon as I can, I'll come back there," he promised. "Back to you. Give me your promise."

She couldn't speak; he seemed to be satisfied with her nod.

And he seemed to understand the tears that misted her eyes and dampened her cheeks as they made love, even at the sweet precipice of rapture. He kissed them away in the aftermath of their passion, holding her to him. And just before she fell asleep, she heard him whisper gently, "I'll come to you at the cove, Kendall, I promise."

When she awakened before dawn, he was gone. Already the day was alive with the roar of cannonfire and the thunder of shelling. The Wilderness Campaign had begun.

In his life, Brent had never seen anything as awful as the Wilderness Campaign.

On horseback, they had started off as one of the earliest units into the fray. The forest had seemed so still, the sky so clear and fresh. He could hear birds, breathe the sweet green smell of the trees and the shrubs.

Midway, they had come across their first action; a rain of bullets had fallen upon them from the left side of the trees. Horses had swung about in panic, the men had quickly dismounted. They'd found their own cover across the road.

Then the cannons had begun.

And the trees had become a blaze.

He had seen Stirling ordering his men to fall back; he had begun the retreat himself, but then he had seen Billy Christian, the little drummer boy from Tallahassee.

Boys weren't supposed to be fighting wars. But Billy had been in this one from just about the beginning, or so Stirling had told Brent. He was just a week shy of his thirteenth birthday, and he'd been pounding out a march beat for the men forever, or so it seemed. He'd been an orphan, his old uncle Josh the only kin he'd had, and Josh had come into the unit.

Josh had died. Billy had stayed.

And now, in the mire of dead men and screaming horses and burning trees and suffocating smoke, Billy was down. Shot in the leg.

Brent heard the boy screaming, and began to ease back

along the burning tinder, keeping a wary eye on the trees above him. He heard the crack of one falling before him and skirted around it; felt the burn against his face as sparks flew. Then he found Billy, saw the wound. Billy opened pain-filled eyes and saw Brent. "Captain, bet you'll stick to water from now on, huh?" he tried to joke. Then another scream tore from him and Brent ripped up his trousers leg to fashion a tourniquet just below his knee. Billy was probably going to lose the leg. Brent could only hope he didn't lose his life.

"Captain, get out of here. The forest is going to blow," Billy warned him.

"Yep, that it is."

Brent hefted down and picked up Billy, carrying him like a baby as he tried desperately to see through the smoke and black powder. He began to stagger forward with Billy's weight, determined he had found his bearings. They were alone in the forest, it seemed. Alone in hell.

A tree cracked and fell behind them. Brent quickened his pace. He was certain he heard hoofbeats just ahead. He started to hurry.

There was a horse, indeed. It was carrying one soldier with a shot-up arm and another with gut-shot. But the injured men stopped when they saw Brent with the boy.

"Sir, we can give you the horse," the gut-shot man offered, pain twisting his features even as he made the gallant offer.

"I've not a mark on me, and you need help fast. You're not giving me a horse, soldier."

"But we can take one more up here before this old nag falls down, sir!" The man with the bloodied arm called out.

"One more will be fine. I can walk," Brent assured them. "If you can just get Billy out of here."

"Aye, Captain!" the man said, saluting. He reached out his arms and Brent set Billy upon the horse. He saluted to the men. "Get going."

The skinny old flea-bitten horse didn't look like it would

quite make it, but the soldier gave it a whack and it started off at a surprising trot out of the field of fire and death.

Brent followed as quickly as he could in their wake. The heat was becoming awful. It was unbearable just to try to breathe.

He lost his bearings briefly, thought he had returned to his direction properly, then thought that he saw some kind of cottage before him through the smoke and haze. He prayed he wasn't wandering in circles. He paused.

And it was then that the tree caught fire behind him. He heard the snap of the flames, heard the cracking. He turned, ready to leap away.

He did so, and avoided the bulk of the tree's weight. But one heavy branch, just beginning to smolder, broke away. He raised his arms, but not in quite enough time to ward off the blow completely. The wood cracked against his skull. Against the grayness and ripping red fire that streaked it, he saw a field of velvet and stars. He fought for consciousness, but he was falling. . . .

He was still alive, he thought moments later. Or else, he was dead, and he had gone to hell, the heat was so intense. He tried to rise. He couldn't fight off the grayness. When he lifted his head, he passed out again.

He couldn't die. He had promised Kendall that he wouldn't die.

Sometimes, when he closed his eyes, he could see her again. She was running down the beach, the luxuriant turquoise water lapping at her bare feet. Her hair was touched by the sun, and he was coming home to her . . .

Then he was in field of fire again. Dying. He struggled up. He had promised her he would live. "Kendall!" he whispered her name; cried it out in the forest.

Someone was above him. He could see a wealth of hair. Kendall, here . . .

But it wasn't Kendall. The hair was gray.

He tried to rise, and saw an old woman with a sad face and skinny frame had come from somewhere. "Ma'am, I've just got to make it out of here," he told her.

"You're half dead, sir," she told him.

He tried to grin. "Only half?"

She smiled. She had been young once. Maybe just before the war.

Her face was gone. She took hold of his ankles. His head bumped against the ground.

Kendall . . .

He had made her a promise. Dear God, he loved her so much. He had to go back to her. He would go back to her, he would go back to her, damn it, but he would live!

The woods seemed to scream with the rise of the fire.

Then the heat was gone, and the pain was gone.

And the world faded to a sweet shade of black. . . .

By midmorning it became apparent that the tavern would soon be directly in the line of battle. Kendall went into the cellar along with the other civilians.

And as the hours passed, the shelling increased. By noon the tavern had actually become part of the Rebel line. The taproom was filled with wounded soldiers and the men who had carried them inside, out of range of enemy fire.

Unable to stand the waiting, Kendall crawled up the cellar stairs. The Rebels seemed surprised to see her, yet they did not protest her company once they realized her usefulness. She bandaged those who were injured, and carried water to those who fought. And listened avidly to the information brought in to the tavern by those leading the infantry troop.

Jeb Stuart's cavalry was all around them, tenaciously holding the line. The cannons grew curiously silent. Kendall learned that neither side dared use such artillery, because the smoke was so thick in the burning forest that cannonfire was likely to kill one's own troops. The combat was now hand to hand.

As darkness descended, there was a lull in the fighting. Cavalrymen drifted into the tavern to find a moment's respite before rejoining their worn and scattered comrades.

Kendall prayed that she would see Brent, and her heart leapt as she recognized the uniforms of the Second Florida Cavalry—and then saw Stirling McClain. She was about to hail him when she saw that he was anxiously scanning the room for her.

"Kendall, dear God, you *are* still here! You've got to get back to Richmond. You can go with the hospital wagons."

"Where's Brent?" Kendall demanded, interrupting him.

Stirling hesitated. "I don't know."

"You and he were together. What has happened to him, Stirling?"

Stirling gripped her shoulders and shook her slightly. "The woods all around us are burning! Men on both sides are dying from the fire as well as from enemy bullets. You can't see your own hand before your eyes, and you don't know friend or foe until you face him."

Kendall broke free from him, nearly hysterical. "I'm going out, Stirling. He's out there somewhere. He might be dying."

She ran past Stirling, tearing for the woods. "Kendall, wait!" he called after her. "The fires are everywhere!"

She heard him running after her, but she didn't care. She raced full into the woods, then paused, spinning about, coughing and choking from the dense smoke. Stirling was right. Between the coming of night and the gray smoke billowing from the red and crackling trees, she couldn't see an inch before her.

"Brent!" she screamed. She was answered by an ominous silence—and then by a sudden roar as a giant oak groaned and snapped beneath the fury of the fire. She screamed, and jumped far back to avoid it, gasping as she tripped over a pile of dead men. A hand grasped her ankle. "Help me, lady, merciful heaven, help me lady."

Kendall gazed down at the pained and sooty face staring into hers. It was that of a young man, twisted in fear and torment. The coat he wore was blue.

"Jesus Christ, *shoot* me, at least. Don't let me burn. Please, have mercy."

"Can you hold on to me?" Kendall gasped.

"Yes, but my leg is all shot up."

Kendall bent down and gripped the man about the waist. Straining hard, she was able to drag him. He screamed out once, but when she paused, he urged her to keep going. "Bless you, ma'am, you're a saint."

"I'm a Rebel," Kendall said dryly.

"A Rebel saint . . ."

The smoke began to thin. Kendall saw people moving slowly about. They were shadows, ghostly shadows in the eerie, doom-filled night.

"Help me!" she cried.

A man came to her. To her horror, she saw that he also wore blue. "Lady," he told her, grappling her human burden from her. "You've got to get out of here. This whole forest is going up like tinder!"

"I . . . I have to find a man," she said.

The Yankee hesitated. "A Rebel?"

Kendall bit her lip, then nodded.

Suddenly the night was illuminated in an orange glow and another great roar split the air. The entire area of trees behind her seemed to blaze together in a massive flame that reached to the heavens.

"You're not going back that way, ma'am, and you're not going to find a thing alive in that direction. Come with me. I'll take you to Lieutenant Bauer."

She felt his grip on her arm, but she didn't care. She was

covered with soot herself now, worn and despairing. Brent had been lost in the fire. Nothing mattered. Nothing at all.

It seemed as if they walked for hours, a party of twenty men carrying what wounded they could take away in stretchers. They had to zigzag continually to avoid the fires. But at last they led her from the forest to an encampment far to the north.

She was brought before a tired, bewhiskered old man in a headquarters tent. She could see that he had been fighting. His blue coat was black and scorched, he stank of smoke—as Kendall was certain she did herself.

"Found ourselves a right pretty Reb, Lieutenant Bauer," said the young Yank who had found her. "What do we do with her now?"

Surprised but compassionate green eyes surveyed her. She must have been a sorry sight, covered with soot, her hair a tangled mass, her shoulders slumped with dejection.

"How did you get into this hell on earth?" the lieutenant asked, shaking his head. "Never mind." He looked back to his man. "If the lady is a Rebel, we'll return her to her side. Arrange a conveyance."

His kindness brought tears to her eyes. "Thank you, sir," she managed to whisper.

"There is enough horror and pain about us," he said briefly, dismissing the problem.

She returned to the Rebel lines on horseback and was handed over to an emissary of Robert E. Lee, but she never did see the southern general. Jeb Stuart had been mortally wounded, and Lee was with his friend arranging to send the great cavalry commander to Richmond.

She was still too numb to care about anything, and she merely stood, swaying before a campfire as her immediate future was decided for her by whispering officers. And then she felt a touch on her arm.

It was Stirling. He turned her into his arms and embraced

her. "Kendall, thank God." He was silent for a moment, then held her away and studied her lifeless eyes. "They're ready to leave for Richmond with some of the wounded, Kendall. You have to go."

She shook her head, blinded by tears. "I can't leave."

"Kendall, you won't help Brent by running into the Yankees again—or by burning to death in the fire. I'll keep in touch with you, but if you really love my brother, take care of yourself. Get back to Florida as soon as you can." Stirling paused once again and held her close. "You could be carrying his child, Kendall."

Kendall doubted that she was, but she didn't tell Stirling that. All the times they had been together, and all the months that had passed . . . she should have had his child. Even that had been denied her.

"Kendall," Stirling said, "you have to go."

"I'll wait in Richmond," she said.

Stirling opened his mouth as if to protest, then shut it. "I'll keep in touch with you, Kendall, I promise."

Stirling was true to his word. She received his letters at least once a month. Brent hadn't been found, Stirling wrote, but neither had his body. Stirling's letters contained hope; he refused to believe that Brent was dead.

So did Kendall. But though his letters urged her to leave Richmond, she continually refused to do so, even when Charlie McPherson arrived at her door, telling her that he could take her to Amy in the *Jenni-Lyn*.

"I'll be back in two months, young lady," Charlie said firmly. "And you'll come with me then. The captain would want that."

Kendall smiled at him vaguely. She knew she wouldn't come.

Months later, as October rolled around, Brent was still

among the missing. Just as he had promised, Charlie McPherson arrived at her door again.

"It's no good, Charlie. I won't leave until I know what has happened to—"

Her words broke off as a man stepped past Charlie, a man strangely out of place in her civilized parlor.

"Red Fox," she whispered, stunned.

He stepped toward her, dark eyes severe and unfathomable, arms strong and secure as he took her gently within them. "You will come, Kendall. When the Night Hawk can, he will come to you at the bay."

"I—"

"I know my friend," Red Fox stated firmly. "And I will take you, his woman, where he would wish you to be."

As she leaned against the Seminole's strength, Kendall remembered Brent's words to her. Yes, when he could, he would come to her at the cove. And she would wait . . . Richmond was growing more dangerous every day. The Yankee yoke about the capital was tightening.

"I'll come," she whispered.

They easily broke through the blockade outside Richmond. Charlie had learned well from his captain.

Throughout the journey, Kendall clung to Red Fox. She trusted him and found his touch comforting.

But one night, beneath the velvet sky and stars, he pulled away from her. "Kendall Moore, I love the Night Hawk. And I feel that he lives. But I am flesh and blood—even if the flesh is red. You are a beautiful woman, and I love you well. You come to me in innocence; yet you tempt me to betray my brother."

Kendall stared at him with wide, startled eyes. And she realized that he did love her, and that he was lonely—just as she was. And if there had never been a Brent McClain, she might have loved Red Fox in every way. He was one of the strongest men she had ever known, in character and person.

But they did both love Brent; and they both believed that he would return.

"I'm sorry," she whispered, backing away from him.

He reached for her, and caught her hand. "No, do not go away. He is my brother; you are my sister. We will not lose our bond of friendship."

"No," Kendall agreed, studying the ageless wisdom in his deep brown eyes. "We will not."

They reached the bay in November. By the start of the new year, things looked extremely grim for the South. Sherman began his infamous March to the Sea, setting Georgia afire with his scorched-earth tactics, destroying everything that couldn't be carried away. Kendall became frightened for her family, and when Charlie stopped at the bay in February, Kendall begged him to try and get into Charleston and bring her mother, sister, and niece south.

Lolly and the baby arrived on a windy March day. Kendall learned that her mother had died at the end of January.

She couldn't really feel pain. She had been numb for so long. And perhaps it was for the best. Her mother would not have had the strength to see the South crumble about her.

Amy Armstrong was delighted with the baby. She cared for little Eugenia often, which was good for Eugenia, because Lolly seemed to be as numb as Kendall. Harry helped her fix up an old deserted cabin to the rear of his property, and Lolly spent most of her time there, polite, but oblivious to all that went on around her. She kept almost completely to herself.

Telegraph and railway ties were broken throughout the South. News came to them infrequently and sporadically. Yet the sense of doom was with them. When Charlie sailed out again at the end of March, Kendall wondered if she would ever see him again.

Spring came. Yet despite its lush beauty, despite the blue clarity of the skies, the days passed in somber gray.

Twenty-two

Spring 1865

Kendall spent as much time as she could at the cove.

She knew as time passed that the others pitied her and thought that she was a fool to keep waiting.

But life without hope would be too bleak to tolerate. As the months drifted by, she knew the chance Brent was alive grew slimmer and slimmer; in her heart, however, she still believed that he was indomitable—and alive.

And that he would come back to her.

She tried to behave rationally. She worked with Amy in the garden, and she sewed and mended and took over much of the housework. But she knew that Amy worried about her; as much as Amy had loved Brent, she believed that he was dead and that it wasn't good for Kendall to live on hope and cling to the past. Lolly had little to say one way or another; she spent long hours cleaning the cabin Harry had given her and trying to make it pleasant for herself and her baby.

Only Red Fox seemed to understand. Kendall knew that he came to the cove sometimes and just watched her before slipping silently away. She was touched by his concern—and grateful for his understanding. Sometimes he asked her to come into the Glades with him, and she always went along, glad that he offered no lectures or opinions on the solitude she so often sought. Red Fox had loved Brent as a blood brother; when she was with him, she felt close to Brent. Since that time aboard the *Jenni-Lyn,* they hadn't touched each other, but their bond of friendship had been too strong to break.

And no matter what anyone said, she would keep waiting.

With her chin resting on her knuckles and her hands on her knees, she sat and stared broodingly out at the sea. April was a pretty month. A pleasant breeze drifted by her while a brilliant sun dazzled the water. The surf seemed to lull away the pain in her heart with its continual flow. She closed her eyes and listened to the sounds around her, the continual surge and ebb of the water, the rustle of the palm leaves, an occasional flutter of birds' wings.

Then she sensed something. She didn't actually hear it; she simply perceived a movement. And she smiled, opening her eyes and staring out to sea again. "Red Fox, you needn't watch me. You know me well enough to realize that I'm not going to jump into the water and drown myself!"

There was no reply, and she felt strange little prickles along her spine. Forewarned by her sixth sense, Kendall slowly turned her head, and her heart seemed to cease its beating, then began to pound furiously.

She should have been stunned, but she wasn't. She had always believed that he lived . . . and that he would come to her. Here. At the cove.

And he was there, really there. In tattered gray with gold trim; alive; as tall and broad and handsomely bronzed as ever. His eyes were like smoke; he merely stared without speech. The naked pain and longing in the wistful gray of his eyes was far more eloquent than any words he might say. ·

"Brent . . ." she whispered, and then she was on her feet, but still she had to stare at him, assure herself that he was there. And then she was running to him, flinging her arms about him, touching him, kissing him; and crying with joy at the sight of him.

For a long while they held each other, and Kendall felt that life was incredibly good. He was solid substance, warm flesh and blood, all the strength in the world as he held her. She felt the gentle spring breeze rustle about them, she felt the heat of the sun, and, caressing them with sound, she heard the lulling song of the surf. For long, long moments they didn't speak, but stood locked, savoring their embrace, the touch of tenderness and love.

At last Kendall pulled away, wiping tears from her cheeks as she challenged him. "Where have you been? Why didn't you write? I was half insane after the Wilderness Campaign—"

"I did send you a message," he told her, studying her features and touching the soft wings of hair that fell over her forehead. "But apparently, too many telegraph wires were down. Nothing got through."

"What happened? Where have you been?"

He shrugged, enveloping her once more. "I was wounded and caught in the fire. I lay there for days, long enough to acquire a ghastly fever. But a woman found me and took me to her home. She told me later that I was delirious for a long time, and then too weak to do more than mutter incoherently. I wasn't able to stand until August, and I didn't get back to Richmond until November. The first thing I did was try to send you a message, but Charlie just told me that it never reached you."

Kendall buried her face against the warm flesh of his neck. "It doesn't matter now . . . You're here. And I always knew you would come, Brent . . ." Her voice trailed away as she felt him stiffen, and she pulled back to meet his eyes with fear and confusion. "What is it, Brent? What—"

"Kendall, we're still at war."

She stared at him for a moment incredulously, then broke

416

from his hold, backing away. *"No!* You're not leaving again! Brent, the war is *over!* We don't get much news here, and what we do get is old. But, Brent, any fool can see that it is all over. Sherman has crushed Georgia! Atlanta was burned. Columbia was burned. It's over! Lee's army is all but wiped out."

"Don't tell me about Lee's army!" Brent exclaimed. "I just left them—and they're still fighting. And Kirby-Smith is still fighting in the West! Kendall, it's more important than ever that supplies get through to those men!"

"No!" Kendall screamed, "I will not let you go again! And what do you think you're going to sail in? Charlie has taken the *Jenni-Lyn* to the Bahamas."

"I came here in the *Rebel's Pride,*" he said softly.

Kendall stared at him in disbelief. The ship *she* had taken—*her* ship—was going to take him away.

"No!" she shouted again, and suddenly she was racing back across the sand, hurling herself against him, beating her fists furiously against his broad chest. "No! The Confederacy has taken all that it is going to take from me! You are not leaving. You are not!"

He caught her fists and secured them against the small of her back, crushing her feminine form to his, but not stilling her wild struggles. "Kendall, I came back to be with the woman I love, not to be ordered about by a shrill harpy!"

"Why? You've been ordering me about for over four years!" Kendall raged, half insane as she fought him. This was the last straw. She had lost him one too many times. She could not bear to lose him again. She would shatter into a thousand pieces. "No, no, *No!"* she shrieked, and her fury was so great that she broke his hold on her and pummeled him with her fists once more.

"Kendall! Stop it!" he demanded. He lunged for her, again securing her wrists and this time catching her ankle with his booted foot to send her thudding to the sand, breathless.

Lithely he cast his own weight over her and used the pressure of his hips and the tangle of his thighs to subdue her writhing form as he stretched her arms high above her head.

"Kendall, if I don't follow orders, I'll be guilty of desertion. And if we don't win this war, there will be nothing left for us. As far as I know, John Moore is still alive and well. If the Yankees win, it will be next to impossible to find a court that will give you a divorce. Kendall, listen to me—our fate is cast with the Confederacy."

"I don't care if I ever get a divorce!" Kendall raged. "It will do me no good if you're dead. Brent, please! We can sail away. We can find refuge in England or in the Bahamas."

"Kendall, neither of us can just sail away, and you know it!"

"I know nothing of the kind!" Tears stung her eyes, and to hide them, she jerked furiously against his grasp, trying to throw him aside and elude him. All she managed to do was tear the top two buttons off her gown and expose the ivory mounds of her breasts beneath. She felt his body quicken and stiffen, and she saw the smolder she knew so well in his eyes.

Moments ago she had been deliriously happy to see him. She would gladly have torn off her clothing to welcome his touch. She had never forgotten the splendor of their passion. Time indeed played tricks on desire. All the cravings, all the hungers held dormant rushed to life at his mere presence, and even now she knew her body would betray all her determination to impose her will on him.

She inhaled sharply. "Brent, don't you dare—"

He more than dared. His mouth claimed hers with a voracious hunger, masterfully stripping away her protests and denials. His force was that of a storm, tempestuous winds defying all obstacles. His tongue sought the nectar of her mouth, plundering and raking, brutally demanding a response.

She held out against him as long as she could, until her breath was gone and her mind swept clear by the force of the raging storm. Her own desires were too strong to deny; the fires within her rose to clash and then meld with his, and she returned his kiss with an angry passion of her own, bitter with the knowledge that she could truly deny him nothing.

She felt his hand delve into the split of her gown. His palm grazed her breast, cupping and cradling it, the skin of his hand feeling rough and provocative on her nipple. The liquid heat began a stormy surge through her, and she trembled, angry but responsive to his touch. She lowered her eyes as he lifted her to tear away the offending gown, his fingers rough and clumsy in their trembling. And then she felt the sand against her naked back as he pulled away her pantalettes. She heard his sharp intake of breath at the sight of her. Time and the bay had been good to her. Her breasts had regained their full, lush curves, as had her hips, while her waist still invited the span of a man's broad hands.

She opened her eyes to his as he began to strip away his own clothing. But when he at last stood naked over her, she closed them once more as a dizziness assailed her. He was as lean and superbly sinewed as a tiger, magnificently broad but trim, his sexuality alive and as hard as his relentless steel-gray eyes.

She loved him, adored him, needed him—and wanted him . . . Forever. If he died, there would be no meaning to life. She had already discovered that during the long months of waiting.

"No!" she yelled suddenly, and sprang to her feet.

"What the damn hell—" he began, reaching for her, but she was too quick. She raced past him, naked, into the brush.

"Kendall!" he shouted with incredulous anger.

She raced through the tangle of sea grapes and palms. But he was too fleet for her. He caught hold of her long hair and

419

jerked her to a halt, then spun her around and crushed her to his naked chest.

"Kendall!"

She kicked and lashed at him, driven by bitterness and frenzy. But his arms locked around her, and together they fell down on a fragrant pile of leaves. She tossed her head, refusing to meet his eyes. "I will not let you die, I will not—"

"Kendall, I will not die!"

"Don't. Please, Brent, don't! I've been trying so hard to learn to live without you. Now you're here, just to leave again. I lived on hope alone. Oh, God, I cannot bear to lose you again. I cannot!"

But suddenly, she could protest no longer. Her arms locked around his neck, and she sought his lips with a fiery passion. Her fingers tangled tightly into his hair; she eluded his lips to press her mouth against his shoulder as she clung to him. She had lied to him; she had never, ever begun to learn to live without him, and she wanted him now, with the sun beating down on them and the leaves caressing their naked flesh. She wanted all of him whenever she could have him, and she would cling to him as long as she could.

"Brent . . ."

"Kendall, oh, sweet Lord, Kendall. I love you. I love you. I've dreamed of you night and day, lived to hold you again, touch you . . . love you."

She felt his knees part her thighs with a firm and agile movement, felt his hands on her as he lifted her to meet his probing thrust. And she cried out her need as the sun seemed to shatter and explode within her, lifting her to the tempest of the wind, the beauty of the storm. His name mingled with her bitter tears as the waves of passion engulfed them in wave after shuddering wave. She sensed everything, the spring air, the caress of the leaves beneath them, the heat of the sun bringing them to a flaring fire of brilliant gold. She knew the masculine scent of him, the wonderful brush of his hard flesh against hers, the muscles of his thighs, the rough hair of his beard, the coarse tendrils on his chest rubbing against her breasts, the sure and vitally strong life of him within her, taking her, filling her, threatening to tear her asunder, yet beautiful all the while. And then she felt that beauty within her soar and crest and fill her with a new liquid heat; one her body answered in rapturous response.

The world slowly ceased to spin. Again she was aware of the sky, the earth, the leaves that were their bed. He shifted his weight, and his fingers tenderly grazed her cheek, but she brushed them away. She had needed him so desperately. But he was going to leave again.

"Leave me," she whispered, shielding her eyes with her arm.

"Kendall, please be sensible."

"I am being sensible!" Again she sprang to her feet—and again he was right behind her. But when he would have touched her, she shook away his hand. "I'm not going to run anywhere naked; I'm going to get my clothing. And be *sensible.*"

"Damn you, Kendall! Go! But I'm not leaving right away! I've got three days."

"I don't care if you've got four weeks!"

"You should take a long, cooling swim!" he shouted after her. "And don't think you can run away. We're going to have this out tonight!"

Kendall found her clothes and donned them quickly. She glanced at the gray trousers, and the gray frock coat. At the tall black boots.

Furiously she grabbed the frock coat and flung it out to sea. The tide brought it back, and she burst into tears. Then she turned away and crept through the brush to avoid the trail—and Brent. She didn't return to Amy's, but walked aimlessly for hours. She wanted to think, but she felt so numb.

When she did begin to think, her head started to pound with a vengeance.

She had to prevent him from leaving.

The sentence repeated itself in her mind time and time again as she walked. When she found herself at the mouth of the river, she sat on the sand and mud bank and stared listlessly at the water. The *Rebel's Pride* lay in the river's mouth, and she wondered if she could find a way to scuttle the ship. She narrowed her eyes and stared at it, then stared idly out at the bay beyond the mouth of the river.

Suddenly her heart pounded viciously within her chest. There was another ship on the horizon, bearing quickly down on them. And it was flying the Stars and Stripes.

She leapt to her feet, blinking furiously. The ship remained on the horizon. Dumbly she stared at it a moment longer. Then she turned to flee, racing as fast as she could, panting in her hurry to reach Amy's.

Amy was calmly working in the garden. She looked up as Kendall approached, dazzling happiness in her eyes. "Kendall, isn't it wonderful? You were right all along about Brent! But where is he?"

Kendall stopped short. "He isn't here?"

"No, he went to look for you."

"Oh, God, Amy! There's a Federal ship heading right for us!"

Amy dropped a handful of flowers. "Oh, Lord! Kendall, go! Take the rowboat up the river and into the swamp. You must hide!"

"I can't—not unless I know where Brent is."

"Brent will be fine—unless he has to worry about you. We didn't want to tell you before, but Harry heard that your husband was back at Fort Taylor. He could be looking for you. You have to get out of here, quickly!"

Kendall felt the world spin about her; the daylight seemed to go black. "John . . ."

422

Amy gave her a push. "Go, Kendall!"

"Wait! I have to get Lolly and the baby. God only knows what he would do to them to spite me."

"Get to the boat, Kendall. I'll get Lolly and the baby. Find a place to hide, Kendall. You know the swamp. And don't come out until one of us comes for you."

"But the Yankees—"

"Won't hurt us, dear. We've nothing they could possibly want. Hurry into the house and get provisions. Then run for that boat. I'll get your sister."

Kendall sank her teeth into her lower lip, drawing blood. She didn't want to go without Brent, but Amy was right. If he believed her safe, he would be far less likely to jeopardize his own life. Amy was already running to warn Lolly. Kendall raced into the cabin, hurriedly filled a tin with fresh water, and stuffed bread and fruit and smoked meat into a satchel she fashioned from a dish towel. All the while she prayed that Brent would appear, but when he didn't, she knew she was out of time.

She raced back to the river and dropped her satchel into the rowboat. A second later, she saw her sister's blond head approaching her through the trees. Then Lolly was hopping into the rowboat, her baby Eugenia howling at her mother's rough treatment. Lolly's eyes met Kendall's without reproach, and Kendall strenuously began to row toward the swamp.

They didn't speak until Kendall had rounded the first bend in the river and found a swamp trail that would take them out of sight of the *Rebel's Pride* and the quickly approaching Yankee vessel.

"Lolly, I'm sorry," Kendall whispered. "I thought you would be safer here. I never knew John might come. He's so vengeful, Lolly. I don't know what he might do."

"Kendall, you did what you thought best," Lolly said placidly.

Kendall moistened her lips and kept rowing with all her strength. "There's a hammock up here where we should be safe. Only the Indians know it."

Lolly smiled. "I trust you, Kendall."

"Don't trust me! I seem to precipitate disaster."

Again, Lolly smiled. "I met your captain, Kendall. He's hardly a disaster! He'll come for us; I'm sure of it."

By nightfall they had reached the hammock. Lolly tried to keep the toddling Eugenia from eating the leaves about them as Kendall strained to create a shelter for them. After an hour of trial and error, she was able to ignite a small fire to shield them from the coolness of the spring night.

"I know that we risk the fire being seen, Lolly," she told her sister, "but it will help keep away the snakes and the insects."

"I'm sure I'd rather a rattler than a Yankee," Lolly murmured, "but do what you think best."

The baby fell asleep in Lolly's arms, but both sisters were too tense to sleep. They talked for hours, and an extreme turnabout seemed to have occurred. Lolly was the strong one now; Kendall poured out her heart, admitting the passion for Brent that defied her will, while Lolly insisted that she was wrong to fight him.

"You can't change a man who is fighting for his ideals, Kendall. You can only pray that he lives." Lolly laughed suddenly. "You must have had some reunion! Look at your dress!"

Kendall blushed as she realized that she was still minus two buttons, and Lolly abruptly sobered. "Kendall, can't you see? This is the end. The time is at hand for someone to claim you. Brent—or John."

Chills crept along Kendall's spine at her sister's words. She stared into her eyes, but Lolly wasn't looking at Kendall; she was staring into the brush.

Kendall turned to follow her gaze—and Lolly spoke again,

her voice filled with horror. "There's an Indian staring at us."

"Red Fox!" Kendall whispered joyously. She ran to him, throwing herself into his arms, finding a security in his strong chest.

"What are you doing here?" he asked her hoarsely.

"The . . . the Yankees have come again," she said, searching out his dark eyes. "And Brent—"

"I know. He returned in the *Rebel's Pride.*"

"How do you know?" Kendall inquired, stunned.

"Because he sought me out this afternoon. Right now he heads for the mouth of the river."

"Alone?" Kendall demanded in horror. He would head straight into a trap. "Oh, my God! I have to find him!"

"You have to stay right here, Kendall," Red Fox said firmly. "I will go for Brent." He glanced beyond Kendall—at the gaping Lolly.

"Who is she?"

"My sister."

Red Fox nodded imperiously. "She will stay with you; I will go. Here, you will take my knife. You know how to use it."

"Yes," Kendall replied, but before the echo of her word faded in the breeze, he was gone.

"An Indian!" Lolly exclaimed, shuddering. "Oh, Kendall, how could you trust a savage?"

"He isn't a savage, Lolly, and that's another long story."

Lolly began to shiver. "Tell it to me, Kendall. Talk to me. We have to do something to endure this waiting."

They talked all night. And when the baby awoke, crying in hunger, they were still talking. Sleep had eluded them both, and dawn was breaking.

In the afternoon, Kendall entertained little Eugenia with a pile of stones, placing them in an empty cup and allowing the toddler to dump them back on the ground. She was amazed by the little girl's beauty. Her eyes were as blue as the clear spring sky, her hair, like her mother's, was as gold as the sun.

Lolly, dozing on and off as she lay listlessly staring up at the sky, opened her eyes and smiled at Kendall. "You're going to make a wonderful mother one day."

Kendall shrugged and tried to answer lightly. "I . . . I don't think I can have children, Lolly."

To her surprise her sister laughed. "Because you've had your captain upon *numerous* occasions during the past years and nothing has happened? Don't be silly, Kendall. When you are together all the time, you'll be a mother someday."

"If I ever see him again," Kendall whispered.

Lolly made no reply.

At nightfall, Kendall decided to light another fire. Lolly and the baby were curled together, fast asleep, but she still couldn't rest. She searched for dry twigs and set to rubbing them together. She was so involved in her task that moments passed before she realized that she had heard a twig snap—and that someone was standing quite close to her.

Slowly, with a sense of foreboding, she looked up. Horror engulfed her. She was staring at John Moore.

The war hadn't changed him. He looked exactly as he had the last time she had encountered him in the swamp. He was the same man she had once come to know so very, *painfully,* well.

She leapt to her feet, staring at him speechlessly, warily. Fear flooded, along with a thousand other emotions, mainly anger and hatred. Time was eclipsed. She couldn't forget the day when he had slaughtered the innocents here in the swamp. Even now, the nightmares of that day sometimes returned to plague her. She couldn't forget that night, how viciously he had taken his revenge on her . . .

"Kendall!"

He spoke her name as softly, as pleasantly, as if he had come upon her at a tea. Then he smiled very slowly. "I knew that I would find you if I searched far enough."

She still couldn't speak. She backed up as he approached her, keeping her eyes fully upon him, afraid to blink.

"It's all come to an end!" he informed her, his voice still soft and pleasant. "Did you think that I would forget you? If so, you didn't give me enough credit. You didn't know me well enough, and, Kendall, I thought that you had! I thought that you knew all there was to know about me! After all, you're my wife. And now we are reunited! What a blessed day. You are mine once again, Kendall. And you will come back with me. We've got so very much lost time to make up together!"

Denial, horror, sprang to her heart. Never. Never now, never after all that she had suffered and survived.

"Why?" she demanded hoarsely of him, shaking her head slightly. She still could not believe that he had found her, that he stood before her. The strangest thing was that he remained a handsome man, and he cut a fine figure in his navy frock coat. His handlebar mustache was dashing, the sharp blue of his eyes contrasted alluringly with his dark, wavy hair. He could have found a woman who would have loved him, and he could have perhaps been happy and—normal.

He could have . . .

Travis had believed that once. Travis had known John most of his life. But even Travis had turned away in the last years, appalled by the changes in John. She wanted to be sorry for him, sorry for the man who had been lost to his own wounded pride. But too much that was unforgivable lay between them, and she felt only fear now, and loathing.

"Why?" He repeated her question, and then smiled. "I don't know, Kendall. I knew that I wanted you from the moment I first saw you. I prayed that you could cure me. I had never seen anyone so beautiful . . ." He shrugged. "I would have payed any price—and I did pay quite a sum! But it was so very obvious from the very beginning that you hated me, that you considered yourself superior. Just like all those braggarts who are now floundering in bloody defeat. The great southern soldiers! You didn't cure me, Kendall. You just twisted a second blade into me. But, Kendall, things have changed since I saw you last. I learned that I'd suffered nerve damage from that fever. But like many a wound, time healed it." He paused, leaning down to look at the still sleeping Lolly and her child. "The brat isn't yours, is she?"

"No!" Kendall assured him, shaking her head vehemently, always wary and afraid of the actions he would take against others because of her. "The baby is my sister's. You can tell by looking at her. Her hair is platinum, like Lolly's."

"You and your sister are both light," he reminded her. "And your Rebel is light-haired as well. Or perhaps I should say that your Rebel *was* light . . ."

"What are you talking about?" Kendall demanded tensely. She was desperately afraid of his answer, and yet, even as she spoke, she tried unobtrusively to glance past his shoulder and discern how he had come—and if he had come alone—but his sardonic smile deepened as he watched the movement of her eyes.

"Ah, the spark of fear alights her glorious blue orbs!" he taunted. "It's nice to see you frightened, Kendall. But no, I haven't seen the notorious Captain McClain—yet. But, you see, the war is over, Kendall. Your General Robert E. Lee surrendered to Grant two days ago. Jeff Davis has fled Richmond, and Florida's loyally-Reb-to-the-heart Governor Milton has committed suicide." John stared at her, his features hard, allowing his information to sink into her mind. What pleasure it gave him to relay such tragedy! "It's gone, Kendall. Your magnificent South, your paradise. It's all ashes and dust now. And if my men don't find McClain and kill him,

428

I will. I can make you forget him, in time. I met a number of engaging southern belles in New Orleans when I was transferred to the Mississippi. It was amazing how willing they were to know and entertain the Union soldiers—they knew we were the ones with the cash to buy silk stockings. But you know, Kendall, even the absolute wonder of finding that I was cured, that I was still a man, it was you I wanted. You with your airs, your passion and fury, and even your hatred. You wanted nothing to do with me, you never did. But it's all going to change, Kendall. You're in debt to me, my love, my *wife*. But that's all right now. We'll have a lifetime in which you can surrender, and pay all your debts. Things will change now. I will make you forget."

"Things can never change!" she whispered sickly. "I will never forget. Dear God, John! I didn't want to marry you, but I didn't hate you until I found out how cruel you could be. Perhaps you've changed, but I can never, never forget the past. Not what you did to me—but what you did to others. It wasn't far from here, John, that you slaughtered people I loved. Women, little children. Babies! And I will never change my heart, John. Whether we've lost the war or not, I love Brent McClain."

"Kendall, that is completely irrelevant. I have found you, and you are coming with me. Now."

"No!" she whispered in furious denial.

"Kendall, there are twenty well-armed men aboard my ship. They'll be behind me any minute. You can't fight me, Kendall. You are my wife—and a vanquished Confederate. A Confederate spy and escaped prisoner, at that. The law is on my side."

The law . . .

Never.

Red Fox had given her his knife. And long ago, he had taught her how to fight. If she could just reach down to the strap around her calf . . .

She smiled and sank down on her haunches, as if she were merely determined to remain right where she was. "John," she told him softly, "I've been fighting for almost four years. Now is no damned different . . ."

Kendall swiftly reached beneath her skirt and whisked out the knife. Maybe he had anticipated her action; maybe he knew the extent of her desperation. He was a step ahead. Before she could spring for him, he knelt beside her sister—his own knife in his hand, the blade at Lolly's throat. Lolly still slept, as innocent, as vulnerable, as an angel.

"Throw your knife at my feet. Now," John ordered flatly.

Kendall swallowed. "You wouldn't stab her, John, damn you, not even you—"

"Throw your blade down. Now!"

She could not be certain just how far he would go and she didn't dare take the risk of testing him now. Defeated, she threw down the blade. Tears swam in her eyes as her shoulders drooped. She had come too far! She had come too far to lose now! She thought of Brent, and of how she had finally been held in his arms after waiting so long, hoping, praying. He had come back to her. The war had kept them apart, but it had never stopped the encompassing growth of their love. She had finally touched him again . . . and run from him in anger.

Yet she had never imagined that she would not see him again, that it could end now, after the waiting and the fighting and the hoping and the praying, like *this!*

He smiled grimly and pocketed her knife, then stood and took a step toward her, his own blade gleaming in the sun. "Carving an A for 'adulterous' on your forehead might have an effect on your arrogance. Or perhaps I should carve it out on your cheek . . ."

He wrenched her to her feet and placed the flat of the blade against her left cheek. She returned his stare, willing herself not to flinch. He slid the cold steel along her throat, threatening, but not quite piercing her flesh. He brought the blade lower, down the valley between her breasts, slitting a button from her dress. "But then again, there are other places where I might carve such a letter, a warning! Perhaps your breast would be the right place. We wouldn't want the neighbors to talk, but then you would think twice before baring yourself to another lover . . ."

Kendall gritted her teeth and winced as the blade pressed harder against her. She couldn't swallow a gasp of pain as the point pressed into her, drawing a thin, sticky trickle of blood. She realized in growing panic that he was serious—and that she was defenseless against him. She was alone with him, an exhausted sleeping woman, and a little child.

"John, no—"

"You have to pay, Kendall. You know that. Sink to your knees like your precious, dying land. Go on, Kendall. Beg me to spare you."

She saw from the ice-cold hardness of his eyes that it wouldn't matter much what she did. She had scorned him twice; once for another man, once for a Yankee prison. He did intend to make her pay.

She remained standing. Her eyes blurred with tears she fought back valiantly. Vaguely, she saw another man approaching them from a small boat drawn up beside the one that had apparently brought John. He was in a blue uniform.

No help for her there. His men had become as vicious as he was himself. They, too, would think that she should pay.

John's anger suddenly burst forth in full fury. "Kendall, so help me God, I will kill you, bitch!" He pressed the point of the blade harder against her breast and twisted it. She cried out with the pain. Her eyes met his as a plea formed on her lips, but she never uttered it. Instead of the gloating triumph she had expected to find in his cold blue eyes, there was a strange, distant gaze.

The knife fell from his hand.

And then John Moore slumped forward, almost knocking her over as he crashed to the ground. Stunned, Kendall followed the descent with wide eyes—and saw that a knife protruded from his shoulder. She looked up.

The man in the uniform was coming toward her. His face was etched with torment and sorrow—and concern.

Travis Deland paused momentarily before Kendall, ascertaining that her wound was superficial. Then he knelt beside John. She saw his shoulders heave, his fists tighten at his sides until his knuckles were white . . . and then suddenly a shattering scream rent the air. A blur swept past Kendall and hurled itself at Travis.

"Damned Yankee! You leave my sister alone! I'll kill you, I'll rip you apart with my bare hands!"

"Lolly!" Kendall screamed. "Wait!"

But it was too late. Lolly and Travis were rolling together on the ground and her golden-haired, *delicate* sister was putting up an admirable fight, exorcising against Travis all of her grief, hate, and anger for the entire war.

Travis was gallantly trying not to hurt Lolly while defending himself—not an easy task. "Cease, shrew!" he bellowed, catching hold of her shoulders and shaking her hard, as if he could shake sense into her.

"Stop it, both of you!" Kendall cried, throwing herself into the brawl. "Travis! Lolly!"

But just as suddenly as she had joined the fray, she was wrenched from it and shoved aside. She knew the touch. Rough or gentle, she would know it anywhere. Brent.

Brent . . .

Who thought that Travis had been attacking them. And he had grappled Travis from Lolly. The two men were rolling in the dirt. The fight had become deadly.

"Thank God!" Lolly cried. "Kill him, Captain McClain, kill the Yank!"

"No!" Kendall shrieked. She looked about her to see that

Red Fox had also come, and stood by the sidelines of the fight. "Red Fox!" Kendall cried. "Stop Brent! Stop him, Travis saved me!"

Red Fox shrugged. "They will not kill each other—"

"Travis might have saved my life and he's my friend!" she stated firmly, rushing toward the men herself again and shouting, "Stop! Damn you both! Stop!"

Fists were flying, and finding their targets with sickening crunches of knuckles against flesh. Desperately Kendall rushed to the water and found a bucket in one of the rowboats. She filled it with cold swamp water, ran back to the fighting pair, and sloshed it over their heads.

Stunned, they both sputtered and lay back, staring up at her with incredulous anger.

"Stay out of this, Kendall!" Brent hissed. "Sweet Jesu, the man attacks you and your sister—"

"The hell I did!" Travis protested.

"He didn't attack us!" Kendall insisted. "And I cannot stay out of this. Travis may have saved my life, and you're beating him to a pulp!"

"I beg your pardon, Kendall!" Travis exclaimed indignantly. "I can fight my own battles, madam! And he isn't doing that damned well!"

"That's right, you're doing just fine!" a sword-edged voice, coming from behind Kendall's back, suddenly interjected. Kendall started to swing around, but discovered that she could not. A bloody hand was suddenly curved around her waist; the razor-sharp blade of a knife quivered against the flesh of her throat. She could barely swallow.

John! They had all forgotten him in the melee, they had assumed him dead. He should have been dead, oh, dear, God, didn't the man ever *die!?*

The fight between Travis and Brent had come to an end. In silence they both stood. Lolly, pale faced, hovered behind

433

the pair. Red Fox, as still as the others, stood by her side. They had all of them forgotten John, presumed him dead.

But now he stood. Half dead perhaps, but with enough life in him to threaten Kendall's own.

"You bloody bastards!" John hissed, glaring at them all, his eyes lighting with a fixed fury on Travis. "All of you— bloody bastards!"

Brent took a step forward, his eyes dark smoke, his features tense. "Let her go! Now!"

"Ah, so there he is at last, the bold, the reckless, the daring, the magnificent Captain McClain!" John mocked. "Seducer of other men's wives! Well, sir, mine will not be worth much when I have finished with her, I do assure you! But then, again, she is mine! Mine, you god-damn Rebel! And now, she is coming home, with me."

The knife was shaking in his hands. Kendall didn't dare breathe. She could almost feel it scraping her vein, cutting down to draw blood . . .

"John!" Travis cried out. "For the love of God, let her go! I'm the one—"

"Ah, yes! There he stands, my lifelong friend! The man who stabbed me in the back! There will be a time to settle old scores with you as well, Travis. But for now, well, Kendall is going to have my full attention. I'm not going to kill her. Not unless you force me to. So keep your distance. My wife is coming home. Into my ever-loving and tender embrace! She'll never be the same again, Reb. I promise. You loved her face once, eh? Look well now! Her breasts were beautiful, well, I knew that, too . . . but then again, they will never be the same. Maybe I'll let you see her again some time, Reb. Maybe we'll all meet up again—in hell!"

He started to back away, toward the boats, dragging Kendall along with him. She almost didn't dare breathe. But even as John began to move, a sound like a low growl suddenly seemed to grow like thunder in the hammock.

And suddenly, Brent was flying after her. Moving like mercury, seeming to fling himself across the space between them with the force and impetus of a tiger. He made his reckless, desperate leap with precision, hurling against John, and knocking him from Kendall to the ground.

John Moore let out a roar of fury, trying to slam the knife into Brent's chest. Kendall screamed, but Brent hadn't needed the warning. He caught hold of John's wrist and slammed it down hard against the ground. The knife flew from John's grasp, sliding into the dirt. Brent drew back a fist, knotting tight in fury, and slammed it into John's face. He stared down at John Moore with glazed gray eyes, with stone-cold, tense features and started to strike him again.

Kendall suddenly screamed out in horror again, running to him, sliding down to her knees in the dirt. "Brent, Brent!"

She didn't want John Moore to live. She had wanted to kill him herself so many times.

But she couldn't bear to watch Brent beat him to death. If he finished the task, something would die within both of them as well.

"Brent, he's down, he's no danger. Brent . . ."

She couldn't even voice what she meant to say. It was the same thing she had felt the day when she had seen him and the others go after the woman who had given them the poisoned pie. Perhaps John deserved to die for his deeds just as the woman had deserved to die for hers. But she didn't want Brent to have to be judge and jury. Not like this.

Brent stared at her. It seemed as if eons passed, as if everyone else in the hammock was dead still, as if even the breeze waited. Then she knew that he understood what she couldn't really explain herself. He sighed. He reached out a hand, stroking her cheek. "God, I love you," he said softly.

He rose, took her hand, and drew her up beside him. He started to walk away with her, away from the man who had caused them so much pain, then they both paused, frozen, as a sudden, violent splash of silver arced past them.

They heard a gasp, and spun back together.

John had been rising—going for the knife in the dirt. His eyes, his mouth were bloodied and swollen; he hadn't cared. He had meant to kill someone—her or Brent, Kendall would never know.

But he had never reached the knife. The hilt of a blade now rose from dead center in his chest, from his heart. Dark crimson stained his uniform, and continued to pump from his now still form, then stopped.

Red Fox walked past Lolly and Travis and Brent and Kendall. He stood over the corpse. John was dead this time; indisputably dead. But it didn't matter. Red Fox knelt down and drew the knife from his heart, and slammed it into the corpse again, hard. "The first for Apolka, my wife, my life. The second for my son. My blood."

Then he rose.

Brent now stood before Travis. "Deland," he said huskily. "I do beg your pardon. But now, sir, please get the hell out of our domain before—"

"Brent!" Kendall cried urgently. "It isn't our domain. Brent, it's over. The war is over."

He stared at her. Blinked. Stared at Travis. Shook his head. "Kendall—"

"General Lee has surrendered!" she insisted. "Travis, tell him, convince him!"

Brent stared at Travis again, hard. Travis nodded solemnly. "I swear it, McClain," Travis said. "Lee surrendered at Appomattox Courthouse on the tenth."

Brent inhaled and exhaled. He still stood as straight as a poker, but he dropped Kendall's hand. His fingers knotted into his palms, white-knuckled.

"Lee isn't the only general. Surely, Kirby-Smith is still fighting in the western arena. It isn't over. It can't be over.

Damn it, it can't be over, it's been too many years, too many lives, too much blood!"

"Too much blood, too many lives!" Kendall agreed, pleading. "Brent, please, it's over!"

There was a silence in the hammock. Then Lolly's baby began to cry.

Brent paused just a moment longer, then started walking toward the boats. He didn't seem to see anything; he walked like a blind man.

"McClain!" Travis called out. "I'm authorized to offer a pardon to any Rebels who cast down their arms!"

Brent paused, then kept on walking for the boats. Kendall started to race after him, but Red Fox caught her arm. "Let him be," he said softly. "He loves you; he would have gladly died for you. In time, he will live for you. Let him accept that the fighting is done. Then he will listen to you."

Kendall stood still, watching as Brent rowed away, her own heart feeling as if it had been torn asunder. She vaguely heard Lolly pick up her crying infant and address Travis with undisguised hostility. "Well, Yank, what have your friends done to the settlement?"

"Nothing!" he snapped. "I told you the war is over. I ordered my men to withdraw."

Lolly walked toward the rowboat that had brought them to the hammock. "An Indian and a Yankee," she muttered. "Kendall, we might as well go home—if the Yankee is telling the truth and we have a home."

"I'm telling the truth," Travis insisted, his own animosity aroused and the shield of his gallantry thin indeed.

"Kendall?" Lolly queried again.

"Not yet," Kendall murmured. She felt no sorrow that John was dead, but she knew that she and Travis would have to bury him.

"Well, then," Lolly murmured. "I guess I'm stuck with the Indian."

Red Fox laughed. "You should take care with savages, Golden-Woman," he said calmly. "But, for your sister, I will take you back."

Kendall watched the two as they settled in the boat. Then she turned to Travis. "You came to save my life, and I know what it cost you."

Travis shrugged, but lowered his lashes over his eyes. "John should have died long ago. He hasn't really lived in years. But he was, at one time, my friend. I pray that he is at peace at last."

"Yes," Kendall murmured.

They set to work, digging with an oar and the water pail. They buried John, and with him they buried the past.

And when they had at last fashioned a cross above the body, they turned to the one remaining boat. And as they rowed back to the settlement, they spoke of the future.

She found Brent at the cove, as she had expected. He was staring out at the sea. She knew he heard her, but he gave no sign.

Kendall sat down beside him. He didn't look her way, and he didn't speak. At length she leaned her head against his shoulder and stared out at the night sea along with him. "I love you," she said softly.

A shudder rippled through him. At last he put an arm around her. "The South is lost, Kendall. The war was all for nothing. We have nothing."

Kendall trembled at the despair in his voice. She placed her hands on his shoulders and knelt before him in the sand, forcing his steel-hard gaze to hers.

"Brent, we have everything."

"Everything!" he exclaimed. "Kendall, I have nothing! South Seas is gone, and I haven't a cent except for Confederate paper that's fit only to start a fire. The old way of life is gone, too. The South is gone."

"Not gone!" Kendall protested. "The land is still here, Brent. Yes, it will have to build anew, but it's here! And we're here, Brent. Oh, Brent, we have lost—but we have also won. We're here, we're alive. And I love you, Brent. Touch me, Brent! I'm alive, and I need you. And at last we can have something—something real, something forever." She clasped his hand, and brought it to nestle between her breasts where her heart was pounding out its beat of life. A sob caught in her throat. "Dear God, Brent, it is over—but we can begin! Please, please . . ."

She collapsed against him, sobbing brokenly. She had lost him along with the war. He could not accept the defeat. He would leave her again, go west to seek out the Rebels who were still fighting.

But after a long moment, she felt his fingers lightly on her hair. Absently, he began to stroke her.

"Kendall, I have nothing to offer you now. Not even a home. I don't even know where the *Jenni-Lyn* is."

"I never had anything until I had you," Kendall whispered. "We can build a home right here. Travis said that little will happen here. No one cares much about a small settlement on the outskirts of a swamp." She hesitated a moment, but grew bolder as his touch lingered possessively on her. "Travis is interested in building a port and starting a shipping business here."

"You're asking me to go into business with a Yankee?" Brent flared, his fingers knotting angrily into her hair.

Kendall winced, but replied with dignity. "No, I'm asking you to consider the proposition of a man who has been a friend to both of us through everything."

She felt him stiffen and then relax. She lifted her head from his chest and wiped the tears from her cheeks with the back of her hand as she met his eyes. They were steel-gray as he scowled, but he reached out to cup her chin in his palm. "All right, I'll consider it."

"Oh, Brent!" Kendall breathed happily, throwing herself against him so that they both fell backward to the sand. She kissed him quickly, before he could protest or turn her aside. His lips were cold and stiff at first, but then his arms wrapped around her, and his mouth formed to hers. Life and warmth and desire came to him, and his lips caressed and subtly savored hers. When she drew away, the hint of a grin had replaced his scowl. "I love you, little Reb," he murmured, his arms still tight around her and his voice husky. "Maybe we do have everything. I will always have the courage and beauty of the South—as long as I have you."

"Oh, Brent," Kendall murmured, leaning her cheek against his chest and feeling the heat and strength of him beneath her fingertips. They lay there awhile beneath the sea grapes and palms, savoring the peace and beauty of the night. Then she spoke again. "Brent, Travis made me another offer."

"Oh?"

She felt his muscles go rigid, and she couldn't resist a secret grin and an urge to draw out the moment. "Yes . . ."

"Kendall!" His arms grew warningly tight about her.

She lifted dazzlingly blue eyes to his. "He offered to marry the two of us aboard his ship. It's quite legal for him to do so."

Brent laughed, and Kendall knew at last that all of their battles were truly over. It would take some time to rebuild their land, and their souls, but true peace was with them.

"Sounds like a good offer," he murmured, drawing her close. She allowed him a kiss, but then tried to squirm away.

"Brent, he'll marry us tonight if you like."

"I like."

"Well?" she demanded.

He drew her closer, gray eyes heavy and sensual. "Soon," he murmured. "'Before I become a married man, I want one last hour beneath the moon with the hoyden who propositioned me all those years ago."

Kendall compressed her lips, but slowly grinned, succumbing to the pressure of his arms. The moon was beautiful . . . and they did need this time together . . . a gentle time. A time to begin the healing . . .

Two hours later, Brent McClain became a married man. Both Rebels and Yankees were in attendance; their respective commanders had ordered them to be civil. And so they stood near one another; blue coats and tattered gray.

The tension was terrible when they first met. Yankees who blamed the Rebels for the years of hardship. Rebels who could not accept the fact that it was over, that the death and bloodshed and destruction had been for nothing . . .

But as God was called upon to witness the marriage, something intangible was brought into being that could not merge blue and gray, but somehow brought home to all of them that the war was truly over at last. The earth had begun to renew itself; it was spring. They didn't have to kill strangers any longer. They could go home.

And when the brief ceremony was over, the men began to mix. They were stiff, there was hostility about them . . . but they were talking about what their lives would be like without war. The more they talked, the more anxious they were for peace to begin.

Brent and Kendall went out on the deck of Travis's ship. The spring breeze cooled them, the smell of the sea was fresh and pungent about them. Kendall pointed across the mouth of the river as she leaned contentedly against him. "Look, Brent."

The *Rebel's Pride* stood at anchor, listing gently in the light current. She was indeed a proud lady as she stood before them, a beautiful silhouette in the night, her masts raised high against the moon. In a strange way, Kendall thought peacefully, it was as if the ship were trying to remind her that all was not really lost. Pride and honor and courage belonged to men and women, not just to the struggling nation that had died in infancy. Pride, honor, and courage were intangible, but she and Brent could hold on to them nonetheless, just as they had held on to their love.

He rested his chin on the top of her head, and she felt his slow smile. Did his thoughts run along with hers? She was certain that they did.

"I'm going to keep that ship somehow," he told her.

And somehow, she knew that he would.

Epilogue

December 1865

The night was dark, the weather cold and damp. There was little holiday spirit about Charleston; the city was being hit hard by the laws of Reconstruction. It was here that the first state had seceded, here that the first shots of the war had been fired.

Painfully, men and women were beginning to put the war behind them. They defied the repercussions against the South, which had been doubled since the assassination of Abraham Lincoln. Many of the stalwart men who had made up one of the finest and most tenacious fighting forces of all time were beginning to look to the business of living once more.

One of these men stood on the wall of the Battery, his rugged face turned seaward, his powerful work-roughened hands stuffed into the pockets of his frock coat. He was a southerner; he would always be a southerner. But he had risen above defeat; he was determined that the South would build anew. It would be different. Nostalgia would often plague him. But he would work for the future, and he would form it with his own hands.

His steel-gray eyes were focused broodingly on the water

as he thought of the years passed. The war had begun here. The loss had begun here . . . but so had all that was shimmeringly beautiful in his life. All that was good. All that was his future.

He smiled, wondering if she would ever fully understand that she was his strength. She thought him indomitable. He wasn't. But when he had almost surrendered to despair, she had been there, giving him back beauty; giving him back the ideal of honor and pride with which to live.

It was cold on the Battery. Why he continued to stare seaward, facing the brisk breeze of winter, he didn't know. He should be seeking shelter inside the comfortable master cabin aboard the *Pride*. A stiff shot of bourbon would warm him . . .

Something, some slight movement, attracted his attention northward along the Battery.

A woman stood there, a silhouette framed by the harbor light and the glow of the moon. She was too far away for him to have actually heard her; the movement alone must have caught his eye.

She stood perfectly still now, her eyes on the sea.

Smiling, he hurried toward her.

"Madam," he began, and she spun to face him with a dazzling smile curving her full rose-colored lips. He slipped his arms around her, and thought for the thousandth time that she was incredibly beautiful. Stunning blue eyes as dark and turbulent as the night sea met his, eyes that hypnotized, framed by lashes of deepest midnight velvet.

"Why are you standing here?" he queried huskily, keeping his arm securely about her shoulder as he led her along the Battery toward the ship.

"Oh, I don't know," she murmured, "just reflecting, I suppose. Oh, Brent! Charleston has changed so sadly!"

His arm tightened about her. "Gaping wounds take time to heal, Kendall."

"I know. I just wish Lolly hadn't been determined to return."

"It's her prerogative, Kendall. How is she?"

"She's bitter. And mad as hell that she could keep her property only because of Travis. She's my sister, Brent, and I love her, but if I were Travis, I'd tell her to go to hell!"

"Kendall!"

"Well, it's true. She's as nasty as a cat to him."

"Well, she is *your* sister."

"And what is that supposed to mean?"

"Nothing, my love, nothing." Brent laughed. "They're both adults. They'll have to solve their own problems."

He paused a moment, taking both her hands in his as they reached the plank to their ship. "Haven't you anything else to tell me?" he demanded, gray eyes shielded as he awaited her answer.

Her lashes fell mischievously over her eyes, and she purposely blinked them in a pretense of innocence. "About what?" she inquired sweetly.

"Kendall," he warned, his grip tightening about her slender hands. "Don't play the belle with me now, love. I want your answer."

She laughed delightedly. "September."

"September?"

"Yes. Dr. Lassiter says the baby will be born around the middle of Sept—"

She didn't finish the word. He swept her off her feet and into his arms, hopping with a lithe and swift movement onto the plank and then to the deck of the *Pride.*

"Brent!" Kendall gasped, wrapping her arms around his neck breathlessly. "What is your hurry?"

"I'm going to be a father!" he replied, spinning around with her in his arms. "Of course, I knew it—but to have it confirmed by Dr. Lassiter—" He broke off as he swept her

445

along to the master cabin and set her on the bed with a flourish. Then he turned and started out the door.

"Brent? Where are you going?" Kendall called after him, perplexity knitting her brow.

He grinned. "To give the order to sail. I want to make love to my definitely pregnant wife. God, I can't wait to hold you!"

"But we don't need to sail!"

"Ah, I seem to have acquired a superstition against making love in Charleston harbor."

"Brent—" she protested.

But he was gone before she could say more. Minutes later he was back. His coat was on the floor before he had closed the door, and in just seconds he stood naked before her, boldly pulling her to her feet and stripping her of her many layers of clothing.

"Brent!" She was half laughing, half protesting his urgency.

He silenced her with a swift kiss. "Darlin', I haven't a thing in the world against making love on the open sea."

Kendall sighed and contentedly lifted her eyes to his. "Neither have I, Captain. Neither have I."